THE GOOD
HOUSEKEEPING
SHORT STORY
COLLECTION

ARROW

Published in the United Kingdom in 1997 by
Arrow Books

1 3 5 7 9 10 8 6 4 2

Copyright © The National Magazine Company Limited 1997

The rights of the authors of this work have been
asserted by them in accordance
with the Copyright, Designs and Patents Act, 1988

Arrow Books Limited
Random House UK Ltd
20 Vauxhall Bridge Road, London, SW1V 2SA

Random House Australia (Pty) Limited
16 Dalmore Drive, Scoresby, Victoria, 3179

Random House New Zealand Limited
18 Poland Road, Glenfield
Auckland 10, New Zealand

Random House South Africa (Pty) Limited
Endulini, 5a Jubilee Road,
Parktown 2193, South Africa

Random House UK Limited Reg. No. 954009

A CIP catalogue record for this book
is available from the British Library

Papers used by Random House UK Limited
are natural, recyclable products made from wood grown in
sustainable forests. The manufacturing processes conform to
the environmental regulations of the country of origin

ISBN 0 09 9227924

Phototypeset in Linotron Ehrhardt 10 on 12pt by Intype London Ltd
Printed and bound in the United Kingdom by
Cox & Wyman Ltd, Reading, Berks

Contents

Foreword

It is often said that women's magazines have kept the short story alive in Britain, and *Good Housekeeping* can certainly claim much of the credit, having regularly published work by some of the greatest writers of the twentieth century.

From the year the magazine was launched in 1922, *Good Housekeeping* readers have consistently been offered short stories by the most famous and interesting writers of the age. From Arnold Bennett or Ellen Glasgow in the 1920s, to H. E. Bates and Somerset Maugham in the 1930s. In the forties, fifties and sixties, the roll call continued, from A. A. Milne, Elizabeth Bowen and Martha Gellhorn, to Paul Gallico and Dorothy Eden. In the seventies, the stars included Margaret Drabble, V. S. Pritchett and Penelope Gilliatt.

The Good Housekeeping Book of Short Stories brings together the best stories published in the magazine during the last two decades of the twentieth century. We have collected twenty-four sparkling stories from such favourites as William Trevor and Rose Tremain, Helen Simpson and Doris Lessing, Edna O'Brien and Maeve Binchy. Each one is a shining example of the short story form. All together they endorse the magazine's commitment to the high quality fiction that has always graced our pages, bringing quiet pleasure to generations of *Good Housekeeping* readers.

I hope you enjoy them all.

Pat Roberts Cairns
Editor

PENELOPE LIVELY

A Dream of Fair Women

Richard Swinton listened to the chairman's introduction, which was satisfyingly eulogistic. He allowed the applause to die down, went to the lectern and arranged his papers in front of him. A full house, he observed, an audience of 80 to 100 or so filling the panelled carpeted upholstered interior of one of the most agreeable public rooms in London. Naturally, for the Brent-Caxton lecture. And for himself. More women than men; his glance swept over the rows of faces – spiky-haired art students, female academics, the smarter coterie from galleries and museums. Provocative black leather, colour supplement chic, the careful neutrality of tweed and muted patterns. Ah, women were so endearingly self-revealing, clothed or unclothed.

He looked quickly at the screen and then at the girl in charge of the slides. The lights were dimmed. He began to speak. This was his *The Nude in Nineteenth Century French Painting* talk, touched up a little for the occasion, but as familiar as an old coat. As he slipped into the opening paragraph he allowed himself to inspect the audience more closely, his eye roving over the faces of strangers and alighting, almost at once, bang in the second row, on that of his third mistress.

There she sat, her hands folded in her lap, gazing at him impassively. Well, no; not at him but at a point about 18 inches behind his left ear. She wore a lilac-coloured suit, white silky shirt and a rope of pearls; she looked very nice – healthy, complacent, older naturally – though not perhaps all of . . . let's see now . . . 51 – no, 53 more like.

He faltered, lost his way for a moment, picked it up again before anyone could have noticed and tapped his pointer for the first slide. Valerie. Well, well. Once upon a time, time out of mind ago, he and she had sunbathed naked on the deserted beach of a Greek island. He could see her now, a delicate prawn pink against the white sand, demanding

1

applications of Ambre Solaire. He still possessed, expediently buried among some old papers that his wife wouldn't be interested in, a photo of her sitting on a rock wearing a yellow bathing costume, nicely tanned by then. And one of himself of which he was rather fond in which the blue of his shirt exactly matched the blue of the cluster of morning glory behind his head; his eyes, in a bronzed face, were becomingly crinkled against the sun – one was, at 30, a good-looking chap, not to put too fine a point on it.

And wearing pretty well at 55. Bit of a paunch (reminded, he drew it in), a few grey hairs, but (compared to some one could name) extremely presentable. He turned to the screen, talking of outlines and skin tones, his pointer wandering across the ivory flank of Ingres's *Grande Odalisque*. It occurred to him – the thought had a certain irony – that in fact he knew the bodies of the great female nudes of European art with greater intimacy than those of any real women. For instance he could not for the life of him now recall much about Valerie's thighs or buttocks, but he could give a perfect account of the form of the Ingres lady – or of Velasquez's *Venus* or Rubens's *Three Graces* or of a score of others. Faces, though, were another matter. He could have conjured up Valerie's face, a trifle blurred perhaps but accurate in essentials, at any point over the years. To glimpse her just now for but a fraction of a second had been enough to recognise her; whereas had it been merely a limb, a torso, a breast that he had seen he would presumably have passed it by without a tremor.

He had not run across her at all in the last 20 years. She had married a wine importer, he remembered hearing at some point, had a child or two, did a bit of up-market cookery journalism – he had found himself reading a piece by her once, in a dentist's waiting room.

How – interesting, touching in a way – that Valerie should attend his Brent-Caxton lecture.

He reached the bottom of another page, paused, put his elbows on the lectern and began to extemporise – the sort of off-the-cuff light discursion with a joke that often came off rather well. Looking down at the upturned faces – less distinct now in the dimmer lighting – he saw the audience

2

respond: smiles here and there, the engaged expressions of people who feel themselves addressed personally. He always enjoyed that feeling of command – indulgent command. It must be akin to the feeling stage actors get on a good night. He had always been a good lecturer; it wasn't something he'd ever had to work at. Of course presumably either you were or you weren't, it was one of those God-given things, like so much in life.

He looked quickly at Valerie – attentive but gazing at the screen, not at him. His gaze passed beyond her towards the centre of the hall and there sitting by the aisle was his first love, Susan.

He dried up completely. Words failed him. He floundered, coughed, retrieved some lame conclusion and fled back to the safety of his text. Christ! What a bizarre really rather entertaining coincidence!

Susan – she of the long flaxen hair with whom he had first known complete unabashed consummation. In cold, stuffy college bedrooms and subsequently in third-class *pensions* in Paris and Avignon. How closely one's early erotic experience had been interwoven with exploration of Europe. France still evoked Susan. And there she was, the flaxen hair no longer flaxen nor long but a rather attractive corn colour, cropped short with a wispy fringe. He looked at her again – caught her eye, he thought, and looked hastily at the screen, where his pointer had summoned up *Le Bain Turc*. Oh yes, it was Susan all right – different as she was now. He began to talk about the painting; that ferment of female flesh, suspended there for inspection, seemed suddenly quite pornographic – he found himself almost embarrassed, indicating a breast here, an armpit there. He cut short his disquisition on the ambiguities of the picture and moved on to the next page.

Susan was wearing some smock-like garment. She looked wholesome, just as she had at 19, more ripely wholesome but still with that wholemeal-loaf-and-cream-cheese aura that had attracted him then, an intriguing antidote to the glossy lipstick and pencilled eyes of the day. A wonderfully compliant girl, one had often regretted her since, up against more difficult women. An adorable creature. And here she

3

was! She painted still, of course, had had the odd exhibition from time to time in small provincial galleries. He had seen her once 15 years or so ago at a Burlington House exhibition, and had introduced her to his wife, who asked rather a lot of questions that evening. Susan's presence today was not, when one came to think about it, all that startling. She was, after all, a painter. Still, she hadn't *had* to come. Touching, again. He felt rather glad, now, that Elizabeth had elected to stay at home on the grounds that she had heard the lecture several times before and she got awfully bored at those receptions afterwards full of milling strangers. There could have been more questions asked; Elizabeth's memory for faces was infallible.

His confidence regained, Richard ventured another departure from the script, inviting the audience at rather greater length than usual to consider the cool gaze of Manet's *Olympia* – 'Isn't it somehow at odds with the rest of her? That calculating stare, a bourgeois stare – you expect to see black bombazine below it, not nudity. Her body invites; her face rejects.' He thought he saw Susan's head tilt to one side a fraction, in consideration; he almost smiled. Thus had she listened to his youthful perceptions in the Louvre and the Jeu de Paume.

She would have observed his progress – the appointments, the publications, the chairmanships of this and that, the CBE. As would Valerie and . . . quite a few others. Benign observation, he imagined – there had not been bitter endings, merely movings on, though perhaps it was he who had usually moved first. One really couldn't quite remember now. It was beginnings you remembered – that moment of ripening interest in another woman. When had one first had that heady realisation that there was no end to them, that it was as though you had been let loose in a strawberry bed? It had seemed thus at 20, and truth to tell one had never really lost that intoxicating sense of possibility. To walk down a crowded street, or to enter a room like this, was still to find oneself scanning with appreciation the wonderful variety of women, in an almost detached way, not necessarily sexual, marvelling simply at that abundance of faces and shapes. Of people. I like women, he thought. I get on with women.

And they like me. Sex aside. Of course, in the fullness of time one had begun to feel a need for stability, and Elizabeth had come along, but even then . . .

Valerie shifted, crossed her legs, smoothed her skirt. Susan was looking down so he would no longer see her face. What were *they* thinking? He felt indulgent and a touch sentimental. And amused. What an absurd situation! And how tiresome that one could share it with no one.

He had arrived now at Renoir; the screen was filled with the glowing fruity flesh of *baigneuses*, the whole room seemed suffused in reflected colour. He summoned them up one after another – the sloe-eyed biddable girls with their pouting nipples. He himself had reservations, he told the audience; one admired the sensuality, the flow of line, but felt ultimately drenched. All the same, look at them . . . and his pointer flicked at a rump here, a bosom there. They showed themselves off one after another – a play of luscious impervious light upon a sheet of canvas. 'In some ways,' said Richard, 'these women seem to me unreal – idealised creatures, manifestations of the painter's imagination. To utter a heresy – they are a nudge or two away from *Playboy.*' He tapped the pointer to dismiss the Renoir houris, turned back to the audience, and saw Elaine, the mistress of his maturity, sitting in the back row.

No. Impossible. He stared, leaning forward a little. But yes, it was she all right. No mistaking her, even at that distance. The shock struck home and he dropped the pointer. The chairman leapt to pick it up. So did Richard. In the ensuing scramble he had time to cleanse his face of the expression of pure horror. Thank God Elizabeth hadn't come; she and Elaine had overlapped for a time, causing problems. But no sooner had horror given way to a flicker of relief than that was replaced by a surge of awful stomach-shrinking doubt. Just what was going on here? Valerie. Susan. And now Elaine. Elaine sitting there large as life looking young and pretty with her hair done differently and large fashionable specs.

He was finding it difficult to continue. He lost his place, mumbled, improvised, picked up the sense again. The audience rustled, embarrassment transmitting itself. This was

5

more than coincidence. It had to be more than coincidence. But how could it be? They don't know each other. How could they know each other? Of course they know vaguely *of* each other . . . Naturally one had let drop this and that to the current girl about others, women find that slightly titillating and anyway it's natural enough to talk of one's past in all its manifestations, and besides one could hardly appear to be a eunuch, it would be neither truthful nor appealing. Of course one had chatted a bit, probably rather specifically on occasion. But surely it was inconceivable that they had . . . It was too absurd to think that they . . . Or was it?

He struggled on with the lecture. Words, somehow, came forth. And the thoughts boiled around in his head. They had set this up, somehow, got together and schemed, laughing at him. What a typically *feminine* thing to do. Like plotting schoolgirls. Let's give Richard the shock of his life. Let's have ourselves a ball. It was so . . . childish . . . that it should just be ignored, except that he couldn't ignore it, stuck up here with them down there goggling at him. And supposing . . . God! – were there any more of them? For a hysterical moment he thought that he was going to discover he had been to bed with every woman in the audience. He stopped talking and took a drink of water. He allowed himself a long pause; he scrutinised the faces in front of him. Please God, no more.

There were no more. That was it. And quite enough. He was now in a cold sweat. He had to find a handkerchief and wipe his forehead. He felt the chairman's anxious eyes on him. Grimly, he made himself go on with the lecture, turn from text to screen, talk of tonal values and composition, address himself to body after body, an eternity it began to seem of displayed flesh, woman after woman with their curves and dimples and shadows, their strategic wisps of material or concealing hand, their carefully arranged limbs and inscrutable faces.

He did not look again at Valerie. Or at Susan. Or Elaine. He could feel their gaze on him like . . . well, like a bunch of harpies, to put it bluntly. What they were going to do, of course, was descend on him afterwards, at this blasted

6

reception which he could not possibly escape. To which he would be led by the chairman, at which a glass would be put in his hand and the audience, eager to get the rest of its money's worth by way of liquor and conversation, let loose upon him. At which point Valerie, Susan and Elaine would converge upon him, grinning hugely, to feast upon his exposure, the target set up and brought down, the fall guy. What fun to ring each other up later and have a laugh about it.

He seriously thought, for a few moments, of feigning illness – dropping his papers, putting hand to head, allowing himself to be escorted from the platform and into a taxi. Going home to a loving and solicitous Elizabeth, who would fuss over him and put him to bed with aspirins and hot water bottles, where he could fall immediately asleep and forget the whole unsettling occasion.

No. Impossible. He hadn't the nerve. Besides . . . He tried to pull himself together – what could they do to him? No one else had any idea of the connection, after all – only he and they knew. No, this was ridiculous, he was playing into their hands getting into a state like this. All he had to do was brave it out, feign imperviousness, appear surprised and friendly if they – if any of them – accosted him.

He delivered the final paragraph of his lecture; the rosy voluptuous girl sprawled on a couch behind his head was extinguished; the lights came on; he acknowledged the applause and was ushered by the chairman down the steps from the platform, out of the door and into the refectory, where waitresses stood about with trays of drinks. The audience surged after them; the room filled up; his attention was required – 'Red or white wine, sir?' 'May I introduce our Provost?' 'Professor Swinton, I just had to say how much I enjoyed . . .'

He looked furtively around. No sign. And then he saw Valerie, 10 feet away, talking animatedly. Oh God! Elizabeth should be here, he thought petulantly, I shouldn't have to cope with this sort of thing on my own, Elizabeth should be here to back me up, to help me make discreet apologies and leave. His panic gave way for a few moments to resentment: Elizabeth was not always as supportive as she ought to be – sitting at home with a book or the telly when one was being harassed like this. It was really too bad of her.

Some woman was chuntering on at him about his Watteau book. He kept looking through the crowd at Valerie; all of a sudden she looked back, raised a hand in greeting and went on with her conversation. What was she up to? Planning some shock assault in her own time? He said, 'Excuse me,' to the Watteau woman and pushed his way to Valerie.

'Hello, Richard. You were awfully rough on poor old Renoir. Do you know John Hailey?'

Her companion began to speak. Richard interrupted, 'I saw you in there. Why did you come?'

Valerie laughed. 'Really! John brought me. I'm afraid I didn't realise who was lecturing till just now.' She was as cool as you like. Laughing at him, no doubt about it. The man must be in it too, whoever he was.

Richard said, 'Susan's here.'

'Susan?'

'Susan Marwood.'

'I'm sorry,' said Valerie. 'Is this someone I should know?'

'Apropos of what you were saying about that Ingres restoration,' said the man, 'I've always felt myself that . . .'

Richard caught sight of Elaine – a glimpse of that unmistakable profile on the far side of the room. He knew now that the thing was to move first. Stand around like a dummy while they worked up to whatever it was they had in mind and he was done for. Get in first – that was the thing – wrong-foot them. He turned his back on Valerie and the man, shouldered his way towards Elaine. Someone seized his arm and said, 'Professor Swinton, I've been dying to ask you if . . .' He shook them off. Elaine had her back to him now, talking to a man he vaguely knew – Walters, that was who, that art critic – and a woman in red. He pushed himself into their group and said, 'Well, Elaine . . .' in a let's-have-no-nonsense voice. The Elaine-figure turned to him the face of a stranger.

'Ah, Richard,' said Walters. 'We were just rubbishing the Hayward exhibition. Have you seen it?' The not-Elaine person stared at him. The woman in red said, 'Oh, Professor

Swinton, you know my brother I think, Tim Rogers, he was saying only the other day that you . . .'

Richard stepped back on someone's foot, felt someone's drink slop on his arm. He could have sworn. Spitting image of Elaine, seen from 35 feet off.

The room was packed. He tried to shove his way through, landed up against a colleague who started to introduce someone, sidled this way and that in an attempt to escape, looked at last at the woman who was being offered to him, started to say, 'Yes, how do you do, I'm frightfully sorry but I'm afraid I've got to rush now . . .' – and the woman was Susan.

Except that she was not. She was wearing Susan's smock dress and had Susan's cropped corn-coloured hair but a bland never-seen-before face and irritating affected voice that was now saying how much she'd always wanted to meet and how thrilled she was and she wondered if.

'I'm sorry,' he said, 'I've got to go.' He waved as though acknowledging some summons, turned, got past another group, found himself blocked again. The noise was frightful, the frenzied amplified insect buzz of a party, women's voices predominating and giving it that upper edge that jarred the ear. Everywhere he looked there were mouths opening and shutting showing teeth and tongues, while elbows and backsides and swinging shoulder bags knocked against him as he tried to head for the exit. He edged his way past emphatic thighs, found his arm up against a squashy bosom, smelt the bathroom smell of bodies, that compound of sweat and perfume, thought he would go mad if he was stuck here another minute. And emerged at last into a sparser area. Where stood Valerie again, alone now, sipping her drink, quite at ease, observing him.

She said, 'You look as though you're in the most awful tizz.'

'I'm perfectly all right.'

'Well, good,' said Valerie. She put her hand to her mouth, deftly smothering a yawn. 'I must be off. I've lost John. Funny meeting up like this. I got quite a shock when I saw who was giving this lecture.' She grinned. 'Anyway, I enjoyed it. I say, are you sure you're all right?'

'I'm fine,' he snapped. 'You're well yourself, I take it?'

She looked attentively at him. 'Extremely well, thank you, Richard.'

'Good night, then.'

'Good night.'

He plunged into the street. Ten yards along the pavement he realised he had forgotten his raincoat. He turned back. A woman was hurrying away in the opposite direction, the shape of her instantly emotive. He stood on the pavement in the rain staring uncertainly at what seemed to be the retreating figure of his wife.

MAEVE BINCHY

Lottery of the Birds

He was a peacock. She knew that the moment she met him. He was looking at his own reflection, not at the picture behind the glass in the frame. He stroked the lapels of his very expensive jacket softly and with pleasure. She knew exactly what she was letting herself in for.

'I'm Ella,' she said simply. 'That is *the* most beautiful jacket. Is it wool?'

He seemed pleased, but not surprised. He talked about the jacket briefly, with unaffected enthusiasm. He had bought it in Italy three weeks ago – but his manners wouldn't let him go on too long.

'I'm Harry,' he said. 'And shouldn't we be talking about your clothes really?'

'Not tonight,' Ella said. 'Tonight I just came straight from the office.'

His smile could have lit the fire that was set in the grate of the art gallery. A fire that was pure decoration.

'It must be a very elegant office, then,' Harry said, and Ella was lost.

She always told herself afterwards that it had been as deliberate an act as she had ever known. She had walked in, eyes wide open, into the situation she had spent most of her adult life trying to rescue her friends from. She had fallen in love with a man who was going to break her heart over and over; she would lose the sympathy, the patience and eventually the company of her friends. Ella, who was known for her self-control and her calm, practical way of looking at things, had fallen for a peacock full of charm. Not even the silliest of them would have thought there was even half a chance with Harry.

But Ella didn't mind. She knew the odds; and then promptly forgot them. She did all the things that the women's magazines used to advise in her mother's day: she was a good listener, she drew him out about himself;

11

she discovered his interests and pretended that they were hers too. She didn't press to meet his family: she didn't impose hers on him.

In fact, it was all so successful that Ella began to wonder whether those old-fashioned ideas about pleasing a man might not be far more helpful than all this modern advice about being yourself, and being equal from the word go. At any rate, she was very shortly Harry's constant companion: she was on his arm at every public event, and in his bed when the night drew to a close.

It was hard work, of course, but then Ella told herself that you don't keep a peacock by your side without a great deal of effort. Anyone could attract a sparrow, she thought, looking without much pleasure at some of the men her friends were going out with. Some of them were indeed like old crows. Only Ella had the peacock, the glorious Harry who turned every head, and she didn't mind when he looked at other women and smiled. They thought he was smiling at them, but he was thinking as much of the actual act of smiling. He knew it made people feel good. He did it a lot. Sometimes he smiled in his sleep, as Ella sat and watched him, his facial muscles stretched into a pleasing, warm half-grin.

She was often awake at night as she learnt the plots of operas. *La Traviata*: that's the one about Alfredo and Violetta, and a series of misunderstandings. *Rigoletto* was the one about the court jester, and *Norma* was the Druid high priestess who did a Romeo and Juliet number with the Romans.

Ella worked for a publishers. She ran it down to Harry: terribly dull people, frightfully boring authors, very tedious and not worth taking up his time. But Harry's job – now that was different: he was in wine importing – *there* was an interesting career for you. Ella made it sound like a magical world. It had involved a lot of studying, more than the opera, even: types of grape, *Appellation Contrôllée*, this vineyard, that importer, this warehouse, that family firm . . . Harry accepted her interest. She was right, it *was* a fascinating business. His previous girlfriends hadn't understood that nearly so well.

He introduced her to his colleagues; her admiration of the business was so obvious she could do him nothing but credit.

The boss and his wife were a cynical, weary couple, who had seen it all, done it all.

'You have a far better chance of nailing him down than the others,' said the boss's wife as she dabbed her nose viciously in the powder room after dinner.

'Oh, heavens, there's no question of that,' Ella protested with a little laugh.

'Keep that kind of line for Pretty Boy,' said the older woman.

Ella felt sorry for her. All she had drawn in the lottery of the birds was a bad-tempered, bald and moulting eagle, not a glorious, multi-coloured peacock.

She went back to the table, where Harry sat, his chin on his hand, in that way that made total strangers stop their conversations and look at him with admiration. The light fell on his fair hair making it shine. Ella's heart soared to think that she had captured this wonderful man.

It pleased her to think that she had a better chance of nailing him than anyone who had gone before – and there were many who had. Sometimes they passed through town.

'An old friend of mine wants me to have a drink in a wine bar,' he would say from time to time.

'Oh, but you must!' Ella was insistent. It would give her time to catch up on some new looming opera. *Fidelio*. This one was by Beethoven, about Leonora, who pretends to be Fidelio. Another three hours of cross-dressing and misunderstanding.

Or on the housework. She hadn't actually moved into his flat, but as near as made no difference. He hated seeing her cleaning, yet he wouldn't employ anyone else to do it. She did it in secretive, hurried darts when he wasn't around. She wanted Harry to think that fresh peaches for breakfast, clean towels in the bathroom and big vases of colourful flowers in clean water sort of happened by themselves when Ella was around.

And because peacocks don't think for too long about the world in general, that's exactly what he thought. He would put his arm around her and say that everything was much *nicer* when she was there.

She took seven shirts of his, every Monday morning, to a very good place just beside her work. No, honestly, darling, she reassured him, I'll be taking my own stuff anyway. He never noticed that everything Ella wore was drip–dry. He thought it was a miracle that his wardrobe was always full of gleaming shirts; he savoured choosing them, holding the ties up against them.

'It used to be very disorganised,' he said with a puzzled frown, shaking his head at the mystery of it all. Ella shook her head too, as if she couldn't believe that things had not always run this smoothly.

She never complained about him at work, or sought advice, so her friends just worried about her to each other and not to her face.

It did not become public until the day she refused to go to the sales conference. For personal reasons. There were no reasons, personal or even global, that allowed you to miss the sales conference. Ella's friends took her aside.

'Come on, what's he doing, what mammoth task has he agreed to do that he needs you to hold his hand?' Clare had been a friend and colleague long enough to speak in that tone. But only just.

'You couldn't be more wrong. Harry didn't ask me not to go, he doesn't even know it's on.'

They looked at each other, shocked. What kind of relationship could you have with a publisher and not know about sales conferences?

'You'll be passed over, Ella, the boys upstairs will never stand for this. No matter what lies you tell them.'

'I won't tell them any lies. I'll just say that it doesn't suit me.'

'Not only are you completely cracked, but you're letting us all down. They'll say women can't cope, that you're premenstrual or having the vapours or that you're pregnant. Lord, you're not, are you?' Clare was aghast.

'No, certainly not.' Ella spoke in a voice too calm, too normal for the crisis she was bringing down on all of them.

Clare waved the others away majestically. 'Let's have a glass of the Emergency Tequila,' she suggested.

'No, honestly, it's too early, I couldn't swallow it,' Ella protested.

'You *are* pregnant,' Clare said. The Emergency Tequila was a ludicrous bottle stashed away at the back of an office drawer for an occasion just like this.

Ella looked at her friend with a great but almost distant affection. Clare was married to an owl, a wise old owl peering over his spectacles with an indulgent look at Clare. In a million years she wouldn't know what it took to hold a man like Harry.

'I can't tell you, you'd feel honour-bound to try to talk me out of it,' Ella said.

Clare looked relieved. At least there was a hint of a smile on Ella's face again; they hadn't seen that for a long time, only a look of grim concentration.

'It's his parents, they're coming up for this *Fidelio*, he's got tickets for all of us.'

'Ella, *Fidelio* will come back again – it's not some new, experimental work that might sink without trace.'

'No, but it's . . .'

'Even his parents will come back again, they're not like Halley's Comet, coming round once every 76 years. You *can't* miss the conference. What about your authors? You can't let them down.'

'Someone else can present their books. Come on, we spend our time telling each other not to believe that we are indispensable . . .'

Clare looked at her in exasperation. It was one thing to realise that you could be replaced: it was another to walk out on your authors. They *expected* you to be at the sales conference, to talk up their books to the reps, who then had to go out and sell them into book shops. Quite apart from what the boys upstairs would say.

'I'm sick of the boys upstairs,' Ella said; and all on her own, Clare opened the Emergency Tequila and drank most of it out of a coffee mug.

Back in the office, Ella faced the silent reproach of Kathy, her assistant.

'I wish you'd change your mind,' Kathy said eventually.

'No, you don't.' Ella was cheerful and brisk. 'This is your big break. It's like the understudy hoping that the decrepit old bat of a leading lady won't be able to go on. Suddenly, a star will be born.'

'It's not remotely like that.' Kathy was cross. 'For one thing you are not a decrepit old bat, no matter how oddly you are behaving. You are only three years older than me if I remember correctly. And anyway, this is not becoming a star, it's taking over all your work as well as my own.'

'You can cope,' Ella encouraged.

'It's not fair, Ella, even if there was a good reason. And how am I going to deal with that madman from Australia?'

'Oh God,' said Ella. 'I'd forgotten the Jackaroo.'

'Well, he hasn't forgotten you.' Kathy was triumphant. 'He has an appointment to see you at five o'clock.'

'Not *this* evening. I can't meet him this evening!'

Kathy lost her temper. 'I think you should play fair with everyone, hand in your resignation, sit at home and plan your hope chest and let the rest of us get on with trying to publish books.'

When Ella was very young, her father had always told her that it was a great virtue to be able to see the other point of view. She used to be able to do that, in fact it was one of her great strengths.

She could imagine what it was like to be an author, or a bookseller, a rival publisher or an office junior. Perhaps of late she had been very preoccupied. She had been seeing another point of view, certainly, but only Harry's. She had been trying to out-guess him, solve the problem before it occurred, wipe away the frown before it started to pucker on his forehead. She looked Kathy straight in the eye.

'You are absolutely right,' she said. And for the first time since she had met Harry, she picked up the phone to tell him that she wouldn't be meeting him.

Harry was astonished. 'Who do you have to meet?' he asked in disbelief.

'This Australian, he's an author. I won't be going to the sales conference, you see, so I have to talk to him about his book and what plans we have for it.'

'But he's an *author*,' Harry said. 'I mean, you're the publisher, he should be pretty bloody grateful that you take any interest in it at all.'

'He is.' Ella's voice was firm.

Harry sounded aggrieved. 'I'd have made other plans, if I'd known. Now I'll be hanging about.'

'Come and join us, then. You and I weren't going to meet until six anyway. Come to the bar beside my office, that's where we'll be, at the back.'

He grumbled a bit. But he said he'd be there.

Ella took her notes on the Jackaroo's book. It was a zany first novel – it was very different from anything else. It was quirky, not in the mainstream. She did regret that she wouldn't be there to explain at the conference how it should be approached. But she had made up her mind. She had not spent all this time taming her beautiful, strutting peacock – making him adapt to a domestic lifestyle and like the idea of her being permanent in his life – just to throw it away. There would be other Jackaroos, other zany first novels, there were sales conferences every six months; but there might never be another shot like this at Harry.

She had never met the man she called the Jackaroo. His manuscript had been very neat, and she had imagined him a small, fussy sort of person – like a penguin, possibly. He had assured her, on the telephone, that he was hopelessly disorganised, but that he happened to be in love with his word processor. He said it had tidied up his mind. Now he wished he could find a machine that would tidy up his house.

'What about a wife?' she had asked him.

'Oh, I have one of those,' he had said.

Or maybe he had said that he *had* had one of those, she couldn't remember. It didn't matter, anyway; all that mattered was that she explain to him that even though *she* wouldn't be there, Kathy would do everything to ensure that the book was appreciated before it set out on its journey with all the other books.

She looked around the bar. Nobody looked remotely like a penguin.

A huge, shaggy man with long hair and a long, droopy coat stood by the bar, sipping white wine.

'I'm looking for a middle-aged trout called Ella,' he said to the barman.

'One middle-aged trout reporting,' she said with a laugh.

'Ella you're different to what I thought!'

'You too.' She wanted to be brisk, get as much of it over as possible, perhaps even all of it, before Harry came in. He looked a reasonable kind of fellow. About as far from a penguin as she could imagine. They sat down together.

'Is it worth my getting a bottle of wine?' he asked. 'I'm timid with publishers, I don't want to assume or presume.'

'You're not timid with publishers – you call them "old trouts".'

'But I was wrong. Is the bottle going too far?'

'But I'm the publisher, I'll get it. Anyway, I've a friend joining us later.'

'You get the second one, then.' He had a wonderful laugh, short, sudden and unexpected but very infectious. She found herself laughing too.

They talked a little about the book. He said it was like a dream, to have made it all the way from the outback to a really smart bar in London, and to find that the old trout he had thought was patting him on the head like a good little colonial was a gorgeous bird.

'You're like a lorikeet, in those lovely blues and oranges,' he said.

'A lorikeet?'

'You've never seen a rainbow lorikeet?' He wondered at the strangeness of it. He told her about the Rosellas and the Fig Parrots and the Noisy Pittas.

'You're making them up!' she pleaded.

Somehow, they hadn't got round to talking about the book by the time Harry arrived.

Harry, in his soft sweater that was exactly the colour of his eyes. But *exactly*. It had taken a lot of choosing and selecting and bringing it out of the shop to the daylight.

Harry said that the bar was a collector's item; he couldn't imagine how they had found somewhere so scruffy.

'I thought it was a smart bar,' said Greg. She had stopped thinking of him as the Jackaroo.

'Oh, well,' Harry said. It didn't mean anything. It could have meant that, if you didn't know better, it was a smart bar, or it might have meant that if you came all the way from Australia, it could possibly look like a smart place. It might have meant, 'Oh, well, it doesn't matter, the main thing is that we're all here having a drink.'

Ella realised that Harry rarely explained himself. Beautiful people didn't have to explain themselves or tell stories. A peacock didn't have to do anything except be a peacock: everyone else did things around him.

She realised what bird Greg reminded her of: an emu, a big scrappy emu . . .

'Tell me what emus are like,' she said; and he told her that they were big, fightless things always looking as if they needed to be put through a car wash – or indeed as if they *were* a car wash. They were innocent and interested in everything, he said. You only had to sit and wave a handkerchief out of the car and a great big mob of them would come meandering through the scrub to investigate.

Ella found that both endearing and funny. She threw her head back and laughed. They sat opposite her, Greg and Harry both looked at her with admiration. But Ella realised that Harry was looking just past her. There was an old mirror behind her. He could see himself nicely.

'Tell me about this sales conference,' Greg asked.

Ella looked straight at him.

'It's next week,' she said. 'I'll be there to hold your hand.'

19

DORIS LESSING

The Italian Sweater

Jealousy had never afflicted the marriage, now 10 years old. It was a good marriage, as they often said, observing how marriages came and went all around them. 'We're not doing too badly, at that,' he might sum up, waiting for her to confirm it with her comic little squeak of a laugh and, 'We're clever, we are. Clever James. Clever Jill.' Then he, 'Clever Jill, clever James.' Then a kiss. Or many.

There was a child, a satisfactory little girl, doing well.

The slump of 1991, or the recession – apparently considered a less alarming word – deprived her of her job as receptionist in a health and beauty salon. It went bust. He would not lose his job, for he was an official in Income Tax. As both joked, someone had to do it. They had to tighten their belts, but not uncomfortably. They did without a holiday and expected to do without another. They did not replace their car. They ate less meat and did not go to parks or museums that charged entrance fees. Like everyone else, they had cupboards stuffed with clothes. Sometimes they remarked, with the same feeling as one which might accompany a venture into quicksand, that it was a pretty bad lookout if defeating the Recession depended on enough people going out and buying goods they didn't need.

She claimed she had plenty to occupy herself. She painted the bathroom and bedroom, and worked in the garden. She and her friends met in each other's houses, not in cafés as in better times.

Often when James asked her how the day had gone she said that she had met Joan, or Betty or Rebecca at the library or in the park. When the couples met complete with husbands, the women might say they had been somewhere or other together.

Then, one evening, there were friends for supper and James remembered Jill had said the women had been for coffee in Norah's house, but when he mentioned it Norah looked blank and Jill flustered and ashamed. The incident was smoothed over by the habit of happiness, or of good manners, that ruled the marriage.

Somewhere or other it had left a small bruise of suspicion. Then, a week or so later James saw his wife in Knightsbridge and that evening remarked to her that he had, and her face convulsed with – well, with what? Yes, it was fear.

And now he was struck into a cold fever of jealousy that at first he did not recognise, and had to say, this is jealousy. It was a region of frightful and elongated images lit redly from smouldering eyeballs, and at once cunning set his face into interested, lying smiles, and he said, 'Then it must have been someone like you. Outside Harrods?' The query trembled unanswered between them as she knit her brows and bit her lips and tried to smile.

Then began a time when he casually – and oh, so obviously, and he knew it himself – questioned her about what she had done in her day. She had gone to the supermarket, or to a film; she had taken the child to a violin class or to visit her best friend, or to the swimming baths.

But in every day it seemed to him there was an unaccounted-for stretch of hours and when he enquired, 'But what did you do after lunch? You didn't collect Joyce from school until 3.45?' – or some similar shameful interrogation, she might look nervous, smile, and send him without knowing she did, beseeching fleeting glances that he saw as confessions.

He hated her. He loved her all over again. Their sex life became what it had been earlier before the attritions of the quotidian set in. At first he was even prepared to be guilty at forcing himself on her who was in love with a rival, but far from shrinking, or showing signs of putting up with him, she responded with a spontaneity of joy he had almost forgotten.

A second honeymoon! And they said it was.

But all the time her guilty looks and smiles tormented him, even more because of their spectacular sexiness together, and he could not let it go.

He saw her again when he did not expect to, entering another Knightsbridge shop, when he was on his way to lunch. He did not go to lunch, but instead into the great shop that was like a town, and wandered about among handbags and hats and scarves, then he saw her on an escalator just above him. He followed her up, with care, stayed on the escalator when she got off, and descended again, and hung about among shoppers, peering everywhere with guilty looks he was afraid would make him seem like a shoplifter.

Just as he was about to leave that floor, he saw a divine creature, a radiant girl, wearing a very short, black suit in some crisp, light material gliding towards him – his wife Jill, her long, elegant legs in pale, shining silver scissoring about as she swerved, posed, stood poised, while three saleswomen stood in a trance of concentration as great as hers. He recognised that look which enclosed her in narcissism. It was the rapt, entranced self-enhancement he saw on her face in her extreme of pleasure, making love. The saleswomen were rapt because his wife was a beauty in that wisp of a black suit. And who was going to pay for it? Not he, her husband, not now in this phase of penny-pinching, nor ever, for that suit was for a rich woman. It must cost hundreds of pounds. She was so pretty. So delicate, so far from the humdrum woman who might paint a ceiling or set out a row of lettuces, bake potatoes. If he was even more consumed with jealousy than before, then he was also feeling – what was it? – compassion, yes, that was it, for he was thinking for the first time of the passing beauty of women and of what that must mean for the possessors of it. How must it feel to slide over your head a few ounces of stuff, and at once become something as exotic as a cactus flower and then lose it all . . . but it was surely time for her to go and get their child from school? She would have to get a move on . . . he sneaked down the escalator, and stood on the pavement on the watch till he saw her, not seeing him, her ordinary self again, in her blue raincoat and a scarf over her head. She jumped on a bus: she was off to pick up the child. She did not carry a parcel: she had not bought the suit. And now, together with the relief, he was indignant at the injustice that prevented her from having the suit which was so right for her. And if she did own it, where would she wear it? Did that mean there were places she went to wearing

such clothes? If so, who did she go with? Up flamed suspicion again . . . he must examine her wardrobe when she
was not there. How? They did not spy on each other.

That evening the family sat at supper, all three of them,
in the well-used, faintly shabby, pleasant kitchen. They ate
salad, baked potatoes, cheese, and a pizza for the little girl,
who soon jumped up and was off to play with the girls next
door. The parents sat on over their coffee, companionably,
not talking. She leaned her head on a slim hand grubby
from cooking and seemed to dream. He knew what it was
she was seeing. What he saw was a rather too thin woman
in her late thirties. She was pale, perhaps a little anaemic?
Her eyes had always been her chief beauty, enormous blue-
green eyes, in delicately moulded lids, edged by gold lashes
which she sometimes did, sometimes did not, paint black.
They were black now, giving an Egyptian hieratic look to
that dreaming face. She wore a faded blue T-shirt and
jeans that had paint smudges on them. Her hair . . . it
occurred to him that those softly gold petals of hair were
excellently cut . . . expensively cut – that hairstyle had not
been achieved at the hairdresser's down the road. Suspicion
was shrivelling him like a poison.

He had to examine her clothes. When? She knew everything he did in the house, just as he knew what she did.
The telephone rang: she was summoned by a neighbour to
discuss some mutual problem, and off she went: she would
be back in a minute, she said. And the little girl might easily
run in and find him . . .

He tore into their bedroom, slid back her cupboard doors,
and at once was enveloped in an odour like warm spicy
bread, a vanilla smell of hair, skin, and hands that reproached
him because of his suspicions of her, his mad, bad imaginings
which this trusting smell of hers told him were nonsense.
But he kept pulling out garment after garment – he knew
each one, they were like shed snakeskins, skins of his own
memory as much as hers.

At this point he almost accepted the truth that was
hammering there on the edge of his poor fevered brain. But
perhaps there was even something quite pleasant about this
fevered state of his? After all, he led a sober enough life,

and the extremes of emotion, for better or worse, did not enliven his days. Or, for that matter, his nights.

They went to bed early and she eagerly came into his arms as he reached out for her. He was holding the exquisite creature he had seen in the big shop, and he yearned and marvelled over that white delicate skin of hers, that had a sheen of love-sweat on it, and her too-thin body, like a stork's or a crane's, made young and vulnerable by his jealousy.

How extraordinary, he thought next morning watching her hustle into her old jeans, an ordinary woman whom no one would notice much at a bus-stop, and then become *that* – what he had seen yesterday.

His was not a job he could leave for a couple of hours without comment. He worked hard. He often did not take a real lunch break, but went out for a quick sandwich. He worked all morning, all afternoon, his mind on what his wife might be doing, and with whom. And then, for the first time in his conscientious life, he invented a domestic crisis and asked for a week off. He had a good deal of leave due to him. And, for the first time, he did not tell Jill.

That evening she seemed to gleam and shine. She was very far away from the little girl, her daughter, and from him. With whom?

Next morning he pretended to go to work as usual. That he did not feel in the least guilty, deceiving this other half of himself, his partner in everything, told him that he was in fact in a bad way. To spy on his own house was impossible. It was kept under observation by a Neighbourhood Watch Committee. Near the bus-stop was a small public garden, and he went there, though it was dangerous: what if someone said to Jill, 'I saw your husband this morning.'

Soon she came running along the pavement like a girl, stepped lightly on to the bus, and went to the front, downstairs. She was smiling, not seeing much. He went up to the top, and when she got off, not in Knightsbridge this time, but near Bond Street, he did too.

This was not an emporium, but a small shop; much more difficult to spy on her. He sauntered up and down the pavement, taking cautious looks in. And there she was, this time in an outfit made for the beach, where they were not going this year – nor any year, not a beach fit for these clothes. She wore pale silk beach pyjamas like those of the Thirties, and a floppy, fine straw hat. Again saleswomen watched her. One brought her a handkerchief to tie at her wrist, another a bright bag, a third coloured beads. Again he saw the close concentration of the women, focused on the body and being of his wife. She was known in this shop which owned the name of one of the world's leading designers. If she was not going to buy these clothes then why . . . but she was so lovely, that was it. These saleswomen sold clothes all day to fat women, ugly women or merely ordinary women, and several times a day they must suffer as some creation lost lustre when it adapted itself to an unsuitable host. But here was this magically pretty creature (his wife) who wore these clothes as they should be worn. That was it . . . And for whom did she model the clothes? And now he had to accept it. For herself. They were day-dreams given substance. He had not known she longed for glamour, for expensive beaches, for parties where she could show off this delicate beauty of hers . . . and perhaps she did not, not really, but only in a part of herself she did not class as important. He hoped at least this was so.

She left that shop, he again followed, and she entered another, in a parallel street and again she paraded in clothes worth hundreds of pounds, and this time customers thought she was a model. The salespeople kept the secret, and Jill played her part. Her husband's heart ached for her, seeing how she was enjoying herself, how well she did it. The dress, which on her looked like a crystalline extension of her body, her movements like a ballerina's, was a pale peachy confec-tion meant to be worn to some important ball and it looked vulgar on the Arab lady who bought it. But never mind. The salespeople, and she his wife, not to mention himself, had seen the dress as it should look and it did not matter about its descent into banality.

He watched her go into a hairdresser whose name was known in five continents. He did not grudge this to her: she must be saving a bit here and there off the housekeeping, but her dragonfly self entitled her to it, and he even under-stood that his not knowing must be part of the fun.

He took the underground a couple of stops to make sure they would not find themselves in the same café. He felt as if he knelt by a deep pool, gazing into it, and there in its depths was his wife, his own Jill, his better half, but in a dimension forever removed from him. He did not know it, but he smiled with tenderness that seemed as strong as the bitter jealousy that had taken itself off.

He could not go home until the usual time. That meant he had several hours to fill. Now he did something he had never even been tempted to do. He went into the men's department of expensive stores and tried on clothes he had never worn in his life. Nor could he wear them now. Where to? In these suits, these jackets, he would be a misfit in his working life, and nothing in his life with his family could accommodate them. He left the big stores, remarking, for he had not known it, since his clothes-buying had been a casual business – that at this level of shops suits and jackets and coats repeated themselves across the city. He entered a shop that was the equivalent of those he had seen Jill in that morning. The prices – well, people had to pay for their fantasies, he could see that. Aided by a youth who saw from one look at him that he was not at home in this place, he put on several sweaters, finally lingering over that was inspired, so it seemed, by Aborigine paintings, a map of another dimension in blues and greens, with a touch of burnt umber and a hint of yellow. Italian. The material was like a supple suede, or thick silk, and the sweater ought really to be framed and hung in the Tate. Much worse had been hung in the Tate.

James was not a bad-looking man, of the tall, lean kind, with a normally humorous (if not recently) smile, and no longer dark, because he was greying. But he looked marvellous in this sweater, no other word for it. It cost . . . he lingered, looking at himself with disbelief. The assistant did too. It was he who offered, 'I'll reduce it . . . it's absolutely right for you.' But it was still far more than he, the family, could afford.

'It's too expensive,' said James. The assistant wanted him to have it. For aesthetic reasons, and probably something more. The languid youth admired him. A variety of pressures James normally knew nothing about turned invisible balances within him – he bought the thing, feeling as if he was accepting calamity.

And now what was he to do with it? He could not take it home. Jill would be appalled: it cost as much as two months' housekeeping. If he took it to the office, whose possession he was as much as he was his family's, in no time that garment would be laid out and admired and exclaimed over. 'Have you won a sweepstake? Won the Pools?' And the questions would be derisive, he knew that. They would think he had gone mad . . . Where could he keep it? He wrapped it up carefully and put it in the bottom drawer of his desk.

That night, he stroked his love Jill's golden hair, touched her soft cheeks, and said helplessly, 'I love you, I love you . . .' And she laughed excitedly and said, 'What's got into you, I'd like to know . . . well, I'm not complaining.'

He stretched his arms out as he lay on his back on the bed and laughed aloud at the excess of emotions that boiled and billowed in him, and saw Jill's flushed face bend over him, and thought what a couple they would make, he and she, in their forbidden clothes, walking together into . . . well, where?

He had four days' holiday left. He did not want them. He did not know what to do with them.

Next day at lunchtime, he went furtively into his office, said he had forgotten something he needed, took out the sweater, put it on in the men's room and sneaked out of the office like a criminal.

Where could he go? He went to the Ritz, sat down where he would be more an observer than observed, and ordered tea. At once he knew that if his sweater was not remarkable here, then everything else about him was wrong – his shoes, his trousers, and even his haircut. Only his Italian sweater belonged, and even that was, perhaps, a bit over the top. Where ought it to be worn? Probably on a yacht with friends. A villa on a sunny coast, in the late evening, when the air was chilled? With people – and this was the point – who cared very much what people wore and who would find this thing a compliment to them. As it was, he felt in the wrong place, and wrongly presented . . . this room was full. People were making a business of having tea and cakes and the rest. No one noticed him ... yes, one did. A young man by himself was watching him ... a young man like the assistant in the shop. Now James was being eyed. Assessed. Priced. This young man was joined by another and both were conscious of James, and looked at his sweater and then at him. James paid for his tea and left. He felt as guilty as if he had robbed a shop, or even his own department.

He took a bus back to the street where the shop was and went in. No customers: after all, this was a Recession. The same languid young man, obviously wishing he had an excuse to be petulant stood staring out at the street. He knew at once why James had come. The two stood staring at each other, James' face an apology and a plea, the young man's at first affronted, ready to accuse.

James said, 'I can't afford it. I must have gone mad.'

The young man's aggressive stance left him. He seemed to brood about the wrongness of the world for a while, then nodded and said nicely, 'Well, I did think at the time ...' He took the garment, which he knew had been worn, found some modish coffee-coloured tissue paper to wrap it in, and returned it to a drawer. Then he looked for James' cheque, still there. He tore it up.

'Believe me,' said James, 'I am really grateful.'

'It happens,' said the young man. Then, 'Well, you can do the same for me some time.'

This preposterousness, with its hinterlands of suggestiveness about which the youth made no bones, eyeing, not to say ogling, James, made them laugh together.

And then, on the laugh, James left the shop and went to his office where he said the domestic crisis was solved. If they wished he could come back tomorrow. They did wish. Income Tax was permanently understaffed. He had only two days off – two days which for ever after he would think of as a dangerous country that might have destroyed him.

To think that a sweater, something woven and dyed and imagined in the mind of some genius or other, could open doors ... just as the pretty clothes his Jill put on could open doors if only ...

But her excursions into fantasy did not go on very long.

After all, there must be a limit to shops even a raving beauty like Jill could enter again and again, to play with her fantasies and those of the salespeople. And where could she go from there – that was the point? There must have come that moment when she, just like James, lost in the feverish world of money and danger, had said to herself, 'But where do I go from here?'

His heart was sore, it mourned for her, for that other self of her which would for ever be unfulfilled. She would go on being his good and loving wife, he would be her good and loving husband, and he would always know when he held her in his arms that somewhere just out of sight danced this other self of hers, as fragile as a butterfly, and she could see that self, and never know that he could too.

For there was no way he could tell her he had spied on her: the fresh and candid air the marriage lived in would not tolerate such a confidence. Interesting though: this wife of his, gardening, cooking, taking the child to school: that other self of hers was one everyone could admire, respect, yearn over – if they caught sight of it. Whereas he in his Italian sweater: well, he could not imagine any setting for it but a disreputable one. Why was that? Surely there was an imbalance here somewhere?

HELEN SIMPSON

The Immaculate Bridegroom

Dawn climbed smiling up from her warm white dream, magnolia petal slippers whispering in the cathedral hush beneath wild silk underskirts, enormously hooped, and bud-studded gypsophila like a mystic cloud of gnats: then reached the top, real life again, and felt her face drop, along with her heart and stomach and the corners of her mouth.

'It's not fair,' she said. She turned her head and stared at the wallpaper – a tangled pattern of briar roses she had seized on for her boudoir 12 years ago, a rare choice allowed by her parents at the onset of adolescence and never regretted. 'What's wrong, darling?' said her mother, Sylvia, appearing with the tea.

'Oh the usual,' grunted Dawn, heaving herself up and jutting out her underlip like a thwarted baby. 'I'm fed up. I want everything to be different.'

'It does seem so unfair,' tutted Sylvia. 'It is,' Dawn agreed.

'Sometimes I curse Roger,' said Sylvia. Dawn gave a soft scream. 'I told you, Mum!' she hissed. 'If you mention his name again, I'll . . .'

'Sorry dear,' said Sylvia. 'I can't help thinking of all those years.'

'Well, don't,' said Dawn, heaving herself out of bed and over to the dressing table. She scowled into its triple mirror, her profile aping the hard-nosed sullenness of a Quattrocento Gonzaga. 'Who knows what might turn up?' said her mother hopelessly.

'Nothing ever does turn up, does it?' said Dawn in injured tones. 'I'll tell you what, Mum, I don't see why Sandra Bailey who was never anything special, and great fat legs, should have her big day and not me.'

'It does seem cruel,' Sylvia agreed. 'We'd manage it much better than Sandra Bailey and her mother. I don't see why you should be done out of it.'

'I don't see why I should be done out of it, either. The most important day of my life.'

'I'm being done out of it too, your big day,' said Sylvia. 'The bride's mother. It's obviously completely unfair.'

Dawn started prowling round the bedroom, abstractedly brushing her hair, which crackled with static under the bristles.

'You're a modern girl,' said her mother. 'You don't have to put up with things.'

'No,' said Dawn. 'I don't.'

'Don't make the mistakes I did,' said Sylvia. 'Too passive. Putting up with things.'

'You're absolutely right, Mum!' said Dawn, pausing by an oppressive poster of Beata Beatrix, taut with the bright-eyed rapture of one to whom the truth has been revealed. Then she sagged. 'But . . . Even so . . . It would be awfully difficult . . .' Sylvia leant forward urgently across the tea tray. 'Nothing worth having's ever easy, Dawn,' she enunciated.

'So you think . . .?'

'Follow your heart's desire.'

'You're right,' breathed Dawn. 'Oh, Mum, I will!'

Dawn's father Harry was less than delighted at her news. 'Do you know what weddings cost?' he grunted.

'Oh you old killjoy,' Sylvia twitted him.

'Do you? Anyway, when did Roger decide to do the decent thing?' said Harry. 'First I've heard of it. Thought he disappeared off the scene years ago.'

'It's not Roger,' said Dawn, pink-cheeked, her eyes starting to brim.

'Then who the hell is it?' said Harry.

'Trust you to be difficult,' snapped Sylvia. 'Can't you see you're upsetting the girl? Marriages are made in heaven. Killjoy. You have to work at a marriage. You wouldn't deny that, I suppose!' She paused for a bitter laugh. 'You wouldn't deny I've had to work at our marriage like some pit pony while you've suited yourself. You wouldn't have the nerve!'

'What?' said Harry.

'Come on, darling,' said Sylvia, 'let's ring your aunts.

31

Your cousins. Tell them the good news. He's thrilled for you really, he just needs time to get used to the idea.'

Once Dawn had found two friends willing to act as bridesmaids, they convened in a wine bar to chew over past weddings and plan this one.

'Amethysts like mauve raindrops,' sighed Milly. 'A pomander affair made of stephanotis and love-in-a-mist looped round her wrist. You can imagine. With her hair.'

Milly sat on the other side of the corridor from Dawn at work. Dawn hadn't known her long but she seemed kind and posh and would know what's what. Also, while she wasn't risibly spotty or funny-looking, neither was she particularly pretty, which was ideal. The same went for Christine on the looks front, though Dawn had known her much longer, since schooldays.

'So tell us about him,' said Christine, draining her glass. 'Where did you meet him?'

'Yes, we don't even know his name!' said Milly. 'So mysterious!'

'Rochester,' said Dawn.

'Rochester?' said Christine. 'What on earth were you doing in Rochester?'

'No,' said Dawn. 'That's his name. Mr Rochester.' She paused. 'Tony.'

'And is he tall, dark and handsome?' enquired Christine sharply.

'Yes,' said Dawn. 'At least, I think so.'

'I should hope so!' said Milly. 'That you do, I mean. That's all that matters, isn't it?'

'Yes,' said Dawn.

The talk turned to the unsatisfactory nature of modern men, the way they seemed to flit around more than they ever used to, never building anything up, never tying themselves down, never amounting to much.

'They take eight or nine of your best years,' snarled Christine. 'Keep you hanging on and hanging on, then they bugger off when crunch time comes. Your Roger was classic, leaving you high and dry at 33. Fantastic.' Dawn looked at her with dislike.

'But Tony's not like that,' said Milly, brightly, at last. 'Hopefully.'

'What does Tony do?' asked Christine.

'He works in finance,' said Dawn. There was a pause. 'High finance,' she added softly.

'And how did he propose?' asked Christine in spite of herself.

'It wasn't in so many words,' said Dawn, her eyes shining. 'It was more we became aware. Both of us. That we'd somehow found our other half. I feel so at home with him. It's almost like being on my own.'

'So when can we meet him?' asked Christine. 'Your other half.'

'The thing is,' said Dawn, 'he has a very responsible job. He's rarely around.'

'Your time together is precious,' suggested Milly.

'Surely he relaxes sometimes,' said Christine.

'Well, he has his . . . his club,' said Dawn.

'Golf?' said Christine. 'How old is he?'

'He does it for his health,' said Dawn, fiddling with her bracelet. 'He has a weak heart,' she added, with a sudden hard look.

After that, wedding preparations started in earnest. Sylvia bought a book on how to do it, packed with nuptial etiquette.

'It's good luck for you to see a sweep on the way to church,' she said. 'Or a grey horse. I don't know which would be more difficult to arrange. Which would you prefer?'

'Milly's got an Edwardian sixpence for my shoe,' said Dawn with satisfaction.

'The bridegroom's function,' read Sylvia, suddenly anxious. 'He buys the ring. That's all right, you can have mine. Call it an heirloom. He provides the bride's mother's corsage. I think I can manage that. Oh, he tips the verger.'

'What's a verger?' asked Dawn.

'It doesn't say,' said Sylvia. 'We'll have to find out.'

'Cooker hood. Nutcrackers. Stepladder,' read Dawn, turning to a list of suggested wedding presents.

'I wouldn't include too many little things like nutcrackers,' said Sylvia. 'People can be very mean. Specially relatives.'

'Music,' Dawn went on, flicking through the pages. She started to hum. 'I quite liked that one Princess Diana had at her wedding. You know, *I Vow To Thee My Country*.'

'That was a real wedding,' crooned Sylvia. 'Just like a fairytale. You can't take that away, you can't say it wasn't perfect. Nothing to do with what came after.'

'No,' agreed Dawn. 'It was above all that. And I liked the wedding in *The Sound Of Music* too, just before the interval. Seven stepchildren, though. Quite a handful.'

'She was good with children, though,' said Sylvia. 'She went on to do *Mary Poppins*.'

'*Arrival Of The Queen Of Sheba*,' said Dawn. 'I'll have that. You remember, Mum; I did it for Grade V. *Dudda dudda dudda dudda dudda dudda dudda dudda da da da da da da da da da da dee da dee da dee DUDDA dudda!*' She ran out of breath and started laughing.

The invitations, spidered with soft silvery italics, took two days to address, owing to the invitees' complicated web of mésalliances, formal and otherwise, tearings asunder, impediments, third-time-roundings, and only the occasional straightforward nuclear smugness to speed things up.

'You see, look,' said Sylvia, 'your cousin Bridget, she was born Bridget Riley, but she married George Filmer.'

'George Filmer!' snorted Harry.

'We all make mistakes,' said Sylvia. 'So they'd have been Mr and Mrs George Filmer, and if he'd died she'd still be Mrs George Filmer. But she divorced, after the Stanley knife incident, so then she was Mrs Bridget Filmer. Not Riley again, mark you, not the name she was born with.'

'Her father's name,' said Harry. 'Now he was a bugger . . .'

'But then she married again, Robert Billington. So now she's Mrs Robert Billington, even though poor Bob's passed away.'

'She did all right out of that,' said Harry. 'All that life insurance. No one ever mentioned seeing a Stanley knife, did they, on the scene, when Bob's body was found?'

'Harry,' said Sylvia. 'I'm warning you. One crack like that at the reception and I'll . . .'

'Do we have to have cousin Bridget?' said Dawn pensively.

'Yes,' said Sylvia. 'She's your flesh and blood. Unfortunately.'

'Mrs Dawn Rochester,' smiled Dawn.

'No,' said Harry. 'Mrs Tony Rochester. You'd have to give him the push before you could call yourself Dawn again.'

'Oh, yes,' said Dawn, looking mildly confused. 'So I would.'

There was no getting round it, said Sylvia, they would have to see the vicar. They couldn't leave it any longer.

Once in his front room, mother and daughter found themselves crouching forward, chins thrust out sincerely, faces reddened by the horrible realisation that what they wanted might not be allowed to happen.

'The thing is, vicar,' said Sylvia, 'Dawn's fiancé has a very responsible job. He's never there.'

'My goodness me,' said the rector. He searched their faces for existential satire, but saw nothing like that beneath the sweat of their embarrassment.

'He's in the world of finance,' Dawn chipped in.

'So we were wondering,' said Sylvia in a rush, 'if by any remote chance he wasn't able to be there on the day, and we're 99.9% sure he will be of course, well, in that event perhaps we could arrange a proxy.'

'A proxy?' said the rector, who had been expecting a double divorcée, say, or a bigamist, but not this.

'Do you remember Prince Arthur? Henry VII's eldest boy?' said Sylvia. 'Well, his father wanted a dynastic marriage with Spain, because the Tudors were new, not really supposed to be there, so he married little Arthur off to the Infanta, but the children were too young to marry really, only seven. So they sent a proxy over to Madrid, to stand in for the prince, who was unwell at the time.'

Sylvia had an encyclopaedic knowledge of the ins and outs of the British monarchy from the Plantagenets onward, acquired during 40–odd years of reading nothing much but Jean Plaidy and Anya Seton.

'On the wedding night,' she continued, 'The proxy touched the Infanta's naked shin with the heel of his bare foot, and that counted as a symbol of the . . .' she lowered her eyes modestly, ' . . . consummation of the marriage. So we were wondering, vicar, if in the unlikely event that Dawn's intended was called away, on her big day I mean . . .'

' . . . by the world of finance . . .'

' . . . by the world of finance, yes, would a . . . a proxy be acceptable to you? Because the boy next door's quite willing to stand in. He's the sort who's naturally unpopular, so he'd do anything for you. We've known him years, Dawn and him used to play French skipping but she's never fancied him. In fact I think he's probably the other way if anything.'

'Oh he is,' said Dawn. 'It's a fact. He came out in January.'

'Oh?' said Sylvia. 'That's news to me.'

'It'd be news to his mother too,' said Dawn. 'He's doing it generation by generation, working back gradually. To the difficult ones. Personally, I wish him well.'

'Excuse me,' said the rector. 'May I interrupt at this point? Well, Sylvia. Well, Dawn. My turn now. I want to let you know where I stand vis-à-vis the horns of your dilemma. And that directly relates to my views on the Church of England.'

'Yes, vicar,' said Sylvia. 'Dawn, sit up straight.'

'Strongly ecumenical though my sympathies are,' continued the rector, 'I cannot help but feel that the Church of England has a superior understanding of life's complexities. We are capable of responding to the changing needs of humanity, indeed to the passage of time itself. We shift. And we are proud to shift. When necessary. You know the story about the oak tree breaking and the reed bending? Well that is what I love about the Church of England – its reediness. Dawn, are you listening?'

'Yes vicar,' said Dawn, who had been thinking she ought to do her nails tonight.

'Now, Dawn, as I see it,' said the rector, 'you are a lamb newly returned to the fold.'

'What, like the prodigal son?' said Dawn, resentfully.

'She's been a good daughter,' said Sylvia.

'I'm sure she has. So I take it you will both agree to come

to church every Sunday until Dawn's wedding and at least every other Sunday for the next five years, by which time I hope you will both be as they say "hooked". On pain of annulment of the marriage if either of you defaults, I'm afraid.'

The night before, Dawn could not sleep. The trouble was, she could not think what he looked like. She could imagine a looming shape in the doorway, a dark brown voice, a muscular thigh. But she could not envisage his face. After a while this bothered her so much that she called out to her mother, who was sitting up late with a fine black felt-tip stroking in a cross-bar on each Order of Service sheet in the line which read: *And did those feel in ancient times.*

'If I'm honest, Mum,' she sniffed, 'I'm not sure how well I really know him.'

'That's only natural, darling,' said Sylvia. 'You're not married yet.'

'But he seems sort of shadowy.'

'Plenty of time for the solid stuff after the wedding. Things should be dreamy before.'

'Am I doing the right thing, though?' wept Dawn. 'What if he turns out to be like Roger? Or Dad?'

'Listen Dawn,' said Sylvia sharply. 'He's an altogether different class of man. He won't.'

'But am I really in love?' she wailed.

'Of course you are!' snapped Sylvia. 'Pull yourself together. What do you want to do? Give the ring back? Call it all off? It's a bit late in the day for that, you know.'

'I know,' said Dawn, trumpeting into a tissue. 'Sorry Mum. It didn't seem quite real for a minute there. Just nerves.'

Four hours of the early part of the morning had been allowed for the preparation of the bride, and that allowance had not proved excessive.

Dawn's colour had been rising steadily since she woke up; she was now very pink indeed under her heated rollers and had almost stopped breathing.

'I think I've got a temperature,' she puffed.

'Excitement,' said Milly knowledgeably, freezing her nail varnish with a fixative spray. 'Don't worry, I've got some green make-up on me. I've done this before. You'll look like an arum lily by the time I've finished with you.'

Sylvia was peeling the price tag from the sole of the bride's gentian satin courts.

'Don't forget to step out of the house on your right foot when you leave for church,' said Milly. 'Or it's bad luck for ever.'

'Oh dear,' said Dawn. 'There's such a lot to remember.'

Milly and Christine, sugar-pink caryatids in sashed and sprigged Swiss lawn, helped Dawn, by now gasping for air like a fish, into the wedding dress. It was a square-necked seersucker gown with leg-o'-mutton sleeves and 182 hand-covered buttons.

'Ooooh,' went the women, with the sigh that people make as fireworks fade.

When Dawn and her father arrived at the church, the rector hurried forward to meet them with a long face.

'I'm afraid I have something of a disappointment for you, my dear,' he said to Dawn.

She recoiled in a rustle of puckered silk.

'You promised,' she hissed, a furious swan on the path. 'You promised!'

'Never fear,' said the rector hurriedly, with a lop-sided smile. 'What I was going to say was, it looks as though our gallant proxy may be called on after all.'

Then Dawn put a hand to her thumping heart and smiled, while Harry turned and waved at the limousine parked by the lych-gate. Out jumped the boy next door, spruce and shy. They shooed him into the church before them, waited a moment and then, at a sign from the rector, the opening chords of *Arrival Of The Queen Of Sheba* cascaded down and they went slowly in.

Just as a camcorder may cause offence during a wedding ceremony, so may an authorial presence. Imagination must supply the dog-rose blushes of the bride beneath her clouding of organdie tulle, the satin slippers moving at the hem

of her dress like blue-nosed mice, and the soaring and crashing of the organ music.

Some guests could not help but notice, however, that what
with the bride's family seated shoulder to shoulder in the
left-hand pews and only the mother of the boy-next-door
on the right, there was something of an imbalance. The
church had lolled like a clumsily ballasted ship.

There was some comment on this at the reception
afterwards.

'Bit of a one-sided wedding,' said an aunt from Birk-
enhead.

'Bit of a one-horse affair all round,' replied Mrs Robert
Billington. 'Not even a sit-down meal.'

'I mean, did you notice,' persisted the aunt, 'our side of
the church was packed, but on the other side nobody but
the next-door neighbour.'

'Ironic, after all these years, to end up with the boy-next-
door,' sniffed Mrs Billington.

'Someone was telling me he was only a stand-in,' puzzled
the aunt.

'A stand-in?' said Mrs Billington. 'A stand-in for what?'
'That's what I said,' the aunt agreed. She shrugged. 'Dawn
makes a lovely bride, though, doesn't she? Bless her.'

Dawn ran whooping through an archway of hands and a
shower of rice, off to the car and away. Sylvia stood and
cried.

'There, there,' said Harry. 'He'll take good care of her.'

And he obviously did. She came back brown as a Sunday
roast – radiant! It was a shame he'd had to carry on from
St Lucia but it would have been foolish not to fly on to the
Philippines to clinch the deal he'd been working on at
the time of their wedding, and Dawn was quite happy about
that.

'I'm not worried,' she said to Milly and Christine at
their post-honeymoon get together to view the wedding
photographs. 'He can look after himself.'

The story should end here, happily ever after so to speak;
unfortunately it is necessary to add a coda.

Such serenity, such newly-wed insouciance, threw the

blow, when it fell, into cruelly sharp relief. News of Tony's demise on foreign shores, a massive coronary at a vital convention, tragic though it was, and of course untimely, trailed clouds of fiscal glory. His actions that day, just before the fatal stoppage, had saved the livelihood of thousands of shareholders, Dawn told them (though it had left her no better off than before since, oddly enough, he had died without leaving a bean). She mopped her eyes and blew her nose with subdued grace.

Widowhood had conferred on Dawn an unexpected gravitas. It became apparent that she was not utterly bereft. Tony had not died without issue, or, at least, not exactly. Dawn grew bulkier by the week and developed a sleepy smile. There was some comfort in this situation, friends remarked; she would have someone to cherish. And if the child were a boy – as indeed proved to be the case – then his father's name, as well as his memory, would live on.

CLARE BOYLAN

Horrible Luck

'And how are you today?' said Mrs Lee.

'Horrible,' said Mrs Lemon.

'What's horrible?' Mrs Lee still had an eye on her newspaper.

'Me luck,' said Mrs Lemon.

Camilla Lee generously detached herself from Auberon Waugh to give her attention to a familiar routine. 'Is it himself?'

Mrs Lemon groaned. 'Haven't seen hide nor hair of himself this past six month. I've been threatened.' She lit a cigarette and commenced a vigorous bout of scrubbing. Turds of ash fell from her gasper and as she cleaned the kitchen counter it was dimmed under a coating of lava. Camilla watched in fascination as the trail of grey ash replaced Frederick's wholesome trail of brown breadcrumbs. Mrs Lemon began to cry. 'It's this letter.' She rooted in her clothing and handed across a sheet of notepaper. Mrs Lee scanned the childish scrawl. It was about St Jude. It enumerated his miracles and favours and attributed oddly material benefits to his supporters – new cars or houses, a big lottery win. It urged the recipient of the note to pass it on to another. '*If you do not do so,*' it unsportingly suggested, '*horrible luck will follow.*'

'It's a chain letter,' Mrs Lee laughed. 'It's just rubbish. Here! We'll throw it in the bin. Have some coffee.'

The two middle-aged women breakfasted together every day. They had nothing in common except their age. Their relationship was based on Mrs Lemon's familiarity with Mrs Lee's underwear, and Mrs Lee's acquaintance with Mrs Lemon's private life. All Mrs Lemon's luck was horrible. Her husband was violent and her children uncontrollable. The woman was so dazed with sedatives and nicotine that she was a fire hazard as well as a terrible housekeeper. Mrs Lee sometimes wondered why she employed her, but Mrs

41

Lemon was both her good deed and her talisman. One needed a good deed to propitiate the gods and she liked having her there for comparison, to think that this was the alternative. She herself had married wisely and kept her looks. Mrs Lemon lumbered back to the table and sat down, rubbing tears from her withered yellow skin. She leaned forward for the sugar and a bolt of ash detached itself and landed in the butter. 'There!' Mrs Lee said kindly.

For some reason the episode bucked her up. It made her count her blessings. Life, she realised, was not merely a matter of luck but of management and she had managed hers superbly. She worked well that morning, dined with pleasure, but without wine, for she was going to a party. It rained when she was emerging late that evening and there weren't any taxis, but a young man with whom she was vaguely acquainted offered her a lift.

'How kind,' Camilla said. She didn't think so at all. She supposed he wanted something. Kim Taylor was young and beautifully made. She admired the selfish curve of his mouth with an edge of temper on it. Young women would think it sensitive. He had a reputation with women. He glanced at her with his piercing turquoise eyes. 'I'm enjoying this,' she thought. She supposed he was anxious to drop her off and be with some girl. This did not make her uneasy. She had her aura too. Mrs Lee was successful and had plenty of money and all men liked that. They drove through the night in silence and comfort, each thinking their own thoughts and well pleased with themselves. She was looking forward to tomorrow, and before that, to her tremendously comfortable bed, with dear old Frederick asleep in it. They had no children and she thought this was probably a good thing. Children rarely understood how pleasant and absorbing the lives of older people could be. She had no idea what the boy was thinking. Well, how could she? He turned slowly and touched her cheek as the rest of the cars edged forward at the lights like greyhounds at a starting line. 'You're very pretty,' he whispered.

'Don't be ridiculous,' she said, rather pleased.

She was woken in the morning, as usual, by a series of trumpeting laments like a ship bewildered by fog, as Mrs

Lemon let herself in and began to unshroud herself of waterproofs. Frederick had gone hours ago, departed at dawn, considerably silent, to make money. The smell of coffee rose through the house. This was the signal for Mrs Lee to get out of bed but as she rose upon an elbow something very peculiar happened. She rolled over, gave a low chortle and then stretched out her body until all the nerves and sinews set up a humming. After that she got up and went downstairs.

There was a moment in the day when she studied her reflection with a new interest. Pretty. It was a long time since anyone had called her pretty. Actually she had never been pretty. She had once been considered handsome but not pretty. The word suggested that its bearer needed no other function except to be. It was a tinkling word. It was . . . absurd. She went out to lunch and successfully snared a year's advertising from a French cosmetic company.

In the middle of the afternoon the phone rang. 'It's Kim.'

'Kim who?' she said. But her heart, fired by a single glass of Chablis, did a silly dance.

'Come to the opera with me?' he said. 'I've got tickets for tomorrow.'

'I can't. I have an engagement.' She took a deep breath and added formally, 'Nice of you to think of me.'

'Cancel your engagement,' he persisted. 'I'll call you in the morning.' And he hung up before she could put him in his place.

She could never have guessed how pleasant it would be, sitting next to his composed beauty and listening to the beautiful music. There was a starkly sexual quality to his self-assurance. When not attending to the music he had the knack of devoting himself completely to her, ignoring the haunted eyes of younger women. 'I'm almost old enough to be his mother,' she reprimanded herself, with a hint of smugness.

On the way home he stopped the car. 'What do you want, Kim?' she said and the young man replied, 'I want to go to bed with you.'

'Don't be ridiculous,' she said again.

He stroked her cheek and her mouth with his finger.

Then he sighed, turned back to the traffic, drove her home in silence. She passed the night in a frenzy of longing.

Mrs Lemon's husband came back and gave her a black eye. She sat at the kitchen table and wept. He went away again. She sat at the kitchen table and wept. Her daughter, 15, got pregnant. Howls dimmed the Hoover's hum and ash gathered in funeral piles. Sharon fell off her boyfriend's motorcycle and she lost the baby. Mrs Lee grieved amid the alien cornflakes. The house looked terrible. Camilla thought she should give Mrs Lemon a few days off and get one of those cleaning agencies in to do a really good job, but Mrs Lemon shook her head, scattering tears and the dust of tobacco leaves. 'I'm better kept busy. I know I haven't been myself. It's me nerves. You've no idea what it's like having a threat hanging over you all the time. I can't get on with my life. I keep thinking something bad will happen.'

Considering the normal run of Mrs Lemon's fortune, Camilla couldn't suppress a small laugh. 'Whatever can you mean?'

'But I threw it out.'

Mrs Lemon excavated the portable black bucket she called her handbag and fished out the crumpled note. 'You have to pass it on. If I don't me luck will be horrible,' Mrs Lemon said stubbornly. 'If I do, there's some other poor soul's misery on my conscience.'

'Now this is plain foolishness and you know it,' Camilla spoke sternly to her domestic. She made a similar speech to Kim Taylor. 'I have to see you,' he had written. There had been notes almost every day – silly, trivial scraps of flattery better suited to a blonde of 19. 'Kim, I do wish you would stop this. I'm a married woman.' She listened hard into the line. 'Look,' she added kindly, 'we could talk about it over a drink.' She put down the phone with a shaking hand. Dear God, he had nearly slipped away.

When he drove her back to his apartment there was the briefly unpleasant sensation that she was losing something of value. It was like watching her credit card slide through a grating in the road. She pushed him off feebly. 'I'm not really used to this sort of thing,' she protested. 'How sweet you are,' he said.

'Darling Milly,' he wrote (no one had ever called her Milly. It too blatantly rhymed with 'silly') . . . 'I dreamed all night of my sweet, delicious nymph. How exquisitely pretty you looked, all dimpled with bliss . . .'

It was mere cajolery. Naturally one did not take such things seriously. All the same, the succulent little tributes did assume a sort of integrity. Camilla was changing. She grew softer. She was so happy that she felt able to dispense this benefit. She could be genuinely nice to Mrs Lemon, for instance, and the poor thing grew less abject, for which her employer awarded her a very nice knitted suit, hardly worn and some advice. 'You have to take control of your life. It is a mistaken belief that you get out of life what you put into it. In fact, you get what you take out of it. Realise your own value. The solution to all your ills lies within your own hands.' So persuasive was she in her new ebullient charm that Mrs Lemon slavishly pursued her prescription. She got a barring order against her husband, though they sometimes met up to go to the pictures, or visited a hotel for sex. She gave up Valium and took up yoga. She asked advice about face creams and once Camilla was touched to see her squirting herself as if to extinguish a fire with her employer's Joy. 'Here!' she said on impulse, 'Take this one for yourself, Mrs Lemon.' And she gave her a half-full bottle of Calèche. 'That one is stale,' Mrs Lemon said. 'And my name is Rosemary.'

Sometimes when she rose from Kim's bed, heavy with gratification and drenched in compliments, she was surprised by her reflection in the mirror, of a tousled middle-aged woman. She expected to see what he described, someone sweet and pretty. And young. In some ways she felt younger than him. She had always been in control of her life but never before had anyone taken control of her. No one had tried to woo her with compliments. They had not understood the burden a successful woman carries, each day having to don her brittle armour of independence. He had recomposed her, had braved the daunting shield to rescue the vulnerable female locked within. She was weary of confrontation and conquest. She wanted to lie down and be praised for the pinkness of her toes. She felt now like a sugar-icing flower on a delicious birthday cake. That is how she *felt*. But what did she think? Camilla was not a susceptible woman, so everyone always said.

'What do you think, Camilla?' A client asked her during an important meeting.

She tried to compose a look of intelligence on her face, which had lapsed into an aspect of carnal vegetation. My breasts, she realised. I was thinking about my breasts. She used to look upon these sturdy organs rather as Mrs Thatcher might, like an advance guard which declared her sex and at the same time avowed that it was not to be trifled with. Now they were heavy flowers that sprang from her ribs, narcotic and exotic. She could never have imagined that breasts could have such personality, could crave and declare. Now she understood the French artists and their models and the nature of the great works that occasionally ensued their alliance; that art might be sex and sex might be art. With an effort of will she brought her mind back to the business of the moment and brought the meeting to a conclusion. 'You are a marvel,' her client told her. 'And you get younger all the time.'

Now and again she got the uneasy feeling that she was indulging her body too much. It was getting the upper hand. She got the odd notion that it sulked if she gave any priority to cerebral issues. The great explosion of happiness and energy that had accompanied the start of her affair was sometimes overtaken by a dreamlike lethargy. The curious idea came to her that Kim had sucked all the steel out of her body and left behind only accessible flesh. Employing his array of compliments, he had filleted her. She was becoming like one of those pallid boneless joints that butchers sell for easy carving. She let her hair grow long and her voice became gentler. When they spoke on the phone it was the merest kitten's mew. Now that she had been made meek she discovered a whole new world of women whom she had not noticed before, young women with eyes of slate and bullet-proof shoulder pads, ever-watchful of successful older women, not to learn from them but to discern their weakness. Once, when she lingered over a lunch with Kim she found that one of these girls had taken over her meeting. When Camilla entered Amy said quite smoothly. 'I hope you're feeling better, Mrs Lee.' Camilla was only sorry for the girl and the aridness of her ambition, compared with the lush tropic of her own heart. While she worked she was assailed by pangs of emotion. Gusts of erotic longing swept her off her feet. Sometimes she felt euphoric and full of energy. At other times she was morbid and breathless and obsessive, as if she had spent all day searching the attic for something that could not be found.

'You're working too hard,' Frederick said.

'Nonsense,' she said quickly, and tears filled her eyes.

He put an arm around her and kissed her fondly. 'You're worn out. You're working late several nights a week. You're getting the demented look career women sometimes have.'

She took a few days off and her languid body availed of the opportunity to come down with flu. Marooned in bed she could not get in touch with Kim and had to content herself with his letters. She was unable to eat anything but licked from the pages the pretty words to which she had become addicted. All she had for company was Mrs Lemon, who hitched up her skirt to show off her new oestrogen patch. 'You should try one,' she crowed. 'It gives you back your libido.'

The malady left her weak and abstracted. When she returned to work she could not concentrate and she frequently burst into tears. She found herself increasingly reliant on young Amy, who had taken her place while she was away. When she went to see the doctor he examined all her lovely parts without remark and then confessed that he did not know what was the matter. 'Of course you don't,' Camilla cried. How could he know, for she had only just realised herself. She had fallen in love.

She phoned Kim right away. 'I've been ill.' Her heart caved in a little for she could tell he had not known, which meant he had not been looking for her. 'I'm better now,' she added quickly.

'We must celebrate,' he said. 'Meet me tonight.'

Something had happened to her during her sickness.

She was not as glossily powerful as she had been before. She painted her face with care and it looked back at her anxiously. She had got too thin. She was beginning to look old.

Kim looked wonderful. He had shed his boyish brashness and assumed a sort of quiet power. In the time they had been acquainted he had grown up. When he put his arms around her, there was real kindness and it was only happiness that stopped her from bursting into tears. She tried to tell him her news but he beat her to it. 'Darling, I've never felt this way before – never until now understood the desire to be one with another person . . . to be married.' Leaving Frederick would be difficult but at least they would not have to live in a garret. Kim was now one of the rising young men in his field. They would have a glorious life. First thing, she would get rid of Mrs Lemon and hire a proper housekeeper. His turquoise eyes were full of tenderness. 'Congratulate me, darling,' he said. 'Her name is Heather.'

She would fire Mrs Lemon anyway, get a woman who could do flowers, make decent coffee, launder silk underwear without bringing it to the boil.

Kim thanked Camilla for helping him to win Heather's heart. Heather was a pure girl. He could not have held out without Camilla's generosity. 'I picked you with great care, darling,' he exulted. 'It had to be someone whose life was already perfectly fulfilled. Otherwise, I would have felt guilty leaving you. I'm not a shit, you know.' 'Why did you write me those letters?' Camilla said very quietly. 'It was a joke, my sweet,' he beamed. 'You knew that. I was careful never to do or say anything that would make you take me seriously. And we did have fun, didn't we?' He showed Camilla a picture of Heather. She was a blonde girl of about 19, very pretty.

Mrs Lemon turned up in a coat made up of many small dead animals stitched together by Dante in his inferno phase. Tufts of ash adorned its collar and a musky aroma surrounded her. She was smoking cannabis now. Camilla had ready a small speech of termination. She handed over a cheque first to soften the blow.

'Bless you, missus,' said Mrs Lemon with an explosion of mirth which scattered ash all over everything. 'I don't need your money. In fact, I have a little something for you – a parting present, if you like. You see I've had a bit of luck on the Pools so I reckon it's time Rosie gave herself a rest.' She watched with happiness as Mrs Lee unwrapped the package which exploded into a parachute of pink nylon. 'Brighten up your night life, if you get my meaning,' said Mrs Lemon with a wink. 'I wouldn't have the cheek to say this only I'm handing in my notice, but we're of an age and it's meant in friendship. You're giving in to your years.'

Oddly, she missed Mrs Lemon. Two other cleaning women came and went in rapid succession and the effort of keeping house along with the demands of her career got her down. Camilla began to think she deserved a rest as much as Mrs Lemon. Frederick was right. She was working too hard. Midway through an appalling day she handed in her notice. Everyone was very understanding.

Except Frederick. She came home to find him standing in the bedroom with a letter in his hand. He regarded her as if she were a stranger. 'I found this,' he said coldly. Camilla had the unpleasant but literal sensation of feeling her world turned upside down. Some violent internal struggle robbed her of breath and drove the blood from her head. Sweet God, she had forgotten to destroy Kim's letters ('sweet, delicious nymph . . !'). Frederick would not even look at her. 'I knew something was wrong, but this . . !' he said with contempt. 'Surely you can't believe in such rubbish?' Too late, she could see where her world lay; not with her lover, nor in contrast with her cleaning woman, nor even in her interesting career but with dear, unobtrusive, reliable . . .

'Frederick!' she humbly said, sinking to her knees.

Frederick watched her in dismay. 'Get up off your knees, old thing. Let me give you a good stiff drink.' He offered her a hand. 'You know it's really nothing to worry about.' His free hand crumpled the note and bowled it into a wastepaper basket. 'Extraordinary really, the things that can upset an intelligent woman. It's only a stupid chain letter.'

PHILIPPA GREGORY

The Playmate

She leaned forward against the constraint of the seat belt. 'I can remember it from here,' she said. 'The trees make a tunnel, a tunnel of green. When I was a little girl we used to sing from here . . .' She sang: '*Under the spreading chestnut tree . . .*' and then broke off with a self-conscious giggle.

'But surely your home was always London?'

She shook her head. 'We lived there – but I called Sussex my home.'

'And did you come down every weekend?' He was curious about her childhood, with that fey, talented mother and the dull stockbroker father. The house in the suburbs had been the father's house, furnished in his style; but the little cottage belonged to the mother. The father hated the little worker's cottage, set back from a muddy lane in a terraced row of red brick, with sprawling roses and hollyhocks. He stayed away while the mother, a difficult, attractive woman, had furnished it – eccentrically – in a ragbag mixture of colours and patterns. She brought her easel and her paints and her little girl almost every weekend in summer, and once or twice – rich, rare events – in winter, too.

'Once it even snowed,' she said, 'and we went tobogganing, on the Downs. I had a tin tray.'

'Your mother tobogganed?' he asked incredulously. She was dead now, a thin, beautiful woman, always wearing velvet in rich, deep colours. She was old by the time he had met her. He had gone to her elegant London flat to interview her and fallen at once under her spell. Daringly, he had asked her if she would come out for dinner. She had looked at him long and hard – that deep, dark blue, provocative look of hers. 'I don't dine with young men. You had much better take Imogen.'

He had taken the daughter to please her – and to secure himself another invitation. Then it was a pattern – he would have tea with the mother and talk about art and criticism and gossip, and then he would take her quiet daughter out for dinner. He could not have said what made the older woman so seductive. It was not her beauty – though much of it still endured in the flirtatious turn of her head and the deep, secretive blue eyes – but the sheer female power of her. Imogen had inherited none of it. 'Dear little Midge,' he thought tenderly. He liked to think of her as she was all those years ago – a little girl, unsubdued by her mother's beauty and talent, sledging on a tea tray on the gentle slopes of the South Downs.

'Did you play alone?'

Midge glowed. 'No, I had a friend in Sussex, a special friend, my very own friend.'

'Who was she?'

'Not she. A boy. He came to do the garden – John Daws.' She smiled. 'Mother called him Jack – jackdaw you see. He was supposed to dig the garden but he used to play with me. Mother said she was hiring a gardener not a nursemaid, but we didn't care. He would take me down to the stream to fish, or we would go and see the sheep or the calves. He let me bring the cows in for milking and play in the dairy. He took me to the mill to see the corn grinding. He let me slide down the chute for the grain and caught me at the bottom!'

'Your mother let you play with a farm boy?' He had to readjust his view of the mother. He would have thought her too fiercely protective of her daughter to let the little girl out without supervision. He would have thought her too snobbish to welcome a friendship with a farm boy.

'She used to say to him, "Fly away, Jackdaw," but then she always let him stay for tea. He would sit on the chair nearest the door and watch Mother make my tea. He would jump up to fetch things for her, lift things for her. Mother liked to do her own cooking in Sussex, it was like a playhouse for her.'

'He came every day?'

'Every single day. Some days we all went out together. We'd take a picnic and he would carry Mother's easel and her paints. We'd go to the stream and the two of us would play while Mother painted. When it was wet we laid out a city of bricks and cards on the floor and Mother sketched us.'

'How old was he?'

'He was halfway between us!' she exclaimed. 'He was 10 years older than me and 10 years younger than mother. I thought that was very special. I was 7, he was 17 and Mother was 27.'

'And how old was your father?'

She looked surprised. 'Oh, we never thought about Father. I don't know. He was older – perhaps 40. You know how it is when you're a child. Everyone is either your playmate or a grown-up.'

'And John Daws was your playmate?'

She was suddenly serious. 'He was my friend, the only friend I ever had.'

'Have you kept in touch?'

'No,' she said slowly. 'I never saw him after I started boarding school. I started at 12, and then Mother's work got so popular that people kept inviting her for the summer: the Riviera, or grouse-shooting in Scotland one year.' She gave an unconscious shiver. 'That was dreadful. All loud men and gossipy women and dead birds. Acres of tiny feathered bodies at the end of every day. More than anyone could ever eat.'

'Did you never come down to Sussex again?'

'She kept promising me . . . but then she was ill, and Daddy rented the cottage to pay for the nurses.'

'So you never said goodbye to John Daws?'

'We were children,' she said firmly. 'We didn't need to say goodbye. At the end of each weekend he'd just say: "See you next week then" – and I'd just say, "Yes." He'd look at Mother and she would smile at him, then he'd tip his cap and go.' She was watching the way the light flickered through the tall beeches on to the road. 'This is the long hill,' she said. 'D'you know, I dream about it still.'

'You must have forgotten him when you went to school,' he suggested. 'You must have made some friends at school.'

She shook her head. The sunlight flickering through the trees gilded her brown hair and then threw her into shadow.

'No,' she said. 'I didn't fit in. I wasn't like the other girls and I didn't know how to learn. They knew about boys and clothes and pop music and I only wanted to get back to Sussex and Jacky Daws.' She hesitated. 'I was so lonely.'

'Didn't you boast about him? You could have called him your boyfriend.'

'I wasn't that stupid,' she exclaimed. 'They would never have understood. They would have turned it into something ugly. He was private. He was my childhood friend, my only friend. I've never told anyone but you. I've never been back until now.'

'I hope it isn't going to be a disappointment,' he cautioned. 'John Daws will be grown up, they may have put a housing estate on your little village green.'

She shook her head. 'It'll be the same,' she said. 'And Jackdaw will be there, just the same.'

He said nothing, watching the road as they breasted the hill and gathered speed down the other side. The road was lined now with thick clumps of coppiced chestnut bushes as impenetrable as jungle. The trees were a bright, rich green. He felt the townsman's unease at the lush fertility of the place.

'Shall you mind if he is married?' he asked. 'Will he be jealous of me, that you are engaged to me?'

She was shocked. 'We were children! It wasn't like that!'

'He was a young man at 17,' he objected. 'Why should he play with a 7-year-old girl?'

She gave a small, sweet smile. 'He just did,' she said simply. 'He was my Jacky Daws. He used to wait for us to come by the lane end and when the car came round the corner, he would jump up on the big running boards and laugh. He was reckless and quick and curly-haired, and he would jump up on the car and laugh when Mother screamed; she always screamed a little bit – as a game. Then when we came in the house we would find the fire laid and ready to light and the tea all ready, and she would say: "Oh, Jackdaw! You are my treasure, my treasure!"'

'And then?'

'Then we'd have tea and he would take me out. We'd go and see the pheasant chicks which his father was rearing, or a bottle-fed lamb in his mother's kitchen. We went on a long expedition to a barn and saw a barn owl's nest one night. We didn't get back till after dark.'

'Wasn't your mother worried?'

She shook her head. 'Not when I was with Jackdaw. And then I would go up to bed and I would hear them talking softly, so as not to wake me. It was lovely falling asleep in the little boxroom with the window open, and the smell of the flowers blowing in, and their voices whispering quietly in the room below. Sometimes he would not leave until the stars were out and the moon was shining, and I would hear them murmuring together, like sleepy wood pigeons cooing.'

'You loved him,' he said flatly.

She paused for a moment. 'He was the only person to ever make me feel important. No one else really saw me. It was always Mother. But Jackdaw was my friend. Just mine.'

'Until me,' he prompted.

She nodded. 'Until you.'

He wondered why the landscape seemed familiar: the easy, arable country of mid-Sussex, the hedges thick with flowers and rich with birdlife, the fields green with a colour-wash of yellow. He realised he knew it from the mother's paintings. He had seen these fields, these very fields, a dozen times under a dozen different skies, in different lights. She had a great gift of making the most prosaic scene into an enchanted world. The shadow of a cloud on growing corn, the speckle of scarlet from poppies on a verge, all combined to give the impression of strangeness and yet familiarity. She'd been a powerful painter, a seductive painter. He wished he had known her at 27, as the farm boy had known her. He felt that if he had known her then, he would never have recovered.

'Right here,' her daughter said.

He signalled and turned the wheel and they were at once engulfed in the deep, sweet-smelling green of a beech wood. She wound down the window and air blew in, colder and damp.

'The river is at the bottom of this hill,' she said. 'We used to fish.'

The lane was narrow, winding between broad-trunked

trees, splashed and speckled with sunlight, filtering through shifting leaves. He had a swift glimpse of the river, a clear sandy bed with sweet water dancing over yellow stones, and then they were driving up the other side of the hill.

'Right here,' she said. 'At the little signpost.'

He could hardly see it. It was a finger-post, grey with lichen, leaning drunkenly backwards. It said 'Woodman Row' in letters which were half eroded by time.

'That's us,' she said, as if she were coming home. She put a hand on his arm to tell him to slow down and he realised that she was half-expecting a curly-haired, reckless youth to sprint from the trees and fling himself at the car.

'He's a grown man now,' he said gently. 'Pushing 40.'

'Yes,' she said. 'Silly of me. I keep forgetting. Everything else is the same, you see.'

He drove slowly down the little track and stopped at the first cottage. She opened the car door and stepped out. There were four cottages. The end two had been knocked into one, which was marred by the bulbous lump of a white aluminium and glass conservatory stuck on the side. He saw her wince and then look down the road to the last cottage.

'Why didn't she leave it to you?' he asked. All the rest of the large estate – the London flat, the paintings, the car, the exotic and expensive jewellery – had been left to her daughter.

'She left it to Jacky Daws,' she said quietly. 'That's how I know he's still here. The lawyers gave him the deeds. I just assumed he'd be here, living here. That's why I thought everything would be the same.'

He slammed the driver's door and locked it. 'I thought we were driving out into the country for a picnic. I thought we were just having a look at the outside of your old home. You never said anything about meeting him.'

She was not listening. She had opened the sagging garden gate and was walking up the path to the cottage. The front door stood open, with sprays of honeysuckle peering curiously inside.

'Now just wait a minute . . .' he said.

She tapped on the open door and then stepped over the threshold into the cool, dim interior.

55

The door opened directly into the kitchen. A man was seated at the kitchen table. A stocky, small man, with iron-grey curly hair. He had a sheet of newspaper spread on the kitchen table and parts of some machine spread out in their own little pools of dark oil. He looked up as she came in and then slowly rose to his feet, wiping his hands on a piece of rag.

'Why, Imogen,' he said gently.

'Jackdaw.'

They stood in silence, scanning each other's face and then he smiled a broad easy smile and waved her into a chair. 'If I'd known you were coming I'd have had something ready,' he said. He moved to the sink and filled a kettle and switched it on.

'This is my fiancé, Philip,' she said.

Jackdaw nodded with a smile. 'I can't shake hands. I'm dirty.'

'I knew you'd be here,' Midge said. In the dimness of the cottage her face was pale. She was smiling, her eyes were bright. 'I knew you would be here.'

He nodded. 'I guessed you'd come sooner or later. But I'd have had tea ready if I'd known it was today.'

'You always had tea ready for Mother and me,' Midge said.

He nodded. 'She liked it so.'

Philip cleared his throat, interrupted the slow rhythm of their speech.

'Why did she leave you the cottage? It's a very valuable asset, isn't it?'

The man shot a swift warning look at him. 'She had no use for it herself,' he said gently.

'She could have left it to Midge. Or given it to a charity.'

'She liked Jackdaw,' the girl interrupted. 'I expect she wanted him to have it.'

The man nodded. 'She was generous.'

'Very generous,' Philip said rudely. 'The place must be worth something like £80,000. Rather a big tip for a gardener, isn't it?'

The man flushed, his pride stung. 'I wasn't just the gardener,' he said. 'I kept everything nice for her. I kept things safe for her. It was always ready for her to come back. I waited for her.'

'You waited?' Imogen asked.

'She never said she was not coming.' They could hear the hurt of the 17-year-old youth in his low voice. 'Every spring it was ready for her, in case she came. Every spring it was ready for her to come home. The garden, the house, and me – waiting for her to come back.' He paused. 'She asked me to wait for her.'

The kettle boiled and the automatic switch clicked off abruptly.

'You loved her!' Philip accused. He could not tolerate the thought of their intimacy, of their cooing like wood pigeons at night, of her asking him to wait for her. She had never asked anything of Philip, except to take Imogen to dinner. She had seemed far beyond him, far beyond all possibility of desire. He knew she had never looked twice at him. But he faced the man as if they were rivals, as if the woman they had both loved were still alive, as if she might ever have been won.

There was a long silence. Outside a jay scolded abruptly and then went quiet. John Daws said nothing. But he looked at Philip as if he understood, as if he recognised a mutual pain.

Imogen rose slowly from her seat, her eyes fixed on John Daws. 'Did you?' she asked. 'Did you love her? Was it her all the time?' She scanned his face as if she could see the bright 17 year old who waited at the corner for the sound of his mistress's car, who waited, and waited, although she had forgotten him altogether. Imogen was staring as if she could see the only happy days of her childhood breaking and reshaping into a new pattern, a pattern of betrayal. Days in which she had not been the centre of love, but had been a diversion or, even worse than that, an alibi. A totally innocent chaperone whose presence had made an adultery possible.

Imogen gave a quick, painful gasp. 'Why?' she cried, in the thin voice of a shocked child. 'Jacky Daws – you were not my friend, you were never my friend! You were her lover! You were her lover and never my friend at all.'

He said nothing – he bowed his head to her as if to confess to the betrayal. Then he raised his eyes and scanned her hurt face.

And both men waited for her to look towards Philip.

JOANNA TROLLOPE

Christmas Wings

The Virgin Mary was in tears.

'I want *wings*, I want *wings*, I want – '

Susie Forrester, who had run a nursery school now for nine years and had already witnessed nine Virgin Marys bottling out of stardom at the eleventh hour, stooped over her.

'Mary doesn't have wings. Mary is too special for wings. Only the angels have wings, and they aren't special, like Mary,' she said.

The Virgin Mary paused mid-howl, and glared at the angels. They wore princessy white robes and had huge white wings edged in sparkly stuff, and more sparkly stuff twisted into large haloes that trembled on ingenious wires above their neatly brushed heads. The Virgin considered her own robe, plain blue, and her headdress, which looked like a tea-towel. She stamped.

'I want *wings*.'

'Very well,' said Susie Forrester, straightening up again. 'You can change places with Daisy. Daisy can be the Virgin Mary and hold Baby Jesus in the very front where all the mummies and daddies can see, and you can go into the back row and be an ordinary angel along with seven other angels.'

The Virgin Mary paused for a second. Then Jason Purdie, the tallest of the angels, moved slightly, and his halo and wings caught the light and shimmered like silver flames. The Virgin Mary tore off her tea-towel and flung it to the floor.

'Stupid Mary,' she said scornfully.

Simon Morris leaned across his stepfather's lap and hissed at his mother, 'I thought *Polly* was going to be Mary!'

Rose looked straight ahead, over the proud parental heads in front of her, at the little stage, brilliantly lit, where a semi-circle of fidgeting angels were crowded around the

59

Holy Family like shoppers around bargains on the first day of the sales.

'She was.'

'But that's not Polly!'

'No,' said Rose, 'that's Daisy Crawshaw. I expect Polly was demoted because she was awful.'

'Never,' said Graham, Simon's stepfather and Polly's father, in too loud a voice.

'Shh!' said all the parents.

Simon slumped in his seat. He'd only agreed to come because Rose and Graham had said he ought to, to show family solidarity when Polly had been chosen as star of the Nativity Play. He had tried to argue that, as Polly was only his half-sister, he only had to show half-solidarity, which meant coming to the school and then sitting in the car playing his Nintendo until it was time to go home. He'd said he'd even say, 'I hear you were great, Poll.'

But Graham had insisted. Graham almost never insisted about anything. Graham was one of the most peaceful blokes Simon had ever come across and not one to come heavy about anything much. But Graham had said, 'Simon, it's Christmas, and Christmas is all about families, and we are a family, and you're coming.'

So here he was in the half-dark, with all these parents and little kids looking at someone called Daisy holding a doll and looking all ready to blub. He craned his neck. He couldn't even see Polly she was so small, although he could see what was probably her halo, which looked bent. He sighed and glanced at his mother's profile. It looked set, as if she were holding something in. It had looked like that a lot lately, not quite angry, not quite sad, but a bit of both.

A piano, rather jangly, struck a chord. The boy playing Joseph leaned forward. He was scarlet with self-consciousness under his checked tea-towel and he spoke in a hoarse whisper.

'We are going to sing to you,' he breathed, 'the Rocking Song.'

There was a squeal and a crash. The uneven rank of angels broke suddenly apart with cries of dismay, and the smallest of them plunged forward into the limelight and seized the Jesus doll from Daisy Crawshaw. The parents gasped in unison.

'I want to be *Mary*!' Polly shrieked.

Simon closed his eyes, groaned and slithered to the dark, invisible haven of the floor.

'I don't even want to talk to you,' Rose said, towelling Polly.

Polly held up a damp, newly bathed rosy face to her mother. 'I'm sweet,' she said firmly.

'No,' Rose said, 'you aren't sweet. You are wilful and selfish and spoilt. I may be responsible for the last defect, but the first two are definitely your own idea.'

Polly drooped. 'I want Daddy.'

'You can't have Daddy. Needless to say, Daddy has been called out to some lambing problem which probably wouldn't arise if people didn't insist on having lambs before Christmas instead of in the spring, which is the proper time for lambing. Where is your nightie?'

'Want 'jamas.'

'Polly,' Rose said, 'what you want means nothing to me. You can go to bed in a dustbin bag for all I care. Why should you, the product of me and a good, kind man, be so frightful, and Simon, the product of me and an appallingly behaved man, be no trouble at all?'

She looked round the bathroom. It was too small, and it needed decorating. The holes in the wall where the towel rail had come off were still unfilled, and there was no new towel rail. In the bathroom where she – or the au-pair girl, she reminded herself, determined upon truth – had once bathed a baby Simon, there had been a carpet on the floor and a gleaming chrome towel rail through which hot water coursed, twenty-four hours a day.

'Not frightful,' Polly said. And then, in an attempt to explain, 'It was the *wings*.'

Rose looked at her. She looked and saw her own childhood face under Graham's russety brown hair, curling, in Polly's case, into soft, round springs.

'I know.'

Polly put her thumb in, holding the corner of the towel against her face, like a comfort blanket.

'I know about wings,' Rose said, leaning forward and kissing her. 'I had them once.'

Polly stopped sucking. 'Where are they?'

'They dropped off,' Rose said, closing her eyes, losing the battle against the injustice and resentment of her thoughts. 'They dropped off, and then Guy took them. Guy, who was Simon's Daddy.'

On the kitchen table, a clingfilmed packet of supermarket minced beef lay waiting smugly to be made into shepherd's pie for supper. Rose had taken it out of the fridge to remind herself, before she went to bath Polly. She didn't, at that moment, at the end of such an afternoon, with Graham out yet again and the cats screaming for food and Simon in a trance of ten-year-old oblivion in front of the television, want to make Shepherd's pie at *all*. And she wanted to have someone notice that she didn't, to have someone say, 'Why should you just go on and on as a one-woman service industry to three other people in this grotty kitchen? It's all wrong, Rose, and deeply unfair. I sympathise with you.'

You're a cow, Rose told herself, finding an onion and a chopping board and tying an apron over her Nativity-Play-watching clothes. It was cow-like to resent the kitchen's shabbiness when Graham had, instead, spent so much money in making her a studio for her pottery. 'It's serious,' he'd said to her of her pottery. 'You're really good. You must take it seriously.'

Guy had never said that to her. Guy had simply thought it an amusing hobby, and had been full of a boastful, but only intermittent, pride when she had made something impressive and stylish for a client of his or a business friend. But if she ever said to him, at a function or a party, 'I think we ought to go because I've left something in the kiln,' he was rude and uncooperative and said he wouldn't leave what they were doing on account of Rose's *hobby*.

Graham never said things like that. Graham was as unlike Guy as he could possibly be. Rose had first met him when a puppy bought by Guy for a far-too-young Simon had been run over in the road and had had two legs broken. Rose had rung the vet and been told that they would send Mr Powers out as soon as he came in from his calls. Rose had waited, sobbing over the poor puppy in the winter afternoon, weeping partly for it and partly because her comfortable, expensive life was such a hollow, unhappy sham, until Graham arrived. He had had to put the puppy to sleep, and had then given Rose some brandy from the decanter in the dining room.

A year later, when Guy had left her for an advertising executive with a flat in Paris, Rose met Graham again in the local supermarket, where he was loading his trolley with sad little quantities of things for one. She took him home for dinner. Before dinner, he sat on the hearthrug with Simon and drew animals for him and explained about cows' stomachs and pigs' feet and birds' eyes. Simon, who was four, said, 'You could be my friend. If you like.'

'I would,' Graham said. 'And I'd like to be your mother's friend, too.'

After her divorce, Rose took Simon to live with Graham in his cottage. Six months later, she married him. He was kind and quiet and he loved her. He said he was sorry the cottage was such a bachelor dump of the dreariest kind, but he had never been much good at either noticing or minding. Rose, drunk on a heady dose of emotional calm and security, said that she didn't mind either.

'You sure?' Graham said, thinking doubtfully about the house she had left behind, about all those floor-length curtains and bathrooms and quietly humming radiators.

'Quite sure,' Rose said, thinking of them, too, but with loathing.

That was over five years ago now, five years in which she had had Polly, thrown her mugs and bowls and vases, and hardly altered Graham's cottage. It was still shabby, it was still too cold in too many places and uncomfortably hot in too few. At first, Rose had had no trouble in not noticing or minding, because of her thankfulness and her gratitude, just as she had barely noticed, and hardly minded, how hard Graham worked in this district of little farms, where there was never, it seemed, a day, and almost never a night, without a crisis. In fact, she had shocked and surprised herself one day when she had heard herself say sharply to Simon, in response to a request that someone might help him with a complicated bit of his model aeroplane, 'Well, it won't be me because I haven't got a minute, and it certainly won't be Graham because he spends every waking hour with his arm stuck up some cow.'

She had gone to Simon later and apologised. He'd had no idea what she was apologising for. She'd explained that she was probably tired and that she would try to help him with his aeroplane. Simon had said it was OK, he'd wait for Graham, if that was OK, too. Rose had gone down to the kitchen and been ashamed and angry. It might be true – it was true – that she had never worked as hard in her life as she was working now in Graham's cottage, with a family and the demands of the local community, but it was also true that she was safe. Hadn't she once said to herself, with a kind of rapture, that she'd joyfully live in a cardboard box just as long as she was emotionally safe?

She tore open the packet of mince and tipped it into the frying pan of onions. With a sense of guilt and irresistible compulsion, like an alcoholic tiptoeing to find a hidden bottle, she thought of that other kitchen, the kitchen she had once had, made of ash and Italian tiles and copper, where the au-pair girl had unloaded the dishwasher and Mrs Tripp had washed and waxed the floor. I hated that kitchen, Rose told herself, I hated it because it was as empty as I was, all outside and no inside. But, she told herself back, it was big and clean and warm and I wasn't always tired in it, I wasn't always –

'Hello,' Graham said, opening the back door.

'Hello,' she said, stirring the mince and not turning round to look at him.

'Don't I get a kiss?'

'I smell of cooking,' Rose said, offering a cheek.

'And I smell of cowshit,' he said, cheerfully. 'Lord,' he said, the condensation in here is awful. New Year Resolution: do the kitchen.'

'Lovely,' Rose said, without enthusiasm.

Graham looked at her. 'You still upset about this afternoon, about Polly?'

'Cross, more than upset.'

He began to take off his waxed jacket. He was laughing. 'It was priceless.'

'Was it?'

'Yes, all those fat-faced, superior parents – '

'But Polly looked so *spoilt*.'

He put his arms around her from behind and nuzzled her neck. 'She looked just like you.'

'Graham!' Rose said furiously, trying to wriggle out of his embrace.

He hung on tighter. 'She did. Adorable and funny and terrified she was going to miss out on something.'

'Is that like me?'

'Sometimes.'

'Let go,' Rose said stonily. She pushed his arms down and went over to the sink and leant on it, staring down at the washing up.

'Rose,' Graham said.

She didn't reply.

'Rose. I've got a confession to make.'

She turned round very slowly. He was standing where she had left him, by the cooker. He looked tired, but still young. He *was* young, for heaven's sake, an over-worked young man with a wife and a child and someone else's son to care for.

'Sorry,' Rose said in a small voice.

He moved his arm slightly, in a gesture of dismissal. 'Forget it. It was tactless anyway. Rose – '

'Yes?'

'I've – I've gone and done something.'

Rose thought, wildly and sickeningly, of adultery and debt and running a child over in the dark. 'What thing?'

'I've asked someone for Christmas.'

Rose gasped. 'But we can't, you know we can't, there isn't room, there isn't – I can't – you know we can't even have your mother, you – ' She stopped. She drew a sharp breath. She said, 'Who have you asked?'

Graham's chin went up a fraction of an inch. 'Guy.'

'*Guy?*' Rose screeched.

'Yes, Guy. I met him about a week ago. In town. He was

rather pathetic. Amelia has left him and he's on his own again. I just thought – '

'What did you think?' Rose said, closing her eyes to stop the kitchen melting and swirling all around her.

'I thought it was pretty bleak for him. And there's Simon. It's only Christmas Eve and Christmas Day after all.'

'We can't have Guy!' Rose cried. 'Guy has champagne and smoked salmon for Christmas. Guy goes skiing in Zermatt. Guy is – '

'Lonely,' Graham said.

Rose moved carefully towards him. She reached past him and pushed the spitting frying-pan off the hotplate. 'Is that all? Is that really the only reason you asked him? No crowing, no triumph?'

'None,' Graham said steadily.

Rose thrust her face almost into his. 'Promise? Promise?' she demanded.

'I didn't ask him, I promise you, to flaunt the fact that I've now got you and he hasn't.'

Rose stepped back. She felt for a kitchen chair, pulled it out from the table and sat down in it. She stared at the wood grain of the table-top, at the smear of yogurt left from Polly's supper, at the scorch where Simon, in a panic, had once dumped a burning pan of baked beans. Guy is coming, Rose thought, Guy is coming here for Christmas!

She leaned on the table and put her hands over her face. A surge of panic rushed up her throat, followed by fear and – and what? – exploding inside her head, by a horrible, wonderful, burst of light.

'It's a Mercedes!' Simon said in wonder. He was staring out of the landing window. 'A Mercedes!'

'So it is,' said Graham, standing beside him.

Simon glanced at his stepfather.

'But quite an old one,' he said hurriedly, miserably anxious to be tactful. 'Not the latest – '

Graham gave Simon's hair a quick tousle.

'No. Not the latest. Shouldn't you go down?'

Simon swallowed. He watched his father get out of the Mercedes, a tall, well-looked-after man in ironed jeans, a polo-neck jersey and a tweed jacket. He liked his father, he knew he did, but it was suddenly appallingly difficult to be expected to like him in front of his mother and Graham. He considered saying this to Graham, and decided that was too difficult, too. He swallowed again.

'In a minute.'

'When you're ready,' Graham said.

He watched Guy Morris stoop inside one of the gleaming car's back doors and bring out a box full of parcels, big red parcels done up with gold ribbon and fat bows on top, like dahlias. He watched Rose go out of the house, a little uncertainly, and cross the weedy drive to greet Guy. Poor Rose. She hadn't known how to dress that morning, nor how to seem. Too much of anything and she might risk upsetting him, Graham. Too little of anything and she might risk letting Guy think she wasn't happy. Graham frowned. Was she happy? He put a gentle hand on Simon's shoulder.

'I think maybe, old son – '

'OK,' Simon said. 'Where's Polly?'

'Putting her wings on.'

'For my dad?'

'I don't know,' Graham said. He took his hand away and put it in his pocket. 'Maybe she just feels like putting them on anyway. You know Poll.'

'Yes,' Simon said. He watched his mother put her face up for his father's kiss. For some reason it was suddenly awful standing beside Graham any longer. 'I'll go down,' Simon said, 'I'll – '

'Yes,' Graham said. 'You go.'

Guy said he thought the cottage was charming, really charming. 'Sixteenth century, is it?'

'Seventeenth, probably,' Graham said. He handed Guy a glass of wine. 'And, as you see, scarcely modernised since then.'

Guy gave a little bark of laughter. He looked round the sitting room. There was a huge fire blazing in the inglenook, and from every beam hung decorations made by Simon and Polly. Polly had also made a very long, very garish paper-chain which she had insisted on hanging across the room at a height she could reach. It was slightly too high to step over and slightly too low to duck under. Simon had helpfully brought the stepladder in to hold the centre up. Guy looked at the stepladder.

'Part of the decoration, Simon?'

Simon went pink. 'Polly made it, you see – '

Guy took a gulp of wine. He winked. 'I look forward to meeting Polly.'

The sitting-room door flew open with a crash. Polly stood in the doorway in her plaid dungarees and her Postman Pat jersey and her wings, tied on with white tapes that went across her front. She had added some of Rose's earrings and shoes.

'Hello,' said Guy, immediately recognising a femme fatale.

'This is Polly,' Rose said, unnecessarily.

Polly tugged at the tapes. 'They wobble,' she hissed.

'Perhaps if you took my shoes off – '

Polly staggered forward, the wings flapping behind her.

'Watch out!'

Polly lurched, shrieked and fell through the paper-chain.

Rose rushed to pick her up. She thought she wouldn't look at Guy, standing there with careful ease, in his cashmere jersey. It had been so disconcerting, kissing him. He smelled of the same aftershave; his cheek and ear and haircut, briefly and intimately in her field of vision while they kissed, were frighteningly familiar.

'At least that solves the problem of the paper-chain,' Graham said.

'Mend it!' Polly shouted, thrashing under her wings.

Rose bore her from the room. Guy grinned down into his wine.

'Family life,' he said jovially, and then, with an inflection of studied seriousness, 'Amelia wanted a family.'

'Did she?' Graham said. He kicked a log on the fire. 'Why didn't you have one then?'

Guy winked at Simon again. 'Not quite my line of country – '

When Rose came back into the room, she said, 'I'm so sorry about that. I've left her having a tantrum in her bedroom. Simon, would you put the stepladder away and then we'll have lunch.' For Guy's benefit she added, 'Christmas is really too much for small children.'

'And chaps on their own,' Guy said. He smiled at Rose. 'Remember those Christmases when Simon was Polly's age?'

The room went very quiet. Rose remembered bottles of scent and bottles of champagne and silky things in tissue paper and Simon in Rupert Bear pyjamas and Guy, furtively telephoning from rooms where he thought she'd never find him.

Simon said desperately, 'I'm hungry – '

'Of course you are,' Graham said. He tipped the last of the wine from the bottle into Guy's glass. 'So am I.'

Guy swallowed his wine. 'Good stuff,' he said. 'Amazing how good supermarket table wine is these days.' He clumped Simon heavily on the shoulder. 'Lunch! I'm starving. Lead on, Macduff.'

At lunch, Guy talked about his business. He said he was probably one of the first people to realise that the future for business didn't lie in the West, nor in the Third World, but in the East. He told several stories, pretending to be Japanese. Rose, pushing her Christmas Eve gammon around her plate but not eating it, realised she had forgotten how good a mimic he was. Graham laughed a lot, quite naturally. Simon laughed, too, rather less naturally. In the middle, Polly came in wearing a summer nightie of flowered lawn, and an anorak, and towing her wings by their tapes. She climbed into her chair, next to Guy, and ate her lunch like an angel.

'Good girl,' Graham said. Polly smirked and lowered her lashes.

After lunch, Guy said he would like to give them all their presents. Simon was rather shocked.

'We shouldn't really, you know, not until Christmas Day.'

'All over Europe,' Guy said, 'you'd have them today. I should know, I'm the travelling man.'

He let Polly distribute the parcels. Her eyes glowed with excitement. Simon, watching, felt a similar glow, but of pride that his father could not only be so funny but had provided these sensational presents. There was wine for Graham and a jersey for Rose – 'Oh my God,' she said when she saw the label – and a doll with a wardrobe of clothes for Polly and for him – well, for him there was a remote-controlled car, a Porsche, as red as a letterbox, as shiny as glass. He felt sick with rapture. Rose was stroking her jersey.

'I think,' Graham said to her, 'you ought to show Guy your studio.'

'Oh – '

'She's doing brilliantly,' Graham said, turning to Guy. 'More commissions every week, especially for fruit bowls. Last year's turnover was – '

'Shh,' Rose said. She put her jersey back into its folds of tissue. Last year's turnover had been in the hundreds. Guy, she had no trouble in recalling, thought only in hundreds of thousands.

'Secret?' Guy said, grinning. 'Never thought of you as an entrepreneur, Rosie.'

Rosie. Only he had ever called her Rosie. She stood up. Polly was talking animatedly to her doll and Simon, like a parent with a precious child who has only just learned to walk, was nursing the Porsche between an armchair and the sofa. She didn't look at Graham; she couldn't.

'Come and see then,' she said to Guy.

It was terribly cold in the studio. Everything was turned off, even the electric kiln which had been Graham's present to her for her birthday three years ago. The unglazed, unpainted bowls and mugs stood on bare shelves against the bare walls, like ghosts. On the table in the centre, beside her potter's wheel, stood a few finished things: a blue and white vase patterned with leaves, a big, shallow dish painted with bright fruit.

'I like that,' Guy said, pointing. 'Looks Mediterranean. French.'

'I sell them for twenty pounds,' Rose said.

Guy whistled through his teeth. 'A bargain!' He looked around him. 'You seem pretty well set up.'

There was a tiny beat. 'I am,' Rose said.

'Cottage, kids, pottery – ' He glanced at her. 'What's it like, being married to a vet?'

'I'm not married to a vet,' Rose said, 'I'm married to Graham.'

Guy put his hands on the table, either side of the bright dish. 'Rosie.'

She waited. She had the sensation, brief and wildly exhilarating, that something was about to happen, something that would change things, decide things.

'Rosie,' Guy said again, bowing his head.

'Yes?'

'Did Graham tell you – Amelia left me.'

A balloon inside Rose deflated with a rush of air. 'Yes.'

'It's really cut me up.'

Rose said coldly, 'Were you faithful to her?'

'Yes! My God, I was. I was faithful to her for seven bloody years!' He banged his fist on the table and the dish jumped. 'Seven years! Seven years of being showered with love and kisses and she leaves me, Rosie, she leaves me!'

Rose took a step back, feeling for something solid to hold on to. 'How dare you.'

He blinked. 'What?'

'How dare you,' Rose said, 'expect me to be sorry for you about Amelia when you couldn't be faithful to me for seven minutes?'

'Hey now, Rosie.'

'Coming in here,' Rose said furiously, 'all swank and presents and showing off about being an international man and then expecting my pity!'

Guy stood up. He looked wounded and thoroughly puzzled. 'But you've got everything,' he said.

'I –?'

'Yes, Rosie.'

She shouted, 'Don't call me Rosie!'

'Why not?'

'Because it reminds me! It reminds me of everything, just as you do, standing there, sodden with self-pity, all mouth and trousers!' She stopped. She put a hand briefly to her face. She said, 'Sorry. Shouldn't have shouted. Not at all Christmassy.' She looked at him, a quick, nervous glance. 'Perhaps you should go and find Simon and spend a bit of time with him.'

Guy nodded. Then he said, a shade too heartily, 'Good idea.'

Graham and Polly were on the sitting-room hearthrug. Graham was solemnly holding Polly's doll upright while Polly, with intense concentration, brushed her shining, auburn nylon hair.

'This doll,' Graham said as Rose came in, 'is imperfectly finished. We've looked. But she has to be a girl, Polly thinks, because of her hair.'

Rose crouched down on the hearthrug beside them. 'He's got to go,' Rose said. 'I can't stand having him here another minute.' Graham said nothing.

'Out there,' Rose said, plucking at the fringe of the rug, 'I remembered everything. It was horrible, as if my flesh suddenly remembered all kinds of things the top layer of my mind had forgotten, things that my flesh will never forget.'

'Hold her still,' said Polly sternly.

'Sorry.'

'Graham – '

'Yes?'

'Will you ask him to go?'

'No,' Graham said. He held the doll out to Polly. 'Take her for a minute, Poll, will you?' He turned to Rose. He put a hand under her chin. He said, 'He had to come. Do you see that? For you, for us. He had to. You weren't remembering straight.'

'So you – '

'Yes,' he said, dropping his hand. 'I asked him deliberately. But you have to send him away. That has to be your decision.'

Rose bent forward until her head touched his shoulder. 'I'm so sorry – '

'Don't apologise,' Graham said. 'You didn't do this on purpose. It just happened. But I don't want it to happen again.'

Polly said, 'I shouldn't cry if I were you.'

'I'm not crying – '

'Well,' Polly said, 'it looks like crying to me.'

Later, they all stood in the doorway while Guy put his suitcases back into his car. He had looked mildly offended but not really surprised when Rose had said, rather clumsily, that she was sorry but it just wouldn't work, having him there for Christmas: they'd all be on edge.

He'd said, 'But where do I go?'

'Why not to your mother? She'd like it. It would be a lovely surprise.' Just in time she'd prevented herself from adding, 'And it will confirm everything she ever thought about me, to her great satisfaction.'

Graham had his arm around Rose. His other arm was loosely around Simon.

'I don't see – ' Simon had said, bewildered.

'I think you will,' Graham told him, 'when you consider how you feel. And how Mum does.'

The wind blew sharply across the flat fields around the cottage and made Rose shiver. Graham tightened his arm. Guy climbed into his car and started the engine.

'Is this the time,' Rose asked, 'when the past stops trying to be the future? Is that what's happening?'

Guy turned the car slowly towards the gate. Graham put his face into Rose's hair. 'Or perhaps it's when the past just finally gives up trying to be anything but the past, when it falls off the back of the lorry.'

Simon waited for Guy's car to slide from view before he leaned, just a very little, against Graham. He looked at Polly. She was holding her doll up into the wind and watching her hair blow about.

'Where are your wings?'

'I broke them,' Polly said. 'I stamped on them until they broke all to pieces.'

'But you liked them!'

'Not much,' Polly said. 'I like Doll now. They were stupid wings.' She glanced at Simon. 'I didn't really like them,' she said, 'and anyway – ' she paused, 'anyway – they didn't even work.'

LESLEY GLAISTER

Ruby Wedding

She brushed her hair one hundred times a night. One hundred crackling strokes. She brushed it until it leapt to meet the brush, long, red strands, live as wires.

When Dorothy was very young, her mother did the brushing, counting every stroke. Which is how Dorothy learned to count. Her mother's brush was heavy and silver-backed and matched the mirror on her dressing-table. It was a rough brush. Dorothy would stare miserably at her own small, mirrored face among the mass of glistening hair; at her mother's face, fierce and rapt, behind her. She gritted her teeth against the tears as the brush raked her scalp, ripped and tore its way through the tangles until, at last, she recognised the end of the incantation: ninety eight, ninety nine, a hundred. Ah . . . And her scalp would tingle and glow as her mother's deft fingers conjured her hair into a long plait, heavy and obedient, hanging down her back.

Later she did the brushing herself with her own set of brushes, red and black and lacquered with birds and fishermen. Oh, yes, sometimes it hurt, but it had to be done. From the root to the tip, one hundred times. And if Dorothy lost count? Then she would begin again.

'A girl's hair is her crowning glory,' her mother said – and in Dorothy's case this was true. It was thick and glossy hair, a dark and foxy red. It was heavy, massy hair. When she let it down, it reached halfway down her thighs, a warm and wavy cloak.

'Better not cut it,' said her mother, in defiance of fashion. 'It's your only real asset.'

Dorothy gazed in the mirror at her pale face – and had to agree. Without the hair she wouldn't be ugly, or even plain, but she would be ordinary and ordinary girls were ten-a-penny. Men – ordinary or otherwise – were not.

Sitting poker-straight on the edge of the bed, Hubert goes into his morning routine. Left leg out straight, swivel

74

foot clockwise 10 times, anti-clockwise 10 times; right leg, likewise. Stand up. Bend and stretch 10 times. Swing arms round.

He catches sight of himself in the mirror on the inside of the wardrobe door, which has swung open with all this activity. His arms fall to his side and he smiles at his own flushed face. He bends and, with a slick flick of the wrist, pops in his teeth.

Not a bad figure he cuts, standing there without a stitch. Perhaps a slight paunch, a little slackness of the chest, a varicose vein or two, but all in all . . . His private parts are all present and correct – if slightly rusty. Yes, Hubert is quite satisfied with himself. At 75, you couldn't expect much better.

'I'm off now,' shouts Dorothy from the kitchen down-stairs.

'Wait on . . .' begins Hubert, but too late – the door bangs. He goes to the window and draws back the lace curtain a fraction. She has her best coat on and is carrying her new handbag. Where the devil is she off to?

A fine morning. Dorothy's heels click satisfyingly on the frosty pavement. She swings her bag in time with her stride. A spry woman I must appear, she thinks. Sprightly. No one would guess I'm past 70.

Her exact age is a secret even to herself: her date of birth creeps forward with the years. She still has hopes for the future, though they've become vague now. She is childless, and to this she attributes her waist – still the 23 inches it was on her wedding day – and her complexion. She has grown through the tales of labour and teething and tantrums and rebellion and acne of her friends, and she has soothed and tutted, with her tummy tucked smugly in and her brow as smooth and clear as tide-washed sand. And now her friends – those that have survived – knit endless shawls for great-grandchildren they never see and Dorothy is very grateful to be spared that irritation.

A tabby cat on a wall stretches up its neck for a stroke. Dorothy tickles it gingerly with the tips of her gloves and it responds with a hungry purr. 'Poor pussy,' she says, and hurries on. She thinks of Hubert at home. A nice loin of pork, she decides.

Hubert has grilled a sausage because it's healthier that way, and a tomato, and is setting himself a nice breakfast place. I could have been, he reflects, a contented bachelor. There is something very satisfying about breakfast alone: a pot of Cooper's chunky marmalade, butter in a china dish, crisp, dry toast, a lone sausage grilled to a turn and the *Telegraph* – unsullied this morning – beside his plate.

There is no need for idle chit-chat. He pours water from the kettle on to the three spoonfuls of Assam in the willow-pattern pot. Nothing namby-pamby about this brew. But there are no lemons. 'Damn Dorothy,' he says.

Roast potatoes and parsnips and petits pois, continues Dorothy. Baked apples and cream. She climbs aboard the bus and surreptitiously flashes her bus-pass at the driver. He doesn't look twice and she is insulted. Still, what does he know, this smooth-cheeked boy who could be her grandson. Could have been, she corrects herself.

The bus is full and she has to sit in the precarious sideways seat if she is to sit at all. She faces a woman with three children. Two of them are boys, wriggling and complaining and banging their shoes against the seat. The third is an anonymous bundle of mauve cable stitch, squashed against its mother's chest. Dorothy crosses her legs and admires the neat boniness of her ankles above her shiny shoes. The woman opposite has ankles that are thick in woolly socks and big, flat shoes that might as well be a man's.

Hubert bisects his sausage exactly. It is a farm pork sausage, an even, comfortable pinky brown with just a fleck of white fat here and there. A perfect sausage. I could have lived my life like this, he thinks, as he chews. Breakfast alone every morning. He sniffs the *Telegraph*. There's something about a newspaper that hasn't been rifled by someone else first. The sun slants through the window and the marmalade glows in its pot. Steam rises from his tea. Paradise, thinks Hubert.

The woman struggles with the boys, who want to stand on

the seat. 'Nearly time to get off,' she says, relieved. 'Our stop next.'

'We're going to see Father Christmas,' one of the boys announces excitedly to Dorothy.

'But it's October!' Dorothy exclaims.

The woman grimaces. 'What can you do?' she says. 'All their friends have been.'

Dorothy's children would have waited calmly for Christmas, hands folded in their laps. Dorothy's children would never have stood on seats or whined or had runny noses or scuffed shoes. Dorothy's children would probably have been girls and proper little girls, too, not like the hoodlums next door.

Dorothy is feeling quite excited herself. She is going to do something drastic today, take Hubert by surprise. 'Be unpredictable,' she read in a magazine in the osteopath's waiting-room, 'if you want to keep your man, if you don't want his eyes to stray.'

Hubert spreads marmalade thickly on his toast and pours another cup of dark tea. He scans the paper. 'Electricians out next, I suppose,' he remarks. But, of course, Dorothy isn't here. This is how it would be if she was dead, he thinks suddenly. This would be the pattern of my grieving: one sausage in a pan, sunshine on the marmalade, no sound but the tick of the clock. Remarks passed unheard, dissolving in the steam of my tea. A stroll to the allotment later, a pie and a pint in the George with a clear conscience. Perhaps I would get a dog, he thinks. Dorothy can't abide dogs.

From next door's garden he can hear the shouts of the children. Nice little girls. He talks to them sometimes, over the fence when he's seeing to the roses. Dorothy doesn't encourage it. Hoodlums, she calls them, but it's only exuberance. Their mother, Dorothy calls a slut. Hubert, privately, disagrees. She's a nice woman, with a warm smile. So what if her hair is a mess? And if she does wear old jumpers with the elbows out? And if she has large, loose breasts that strain wantonly against the wool? Hubert doesn't mind.

Children might have done Dorothy good, he reflects. There would be grandchildren now, to shout over the fence to the lovely hoodlums. I might have been a good father, given half a chance, he thinks, and he feels angry with Dorothy. This is not fair, and he knows it. That side of things never got off the ground, not really, and it was his fault as much as hers.

He squeezes his old man's parts affectionately and remembers the Dorothy he married. She had long, red hair then, masses of it. It was with her hair that she had snared him, a fisherwoman with a luxurious net. It was a dark, rich red. And there was miles of it, as he found out on their wedding night when she sat before the dressing-table and allowed him to brush it for her. It felt alive, that hair, that warm, red shawl through which her shoulders glowed a pearly white. It crackled under the brush and rose to meet his passionate face as he buried himself in the warm, red waviness of it.

But it was a damn nuisance that hair, if the truth be told. It got everywhere. He was always lying on it in bed and angering her, getting it caught in the crook of his arm when he turned from her to sleep and making her shriek. Dorothy insisted on brushing it one hundred times before she'd get into bed beside him, and if he talked and interrupted she'd click her tongue and start all over again. Often, his desire had waned and he'd fallen asleep by the time she'd finished.

On Sunday mornings, there was the solemn ritual of the shampoo, and she would leave long hairs stuck to the sides of the bath. Strange how the hair that seemed so lovely when rooted in her scalp became so distasteful once detached. Once he had discovered one curled in his Yorkshire pudding like a baked serpent, and found himself quite unable to swallow another mouthful.

Has he really forgotten?, wonders Dorothy, or will there be flowers when I get home or, even better, something more lasting? A piece of jewellery would be very acceptable, something with rubies. For it is 40 years – though no one would ever believe it. She smiles at her trim reflection in the jeweller's window, and then looks through herself at a ruby brooch in the shape of a single red rose. But even a real rose would do, she thinks, as long as he hasn't really forgotten. There's a bottle of claret in the cellar, she remembers, and what could be more appropriate? She anticipates the celebration they will have, the delicious tender meat, the wine ruby red in the crystal glasses. How it will glow in the candlelight! How she will glow and remind him of the young woman he married.

It is a fine morning. The frost is dissolving now in the kind October sun. There are cobwebs glistening on the cotoneaster berries which shine red in the sun. Like blood, thinks Hubert, like rubies. He potters about, listening to the shouts of the girls next door and the murmurs of their mother.

'Lovely morning,' he says over the fence.

The woman, Greta, stops digging and rests one foot on her fork. 'Wonderful,' she says. 'I'm just putting in some bulbs.'

'Hello, mister,' shout the children. Their cheeks are rosy and their eyes bright. 'We're digging too!' says one.

'See my trowel,' says the other.

'That's a good trowel,' says Hubert.

'We're going to the park later,' she says. 'It's Mum's birthday and we're having a picnic lunch.'

'Many happy returns,' says Hubert.

'You come, too,' says one of the girls. 'Mum, the old man can come, too, can't he?'

Greta laughs. 'Of course he can, if he wants to.'

Hubert is embarrassed. 'Oh, you wouldn't want me tagging along.'

'Honestly, if you'd like to. A bit of adult company would be nice.'

'Oh, no, I couldn't possibly impose.'

'Please,' say the girls, 'please, please, please.'

'Well . . .' Hubert considers. Why not? Dorothy will be furious, of course, but then she's out. There is no particular reason to be here when she gets back. Let her stew, he thinks. 'I would be honoured,' he says.

'Good,' says Greta. 'That's that sorted then. We'll set off about twelve.'

'Looking forward to it,' says Hubert. 'I'll see you later.' He goes back into the house, a smile upon his face. It's not a bachelor I should have been at all, he reflects, it's a grandfather.

Dorothy has reached her destination. Usually, she visits the local hairdresser for a trim, which is all that her long, white hair requires. It is easy hair now, not so luxuriant. It is easy to twist into a white tail and fold into a neat pleat, fastened firmly to her scalp with steel pins. But, today, Dorothy wants something different.

'I want it dyed red,' she says to the young man. 'A bright auburn, my original colour.'

The young man combs Dorothy's hair through. 'I don't know,' he says. 'I don't really think . . .'

'Think what?'

'I don't think it would suit . . .'

'Not suit!' exclaims Dorothy. 'But that's my original colour!'

The young man hesitates. 'I'll fetch Suzanne,' he says, and flees.

In the mirror, Dorothy can see the young man and Suzanne talking. They are both looking at her and shaking their heads. Silly young fools, she thinks. She stretches out her elegant hands and regards them fondly. There are a few brown stains upon their backs but, still, they are good hands with slim wrists and straight fingers. Her wedding ring shines a warm gold against the whiteness of her skin.

'Excuse me, madam,' says Suzanne through her scarlet lipstick. 'My colleague has asked me to give you a compli- mentary beauty advice session.'

'Thank you,' says Dorothy frostily, 'but I don't require advice. I know exactly what I want. I want my hair brought back to its original colour, the colour it was on my wedding day. That boy had the nerve to suggest that it wouldn't suit me! My own colour!'

'But you see, madam,' says Suzanne, as if to a child, 'as we age, it isn't just our hair that loses pigment, it's our skin, too. So your original shade simply won't suit you any more. We could do you a rinse, though. What about a nice soft apricot?'

'Red,' says Dorothy firmly. 'Bright red.'

'And, also, if I may say so,' continues Suzanne unabashed, 'your hair is very fine and, well, getting a little sparse. A dye might actually damage your scalp. Look, madam.'

Suzanne produces a mirror and shows Dorothy a terrible sight, a sight she never asked to see: the back of her head. She can clearly see the shape of her scalp gleaming pink through the ragged white stuff that had once been her only real asset. Dorothy shuts her eyes.

'Red,' she says.

'But, madam . . .'

'Am I to understand that you are refusing to do my hair?' asks Dorothy. Suzanne looks nervously around, for Dorothy's voice is loud and querulous and other clients are beginning to fidget and look.

'No, of course not, madam,' she says. 'But please understand this. If you insist on a particular treatment against our advice, then we cannot accept responsibility for the results.'

'Understood,' says Dorothy. 'Now, let's get on with it. I haven't got all day.'

In the kitchen, Hubert is getting a move on, too. He has already spent half an hour in the bathroom, trimming the hairs that protrude from his nose and ears in honour of the occasion. He has chosen a beige silk cravat to hide the tortoise wrinkles on his neck. He has been back outside and chosen three miraculous blooms, three roses that have braved the frost. They are deep red roses, velvet rich, their secret folds almost black.

He has a sudden, terrible urge to force his finger into the cool dark velvet of them, but resists. They are perfect. Greta will appreciate them for they are living, growing things. He finds a card and writes in his careful hand: 'To you on your special day. With love.' His hand trembles and there is a messy trail of ink. He feels embarrassed by the strength of his feeling. Perhaps she will think him just a feeble old man. Pathetic. Perhaps he will throw the card away after all. He places it on the table beside the roses just for now.

He searches in the cupboard for a contribution towards the picnic, but finds nothing suitable. Ah, he thinks, I know. There's a bottle of claret in the cellar. It is the final bottle of a case eked out over years of too few worthy occasions. He opens the cellar door and fumbles for the light.

Dorothy's eyes are red. She has spent a long time locked in the lavatory in Debenhams, weeping. Suzanne was right.

Her hair is hideous. Handfuls of it fell out in response to the dye, and what is left is a fierce acidic orange that clashes with the painful scarlet mess that is her scalp. Not only does it look terrifying, but it is also too painful to touch. Suzanne refused payment for the treatment and hustled her out of the back door with a towel over her head. 'Told you so,' said her eyes, and Dorothy was humble. She had been wrong, and now she looked a nightmare.

In the cellar, Hubert has what Dorothy calls one of his funny turns. Red berries like beads of blood, he thinks, like rubies, like drops of wine. Red cheeks and petals and cool velvet folds. He stands, swaying, the cold, gritty neck of the bottle clutched in his hand. Rubies and wine and blood, he thinks, and the bottle slips from his hand and smashes on the floor.

With the noise, Hubert comes to. He looks at the ruby puddle spreading across the floor. He thinks wildly of mops and buckets and Dorothy's face when she discovers their loss. But there is no time to do anything for there is the ring of the doorbell and the scuffle of children on the doorstep. He leaves the precious wine to soak into the floor, the shards of glass to glitter in the dimness, and climbs the stairs.

When he opens the door, he sees that Greta's eyes are as bright and eager as her children's and look scarcely older.

'We've got chocolate cake!' announces one of the girls.

'And cola,' adds the other.

'I should wrap up warm,' says Greta. 'It's getting really nippy.' And, indeed, the sun has vanished and the sky is old and grey behind their bright faces. I am just an old man, thinks Hubert, an old man who must wrap up against the cold.

'I've brought a Thermos of soup,' says Greta. 'I thought you might prefer that to cola!' Her cheeks are as red as her daughters'. He imagines handing her the roses. How touched she would be to receive this gift from such an old man. Her woollen breasts are hidden inside her coat. The edge of her ear is a delicate pink, cold.

'I don't think, after all, that I will come,' he says. And he can clearly see the relief that flickers across Greta's face before she says, 'Oh, what a shame!'

And the girls don't care. 'Come on, Mum,' they whine.

'Some other time,' says Greta. 'We'd better go before it starts to rain!'

'Yes,' says Hubert as they go. 'Some other time.' He shuts the door. In the hall mirror his face is grey. I'd better get that wine mopped up, he thinks.

Dorothy hesitates outside the house. Whatever will Hubert say? It was romance she had in mind when she set out this morning, the intention to surprise. I will bathe my head and use a soft, silk scarf as a turban, she decides, and I will cook a dinner so superb that it won't matter how I look. After all, I'm an old woman now and should not be vain. I must hurry in, she thinks, and defrost the loin.

Going down the cellar steps, Hubert feels old and stiff: he feels his age. The low room is heady with the robust smell of claret. The mop feels unwieldy. He pauses and closes his eyes. The secret black folds of the rose, he thinks, the delicate edge of a cold ear. He drops the mop on the floor and, somewhere, vaguely, he feels his knees give way. Loose breasts against a woollen jumper, he thinks, and the bright eyes of children. Hubert sinks to the floor.

He dies contentedly, the odour of fine wine in his nostrils, his face cradled on the shards of the treasured bottle, the dark stain of the wine spreading around him. Berries and breasts and roses are the last traces of thought in his mind, rubies and wine and blood.

Dorothy finds the roses on the table and the oddly worded card. Our day, surely, she thinks. But never mind, he has not forgotten, bless his heart. And perhaps there will be something more lasting, later. She picks up a rose and sniffs, but there's no odour. A thorn pierces her finger and a bright drop of blood oozes out. She licks it with the tip of her tongue.

Although the roses have no scent, there is a funny smell in the kitchen, like wine, which reminds Dorothy that if she really wants to please Hubert, she had better decant the claret in good time. It must have time to breathe . . .

RUTH RENDELL

Long Live the Queen

It was over in an instant. A flash of orange out of the green hedge, a streak across the road, a thud. The impact was felt as a surprisingly heavy jarring. There was no cry. Anna had braked, but too late, and the car had been going fast. She pulled in to the side of the road, got out, walked back.

An effort was needed before she could look. The cat had been flung against the grass verge which separated road from narrow walkway. It was dead. She knew before she knelt down and felt its side that it was dead. A little blood came from its mouth. Its eyes were already glazing. It had been a fine cat of the kind called marmalade because the colour is two-tone, the stripes like dark slices of peel among the clear orange. Paws, chest and part of its face were white, the eyes gooseberry green.

It was an unfamiliar road, one she had only taken to avoid road works on the bridge. Anna thought, I was going too fast. There is no speed limit here, but it's a country road with cottages and I shouldn't have been going so fast. The poor cat. Now she must go and admit what she had done, confront an angry or distressed owner, an owner who presumably lived in the house behind that hedge.

She opened the gate and went up the path. It was a cottage, but not a pretty one: of red brick with a low, slate roof, bay windows downstairs with a green front door between them. In each bay window sat a cat, one black, one orange and white like the cat which had run in front of her car. They stared at her, unblinking, inscrutable, as if they did not see her, as if she was not there. She could still see the black one when she was at the front door. When she put her finger to the bell and rang it, the cat did not move, nor even blink its eyes.

No one came to the door. She rang the bell again. It occurred to her that the owner might be in the back garden and she walked round the side of the house. It was not really a garden but a wilderness of long grass and tall weeds and wild trees. There was no one. She looked through a window into a kitchen where a tortoiseshell cat sat on top of the fridge in the sphinx position, and on the floor, on a strip of matting, a brown tabby rolled sensuously, its striped paws stroking the air.

There were no cats outside as far as she could see, not living ones at least. In the left-hand corner, past a kind of lean-to coal shed and a clump of bushes, three small wooden crosses were just visible among the long grass. Anna had no doubt they were cat graves.

She looked in her bag and finding a hairdresser's appointment card, wrote on the blank back of it her name, her parents' address and their phone number, and added, 'Your cat ran out in front of my car. I'm sorry, I'm sure death was instantaneous.' Back at the front door, the black cat and the orange and white cat still staring out, she put the card through the letter box.

It was then that she looked in the window where the black cat was sitting. Inside was a small over-furnished living room which looked as if it smelt. Two cats lay on the hearth rug, two more were curled up together in an armchair. At either end of the mantelpiece sat a china cat, white and red with gilt whiskers. Anna thought there ought to have been another one between them, in the centre of the shelf, because this was the only clear space in the room, every other corner and surface being crowded with objects, many of which had some association with the feline: cat ashtrays, cat vases, photographs of cats in silver frames, postcards of cats, mugs with cat faces on them and ceramic, brass, silver and glass kittens. Above the fireplace was a portrait of a marmalade and white cat done in oils, and on the wall to the left hung a cat calendar.

Anna had an uneasy feeling that the cat in the portrait was the one that lay dead in the road. At any rate, they were very alike. She could not leave the dead cat where it was. In the boot of her car were two plastic carrier bags, some sheets of newspaper and a blanket she sometimes used for padding things she did not want to strike against each other while she was driving. As wrapping for the cat's body the plastic bags would look callous, the newspapers worse. She would sacrifice the blanket. It was a clean dark blue blanket, single size, quite decent and decorous.

The cat's body wrapped in this blanket, she carried it up the path. The black cat had moved from the left-hand bay and had taken up a similar position in one of the upstairs windows. Anna took another look into the living room. A second examination of the portrait confirmed her guess that its subject was the one she was carrying. She backed away. The black cat stared down at her, turned its head and yawned hugely. Of course it did not know she carried one of its companions, dead and now cold, wrapped in an old car blanket, having met a violent death. She had an uncomfortable feeling, a ridiculous feeling, that it would have behaved in precisely the same way if it had known.

She laid the cat's body on the roof of the coal shed. As she came back round the house, she saw a woman in the garden next door. This was a neat and tidy garden with flowers and a lawn. The woman was in her 50s, white-haired, slim, wearing a twin-set.

'One of the cats ran out in front of my car,' Anna said. 'I'm afraid it's dead.'

'Oh dear.'

'I've put the – body, the body on the coal shed. Do you know when they'll be back?'

'It's just her,' the woman said. 'It's just her on her own.'

'Oh, well. I've written a note for her. With my name and address.'

The woman was giving her an odd look. 'You're very honest. Most would have just driven on. You don't have to report running over a cat, you know. It's not the same as a dog.'

'I couldn't have just gone on.'

'If I were you I'd tear that note up. You can leave it to me, I'll tell her I saw you.'

'I've already put it through the door,' said Anna.

She said goodbye to the woman and got back into her car. She was on her way to her parents' house where she would be staying for the next two weeks. Anna had a flat on the other side of the town but she had promised to look after her parents' house while they were away on holiday, and – it now seemed a curious irony – her parents' cat.

If her journey had gone according to plan, if she had not been delayed for half an hour by the accident and the cat's death, she would have been in time to see her mother and father before they left for the airport. But when she got there they had gone. On the hall table was a note for her in her mother's hand to say that they had had to leave, the cat had been fed and there was a cold roast chicken in the fridge for Anna's supper. The cat would probably like some too, to comfort it for missing them.

Anna did not think her mother's cat, a huge fluffy creature of a ghostly whitish-grey tabbyness, named Griselda, was capable of missing anyone. She could not believe it had affections. It seemed to her without personality or charm, to lack endearing ways. To her knowledge, it had never uttered, beyond giving an occasional thin squeak that signified hunger. It had never been known to rub its body against human legs, or even against the legs of the furniture. Anna knew that it was absurd to call an animal selfish, an animal naturally put its survival first, self-preservation being its prime instinct, yet she thought of Griselda as deeply, intensely, callously selfish. When it was not eating, it slept, and it slept in those most comfortable places where the people that owned it would have liked to sit, but from which they could not bring themselves to dislodge it. At night it lay on their bed and if they moved, dug its long sharp claws through the bedclothes into their legs.

Anna's mother did not like hearing Griselda referred to as 'it'. She corrected Anna and stroked Griselda's head. Griselda, who purred a lot when recently fed and ensconced among cushions, always stopped purring at the touch of a human hand. This would have amused Anna if she had not seen that her mother seemed hurt by it, withdrew her hand and gave an unhappy little laugh.

When she had unpacked the case she brought with her, had prepared and eaten her meal and given Griselda a chicken leg, she began to wonder if the owner of the cat she had run over would phone. The owner might feel, as people

87

bereaved in great or small ways sometimes did feel, that nothing could bring back the dead. Discussion was useless and so, certainly, was recrimination. It had not in fact been her fault. She had been driving fast, but not *illegally* fast, and even if she had been driving at 30 miles an hour she doubted if she could have avoided the cat which streaked so swiftly out of the hedge.

It would be better to stop thinking about it. A night's sleep, a day at work, and the memory of it would recede. She had done all she could. She was very glad she had not just driven on as the next-door neighbour had seemed to advocate. It had been some consolation to know that the woman had many cats, not just the one, so that perhaps losing one would be less of a blow.

When she had washed the dishes and phoned her friend Kate, she wondered if Richard, the man who had taken her out three times and to whom she had given this number, would phone, and having decided he would not, she sat down beside Griselda, not *with* Griselda but on the same sofa as she was on, and watched television. It got to 10pm and she thought it unlikely the cat woman – she had begun thinking of her as that – would phone now.

There was a phone extension in her parents' room but not in the spare room where she would be sleeping. It was nearly 11.30pm and she was getting into bed when the phone rang. The chance of it being Richard, who was capable of phoning late, especially if he thought she was alone, made her go and answer it.

A voice that sounded strange, thin and cracked, said what sounded like, 'Maria Yackle.'

'Yes?' Anna said.

'This is Maria Yackle. It was my cat that you killed.'

Anna swallowed. 'Yes. I'm glad you found my note. I'm very sorry, I'm very sorry. It was an accident. The cat ran out in front of my car.'

'You were going too fast.'

It was a blunt statement, harshly made. Anna could not refute it. She said, 'I'm very sorry about your cat.'

'They don't go out much, they're happier indoors. It was a chance in a million. I should like to see you. I think you should make amends. It wouldn't be right for you just to get away with it.' Anna was very taken aback. Up till then the woman's remarks had seemed reasonable. She did not know what to say.

'I think you should compensate me, don't you? I loved her, I love all my cats. I expect you thought that because I had so many cats it wouldn't hurt me so much to lose one.'

That was so near what Anna had thought that she felt a kind of shock as if this Maria Yackle, or whatever she was called, had read her mind. 'I've told you I'm sorry. I am sorry, I was very upset, I *hated* it happening. I don't know what more I can say?'

'We must meet.'

'What would be the use of that?' Anna knew she sounded rude but she was shaken by the woman's tone, her blunt, direct sentences.

There was a break in the voice, something very like a sob. 'It would be of use to me.'

The phone went down. Anna could hardly believe it. She had heard it go down but still she said several times over, 'Hallo? Hallo?' and 'Are you still there?'

She went downstairs and found the telephone directory for the area and looked up Yackle. It wasn't there. She sat down and worked her way through all the Ys. There were not many pages of Ys, apart from Youngs, but there was no one with a name beginning with Y at that address on the rustic road among the cottages.

She could not get to sleep. She expected the phone to ring again, Maria Yackle to ring back. After a while she put the bed lamp on and lay there in the light. It must have been 3am, and still she had not slept, when Griselda came in, got on the bed and stretched her length along Anna's legs. She put out the light, deciding not to answer the phone if it did ring, to relax, forget the run-over cat, concentrate on nice things. As she turned face-downwards and stretched her body straight, she felt Griselda's claws prickle her calves. As she shrank away from contact, curled up her legs and left Griselda a good half of the bed, a thick rough purring began.

89

The first thing she thought of when she woke up was how upset that poor cat woman had been. She expected her to phone back at breakfast time but nothing happened. Anna fed Griselda, left her to her house, her cat flap, her garden and wider territory, and drove to work. Richard phoned as soon as she got in. Could they meet the following evening? She agreed, obscurely wishing he had said that night, suggesting that evening herself, only to be told he had to work late, had a dinner with a client.

She had been home for 10 minutes when a car drew up outside. It was an old car, at least 10 years old, and not only dented and scratched but with some of the worst scars painted or sprayed over in a different shade of red. Anna, who saw it arrive from a front window, watched the woman get out of it and approach the house. She was old, or at least elderly – is elderly older than old, or old older than elderly? – but dressed like a teenager. Anna got a closer look at her clothes, her hair and her face when she opened the front door.

It was a wrinkled face, the colour and texture of a chicken's wattles. Small blue eyes were buried somewhere in the strawberry redness. The bright white hair next to it was as much of a contrast as snow against scarlet cloth. She wore tight jeans with socks pulled up over the bottoms of them, dirty white trainers, and a big loose sweatshirt with a cat's face on it, a painted, smiling, be-whiskered mask, orange and white and green-eyed.

Anna had read somewhere the comment made by a young girl on an older woman's boast that she could wear a mini-skirt because she had good legs: 'It's not your legs, it's your face.' She thought of this as she looked at Maria Yackle, but that was the last time for a long while she thought of anything like that.

'I've come early because we shall have a lot to talk about,' Maria Yackle said and walked in. She did this in such a way as to compel Anna to open the door further and stand aside. 'This is *your* house?'

She might have meant because Anna was so young, or perhaps there was some more offensive reason for asking.

'My parents'. I'm just staying here.'

'Is it this room?' She was already on the threshold of Anna's mother's living room.

Anna nodded. She had been taken aback but only for a moment. It was best to get this over. But she did not care to be dictated to.

'You could have let me know. I might not have been here.'

There was no reply because Maria Yackle had seen Griselda.

The cat had been sitting on the back of a wing chair between the wings, an apparently uncomfortable place, though a favourite, but at sight of the newcomer she had stretched, got down and was walking towards her. Maria Yackle put out her hand. It was a horrible hand, large and red with rope-like blue veins standing out above the bones, the palm calloused, the nails black and broken and the sides of the forefingers and thumbs ingrained with brownish dirt. Griselda approached and put her smoky whitish muzzle and pink nose into this hand.

'I shouldn't,' Anna said rather sharply, for Maria Yackle was bending over to pick the cat up. 'She isn't very nice. She doesn't like people.'

'She'll like me.'

And the amazing thing was that Griselda did. Maria Yackle sat down and Griselda sat on her lap. Griselda the unfriendly, the cold-hearted, the cat who purred when alone and who ceased to purr when touched, the ice-eyed, the standoffish walker-by-herself, settled down on this unknown, untried lap, having first climbed up Maria Yackle's chest and on to her shoulders and then rubbed her soft ears and plump furry cheeks against the woman's sweatshirt with the painted cat face.

'You seem surprised.'

Anna said, 'You could say that.'

'There's no mystery. The explanation's simple.' It was a shrill harsh voice, cracked by the onset of old age, articulate, the usage grammatical, but the accent raw cockney. 'You and your mum and dad too, no doubt, you all think you smell very nice and pretty. You have your bath every morning with bath essence and scented soap. You put on talcum powder and spray stuff in your armpits, your rub cream on your bodies and squirt on perfume. Maybe you've washed your hair too with shampoo and conditioner and what-do-they-call-it? – mousse. You clean your teeth and wash your mouth, put a drop more perfume behind your ears, paint your faces – well, I daresay your dad doesn't paint his face, but he shaves, doesn't he? More mousse and then aftershave.

'You put on your clothes. All of them clean, spotless. They've either just come back from the dry-cleaners or else out of the washing machine with biological soap and spring-fresh fabric softener. Oh, I know, I may not do it myself but I see it on the TV.

'It all smells very fine to you but it doesn't to her. Oh no. To her it's just chemicals, like gas might be to you, or paraffin. A nasty strong chemical smell that puts her right off and makes her shrink up in her furry skin. What's her name?'

This question was uttered on a sharp bark. 'Griselda,' said Anna, and, 'How did you know it's a she?'

'Face, look,' said Maria Yackle. 'See her little nose. See her smily mouth and her little nose and her fat cheeks? Tom cat's got a big nose, got a long muzzle. Never mind if he's been neutered, still got a big nose.'

'What did you come here to say to me?' said Anna.

Griselda had curled up on the cat woman's lap, burying her head, slightly upward turned, in the crease between stomach and thigh. 'I don't go in for all that stuff, you see.'

The big red hand stroked Griselda's head, the stripy bit between her ears. 'Cat likes the smell of me because I haven't got my clothes in soapy water every day, I have a bath once a week, always have and always shall, and I don't waste my money on odorisers and deodorisers. I wash my hands when I get up in the morning and that's enough for me.'

At the mention of the weekly bath, Anna had reacted instinctively and edged her chair a little further away. Maria Yackle saw, Anna was sure she saw, but her response to this recoil was to begin on what she had in fact come about: her compensation.

'The cat you killed, she was 5 years old and the queen of

the cats, her name was Melusina. I always have a queen. The one before was Juliana and she lived to be 12. I wept, I mourned her, but life has to go on. The queen is dead, I said, long live the queen! I never promote one, I always get a new kitten. Some cats are queens, you see, and some are not. Melusina was 8 weeks old when I got her from the Animal Rescue people, and I gave them a donation of £20. The vet charged me £27.50 for her injections, all my cats are immunised against feline enteritis and leptospirosis, so that makes £47.50. And she had her booster at age 2 which was another £27.50, I can show you the receipted bills, I always keep everything, and that makes £75. Then there was my petrol getting her to the vet, we'll say a straight £5 though it was more, and then we come to the crunch, her food. She was a good little trench- erwoman.'

Anna would have been inclined to laugh at this ridiculous word, but she saw to her horror that the tears were running down Maria Yackle's cheeks. They were running unchecked out of her eyes, over the rough red wrinkled skin, and one dripped unheeded on to Griselda's silvery fur.

'Take no notice. I do cry whenever I have to talk about her. I loved that cat. She was the queen of the cats. She had her own place, her throne, she used to sit in the middle of the mantelpiece with her two china ladies-in-waiting on each side of her. You'll see one day, when you come to my house.

'But we were talking about her food. She ate a large can a day, it was too much, more than she should have had, but she loved her food, she was a good little eater. Well, cat food's gone up over the years of course, what hasn't, and I'm paying 50p a can now, but I reckon it'd be fair to average it out at 40p. She was 8 weeks old when I got her, so we can't say five times 365. We'll say five times 355 and that's doing you a favour. I've already worked it out at home, I'm not that much of a wizard at mental arithmetic. Five 355s are 1775, which multiplied by 40 makes 71,000p. Add to that the £80, plus the vet's bill of £9 when she had a tapeworm, and we get a final figure of £799.'

Anna stared at her. 'You're asking me to give you nearly £800.'

'That's right. Of course we'll write it down and do it properly.'

'Because your cat ran under the wheels of my car?'

'You murdered her,' said Maria Yackle.

'That's absurd. Of course I didn't murder her.' On shaky ground, she said, 'You can't murder an animal.'

'You did. You said you were going too fast.'

Had she? She had been but had she said so?

Maria Yackle got up, still holding Griselda, cuddling Griselda, who nestled purring in her arms. Anna watched with distaste. You thought of cats as fastidious creatures but they were not. Only something insensitive and undiscerning would put its face against that face, nuzzle those rough, grimy hands. The black fingernails brought to mind a phrase, now unpleasantly appropriate, that her grandmother had used to children with dirty hands: in mourning for the cat.

'I don't expect you to give me a cheque now. Is that what you thought I meant? I don't suppose you have that amount in your current account. I'll come back tomorrow or the next day.'

'I am not going to give you £800,' said Anna.

She might as well not have spoken.

'I won't come back tomorrow, I'll come back on Wednesday.' Griselda was tenderly placed on the seat of an armchair. The tears had dried on Maria Yackle's face, leaving salt trails. She took herself out into the hall and to the front door. 'You'll have thought about it by then. Anyway, I hope you'll come to the funeral. I hope there won't be any hard feelings.'

That was when Anna decided Maria Yackle was mad. In one way this was disquieting, in another a comfort. It meant she was not serious about the compensation, the £800. Sane people do not invite you to their cat's funeral. Mad people do not sue you for compensation.

Although no note awaited her on the doorstep, no letter came and there were no phone calls, Anna knew the cat woman would come back on the following evening. Richard had advised her to go to the police if any threats were made. There would be no need to tell them she had been driving very fast. Anna thought the whole idea of going to the police bizarre. She rang up her friend Kate and told her all about it and Kate agreed that telling the police would be going too far.

The battered red car arrived at 7pm. Maria Yackle was dressed as she had been for her previous visit, but because it was rather cold, wore a jacket made of synthetic fur as well. From its harsh too-shiny texture there was no doubt it was synthetic but from a distance it looked like a black cat's pelt.

She had brought an album of photographs of her cats for Anna to see. Anna looked through it – what else could she do? Some were recognisably of those she had seen through the windows. Those that were not, she supposed might be of animals now at rest under the wooden crosses in Maria Yackle's back garden. While she was looking at the pictures, Griselda, Anna's mother's cat, came in and jumped on to the cat woman's lap.

'They're very nice, very interesting,' Anna said. 'I can see you're devoted to your cats.'

'They're my life.'

A little humouring might be in order. 'When is the funeral to be?'

'I thought on Friday. Two o'clock on Friday. My sister will be there with her two. Cats don't usually take to car travel, that's why I don't often take any of mine with me, and shutting them up in cages goes against the grain, but my sister's two Burmese love the car, they'll go and sit in the car when it's parked. My friend from the Animal Rescue will come if she can get away and I've asked our vet but I don't hold out much hope there. He has his goat clinic on Fridays. I hope you'll come along.'

'I'm afraid I'll be at work.'

'It's no flowers by request. Donations to the Cat's Protection League instead. Any sum, no matter how small, gratefully received. Which brings me to money. You've got a cheque for me.'

'No, I haven't, Mrs Yackle.'

'Miss. And it's Yakob. J,A,K,O,B. You've got a cheque for me for £799.'

'I am not giving you any money, Miss Jakob. I'm very very sorry about your cat, about Melusina, I know how fond you were of her, but giving you compensation is out of the question. I'm sorry.'

The tears had come once more into Maria Jakob's eyes, had spilled over. Her face contorted with misery. It was the mention of the wretched thing's name, Anna thought. That was the trigger that started the weeping. A tear splashed on to one of the coarse red hands. Griselda opened her eyes and licked up the tear.

Maria Jakob pushed her other hand across her eyes. She blinked. 'We'll have to think of something else then,' she said.

'I beg your pardon?' Anna wondered if she had really heard right. Things couldn't be solved so simply.

'We shall have to think of something else. A way for you to make up to me for murder.'

'Look, I will give a donation to the Cats' Protection League. I'm quite prepared to give them – say £20.' Richard would be furious but perhaps she would not tell Richard. 'I'll give it to you, shall I, and then you can pass it on to them?'

'I certainly hope you will. Especially if you can't come to the funeral.'

That was the end of it then. Anna felt a great sense of relief. It was only now that it was over that she realised quite how it had got to her. It had actually kept her from sleeping properly. She phoned Kate and told her about the funeral and the goat clinic and Kate laughed and said, poor old thing. Anna slept so well that night that she did not notice the arrival of Griselda who, when she woke, was asleep on the pillow next to her face, but out of touching distance.

Richard phoned and she told him about it, omitting the part about her offer of a donation. He told her that being firm, sticking to one's guns in situations of this kind, always paid off. In the evening she wrote a cheque for £20, but instead of the Cats' Protection League, made it out to

Maria Jakob. If the cat woman quietly held on to it, no harm would be done. Anna went down the road to post her letter, for she had written a letter to accompany the cheque, in which she reiterated her sorrow about the death of the cat and added that if there was anything she could do, Miss Jakob had only to let her know. Richard would have been furious.

Unlike the Jakob cats, Griselda spent a good deal of time out of doors. She was often out all evening and did not reappear until the small hours, so that it was not until the next day, not until the next evening, that Anna began to be alarmed at her absence. As far as she knew, Griselda had never been away so long before. For herself she was unconcerned, she had never liked the cat, did not particularly like any cats, and found this one obnoxiously self-centred and cold. It was for her mother, who unaccountably loved the creature, that she was worried. She walked up and down the street, calling Griselda, though the cat had never been known to come when it was called.

It did not come now. Anna walked up and down the next street, calling, and around the block and further afield. She half-expected to find Griselda's body, guessing that it might have met with the same fate as Melusina. Hadn't she read somewhere that nearly 40,000 cats are killed on British roads annually? On Saturday morning she wrote one of those melancholy lost cat notices and attached it to a lamp standard, wishing she had a photograph. But her mother had taken no photographs of Griselda.

Richard took her to a friend's party and afterwards, when they were driving home, he said, 'You know what's happened, don't you? It's been killed by that old mad woman. An eye for an eye, a cat for a cat.'

'Oh, no, she wouldn't do that. She loves cats.'

'Murderers love people. They just don't love the people they murder.'

'I'm sure you're wrong,' said Anna, but she remembered how Maria Jakob had said that if the money was not forthcoming she must think of something else, a way to make up to her for Melusina's death, and she had not meant a donation to the Cats' Protection League.

'What shall I do?'

'I don't see that you can do anything. It's most unlikely you could prove it, she'll have seen to that. You can look at it this way, she's had her pound of flesh . . .'

'Some 15lb of flesh,' said Anna. Griselda had been a large, heavy cat.

'OK, 15lb. She's had that, she's had her revenge, it hasn't actually caused you any grief, you'll just have to make up some story for your mother.'

Anna's mother was upset but nowhere near as upset as Maria Jakob had been over the death of Melusina. To avoid too much fuss, Anna had gone further than she intended, told her mother that she had seen Griselda's corpse and talked to the offending motorist who had been very distressed. A month or so later Anna's mother got a kitten, a grey tabby tom kitten, who was very affectionate from the start, sat on her lap, purred loudly when stroked and snuggled up in her arms, though Anna was sure her mother had not stopped having baths or using perfume. So much for the Jakob theories.

Nearly a year had gone by before she again drove down the road where Maria Jakob's house was. She had not intended to go that way. She had been given directions to a smallholding where they sold early strawberries on a roadside stall but she must have missed her way, taken a wrong turning and come out here.

If Maria Jakob's car had been parked in the front she would not have stopped. There was no garage for it to be in, it was not outside, therefore the cat woman must be out. Anna thought of the funeral she had not been to, she had often thought about it, the strange people and strange cats who had attended it.

In each of the bay windows sat a cat, a tortoiseshell and a brown tabby. The black cat was eyeing her from upstairs. Anna did not go to the front door but round the back. There, among the long grass, as she had expected, were four graves instead of three, four wooden crosses and on the fourth was printed in black gloss paint: *Melusina the Queen of the Cats, murdered in her sixth year. R.I.P.*

That 'murdered' did not please Anna. It brought back all

the resentment at unjust accusations of 11 months before. She felt much older, she felt wiser. One thing was certain, ethics or no ethics, if she ever ran over a cat again she'd drive on, the last thing she'd do was go and confess.

She came round the side of the house and looked in at the bay window. If the tortoiseshell had still been on the windowsill she probably would not have looked in, but the tortoiseshell had removed itself to the hearth rug.

A white cat and the marmalade and white lay curled up side by side in an armchair. The portrait of Melusina hung above the fireplace and this year's cat calendar was up on the left-hand wall. Light gleamed on the china cats' gilt whiskers and between them, in the empty space that was no longer vacant, sat Griselda.

Griselda was sitting in the queen's place in the middle of the mantelpiece. She sat in the sphinx position, with her eyes closed. Anna tapped on the glass and Griselda opened her eyes, stared with cold indifference and closed them again.

The queen is dead, long live the queen!

GILLIAN TINDALL

Journey of a Lifetime

She was packing to go away, not just for a holiday this time but for a long while: there was so much still to do. Distractedly she filled suitcases with her own clothes and her husband's; she had said that she would pack for him, as he would be busy at work; then they could leave in the evening as soon as he got home. But she kept remembering more things that must go in, not just isolated objects but whole ranges of things, whole departments of life. And not only things that needed packing but other matters that should be attended to in different ways: the gas, the electricity, stuff at the cleaners . . . and what about the cats? What arrangement had she made about them?

The usual one, surely, but she could not be certain – and there was so little time . . . She looked at her watch. The afternoon was rapidly passing. She suddenly knew that she ought to put polythene sheets over the furniture as well. And go and see their neighbour before leaving. And the jobbing gardener . . . And were there still outstanding bills to pay?

But what really distracted her, preventing her from concentrating on the packing while yet making it imperative that she should get it done *now*, without further muddle or delay, was the awful knowledge that she had not yet got the plane tickets. She surely should have done? It must have been her responsibility, and her husband would be relying on her having done so with her usual competence. Or no – wait: did he perhaps have his own ticket already, as he sometimes did, provided by the firm? If so, it was just her ticket that she had, idiotically, failed to order. She had certainly meant to.

Six o'clock. That was when their travel agent closed. (Her busy life was organised upon a series of fixed props: 'their' travel agent, jobbing gardener, carpenter, plumber, locksmith, cleaner, neighbour, little-man-round-the-corner, grocer-who-delivers.) The travel agent was so helpful, if only she could get down to him before six all might yet be well. But further suspicion nagged: when did the plane actually leave? Much later than six? Possibly. But they would still have to get out to the airport . . .

She realised that she had yet to wash her hair. And she must wash it. It was, for some reason, crawling with insects and coming out in handfuls. The strands disintegrated between her fingers with a nameless corruption. She tried to scream, but no sound came.

She woke. Relief seeped through her. It was not late afternoon but early in the morning. She had the whole day to do things, and her husband would do his share; he was not going to work. He was asleep beside her now, and in fact he would not be going to work any more on a regular basis ever again, as he had recently retired. That was the reason they were able to make this extended trip: months and months slowly encircling the world in modest, economical stages, staying with this old friend here, looking up that erstwhile work-contact there. It was going to be the journey of a lifetime.

And of course she hadn't failed to pick up the tickets. They were all there, a whole folder of them, along with the passports, visas, health certificates and other necessary papers, sitting safe in the desk drawer, and had been for the last fortnight.

'I had a ghastly dream,' she said to her husband when he stirred. 'I'm so glad to wake up.'

'What dream?' he said dutifully, sleepily.

'My hair was coming out in handfuls,' she said, after a pause. She decided not to bother with the rest, which was indeed rapidly fading.

He snorted, secure in his own baldness.

'Is that all? You always were a vain woman.'

Well before six in the evening they were ready to leave. Their plane did not take off till the following morning, but they had decided to avoid an exhaustingly early start then by spending the night at the airport hotel. Long ago, she recalled, they had thought nothing of setting out in the dark after a bare three or four hours' sleep, or driving long distances across foreign countries. And that had been in the days when the children were still living with them and needing them. But as you got older your reserves of energy depleted, they had each separately discovered, however brisk and active your outward life.

Now the luggage, the lightweight matching set they had bought the year before with this trip in mind, was outside in the boot of the car. Not their own car – that they had lent to their youngest son. Or supposedly lent. In practice, when they finally got home again, they might let him keep it and get themselves a replacement. They could still afford it, and he was working so hard to get his own company off the ground. Graphic design. A lot of competition in that field, of course. Oh well. He had never (they said to one another) cost them as much as his older brother and sister had, with their long training in medicine and law respectively. And as it happened (though they did not actually say this to each other) he had always been the sweetest-natured of their children.

So the car outside had been lent by a kindly neighbour. They would leave it at the airport, post him the parking ticket, and he would collect at his convenience. All their lives they had been good at making efficient arrangements of this sort with other like-minded people.

'Are we under starter's orders?' said her husband. It was his set phrase for departures, sanctioned by years of use in this context, but produced originally from goodness knows what extinct period of his life or passing relationship: he had never, to her knowledge, been a racing man.

'Yes . . .' she said slowly, preoccupied with a mental review of the contents of her shoulder bag: passports – he had the tickets now – her own travellers' cheques, cash in useful dollar bills (carried separately from the cheques), airsickness pills, short-acting sleeping pills (for jet lag), jersey, spare blouse and change of underwear (in case the main luggage got delayed or even lost), assorted reading matter, toothbrush, tissues, make-up, her locket with the children's baby hair in it, without which she never travelled any distance . . . She would have unhesitatingly repudiated any suggestion

102

that she was a superstitious woman, yet the locket had become her talisman, a combination of charm and private identity tag.

'Yes,' she said again, with conscious decision. 'Ready, I think. Let's sit down a moment.'

They sat. He – not a superstitious man either, and not a believer in anything if you took him at his own word – counted out loud to three. Then they were officially off.

As he went to the cupboard under the stairs to set the burglar alarm, she made a hasty retreat out of their own front door. She had never really got used to the alarm, or learnt to treat it nonchalantly as he did. She knew that in practice, once the alarm was set, they had a full half-minute to shut the front door behind them, but she found herself unrealistically scared of cutting her exit fine and risking (horrors!) that before the latch had clicked to the alarm would start to ring. 'Well, it wouldn't be the end of the world if it did,' her husband would tell her, maddeningly deliberate in his moves, refusing to panic (as he put it). She knew that he was correct. But it was as if, in the depths of her mind, the 30-second bleeper in the alarm box was counting out something other, and more significant, than the mere time allowed for shutting the door.

Thus, in a passing flurry of anxiety and urgency, she got herself out of the house – her beloved house, which she would not see again for months – and into the borrowed car. She had thought she would very much mind leaving home this time. Yet, once in the strange car, they seemed to have left already.

The suburban avenue where she knew so many of the occupants by sight or name ... then the parade of shops along the main road where she was an habitual customer ... These passed by behind the closed windows of the car like a film which was nothing to do with her. Impossible, now, to envisage stopping, calling in for a packet of biscuits or the evening paper, or even to say 'goodbye'. They had officially departed, and were in an element of their own. They turned their faces to the west. The thickening rush-hour traffic was going the opposite way to them, cars with other people who were caught in the old life, who, at the next dawn, would be asleep in their own beds, not flying off above the clouds into the brightness without frontiers.

In the airport hotel they were in the standard room: she had been in it many times before, accompanying her husband on business trips. In Glasgow, Frankfurt and Milan she had been in it, in New York, Pittsburg, Hong Kong and Tokyo. She knew the bathroom alongside the entrance, with its thick towels, gift-wrapped shower cap and sachets of shampoo, knew the twin beds with the television control panel between them, the twin padded chairs and low table, the large sidelit mirror above what he always claimed was a desk and she maintained was meant as a dressing table. She knew too the soundless, odourless, temperature-less night, with its galaxy of lights below, beyond the double-glazed windows. It was almost like being up in a plane already. Unlike a house, let alone your own house, where there were things making silent demands all round you, there was almost nothing to do in that room. At the very most, you might make a phone call, and wash out your tights ready for the next morning, before stretching yourself on the bed with a traveller's paperback. Amazingly restful, not only for the body but also for the mind. Like Eternal Rest. A fragment of the Victorian dream of heaven.

But only a fragment. Because the next day always came. One never had long, not long enough really, to repose in that room. She prepared to luxuriate in the brief time allowed. But her husband seemed restless. He got himself an expensive Scotch from the minibar, then left it standing getting warm under the lamp while he fiddled with his camera. Presently he said abruptly:

'I think I'll just write the odd letter.'

'Oh? I thought you'd got all your post done before you left.' He was punctilious about that sort of thing.

He said, in the remote voice of one who does not want to be questioned further:

'I thought I'd just drop a line to each of the children. Sort of – let them know we're off.'

The children. Goodness. He'd hardly ever written to the children. Even when they were away at college – or now, when their eldest son was a doctor at a hospital in the North.

He was always happy to chat to them on the phone, but writing had been tacitly regarded as her task. She thought of saying, 'But they know we're leaving tomorrow. We've seen or spoken to all of them in the last three days.' She thought of saying, 'But you haven't anything to tell them yet. Why not wait till we land in Cairo?' Naturally she said neither. He had been on edge these last few days, tense, withdrawn, not like himself. She opened her book.

What did he usually do in the hotel room at these times? Of course, she realised, on all previous trips within her experience he had had paperwork to do. A file to go through for someone he was due to meet in Frankfurt, Milan or Tokyo. A memo to write up for someone back at home.

But now there were no more files and memos. No more, ever. For the first time, as she lay on the smooth, firm bed under the diffused lights, the reality of her husband's retirement – effectively masked during the unnaturally busy weeks before their departure – came home to her. Something akin to panic stirred within her. What would he do? What would he ever do?

No, she would not think about that now. In any case she had no time to. Weeks – months – out of ordinary time lay ahead of them, a period of repeated departures into the brightness, a succession of arrivals at alien, pristine places, untarnished by experience. No space, in such a life-outside-life, for worry or doubt or long-term dread. All that could wait for the unimaginably distant day of their return. Meanwhile each new stage would be like that lovely hymn – *Morning has broken – like the first morning* . . .

Soothed because it was a hymn, and went back to her childhood, she let the book fall and dozed a little. The past day had, cumulatively, been very tiring, she thought between one absence and another. And she had not slept well the night before. That dream . . . With his back to her, her husband sat and wrote steadily to their children on hotel paper, as if imparting something unprecedented she could not guess or share.

Then, when she woke again, time was no longer spacious but very thin, a mere slice of cold blue light, sharp to the eyes. It was as if it were already compressed by the day ahead which would be no true day, mere hours without weight or character, unnaturally accelerated as they were carried eastwards, into the future.

As the desk clerk handed back the credit card to him, she said to her husband:

'Did you pay the Barclaycard bill up to date?'

'I paid all the bills,' he said, using again that flat, remote voice of one who has temporarily severed contact.

With another small, sudden excess of panic she thought: Oh, I hope he doesn't keep being – like this – while we're away. We'll be together all the time. And if he's – like this – it'll be so lonely . . .

But in the coach going to the terminal he uncharacteristically took her hand a moment and squeezed it.

The terminal at that unreal hour was almost empty, many of the desks still closed. They skirted round one straggling queue of dark-skinned people with copious luggage, and reached their own check-in. There was no one there but the airline clerk.

An experienced traveller, her husband inquired if the bulkhead seats were taken yet and, having secured them, turned back to her triumphantly:

'There, I said we might get those if we turned up in good time. Lots of room for our legs.' To the clerk, he added hopefully: 'Is there a good chance of the third seat that side staying empty? I don't imagine that the flight's full, is it?'

'The flight *is* full, Sir, as it happens.'

'Oh – how odd. But I thought . . . Oh well.'

The clerk, tapping his computer, made no reply. Their suitcases jolted off down the ramp. As always, she watched them go with a faint pang.

'These are your boarding cards, Sir. Boarding will start in approximately one hour from now. Gate 23.'

'Good. Thank you. We'll go and get some breakfast.'

She was glad that his withdrawn mood had passed. He seemed now almost unnaturally cheerful.

She did not want breakfast. She discovered that she actually felt slightly sick and strange, what she had all her life known as that going-back-to-boarding-school feeling that she tended to get before journeys. She called it that to herself because she had always supposed it was an emotion left over from the unhappiness of youth, long rendered obsolete by the layers of security and happiness that had accrued around her in adult life. But now, as she followed him docilely towards the café, it occurred to her that it did not actually feel like an emotion from the past. No, it was more like a rehearsal for something else. Something long foreseen but still to come.

He had porridge and a croissant and coffee. She had tea. They bought two newspapers and, with abstracted minds, read through British news which already seemed to have become thin and strange like the morning light, artificial approximations of news and daylight rather than the genuine thing.

Later, past Customs and security checks, as they waited on the Departure side amid acres of padded seats, she suddenly said:

'It's not on the monitor.'

'What?'

'Our flight. It ought to be on the monitor by now – it's nearly the time that we were told for boarding. But it isn't there.'

He got up himself to study the nearest television screen, fished out the boarding cards to check. She saw him accost a man in uniform, and saw from the man's stance and expression that he was unconcerned by their plight but seemed to be gesturing towards the galleries that led to the departure gates.

With that tightening in her stomach again, she thought wildly: we've miscounted the time, got confused getting up so early – mislaid an hour, even. It must be much later than we thought. Perhaps we've missed the plane . . .

He came back to her, walking deliberately, wearing the aloof expression of one refusing to be made anxious, but he gathered up his own bag quickly.

'He says we'd better get down to Gate 23 now. Says the monitors don't always work as they should.'

She was already on her feet, her own bag on her shoulder.

'But there've been no announcements or anything . . . None that we've heard, anyway.'

'Quite.'

They passed rapidly down the galleries, their way speeded by moving belts; they spared hardly a glance at the unrealistic décor of life that still anachronistically and pointlessly continued beyond the toughened glass screens. As if in perfunctory approximation to traditional British weather, a little soundless rain seemed to be falling.

In the boarding lounge for Gate 23 there was an oddly nondescript collection of people, among whom no particular nationality or race seemed to predominate. Some, like themselves, carried only compact manageable baggage. But some were monstrously laden with supernumary cases and plastic bags, struggling under weights they could hardly lift. Why did the airlines, who theoretically had rules about one piece of hand luggage only, allow this situation? It wasn't even kind, she thought, to let passengers be so foolish: precious possessions should not become a grievous burden.

With the mixture of amusement and disapproval customary between them at these moments, she drew her husband's attention to their laden companions, adding – 'Lots of them are quite old too, poor things. One wonders why on earth they need to travel with all that stuff?'

Her husband did not answer directly, but said after a moment, in a strained voice:

'There are no children on this flight.'

'Well, that's rather a relief,' she said, determinedly bright now that he seemed to have become withdrawn again. 'I mean, it's not that I want to be the sort of person who objects to sitting next to a child on a plane, but when you've spent years bringing up your own children and turning them into reasonable human beings . . .'

He said in the same voice, as if he had not heard her:

'There are not many people here under 50, for that matter.'

She looked around, and saw what he meant. A silence fell between them. It prolonged itself.

Then they were standing in line. An announcement was now, belatedly, crackling over the loudspeaker; it must – it could only be – their flight being called, but the sound was distorted and people were fussing with luggage and talking all round them; it was impossible to hear properly what was being said.

As they reached the dark-faced official who was collecting parts of the boarding cards she had a strong helpless desire to say No! – No, there must be some mistake, that this could not be their flight – that it was not time yet, not for a number of years; that anyway she did not want – that husband wouldn't want – that they hadn't meant –

No use. She could not speak. She saw her husband, at her side, surrender the cards. Too late. They entered the short tunnel that led to the plane.

Heads high, united in a sudden wordless comprehension of which they would now never speak, since there would be no time in which to speak, they entered the aircraft together: a good-looking couple but almost old, suitably equipped for the journey of a lifetime, only lightly laden with the cares of that life, owing nothing; ready, you might say, to go. Or as ready as human beings ever are. At any rate, she thought, in the sudden courage of defeat, they were prepared.

Hardly had they stowed their bags away and seated themselves, than the doors of the plane were closed and the engines revving. The acceleration of time was already taking place.

As they rose into the air, the grass and tarmac and cars and roofs and trees and roads and reservoirs and meadows falling effortlessly away from them forever, that new brightness that she had so long fearfully foreseen, that morning breaking like the first morning, invaded the plane, dazzling her so that she shut her eyes.

Then, for the second time in two days, she opened them on a different realisation. And relief seeped through her.

ALISON LURIE

Fat People

I've never run into any spooks in sheets, no headless horsemen, haunted mansions, nothing like that. But there was something weird once . . .

It was a while ago, when Scott went to India on that research grant. What happened at first was that I began noticing fat people. I saw them snatching the shrimps and stuffed eggs at parties; I saw them strolling along Cayuga Street with the swaying sailor's gait of the obese, and pawing through the queen-size housecoats in JC Penney. They were buying tubs of popcorn at the flicks, ahead of me in line at the post office and pumping self-serve gas into their pick-up trucks when I went to the garage.

I didn't pay much attention at first; I figured that since I was dieting I'd become more aware of people who should be doing the same. My idea was to lose 15lb while Scott was away because of what he'd said just before he left.

We were at the county airport on a cold, weepy day in April, waiting for Scott's plane and trying to keep up a conversation, repeating things we'd already said. I'd seen Scott off on trips before; but this time he'd be gone over three months. He was saying he wished I were coming, and promising to wire from Delhi and write twice a week, and telling me he loved me and reminding me again to check the oil on the Honda. I said I would, and was there anything else I should do while he was away?

Then the flight was announced and we grabbed each other. But we were both wearing heavy quilted jackets, and it didn't feel real. It was like two bundles of clothes embracing, I said, all choked up. And Scott said, 'Well, there is one thing we could both do while I'm gone, Ellie; we could lose a few pounds.' He was kissing my face and I was desperately trying not to break down and howl.

Then Scott was through the skeleton frame of the x-ray scanner and out the door, and then he was crossing the wet tarmac under the dark lump of his carry-on bag and climbing the steps. It wasn't until I'd gone back to the main waiting room and was standing inside the teary steamed-up window watching Scott's plane shrink and blur into fog that I really registered his last remark.

I drove back to Pine Grove Apartments and dragged off my fat coat and looked at myself in the mirror on the back of the closet door. I knew I was a big girl, at the top of the range for my height, but it had never bothered me before. And as far as I knew, it hadn't bothered Scott, who was hefty himself. Maybe when he suggested we lose a few pounds he was just kidding. But it was the last thing I'd hear him say for three months. Or possibly forever, I thought, because India was so far away and full of riots and diseases, and maybe in one of the villages he was going to they wouldn't want to change their 1000-year-old agricultural methods, and they would murder Scott with long wavy decorated knives or serve him curry with 1000-year-old undetectable poisons in it.

I knew it was bad luck to think that way, Scott had said so himself. I looked back at the mirror again, turning sideways. Usually I was pleased by what I saw there, but now I noticed that when I didn't breathe in, my tummy stuck out as far as my breasts.

Maybe I had put on some extra pounds that winter. Well, it should be easy to take them off. It could be a project, something to do while Scott was gone. I wouldn't write him about it, I'd save it for a surprise when he got back. 'Wow, Ellie,' he would say, 'You look great.'

Only it turned out not to be as easy as all that. After two weeks, I weighed exactly the same. One problem was that all our friends kept asking me over and serving meals it would have been a shame to refuse, not to mention rude. And when I didn't have anywhere to go in the evening, I started wandering around the apartment and usually ended up wandering into the kitchen and opening the fridge, just for something to do.

It was about then that I began to notice how many fat people there were in town. All sorts and all ages: overweight country-club types easing themselves out of overweight cars;

street people shoving rusted grocery carts jammed with bottles and bundles. Fat, old men like off-duty Santa Clauses waddling through the shopping mall, fat teenagers with acne, and babies so round and plump they could hardly get their thumbs into their mouths.

Of course I'd seen types like this before occasionally, but now they seemed to be everywhere. At first I put it down to coincidence, plus having the subject on my mind. It didn't bother me; in a way it was reassuring. When some bulgy high-school senior came for an interview at the college, and tried to fit their rear end on to the chair by my desk, I would think as I smiled nicely and asked the standard questions, well, at least I don't look like that.

My folks knew I was trying to lose weight, and wanted to help, but they only made it worse. Every time I went over to the house for Sunday dinner Dad would ask first thing if I'd heard from Scott. It got to be over three weeks, and I still had to say 'No, nothing since the telegram,' and remind them we'd been warned how bad the mail was.

Then we'd sit down to the table and Mum would pass my plate, and there'd be this measly thin slice of chicken on it, and a bushel of cooked greens, as if I was in some kind of concentration camp for fatties. The salads all started to have sour low-cal dressing, and there was never anything but fruit for dessert: watery melon, or oranges cut up with a few shreds of dry coconut on top, like little undernourished white worms.

All through the meal Mum and Dad wouldn't mention Scott again, so as not to upset me. There was nothing in the dining room to remind anybody of Scott either, and of course there wasn't any place set for him at the table. It was as if he'd disappeared or maybe had never even existed. By the time dinner was over I'd be so low in my mind I'd have to stop on the way home for a pint of chocolate marshmallow.

I'd hang up my coat and turn on the television and measure out exactly half a cup of ice cream, 105 calories, less than a bagel. I'd put the rest in the freezer and feel virtuous. But when the next commercial came on I'd open the freezer and have a few more spoonfuls. And then the whole process would repeat, like a commercial, until the carton was scraped clean down to the wax.

It got to be four weeks since Scott had left, and I still didn't weigh any less, even when I shifted my feet on the scale to make the needle wobble downwards. I'd never tried to lose weight before; I'd always thought it was ridiculous the way some people went into agonies over diets. I'd even been kind of shocked when one of my married friends made more fuss about taking a second slice of peach pie than she did about taking a lover. Displaced guilt, I used to think.

Now I was as hysterical about food as any of them. I brooded all afternoon over a fudge brownie I hadn't had for lunch, and if I broke down and ordered one I made up excuses for hours afterwards. 'I didn't promise Scott I'd lose weight,' I would tell myself, or 'It's not fair asking someone to give up both food and love at the same time.'

I started to read all the articles on losing weight that I used to skip before, and I took books out of the library. Over the next couple of weeks I tried one crazy diet after another: no-carbohydrate, no-fat, grapefruit and cornflakes, corned beef and bananas and skimmed milk. Only I couldn't stick with any of them. Things went wrong at night when I started thinking about how I'd written nine letters to Scott and hadn't got one back. I'd lie in bed asking myself where the hell was he, what was he doing now? And pretty soon I'd feel hungry, starving.

Then I kept asking myself, especially when I chewed through some dried-out salad or shook Sweet-N-Low into my coffee, was what Scott, assuming he was still alive, was eating over there on the other side of the world. If he wasn't on a diet, what was the point? I would think, watching my hand reach out for the blue-cheese dressing or the Half-and-Half cream. 'He hadn't meant it seriously,' I'd tell myself.

But suppose he had meant it? Suppose Scott was becoming slimmer and trimmer every day; what would he think if he knew I hadn't lost a pound in nearly five weeks?

Trying to do it on my own wasn't working. I needed support, and I thought I knew where to find it. There was a young woman in the Admissions Office called Dale. She was only a couple of years older than me, maybe 26, but in two months she'd just about reorganised our files, and she obviously had her life under control. She was a brunette, with a narrow neat little figure and a narrow neat little poodle face; you got the feeling her hair wouldn't dare get itself mussed up, and she'd never weigh one ounce more than she chose to.

I figured that Dale would have ideas about my problem, because she was always talking about interesting new diets. And whenever some really heavy person came in she'd make a yapping noise under her breath and remark later how awful it was for people to let themselves go physically. 'Heaven knows how that hippopotamus is going to fulfill his athletic requirement,' she would say, or 'That girl's mother ought to be in a circus, she hardly looked human,' and I'd think, do I look human to Dale?

So one day when we were alone in the washroom I let on that I was trying to lose some weight. Dale lit up like a fluorescent tube. 'Yes, I think that's a good idea, Ellie,' she said, looking from herself to me, poodle to hippo, in the mirror over the basins. 'And I'd like to help you, okay?'

'Okay, thanks,' I said. I didn't have any idea what I was getting into.

On our way back to the office, Dale explained to me that overweight was a career handicap. It was a known fact that heavy people didn't get ahead as fast in business. Besides, fat was low-class: the Duchess of Windsor had said you could never be too rich or too thin. When I told her there wasn't much danger of my ever being either one, Dale didn't laugh. She printed her Duchess of Windsor line out in computer-graphic caps, and fastened it on the side of my filing cabinet with two pineapple magnets.

The next thing Dale did was persuade me to see a doctor to make sure I was healthy, the way they tell you to do in the diet books. Then she started organising my life. She got me enrolled in an aerobics class, and set up a schedule for me to jog every day after work, regardless of the weather. Then she invited herself over to my apartment and cleaned out the cupboards and icebox. Bags of pretzels and fritos, butter and cream cheese and cold cuts, a loaf of cinnamon-raisin bread, most of a pound of Jones bacon – Dale packed everything up, and we hauled it down to the local soup-kitchen. I kind of panicked when I saw all that lovely food disappearing, but I was hopeful too.

The next day Dale brought in a calorie-counter and planned my meals for a week in advance. She kept a chart, and every day she'd ask how much I'd weighed that morning and write it down.

Only the scale still stuck at the same number. If there was nothing in the apartment, there was always plenty in the grocery. I'd go in for celery and cottage cheese and Rye-Krisp, but when I was pushing the cart down the last aisle it was as if the packages of cookies on the shelves were crying out to me, especially the chocolate-covered cookies. I could almost hear them squeaking inside their cellophane wrappers, in these little high sugary voices: 'Ellie, Ellie! Here we are, Ellie!'

When I confessed to falling off my diet, Dale didn't lose her cool. 'Never mind, Ellie, that's all right,' she said. 'I know what we'll do. From now on, don't you go near a supermarket alone. I'll shop with you twice a week on the way home.'

So the next day she did. But as soon as she got a little ahead of me in the bakery section, I began drifting towards a tray of apricot croissants. Dale looked round and shook her poodle curls and said, 'Naughty, naughty,' – which kind of made me feel crazy, because I hadn't done anything naughty yet – and then she grabbed my arm and pulled me along fast.

There'd been several fat people in the store that day, the way there always were lately. When we were in line at the checkout with a load of groceries only a rabbit could love, I noticed one of them, a really heavy blonde girl about my own age, leaving the next register. Her cart was full, and a couple of plump bakery boxes, a carton of potato chips, and a giant bottle of Coke were bulging out of her bags. As she came past, the fat girl picked up a package of chocolate bars, tore it open, and half-smiled in my direction as if she was saying, 'Come on, Ellie, have one.'

Looking round at Dale, I figured she would make some

negative comment, but she didn't. Maybe she hadn't seen the fat girl yet. The funny thing was, when I looked back I didn't see her either; she must have been in a big rush to get home. And she was going to have a really good time when she got there, too, I thought.

Another week dragged by full of carrots and diet soda and frozen Weight-Watchers dinners, and no news from Scott. My diet wasn't making much progress either. I'd take a couple of pounds off, but then I'd go out to dinner and put three or four back on. Instead of losing I was gaining.

I was still seeing fat people too, more and more of them. I tried to convince myself it was just because they weren't disguised inside winter clothes any longer. The only problem was, the people I was seeing weren't just heavy, they were gross.

The first time I knew for sure that something strange was going on was one day when I was in the shopping plaza downtown, sitting on the edge of a planter full of sticky purple petunias and listening to a band concert instead of eating lunch, which had been Dale's idea naturally. I was feeling kind of dizzy and sick, and when I touched my head it seemed to vibrate, as if it wasn't attached to my body too well.

Then I happened to glance across the plaza, and through the window of the Home Bakery I saw two middle-aged women, both of them bulging out of flowered blouses and slacks as if they'd been blown up too full. I couldn't make out their faces well because of the way the light shimmered and slid on the shop window; but I could see that one of them was looking straight at me and pointing to a tray of strawberry tarts: big ones with thick ruby glaze and scallops of whipped cream. It was as if she was saying, 'Come and get it, Ellie.'

Without even intending to I stood up and started to push through the crowd. But when I reached the bakery there weren't any fat women, and I hadn't seen them leave either. There'd been a moment when I was blocked by a twin stroller; but it still didn't make sense, unless maybe the fat women hadn't really been there. Suddenly I started feeling sick to my stomach. I didn't want a strawberry tart any more; I just wanted to go somewhere and lie down, only I was due back in the Admissions Office.

When I got there I said to Dale, making my voice casual, 'You know something funny, I keep seeing all these really fat people around lately.'

'There are a lot of them around, Ellie,' Dale said. 'Americans are terribly overweight.'

'But I'm seeing more. I mean lots more than I ever did before. I mean, do you think that's weird?'

'You're just noticing them more,' Dale said, stapling forms together bang-bang. 'Most people block out unpleasant sights of that sort. They don't see the disgusting rubbish in the streets, or the way the walls are peeling right in this office.' She pointed with her head to a corner above the swing doors, where the cream-coloured paint was swollen into bubbles and flaking away; I hadn't noticed it before. Somehow that made me feel better.

'I guess you could be right,' I said. I knew that Dale was getting impatient with me. She'd stopped keeping my weight chart, and when we went shopping now she read the labels on things aloud in a cross way, as if she suspected I was cheating on my diet and had a package of shortbread or a box of raisins hidden away at home, which was sometimes true.

It was around that time that eating and sex started to get mixed up in my mind. Sometimes at night I still woke up hot and tense and longing for Scott; but more often I got excited about food. I read articles on cooking and restaurants in a greedy lingering way, and had fantasies about veal paprika with sour cream and baby onions, or lemon meringue pie. Once after I'd suddenly gone up to a pushcart and bought a giant hotdog with ketchup and relish I heard myself saying half aloud, 'I just had to have it.' And that reminded me of the way men talked in tough-guy thrillers. 'I had to have her,' they always said, and they would speak of some woman as if she was a rich dessert and call her a dish or a cupcake and describe parts of her as melons or buns. Scott isn't really a macho type, but he's always liked reading thrillers; he says they relax him on trips. And when he got on the plane that awful day he'd had one with him.

He'd been gone over six weeks by then, and no news since the telegram from Delhi. Either something really terrible had happened to him or he deliberately wasn't writing. Maybe while I was cheating on my diet, Scott was cheating on me, I thought. Maybe he'd found some Indian cupcake to relax him. As soon as I had that idea I tried to shove it out of my head, but it kept oozing back.

Then one sunny afternoon early in June I came home from work and opened the mailbox, and there among the bills and circulars was a postcard from Scott. There wasn't any apology for not writing, just a couple of lines about a beautiful temple he'd visited, and a scrawled 'love and kisses'. On the other side was a picture of a sexy over-decorated Indian woman and a person or god with the head of an elephant, both of them wearing smug smiles.

As I looked at that postcard something kind of exploded inside me. For weeks I'd been telling myself and everyone, 'If only I knew Scott was all right, I'd feel fine.' Now I knew he was all right, but what I felt was a big rush of suspicion and fury.

Pictures from the coffee-table books on India that Scott had borrowed from the library crowded into my mind. I saw sleek prune-eyed exotic beauties draped in shiny silk and jewels, looking at me with hard sly expressions; and plump nearly naked blue gods with bedroom eyes; and close-ups of temple sculptures in pockmarked stone showing 1001 positions for sexual intercourse. The idea came to me that at that exact moment Scott was making out in 1000 different positions with some woman who had an elephant's head or was completely blue. I knew that was crazy, but still he had to be doing something he didn't want to tell me about and was ashamed of, or he would have written.

I didn't go on upstairs to the apartment. Instead I got back into the car, not knowing where I was going till the Honda parked of its own volition in front of a gourmet shop and café that I hadn't been near for weeks. There were five other customers there, which wasn't unusual at that time of day. The unusual thing was, all of them were fat; and not just overweight: humongously huge. All of them looked at me in a friendly way when I came in, as if maybe they knew me and had something to tell me.

For a moment I couldn't move. I just stood there stuck to the indoor-outdoor carpeting and wondered if I was going out of my mind. Five out of five; it wasn't reasonable, but there they were, or anyhow I was seeing them.

The fat people knew about Scott, I thought. They'd known all along. That was what they'd been trying to say to me when they smiled and held up cones or candy bars: 'Come on, honey, why should you deny yourself? You can bet your life Scott isn't.'

A huge guy with a grizzly-bear beard left the counter, giving me a big smile, and I placed my order. A pound of assorted butter cookies, a loaf of cinnamon bread, and a date-walnut coffee ring with white sugar icing. As soon as I got into the car I tore open the box and broke off a piece of the coffee ring, and it was fantastic: the sweet flaky yellow pastry, and the sugar-glazed walnuts; a lot better than sex with Scott, I told myself.

For the next four days I pigged out. I finished the cookies and coffee ring that same evening, and on Friday afternoon I sneaked over to the grocery without telling Dale and bought everything I'd dreamt about for weeks: bacon and sausages and sliced Virginia ham, butter and sour cream and baking potatoes, pretzels and barbecue potato chips and frozen french fries. And that was just the beginning.

When I went in to work Monday morning with a box of assorted jelly doughnuts, I let Dale know I was off my diet for good. Dale tried to shove me back on. It didn't really matter about the weekend binge, she yipped. If I skipped lunch all week and cut down on dinner and jogged two miles a day I'd be back on track.

'I don't want to be on track,' I told her. 'Eight weeks Scott has been away in India, and all I've had from him is one disgusting postcard.'

Dale looked pained and started talking about self-respect and self-image, but I wasn't having any. 'Leave me alone, please,' I said. 'I know what I'm doing.'

Two days and a lot of pork chops and baked potatoes and

chicken salad and chocolate almond bars and cherry pie later, I walked into my building, steadied a bag of high-calorie groceries against my hip, and opened the mailbox.

Jesus, I practically dropped the bag. The galvanised-metal slot was crammed with fat white and flimsy blue airmail letters from India. Most of them looked as if they'd been opened and read and crumpled up and walked on, and they were covered with stamps and cancellations.

An hour later, sitting on my sofa surrounded by two months' worth of Scott's letters, I faced facts. He was dieting: his second letter said so, mentioning that he didn't want to look overfed when he walked through a village full of hungry people. All right. I had three weeks, which meant – I went into the bathroom and dragged out the scale from the bottom of the cupboard where I'd shoved it on Friday – which meant, oh God, I'd have to lose over 4lb a week just to get back to where I was when Scott left.

It was an awful three weeks. I had cereal and skimmed milk and fruit for breakfast and lunch, to get through work, but otherwise I didn't eat anything much. Pretty soon I was blurred and headachy most of the time, in spite of all the vitamins and minerals I was scoffing down, and too tired to exercise. And I was still behind schedule on losing weight.

What made it worse was the fat people. I was seeing them again everywhere, only now they didn't look happy or friendly. 'You're making a big mistake, Ellie,' they seemed to be telling me at first. Then they began to get angry and disgusted. 'Sure, he wrote you, stupid,' their expressions said. 'That doesn't prove he's not helping himself to some Indian dish right this minute.'

I quit going out after work; I didn't have the energy. Mostly I just stayed home drinking diet soda and re-reading Scott's letters, kind of to prove to myself that he existed, I guess, because there hadn't been any more. Then I'd watch a little television and go to bed early, hoping to forget about food for a while. But for the first time in my life I was having insomnia, jolting awake in the small hours and lying there starving.

The day Scott was due back, I woke up about 4am and

couldn't doze off again even with Valium. For what seemed like hours I thrashed around in bed. Finally, I got up and opened a can of diet soda and switched on the TV. Only now, on all the channels that were still broadcasting, everybody was overweight: the punk MTV singers, the comics in an old black-and-white film. On the weather channel I could tell the girl was hiding thighs like hams under the pleated skirt she kept swishing around as she pointed out the tornado areas. Then the picture changed and a soft plump guy smiled from between chipmunk cheeks and told me that airports were fogged in all over Europe and Scott would never get home.

I turned off the television, dragged on some jeans and a T-shirt, and went out. It was a warm June night full of noises: other tenants' air conditioners and fans, traffic out on the highway; and planes overhead. There was a hard wind blowing, which made me feel kind of dizzy and slapped about, and it was that uneasy time just before dawn when you start to see shapes but can't make out colours. The sky was a pale sick lemon, but everything else was lumps of blurred grey.

Pine Grove Apartments is surrounded on three sides by an access road, and I'd just turned the corner and was starting towards the dead end. That was when I saw them, way down by the trees. There was a huge sexless person with long stringy hair waving its arms and walking slowly towards me out of the woods, and behind it came more angry fat grey people, and then more and more.

I wanted to run, but I knew somehow that if I turned round the fat people would rush after me the way kids do when you play Grandmother's Footsteps, and they would catch me and, God, I didn't know what. So I just backed up slowly step-by-step towards the corner of the building, breathing in shallow gasps.

They kept coming out of the woods in the half-light, more and more, maybe 10 or 20 or 50, I didn't know. I thought I recognised the women from the bakery, and the big guy with the beard. And then I realised I could hear them too, kind of mumbling and wailing. I couldn't take it

121

any more, I turned and raced for home, stumbling over the potholes in the drive.

Well, somehow I made it to the apartment, and slammed the door and double-locked it and put on the chain, and leaned up against the wall panting and gulping. For what seemed like hours I stood there, listening to the sounds of the fat people coming after me, crowding up the stairs, all grey and blubbery, and roaring and sobbing and sliding and thumping against the walls and doors.

Then the noises started to change. Gradually they turned into the wind in the concrete stairwell and the air conditioner downstairs and the 6.30am plane to New York flying over the complex and a dog barking somewhere. It was light out now, nearly 7 o'clock. I unbolted my door and eased it open a slow inch. The hall was empty.

I still felt completely exhausted and crazy, but I got myself dressed somehow and left for work. On the way I took a detour in the Honda round the corner of the building. At first I was afraid to look, even though I was safe inside the locked car. At the edge of the woods where the mob of fat people had been there was nothing but some big old bushes blowing about.

That evening Scott came home, 10lb overweight. A couple of days later, when he was talking about his trip, he said that Indian food was great, especially the sweets, but the women were hard to talk to and not all that good-looking.

'A lot of Indians are heavy too, you know,' he told me.

'Really?' I asked. I wondered if Scott had had some spooky experience like mine, which I still hadn't mentioned: I didn't want him to think I was going to crack up whenever he left town.

'It's a sign of prosperity. You notice them especially in the cities, much more than in this country. I mean, you don't really see that many fat people around here for instance, do you Ellie?'

'No,' I agreed, cutting us both another slice of pineapple upside-down cake. 'Not lately, anyhow.'

EDNA O'BRIEN

Another Time

It happens to one and all. It is given many names, but those who have it know it for what it is – the canker that sets in and makes one crabbed, finding fault with things, complaining, full of secret and not-so-secret spleen. Nelly knew it. She knew she was in trouble after that dream. She dreamed that one of her children had stripped her of everything, even her teeth, and when she wakened she decided that it was time to get away. 'Get away, get away,' she said several times to herself as she hurried up the street to a travel agent to look at brochures. In a small, unprepossessing office she saw posters of walled cities, all of which were gold-coloured; she saw churches, canals, castles; and each one filled her not with expectations but with doom. It was as bad as that. Suddenly it came to her. She would go home – not to her own people but to a small seaside town about 20 miles from there, a place she had always yearned to go to as a child, a resort where some of the richer people had cottages. It was remote and primitive, on the edge of the Atlantic, the white houses laid out like kerchiefs. She had seen photos of it, and it had for her a touch of mystery, a hidden magic; it was a place where people went when they were happy – newlyweds and those who got legacies. There was a jetty across, so although an island, it was not cut off completely, and she was glad of that. The ocean could pound or lap on three sides and yet she had a link with the land, she could get away. Getting away preoccupied her, as if it would lead to redemption.

As she crossed the threshold of the bedroom in her hotel, she saw that it did not bode well. It was a tiny room, with a tiny sagging bed, bits and pieces of tasteless furniture, and a washbasin in one corner with a vein of rust running down from one of the taps. The coat hangers were of metal, and either they were buckled or their hooks were so attenuated that they looked like skewers. A view of the ocean, yes, but it was not an expanse, more a sliver of grey-green sulky sea.

It will get better, she thought, fearing that it wouldn't. She could hear the man in the next room as she hung her clothes. He was coughing. He's lonely, she thought, that's why he's coughing. After she had hung her clothes, she put on a bit of make-up before going down to have a drink with the owners. The owners had welcomed her and asked her to have an early drink before dinner. On impulse, she gave them the bottle of champagne that she had bought at the airport, and now she wished she hadn't. They seemed so taken aback by it – it was too patrician – and it was not chilled.

Opening the champagne took quite a while, because the husband was more interested in telling her about some of his more exotic travels than in wheedling the cork out. The wife was a bit heavy and had a sleepy, sad face with big spaniel eyes. They seemed to have no children, as children were not mentioned. The husband held forth about jobs he had held in Borneo or Karachi or wherever – that was when he was in oil. Then at length he had decided to settle down, and he found himself a wife, and they came back to Ireland, to their roots, and bought this hotel, which was something of a legend. The previous owner was an eccentric and made people do morris dancing and drink mead.

No morris dancing now, Nelly thought as they lifted their glasses. They were tiny glasses – sherry glasses, really – and the champagne was tepid. Just as the cork flew out, a tall boy had come in from the kitchen and stared. He was a simpleton – she could tell by his smile and the way he stared and then had to be told by the wife to go back in to mind the cabbage.

'Go in, Caimin,' she said.

'Yes, Ma'am,' he said, coveting the green cork, with its dun-gold paper. The husband was telling Nelly that she had picked a most unfortunate evening for her first dinner. They were overbooked, jam-packed. A party of 12 at one table alone. He himself had not taken the booking; a silly young girl had taken it over the phone. He apologised in advance. Nelly looked around the dismal room, with its checked

124

tablecloths and kitchen chairs, and was not regaled by what she saw. There were empty wine bottles above the sideboard and all along the wall ledge. They were green and dusty and served no purpose whatsoever, and she supposed that the champagne bottle would go up there somewhere and be just as useless.

He wasn't pouring fast enough for her. She wanted to drink in great gulps, to forget her surroundings, to be removed from them, to forget the impulse for her coming, and to blot out the admission that she had made a mistake.

'We reserved you that table,' he said, pointing to a table in the corner, close to the window, with a view of the road outside. The road was covered with mist and the summer evening could easily pass for October or November. Suddenly radio music and loud voices came from the kitchen, and then a buxom girl emerged followed by another girl with long plaits. They had come to lay the tables. They were big, strapping girls, and they more or less slung the plates and the cruets onto the tables and made a great clatter with the cutlery box. They eyed Nelly sitting there with the boss and the Mrs, and one of them whispered something to the other – probably about her being a big shot, maybe even someone from the Tourist Board. Occasionally they would laugh, and the simpleton would rush from the kitchen, holding a ladle or a saucepan in his hand, to join in the levity.

Soon the wife rose, put her hands to her chest, and said very formally, 'Duty calls.' Then the husband picked up the bottle of champagne and said, 'We'll chill the rest of this for you. You can have it with your meal.'

As she turned the key in her bedroom door, Nelly met her neighbour. He wore a suit and a cap, and it was clear that he was not accustomed to being on holiday. His first remark was how beautiful the hotel was – a palace. A palace! A bit of dark landing with linoleum and off-white doors, like hospital doors, leading to the rooms; a sickly maidenhair fern in a big brass jardinière. He spoke with a clipped Northern accent as he enlarged on the glories of the place, the seashore where he had just been walking, the peace and quiet, and the big feeds. He was on his way to the public house for a few jars before dinner. Would she care to join him? She realised that he had been waiting to pounce, that he must have heard of her arrival – a woman on her own – and that he had assumed they would become friends. She declined. He asked again, thinking she said no only out of courtesy. She declined more firmly. She saw the smile leave his face. She saw the scowl. He could hardly endure this rebuff. His anger was rising. He pulled his key from his pocket and, for no reason, proceeded to open his door again. Anything to withhold his rage. They were from the same country, God damn it; just because she lived abroad in England was no reason to snub him. She could read his inner thoughts and guess his outrage by the obsequiousness of what he then said.

'Aah, thanks a lot,' he said, and repeated it twice over, when in fact he wanted to strike her. He had reverted to some shaming moment when he had thanked a superior whom he really hated.

I have made an enemy, she thought as she entered her room. She went straight to the washbasin and splashed her face fiercely with douches of cold water.

Dinner was indeed a boisterous affair. The party of 12 was mostly children, ranging from teenagers to a baby in a high chair. The mother addressed each child by name, over and over, sometimes admonishing, sometimes approving, so that Nelly soon knew that the baby was called Troy, short for Troilus, and would have to eat those mashed potatoes before he got his mashed banana. The mother was a strong, bossy woman, and without these hordes of children to address she would have been lost; she would have had no part to play.

'Eat that stew, Kathleen,' she would call, backing it up with a glare. It was mutton stew, with potatoes and onions floating in the thickened parsley sauce. Big helpings were on the plates, and the extra vegetables were piled in white enamelled dishes, like soap dishes. The champagne on Nelly's table seemed absurd. Each time she poured, she looked away, so as not to be seen, and gave her gaze the benefit of the road in the rain. Most of the other guests drank soft drinks or milk, but one quiet couple had a bottle of wine. The man who had invited her to the public house ate alone and never once looked in her direction. In fact, when he entered the room he made a show of saluting one or two other people and deliberately ignored her. He drank tumbler after tumbler of milk with his stew. The waitresses, in some show of bravura, had put flowers in their hair, bits of fuchsia, and it was clear by the way they giggled that they thought this to be very scandalous. All the guests resented the interlopers who made such a fuss and such demands – asking for more napkins and for orangeade, some begging to be let down from the table, others slapping their food into plump pancakes, others simply whingeing. A German au pair, who sat among the children, occasionally poured from a water jug but otherwise did not pay much attention to their needs. The waitresses dashed about with second helpings and then brought big slabs of rhubarb pie, each decorated with a whorl of cream so whipped that it seemed like an imitation chef's hat. The owner came into the room and went from table to table – except, of course, to the rowdy table – apologising to his guests for the invasion, assuring them that it would not happen again. 'End of story . . . end of story,' he kept saying, giving the intruders a stern look. The irate mother, sensing rebuff, ordered a pot of tea and a pot of coffee while telling some of her children to go out and play in the grounds. Meanwhile the whipped cream was leaking into the rectangles of rhubarb pie.

All the guests were given a complimentary glass of port wine, and by the time Nelly had finished hers she was the only one left. The room was almost in darkness and it was dark outside. She kept waiting for the candle stump to sputter out, as if that were to be the signal to go upstairs. Already she was thinking that she had only five more dinners to endure and that she would be going home Saturday. Home now seemed like a nest, with its lamps and its warmth. The simpleton gave her a start as he appeared over her, a big clumsy figure in a sheepskin jacket.

'Will you be here tomorrow?' he asked. He had a muffled voice, and there was a stoppage in his speech. It was as if he had too much saliva.

'I'm afraid I will,' she said, and hoped she didn't sound too peeved.

'I'm glad you'll be here. You're a nice lady,' he said as he shuffled out, and, rising, she picked her way between the tables, certain that she was about to break down.

In the morning things seemed quite different – sparkling. The sea was bright, like a mirror with the sun dancing on it, and there was nothing to stop her going down there and spending the whole day walking and breathing – getting rid of the cobwebs, as she put it. She would pack a basket and bring down her things. She would write cards to her sons and her friends; she would read, reread, and, after the few days, she would be something of her former, self – cheerful, buoyant, outgoing.

The sand was a pale, biscuit colour that stretched way ahead of her – to the horizon, it seemed. The people dotted here and there were like figures in a primitive painting. Those in red stood out, both the toddlers and the grown-ups; red was the one splash of colour in this pale gold, luminous universe. The sea was a baby blue and barely lapped. It seemed so gentle, not like the sea that roared and lashed but like an infinite and glassy terrain one might scud over. There were dogs, too – the local dogs resenting the dogs that had come with the newcomers, snarling until they got to know them. Some people had erected little tents, obviously intending to settle for the day. Some walked far out to sea, and a few stalwarts were bathing or paddling. Although sunny, it was not yet a hot day. She would walk forever; she would gulp the air with her mouth and her whole being; she would resuscitate herself. Here and there, as she looked down at the sand, she would see empty cans, or seaweed, or little bits of sea holly in clumps – shivering but tenacious.

'I am walking all my bad temper away . . . I am walking my bad temper away,' she said, and thought, How perfect the isolation, the sense of being alone. She loved it – the near-empty seashore, the stretch of sand, the clouds racing so purposefully, and now the sea itself, which had changed colour as if an intemperate painter had just added blue and green and potent violet. The colours were in pockets, they

128

were in patches, and even as she looked there were transmutations – actual rainbows in the water, shifting, then dissolving. She would walk forever. There wasn't a boat or a steamer in sight. As she looked back at the town, its cluster of white cottages seemed like little rafts on a sea, on the sea of life, receding. People she met smiled or nodded, to compliment her on her stride, and the good thing was that she always saw them as they came toward her, so that she was not taken by surprise. Yet it was a jolt when a woman ran up to her and took her hand. She recognised Nelly from the short time when she had been a television announcer.

'You disappeared so suddenly,' the woman said, and Nelly nodded. She had given up her glamorous job for a man, even though she knew she was throwing in her lot with a black heart.

'We might see you in the pub tonight. There's a singsong,' the woman said, and, though smiling, Nelly quivered inwardly. She did not want to meet people, especially those who had known of her in the past; she had put an iron grille over all that, and yet this very encounter was disturbing, as if the weed and bindweed of the past were pushing their way up through the gates of her mind. As she walked on, she found herself remembering her marriage day – two witnesses and a half-bottle of champagne. She remembered living in a big, draughty house in the country, and her morning sickness, which at first she did not understand. But it was as if she were recalling a story that had happened to someone else. In a way, she remembered her divorce far better, because she had had to fight. Once, with a solicitor, she had gone to a suburb of London where she hoped a former housekeeper would testify to her having loved her children; a more recent incumbent had sworn affidavits against her and said she was a wicked woman. In that little sitting room in Tooting, waiting for what was going to be crucial, she sat with the solicitor while the mother put her noisy children to bed. There was a terrible smell, something being cooked.

'Is it a horse they're boiling?' the solicitor said, and she laughed, because she knew he had put himself out of his way to come with her, and that he loved her a little, and that, of course, he would never say so. When the housekeeper came in and kissed her, the kiss itself a guarantee of friendship and loyalty, the solicitor beamed and said. 'We're there . . . we're home and dry.' She got her children in the end.

Then there were the years of birthdays and train sets and Christmases and measles and blazers that they grew out of, and then their going away to boarding school and the raw pain of that first rupture, that first farewell. Not for ages had she allowed herself such a glut of memory, such detail.

Yet she was not crushed by these things, and quite gaily she asked aloud what happened to that blue dress with the tulip line, and where was the Georgian claret jug that she had bought for a song. Where, oh where?

Up on the road, there were several cars and a loudspeaker announcing something. Although it was loud, it was senseless. She was a long way from the hotel but she had her bearings. She knew she could either turn right to head for the one shop and the telephone kiosk or turn left for her hotel and the new chapel beyond it, which had modern stained-glass windows. She felt hot and her throat was parched – she longed for something. She believed that she longed for lemonade. She could taste it again as she had tasted it in childhood, so sweet and yet so tart. The sun shone with a flourish, and the flowers in the cottage gardens – the dahlias, or the devil's pokers, or whatever – seemed to be glistening with life. She stopped by a garden where a yearling calf was letting out a loud lament. He had two wounds where his horns had recently been removed. They were full of flies. He tried with his head to toss them away, but they had sunk into the wounds, which were covered with some sort of purple ointment. The animal bawled and tossed and even leapt about, and so moved was she to pity that she began to shout, 'Are you there? Are you there?'

Eventually a young man came out, holding a mug of tea. He seemed surprised to have been called.

'He's itchy,' she said, pointing to the yearling.

130

'He's a devil,' the young man said.

'He's in agony,' she said, and asked if he could do something.

'What can I do?' he said, annoyed that she had summoned him like this.

'I'll help you,' she said, gently, to coax him.

'I have just the thing,' he said, and he ran to the house and came back with a giant canister of wasp repellent.

'Oh, not that,' she said, grabbing it from him and explaining that the flies would wallow in the wounds and dement the poor animal even more. She made him fetch a strip of cardboard, then hold the beast, which bucked and reared while she edged the flies out, pushing them onto the clay and watching them stagger from their somersaults. The man was so impressed by her expertise that he asked if she was a vet.

'Hold him, hold him,' she said, as there was the second wound that she had to tackle. That done, they drove the animal through a side gate, over some cobbles, and into a dark manger. As the man closed the door, the animal yelled to be let out, its cry saying that daylight, even delirious daylight with flies and pain, was preferable to this dark dungeon.

'I told you he was a devil. He never lets up,' the man said, as he motioned her into the house. There was nobody in there, he assured her, his mother being dead. The few flowers in the flower bed, and the gooseberry bushes, had, as she imagined, been sown by his mother. There was also a ridge of flowering potatoes. He went to England for a time, worked in a car factory there, but he always came back in the summer, because he needed the fresh air. He bought a calf or two and sold them when he left.

'Would you marry me?' he said suddenly. She knew that he did not really mean such a thing, that he meant 'Stay for a bit and talk to me.'

'I am married,' she lied.

'You've no wedding ring,' he said, and she looked down at her hand and smiled, and said she must have forgotten to put it on. Then she excused herself, saying that she had to be back at the hotel, because of a phone call.

Caimin met her at the door. She had had a visitor, a woman. The woman had waited and waited. He handed her a note. It said 'Hi. Long time no see. I'll call back around four. Gertie.' Who was Gertie? Gertrude. She could only think of Hamlet. Suddenly she was shaking. She could not see anyone. She did not want to meet this Gertie, this stranger.

'Tell her I've gone . . . gone,' she said as she flew up the stairs to her room. Even the disgruntled neighbour, who was on his way out, seemed to sense her disquiet. He smiled, and waved a golf club, proudly. She hated the hotel even more now – the awful washbasin, the stained furniture. She hated it not so much for its own pitiable sake as for what it reminded her of – the rooms and landings of childhood, basins and slop buckets that oozed sadness. It seemed as if the furniture of those times, and her failed marriage, and the flies in the raw wounds, and the several mistakes of her life had got jumbled together and were now hounding her, moving in on her in this place. Various suggestions offered themselves, such as to go back to London to her own house and never leave it again, or to go to the house where she was born and exorcise her fury, though she had been back there a few times and was almost indifferent to the sight of it. She saw briars, she saw gates in need of paint, she saw the outside gable wall over which her mother had so lovingly planted a creeper, and she saw the hall door with the pad-locks that her brother had put there to keep her and others out. Bastard, she thought, and wished she could scrawl it somewhere for him to see. Her maggot brother.

'This won't do,' she said, sitting on the bed, reliving old hatreds, fresh and vigorous as when first incurred. Coming back had set off this further welter of rage, like a time bomb.

'What is it?' she asked aloud, wondering what particle in the brain is triggered by some smell, or the wind, or a yearling in pain, or a voice sodden with loneliness that says, without meaning it, 'Would you marry me?'

She might have known it: there was a knock on the door, Caimin calling her, saying she had a visitor, saying it with excitement, as if she should be pleased.

He had completely misunderstood her instructions, her clamour to be left alone. Out she went, fuming, about to tell him to send the stranger away, but the stranger was standing there beside him – a largish woman in a raincoat, with grey hair drawn back severely in a bun. 'Hay fever,' Nelly heard herself saying, to account for the tears, and for the crumpled handkerchief that she was holding. Caimin left them together on the landing and shuffled off like a dog that knows it has done something wrong.

'You don't remember me,' the woman was saying. She was breathless, as if she had run, so eager was she to be there. Bringing her face closer, she allowed Nelly to scan it, pleased to present this challenge. Nelly realised it must be someone from her nearby home. She tried to recall all her school friends, tried to picture them at their desks, or in the choir on Sundays, or in the school photo that they had all received when they left. This face was not among them.

'No,' she said finally, feeling a little baffled.

'I'm Gertie . . . Mrs Conway's niece. She owned the hotel in your town,' the woman said with a nervous smile. Her excitement was fading and she realised that she was not welcome. She began apologising for barging in, explaining that a woman in the shop said she had seen Nelly Nugent walking on the seashore.

'Mrs Conway's niece,' Nelly said, trying not to bristle. Of course. Gertie's aunt had also owned a house here. They used to come for weekends, had houseparties.

'Gertie,' she whispered, remembering the vivid young girl who had come often to stay at her aunt's hotel. She had served behind the counter like a grown-up, and had the opportunity to meet all the men, to flirt with them. Being Gertie, she had snatched the prize of them all.

Yes, she remembered Gertie. She remembered precisely when she had first seen Gertie – unexpectedly, as it happened. She was about to leave her home village, to go to the town to learn shorthand, and an older girl – Eileen, who lived up the country – had promised her a dress that she had become too fat to wear. It was black grosgrain and it had long sleeves – that was all she knew. She walked to Eileen's on a summer's day, after lunch, and twice had to ask the

133

way, as there was more than one family of the same name. She remembered that she had to cross a stream to get to the house, and; yielding to a bit of fancy because of the sunshine and thought of the dress, she took off her shoes and dipped her feet in the water, which she felt to be like liquid silver washing over her insteps and toes. The dress fitted her perfectly. In fact, it fitted her so well and gave her such allure that Eileen put her arms around her and, almost in tears, said, 'Hold on to your looks, Nell. Whatever you do, hold on to your looks.' That was 30-odd years ago. Walking down the country road, all alone, she was so sure of herself and her beauty then; she even believed that the trees and the gates and the walls and the brambles partook of it. Along with the dress, Eileen had given her an old handbag, in which there was a little mirror with a tortoise-shell frame tucked inside one of the flaps. From time to time, she ran the looking glass down the length of the dress to see the flair and the grosgrain reflected.

As she neared the town, she decided to do it. It would have been inconceivable on the way up to the country, but now she was a different person – sophisticated, assured – and anyhow she was going away. She decided to seek him out at his lodgings. It was a house not far from the chapel – one of the five or six terraced houses with a tiled hallway and a stained-glass fanlight over the door that shone ruby or blue or green floating patterns on the floor, depending on the position of the sun. The landlady, a thin and inquisitive woman, answered the timid knock, and upon hearing the request said, 'He's having his tea.' Nelly stood her ground; she had come to see him and she was not going away without seeing him. He was the new teacher in the technical college and had many skills. He was swarthy and handsome and he had made an impression on most of the young girls and the women. Many had boasted of having had conversations with him, and promises to learn tennis from him, or woodwork, or the piano accordion. 'I won't keep him long,' she said to the landlady, who was running her tongue all around her teeth, her upper and her lower teeth, before deciding to consider the request.

He sauntered toward her – his red sweater seeming so

dashing – with a puzzled smile on his face. The moment he stood in front of her with that look of pleasant inquiry, she registered two things: that his eyes were a dark green that gave the semblance of brown, and that she was not going to be able to say why she had called on him, had him routed from his tea table. She saw, too, that his eyes took in every feature of her, that he knew why she had come, knew that she was smitten, knew that she was embarrassed, and felt a certain animal pleasure, a triumph, in those things, and was not in the least bit discomfited. He stood there smiling, studying her face, not in any hurry to break the silence.

'I wondered about your night classes,' she said, even though he, like everybody else, had probably heard the news that she was going to the city to train as a secretary. 'I mean, my mother wondered,' she then said, becoming even clumsier by adding that her mother felt that women should be able to take the woodwork class just the same as men.

'Agreed,' he said with that pleased, tantalising smile. Indeed, one little cautionary part of her recognised him as being rather smug, but it was not enough to dampen the flush of attraction and excitement that she felt toward him. She had felt it for weeks, ever since he came – sighting him on his way to or from Mass, or on his bicycle, or in his tweed jacket with the leather patches on the elbows, or on the hurley pitch in his togs, where he stumbled and fell but always got up again to tackle an opponent. It was obviously time for her to leave, because she had said her piece. Yet she lingered. He put a finger to a tooth where a piece of raisin had stuck.

Raisins, he declared, were the bane of his life, as he picked at it assiduously. Then, from the kitchen, she heard his name called: 'Vincent . . . Vince.' It was not the landlady's voice, it was another voice – coyer and younger. Then, in the doorway, Gertie appeared – a girl a bit older than herself – running her hands up and down the jamb, caressing it and smiling at them. She wore trousers that clung to her. They were of a black hairy stuff, like angora. She was like a cat. Like a cat, she stroked the door, ran her fingers along it as if she were running them over his body. He basked for a moment in the excitement of it, poised as he was between two doting creatures – one assured, the other lamentably awkward.

'Your tea is getting cold,' Gertie said.

'How cold?' he asked, amused.

'So–so cold,' she said saucily.

'He always talked about you,' Gertie was saying to her now, as if she guessed every particle of thought that had passed in a swoop through Nelly's mind. 'When we had a card party or a Christmas party, he always boasted that he knew you. You were a feather in his cap, especially after you appeared on television.'

'How is he? . . . How are you?' Nelly asked. She remembered hearing about their engagement, their lavish wedding preparations, and especially their coming to this very spot for a prolonged honeymoon. In fact, without her realising it, in some recess of her mind, this place was always their preserve.

'Oh, he died . . . Didn't you know? He died suddenly . . .' Gertie said very quietly, her voice trailing off, suggesting that there were many other things she would have liked to say, such as what his death had meant to her, and how happy or unhappy their marriage had been.

'He liked the ladies,' she said then. There was something so incredibly gentle about it that all of a sudden Nelly embraced her and invited her to stay and have tea, or a drink, or whatever.

'I can't,' Gertie said, and explained that a woman friend had driven over with her for the day, and that the woman was outside, waiting in the car. 'Another time,' she said. But they both knew there would probably not be another time.

'And you kept the figure,' Gertie said, then drew her coat open to show her own girth, to pay Nelly a belated compliment. Then she was gone, hurrying down the stairs, the belt and buckle of her open raincoat trailing behind her.

Nelly stood stunned, tears in her eyes. She felt as if doors or windows were swinging open all around her and that she was letting go of some awful affliction. Something had happened. She did not know what it was. But soon she would know. Soon she would feel as she had felt long ago – like a river that winds its way back into its first beloved enclave before finally putting out to sea.

ANGELA HUTH

Mother of the Bride

After much deliberation, Mrs Hetherington decided against taking any tranquillisers. Better, she thought, to witness the whole thing with a clear mind than through an unreal calm induced by pills. If a tear should come to her eye – why, that was the prerogative of every bride's mother. Few people would see and those who did might understand.

When she had taken her decision, Mrs Hetherington had not envisaged the strength of emotion that would affect her on the Big Day. So it was with some surprise, here and now in the church, the journey up the aisle having been accomplished with dignity on the arm of her brother John, that she felt frills of sweat at the back of her knees. And her hands, stuffed into navy gloves one size too small, trembled in a disconcerting fashion.

She had chosen to wear navy with the thought that it was the most appropriate colour for her particular role at the wedding. Nobody could accuse her of trying to steal the bride's thunder – as did so many mothers, perhaps unconsciously – and yet, if they observed her closely, Mrs Hetherington's friends would see that her clothes conveyed the quiet chic she had always managed to achieve. She had chosen them with care: silk dress, matching coat, straw hat bearing the only small flourish of which she could be accused – an old fashioned rose on its moiré band. On a November morning of early snow she had taken shelter in Debenhams and come upon the whole outfit, piece by lucky piece: even bag, shoes and gloves. In the small changing-room she had examined her appearance with the sort of critical eye no bride's mother can afford to be without. How would it all look five months hence under a blue April sky? Mrs Hetherington would have liked to have asked Alice's opinion – after all, it was by tradition supposed to be Alice's day – but her daughter was off on a 'holiday' raising funds for overseas famine relief. She was funny like that, Alice. No interest in appearance – never had had. It had been all Mrs Hetherington could do to persuade her daughter in March – cutting it pretty tight – to concentrate on her own wedding dress. No: Alice had never so much as asked her mother what she was going to wear, and in all the flurry of getting ready it was unlikely that she had noticed. Or even cared.

Precisely what Alice did care for, Mrs Hetherington was sometimes at a loss to know. As a child she had been straight-forward enough – ordinary, really, except for her freckles. A fondness for rabbits rather than ponies; some talent at the high jump, which petered out at puberty; an inclination towards history, which petered out after O levels; and no traumas that Mrs Hetherington could recall. Except perhaps for the time Alice had thrown scrambled egg at her father on the last morning of their holiday at Brancaster, calling him a fuddy-duddy (and worse) for not allowing her to stay at the village disco later than midnight. But that had been an exceptional time, and David had made his point clumsily, Mrs Hetherington had to agree. She put the incident down to teenage wilfulness and considered herself lucky she had such a comparatively easy offspring.

It was only when she thought about it later that it occurred to her that Alice's 'distance', as she called it, dated from that holiday. This 'distance' itself was so hard to define that Mrs Hetherington refrained from mentioning it even to David, lest he should consider her ridiculous. But to Mrs Hetherington, who could never be accused of insensitivity, the widening gap between their daughter and her parents seemed noticeably to develop. It wasn't that Alice changed in any outward way: she remained the polite, willing, quiet creature she had always been, dutiful to her parents and apparently content to come home most weekends. But of her weekday life in London Mrs Hetherington had always been a little unclear and never remembered, somehow, to ask. She shared a flat with an old school friend in Shepherd's Bush: not a very salubrious part of London, but still. What she got up to in the evenings Mrs Hetherington had no idea, though several times when she had rung after nine at night Alice had been in, giving rise to the comfortable thought that at least her daughter spent many evenings at home watching television. Once, when Mrs Hetherington had conversationally mentioned a demonstration in Trafalgar Square that had been given much attention in the papers, Alice casually remarked that she had been there and it wasn't half as bad as the publicity made out. Well, thought Mrs Hetherington at the time, Alice must have been passing. She had never been a political girl, that was for sure. She could happily have bet her bottom dollar that Alice would have no interest in the terrible carryings-on of the National Front, or those dreadful militants.

As for men in her daughter's life, Mrs Hetherington would hover – not out of curiosity, of course, but from natural anxiety about what was going on. If Alice had any boyfriends she never brought them home. Mrs Hetherington could not understand why. She had always made it clear she was eager to entertain any of Alice's friends. 'Do bring whoever you like to stay, darling,' she would say every Sunday evening Alice was at home. But Alice would always reply she preferred her weekends alone.

Then, out of the blue, no warning, there had been the event of Alastair. Mrs Hetherington would never forget it. Glancing at the stained-glass windows above the altar, whose unkind colours recharged the tears in her eyes, she remembered that occasion once again. Alice had not acted in the most thoughtful way, it had to be admitted. Not a warning telephone call even. Just, that Friday evening, arriving with him.

'Thought you wouldn't mind, Mum,' she said, 'if I brought Alastair Mead. We're going to get married.'

David, bless him, had taken it very well. Fetched the last bottle of Krug from the cellar and was talking easily to Mr Mead, about mortgages, within moments. (Mr Mead, it seemed, was something to do with mortgages 'for the bread and butter,' Alice said. In his spare time, his real vocation, he raised money for famine relief.) Their conversation gave Mrs Hetherington time to study her future son-in-law: she saw a shortish, chunky figure, head slightly too big for his body, the loose smile of lips not quite in control, falling socks. She sipped rapidly at her drink to conceal her disappointment. In her heart of hearts she had always hoped her son-in-law would cut something of a dash: the brutal truth about Mr Mead was that he would not turn a head in the most plebeian crowd. Still, he had been to Charterhouse, as he let drop with his second glass of champagne, and perhaps his charm lay in his mind. He must be given a fair chance, Mrs Hetherington told herself, and in time Alice might wean him off tweed ties. Dreadful to be so prejudiced by appearances, but Mrs Hetherington knew that she hated Alastair Mead, both for himself and for his proprietory talk about Alice. But she smiled bravely, and no one could have guessed her feelings.

Next morning the two of them appeared at breakfast blatantly haggard. Well, Mrs Hetherington and David had done a bit of passage-creeping in their time, but at least they had the decency to disguise the effects of their naive kisses next morning. With a shudder, Mrs Hetherington handed Alastair a kipper. He should have known better than to lay hands on Alice the first night under her parents' roof. Also, he had cut himself shaving and a thread of blood looped down his chin to join a clot of dried toothpaste in the corner of his mouth. All distasteful to her, poor man. In 29 years, David had never cut himself shaving: it wasn't necessary. As for Alice, she could have combed her hair, surely, and done something to conceal her satiated state. It wasn't that Mrs Hetherington disapproved of sex before marriage, naturally: everyone did it these days and Alice, she had no doubt, had relinquished her virginity some years ago. But up to now she had had the tact to protect her mother from evidence of her affairs. Would that she had not let matters slip just because she had an engagement ring – and a very minor pearl, at that – on her finger. Mrs Hetherington's thoughts were only interrupted by Alastair's irritating pecking at his kipper, and his boring remembrances of childhood kippers in Scotland, implying criticism of the MAC Fisheries pedigree of the present fish. In all, Mrs Hetherington found the whole weekend a trial. She could not deny the probity of Alastair's character, but kept furiously to herself the disappointment at his lack of humour and style. Worst of all, he supported Alice in her desire for a quick register office wedding. But on that point Mrs Hetherington was adamant,

141

unbudgeable. It was to be a white wedding with all the trimmings, for her sake if not for theirs.

The organ played Bach, swelling to greet Mrs Hetherington's present feeling of satisfaction as she reflected on her efforts in the past months. She had tried, and she had triumphed. There was genuine love in her heart, now, for her son-in-law. Even admiration. The way he worked such long hours in his mortgage business and then gave up his weekends to famine relief. His solid principles: only live in the way you can afford (they were to start off in a small rented house in Twickenham) and put work before pleasure. He had planned with touching care a honeymoon trip around Inverness. Mrs Hetherington wouldn't have cared for any such thing herself, of course: she and David had cruised to Panama. However, Alice seemed happy in general. And, in trying to see Alastair through her daughter's eyes, Mrs Hetherington had almost certainly succeeded in discovering his charm – if devotion counts as a charm. She found it hard to forgive his dandruff and his anorak, a particularly nasty blue – but they were unimportant externals, weren't they? It was his character that counted and, by God, by now, she loved that. She really did. The love had been flamed by others' approval: his prospects, his solidity, his charity. But no matter how it had been come by, it was there. The real love of Mrs Hetherington for her son-in-law Alastair Mead.

She glanced at the gold watch embedded in her wrist. Only a minute to go. Very moving, the music, whatever it was. Half an hour ago she had witnessed the poignant sight of Alice struggling into her white satin. She looked – cliché or not – radiant. Alastair was a very lucky man. Mrs Hetherington let her eyes fall upon his back view. He had had a haircut, it seemed. And he looked a little taller in his morning suit. Rather endearing, the way he kept nervously whispering to the best man. Of course – and this was a wicked and secret thought – in Mrs Hetherington's experience of weddings, Etonians undoubtedly made the least nervous bridegrooms. She'd noticed over the years. (David, in the Guards Chapel, had been wonderfully untrembling, giving her courage.) But given the less noble training of

Charterhouse, Alastair wasn't doing too badly so far. Straight shoulders, almost as if he'd been in the army. Mrs Hetherington wished her brother, who was still in the army, could contain his asthmatic wheezing, irritating at such a solemn time. Still, the marguerite trees at the altar had been an inspiration. (Hers.) Oh dear God, where were they? A minute late and her left shoe was hurting.

She heard the hush that precedes a bride's entrance. With a supreme effort of will, Mrs Hetherington remained facing the altar. Alastair, weaker, turned. His face was pale, the jowls loosened by trepidation. Dear Alastair. Would he were just a few inches . . . But all right so long as Alice never wore stilettos. Had David ordered enough champagne? And Alice's heart: was it beating like her own? Funny how such disparate thoughts topple over one another at such moments. What on earth could they be *doing*? Darling Alice, she had been such a loving daughter.

Glorious things of Thee are spoken . . .

Ah, they must be on their way at last. Oh my Alice . . . the way she laughed in the bath so much at 2; and how she cried that time she fell off her bicycle into the shrubbery at 4. And all those things she had made at school: painted fir cones and potato-cut calendars. No better presents in the whole world, were there? Impossible to think of her as a married woman. Oh dear, they must be halfway up the aisle by now. Well at least Alice wouldn't be in fearful anticipation of It, as Mrs Hetherington herself had been. Rather a shame, really, that particular excitement already over. But it was awful to be thinking of her own daughter in such terms at all, wasn't it? And here she was at last, misty faced under her veil. Pity about no posy of gardenias, as Mrs Hetherington would have liked, but Alice had insisted on the austerity of a prayer book. Anyway, she was beautiful. Well, almost. David's handsome bones were a bit strong on a girl, perhaps: it had to be said Alice's face was not one of infinite delicacy. But today it was at its best, all for Alastair Mead.

'Let us pray,' said the vicar.

Navy patent bow dug less into her foot now she was on her knees. Thank God. Thank God for having given her a daughter like Alice. That time she had been so homesick at her finishing school in Paris – oh God forgive me for all my inadequacies as a mother. Darling Alice forgive me too and try to be happy. Try to keep those promises like Daddy and I have done. It may be awfully boring sometimes, but it's worth trying. And don't desert us. Why didn't I put my handkerchief up my sleeve instead of in my bag – it would make too much noise, opening it. Mustn't sniff . . . Come home whenever you want to and bring your friends. And I promise to be a good grandmother. Babysit at any time. Oh you were such an adorable baby, and so good. Mrs Alastair Mead. Well, who on earth would want their daughter to marry a flashy duke? Who'd really want their daughter to be a sudden duchess?

They were in their seats now, listening to the address. It was a little hard to hear, even here in the front row: something about the importance of putting someone else *first*, for the rest of your life. Very moving. Pity those further back wouldn't be able to hear the message. But then the servants of God were inclined to mumble too humbly. Putting Alastair Mead *first*: what a thought. Who on earth could want . . .? Mrs Hetherington glanced at her husband, firm beside her, slight smile. Dear David: his handsome rugged face, the calm of a good colonel in all crises. Though naturally this wasn't a crisis, was it. But a very happy day.

There was much kissing in between signing the register. Alastair's cheek was damp with nervous sweat. He smelt of the worst kind of aftershave. Alice glowed at him, brown mascara blotting her eyelashes. No words: what could Mrs Hetherington say? Thank goodness this part of it was nearly over. Called upon to be efficient at the reception, her role would come more easily. It was all this hovering about, second lead to the star, that caused the strain. Stiffly, she followed David back to their pew, eyes down, aware of the blur of wedding hats and curious faces. Mean thought: mostly *their* friends. The Meads' side was half empty . . .

Optimistic blast of the organ. Finale. Darling Alice. As she appeared on Alastair's arm Mrs Hetherington briefly shut her eyes to protect the scalding balls. On opening them she felt them lashed with tears in spite of all the self-control. Perhaps she should have taken a pill after all.

Alice smiling, now. Alastair smiling. Stupid acid smile of triumph at his catch. For after all, Alice *was* something of a catch. Sparkle of dandruff on his shoulder. Wedding socks no doubt wrinkled. God forgive her, but Mrs Hetherington couldn't love him any more. Her first instincts had been right. Nothing could alter the fact that he was a humourless dreary prig: there was not a single thing about him over which she could rejoice.

Still, sons-in-law are sent to try us, and she would battle on. She let Alastair's dreadful father, pink-eyed, take her arm. She gave a wonderful smile to the congregation at large, acknowledging the happiness of the day. And with eyes never leaving the distant white cloud that was her beloved daughter, refusing to limp in spite of the agony of her shoe, she made the kind of irreproachable journey down the aisle which can only cause the wedding guests to observe: what a perfect mother of the bride.

WILLIAM TREVOR

The Third Party

The two men met by arrangement in Buswell's Hotel. The time and place had been suggested by the man who was slightly the older of the two; his companion had agreed without seeking an adjustment. Half past 11 in the bar: 'I think we'll spot one another all right,' the older man had said. 'Well, she'll have told you what I look like.'

He was tall, acquiring bulkiness, a pinkish brown sunburn darkening his face, fair curly hair that was turning grey. The man he met was thinner, with spectacles and a smooth black overcoat, a smaller man.

Lairdman this smaller man was called; the other's name was Boland. Both were in their early 40s.

'Well, we're neither of us late,' Boland said in greeting, the more nervous of the two. 'Fergus Boland. How are you?' They shook hands. Boland pulled out his wallet. 'I'll have a Jameson myself. What'll I get you?'

'Oh, only a mineral. This time of day, Fergus. A lemonade.'

'A Jameson and a lemonade,' Boland ordered.

'Sure,' the barman said.

They stood by the bar. Boland held out a packet of cigarettes. 'D'you smoke?'

Lairdman shook his head. He cocked an elbow on to the bar, arranging himself tidily. 'Sorry about this,' he said.

They were alone except for the barman, who set their two glasses in front of them. They weren't going to sit down; there was no move to do so. 'A pound and tenpence,' the barman said, and Boland paid him. Boland's clothes – tweed jacket and corduroy trousers – were wrinkled: he'd driven more than 100 miles that morning. 'I mean I'm really sorry,' Lairdman went on, 'doing this to anyone.'

'Good luck.' Boland raised his glass. He had softened the colour of the whiskey by adding twice as much water. 'You never drink this early in the day, I suppose?' he said, con-

146

strainedly polite. 'Well, very wise. That's very sensible: I always say it.'

'I thought it mightn't be a drinking occasion.'

'I couldn't face you without a drink in, Lairdman.'

'I'm sorry about that.'

'You've lifted my wife off me. That isn't an everyday occurrence.'

'I'm sorry – '

'It would be better if you didn't keep saying that.'

Lairdman, who was in the timber business, acknowledged the rebuke with a sideways wag of his head. The whole thing was awkward, he confessed, he hadn't slept a wink the night before.

'You're a Dubliner, she tells me,' Boland said, the same politeness to the fore. 'You make blockboard: there's money in that, no doubt about it.'

Lairdman was offended. She'd described her husband as clumsy, but had added that he wouldn't hurt a fly. Already, five minutes into the difficult encounter, Lairdman wasn't so sure about that.

'I don't like Dublin,' Boland continued. 'I'll be frank about it. I never have. I'm a small-town man, but of course you'll know.'

He imagined his wife feeding her lover with information about his provincialism. She liked to tell people things; she talked a great deal. Boland had inherited a bakery in the town she had referred to, one that was quite unconnected with the more renowned Dublin bakery of the same name. A few years ago it had been suggested to him that he should consider retitling his, calling it Ideal Bread and Cakes, or Ovenfresh, in order to avoid confusion, but he saw no need for that, believing indeed that if a change should come about it should be made by the Dublin firm.

'I want to thank you,' Lairdman said, 'for taking all this so well. Annabella has told me.'

'I doubt I have an option.'

Lairdman's lips were notably thin, his mouth a narrow streak that smiled without apparent effort. He smiled a little now, but shook his head to dispel any misconception: he was not gloating, he was not agreeing that his mistress's husband

147

had no option. Boland was surprised that he didn't have a little chopped off moustache like so many Dublin men had.

'I thought when we met you might hit me,' Lairdman said. 'I remarked that to Annabella, but she said that wasn't you at all.'

'No, it isn't me.'

'That's what I mean by taking it well.'

'All I want to know is what you have in mind. She doesn't seem to know herself.'

'In mind?'

'I'm not protesting at your intentions where my wife is concerned, only asking if you're thinking of marrying her and if you have some kind of programme. I mean, have you a place up here that's suitable for her? You're not a married man, I understand? I'll have another JJ,' Boland called out to the barman.

'No, I'm not a married man. I never have been. What we were hoping was that − if you're agreeable − Annabella could move into my place more or less at once. It's suitable accommodation all right, a seven-room flat in Wellington Road. But in time we'll get a house.'

'Thanks,' Boland said to the barman, paying him more money.

'That was my turn,' Lairdman protested, just a little late. She wouldn't care for meanness, Boland thought, when it began to impinge on her, which it would: these things never mattered at first.

'But marriage?' he said. 'It isn't easy, you know, to marry another man's wife in Ireland.'

'Annabella and I would naturally like to be married one day.'

'That's what I wanted to put to you. How are you suggesting that a divorce is fixed? You're not a Catholic, I'm to understand?'

'No.'

'No more am I. No more is Annabella. But that hardly matters, one way or another. She's very vague on divorce. We talked about it for a long time.'

'I appreciate that. And I appreciated your suggestion that we should meet.'

148

'I have grounds for divorce, Lairdman, but a damn bit of use they are to me. A divorce'll take an age.'

'It could be hurried up if you had an address in England. If the whole thing could be filed over there we'd be home and dry in no time.'

'But I haven't an address in England.'

'It's only a thought, Fergus.'

'So she wasn't exaggerating when she said you wanted to marry her?'

'I don't think I've ever known Annabella to exaggerate,' Lairdman replied stiffly.

Then you don't know the most important thing about her, Boland confidently reflected – that being that she can't help telling lies, which you and I would politely refer to as exaggerations. He believed that his wife actually disliked the truth, a rare attribute, he imagined, in any human being.

'I'm surprised you never got married,' he said, genuinely surprised because in his experience cocky little men like this very often had a glamorous woman in tow. He wondered if his wife's lover could possibly be a widower: naturally Annabella would not have been reliable about that.

'I've known your wife a long time,' Lairdman retorted softly, and Boland saw him trying not to let his smile show. 'As soon as I laid eyes on Annabella I knew she was the only woman who would make sense for me in marriage.'

Boland gazed into his whiskey. He had to be careful about what he said. If he became angry for a moment he was quite likely to ruin everything. The last thing he wanted was that the man should change his mind. He lit a cigarette, again offering the packet to Lairdman, who again shook his head. Conversationally, friendly, Boland said:

'Lairdman's an interesting name – I thought that when she told me.'

'It's not Irish. Huguenot maybe, or part of it anyway.'

'I thought Jewish when she told me.'

'Oh, undoubtedly a hint of that.'

'You know the way you're interested when you're told about a relationship like that? "What's his name?" It's not important, it doesn't matter in the least. But still you ask it.'

'I'm sure. I appreciate that.'

When she said his name was Lairdman, Boland had remembered the name from his schooldays. He'd guessed that the man she was telling him about was a boy he couldn't quite place. But knowing the name, he'd recognised in Buswell's bar the adult features immediately.

' "Where did you meet him?" That doesn't matter either. And yet you ask it.'

'Annabella and I – '

'I know, I know.'

At school Lairdman had been notorious for an unexpected reason: his head had been held down a lavatory while his hair was scrubbed with a lavatory brush. Roche and Dead Smith had done it, the kind of thing they tended to do if they suspected uppitiness. Roche and Dead Smith were the bullies of their time, doling out admonitions to new boys who arrived in the summer or winter terms rather than the autumn one, or to boys whose faces they found irritating. Lairdman's head had been scrubbed with the lavatory brush because he kept his hair tidy with perfumed oil that was offensive to Dead Smith.

'I think we were at school together,' Boland said.

Lairdman almost gave a jump, and it was Boland, this time, who disguised his smile. His wife would not have remembered the name of the school in question, not being in the least interested: the coincidence had clearly not been established.

'I don't recollect a Boland,' Lairdman said.

'I'd have been a little senior to yourself.' Deliberately, Boland sounded apologetic. 'But when she said your name I wondered. I was one of the boarders. Up from the country. Terrible bloody place.'

Thirteen boarders they'd been, among nearly 100 day boys. The day boys used to come noisily up the short, suburban avenue on their bicycles, and later ride noisily away. They were envied because they were returning to warmth and comfort and decent food, because after the weekends they'd talk about how they'd been to the Savoy or the Adelphi or even to the Crystal Ballroom. The boarders in winter would crouch around a radiator in one of the classrooms; in summer they'd walk in twos and threes around the playing fields. The school matron, a Mrs Porter, was also the cook, but regularly burnt both the breakfast porridge and the barley soup she was given to producing as the main source of sustenance in the evening. An old boy of the school, occupying an attic at the top of a flight of uncarpeted stairs that led out of one of the dormitories, was the junior master, but appeared to have acquired neither privilege nor distinction through that role: he, too, sat by the radiator in the classroom and dreaded the cooking of Mrs Porter. The bachelor headmaster, a boxer in his time – reputed to have been known in ringside circles as the Belted Earl, an obscurely acquired sobriquet that had remained with him – was a Savonarola-like figure in a green suit, sadistically inclined.

'Oh, I quite liked the place,' Lairdman said.

'You were a day boy.'

'I suppose it made a difference.'

'Of course it did.'

For the first time Boland felt annoyed. Not only was the man she'd become involved with mean, he was stupid as well. All this stuff about an address in England, all this stuff about giving up a seven-room flat, when if he had an iota of common sense he'd realise you didn't go buying houses for the likes of Annabella because in no way whatsoever could you rely on her doing what she said she was going to do.

'I've always thought, actually, it supplied a sound education.' Lairdman was saying.

The awful little Frenchman who couldn't make himself understood. O'Reilly-Flood, whose method of teaching history was to give the class the textbook to read while he wrote letters. The mathematics man who couldn't solve the problems he set. The Belted Earl in his foul laboratory, prodding at your ears with the sharp end of a pair of tweezers until you cried out in pain.

'Oh, a great place,' Boland agreed. 'A fine academy.'

'We'd probably send our children there. If we have boys.'

'Your children?'

'You'd have no objection? Lord no, why should you? I'm sorry, that's a silly thing to say.'

'I'll have another,' Boland requested of the barman. 'How about your mineral?'

'No, I'm OK, thanks.'

This time he did not mention, even too late, that he should pay. Instead he looked away, as if wishing to dissociate himself from an overindulgence in whiskey on an occasion such as this, before it was yet midday. Boland lit another cigarette. So she hadn't told him? She'd let this poor devil imagine that in no time at all the seven-room flat in Wellington Road wouldn't be spacious enough to contain the family that would naturally come trotting along once she'd rid herself of her provincial husband. Of course there'd have to be a divorce, and of course it would have to be hurried up: no one wanted a litter of little bastards in a seven-room flat or anywhere else.

'Good man yourself,' he said to the barman when his whiskey came. If he ended up having too much to drink, as indeed might happen, he'd spend the night in the hotel rather than drive back. But it was early yet, and it was surprising what a heavy lunch could do.

'I'm sorry about that,' Lairdman repeated, referring again to his slip the tongue. I wasn't thinking.'

'Ah, for heaven's sake man!'

Boland briefly touched him, a reassuring tap on the shoulder. He could hear her telling him that the reason for their childless marriage had long ago been established. 'Poor old fellow,' she'd probably said, that being her kind of expression. She'd known before their marriage that she couldn't have children; in a quarrel long after it she'd confessed that she'd known and hadn't said.

'Naturally,' Lairdman blandly continued, 'we'd like to have a family.'

'You would of course.'

'I'm sorry that side of things didn't go right for you.'

'I was sorry myself.'

'The thing is, Fergus, is it OK about the divorce?'

'Are you saying I should agree to be the guilty party?'

'It's the done thing, as a matter of fact.'

'The done thing?'

'If you find it distasteful – '

'Not at all, of course not. I'll agree to be the guilty party and we'll work it out from there.'

'You're being great, Fergus.'

The way he was talking, Boland thought, he might have been drinking. There were people who became easy-going, who adopted that same kind of tone, even if they'd only been drinking with someone else: he'd often heard that but he'd never believed it. A sniff of someone else's glass, he'd heard, a vapour in the air.

'Do you remember the cokeman they used to have there? McArdle?'

'Where was that, Fergus?'

'At school.'

Lairdman shook his head. He didn't remember McArdle, he said. He doubted that he'd ever known anyone of that name. 'A cokeman?' he repeated. 'What kind of a cokeman? I don't think I know the word.'

'He looked after the furnace. We called him the cokeman.'

'I never knew that person at all.'

Other people came into the bar. A tall man in a gabardine overcoat who opened an *Irish Times* and was poured a glass of stout without having to order it. An elderly woman and two men who appeared to be her sons. A priest who looked around the bar and went away again.

'You wouldn't have noticed McArdle because you weren't a boarder,' Boland said. 'When you're weekends in a place you notice more.'

'I'm sorry I don't remember you.'

'I wouldn't expect you to.'

She'd be imagining this conversation, Boland suddenly realised. It was she who had suggested this bar for their meeting, speaking as if she knew it and considered it suitable. 'I think I'll go up and see Phyllis,' she used to say, saying it more often as time went by. Phyllis was a friend she had in Terenure, whose own marriage had ended on the rocks and who was suffering from an internal complaint besides. But of course Phyllis had just been a name she'd used, a stalwart friend who would cover up for her. For all he knew, Phyllis might never have been married, her internal system might be like iron. 'Phone me,' he used to say, and obediently and agreeably his wife would. She'd tell him how Dublin looked and how Phyllis was bearing up. No doubt she'd been sitting on the edge of a bed in the seven-room flat in Wellington Road.

'It's really good of you to come all this way,' Lairdman said with a hint of finality in his voice, an indication that quite soon now the encounter should be brought to an end. 'I really appreciate it. I'll ring Annabella this afternoon and tell her we know where we stand. You won't mind that, Fergus?'

'Not at all.'

Boland had often interrupted such a telephone conversation. He would walk into the hall and there she'd be, knees drawn up on the second step of the stairs, the receiver strung through the banisters. She'd be talking quite normally in her slightly high-pitched voice, but when he stepped through the hall door she'd wave a greeting and begin to whisper, the hand that had waved to him now cupped around the mouthpiece. He'd often wondered what she imagined he thought, or if she achieved some tremor of satisfaction from the hushed twilight of this semi-surreptitious carry-on. The trouble with Annabella was that sooner or later everything in the world bored her. 'Now I want to hear,' she would soon be saying to Lairdman, 'every single thing since the moment you left the house.' And the poor man would begin a long history about catching a bus and passing through the entrance doors of his blockboard business, how he had said good morning to the typist and listened to the foreman's complaint concerning a reprehensible employee, how he'd eaten a doughnut with his 11 o'clock coffee, not as good a doughnut as he'd eaten the day before. Later, in a quarrel, she'd fling it all back at him: who on earth wanted to know about his doughnuts? She'd screech at him, her fingers splayed out in the air so that her freshly applied crimson nail varnish would evenly dry. She had a way of quarrelling when she was doing her nails, because she found the task irksome and needed some distraction. Yet she'd have felt

154

half-undressed if her fingernails weren't evenly painted, or if her make-up wasn't right or her hair just as she wanted it.

'I'll be able to say,' Lairdman was stating with what appeared to be pride, 'that there wasn't an acrimonious word between us. She'll be pleased about that.'

Boland smiled, nodding agreeably. He couldn't imagine his wife being pleased since she so rarely was. He wondered what it was in Lairdman that attracted her. She'd said, when he'd asked her, that her lover was fun; he liked to go abroad, she'd said, he appreciated food and painting; he possessed what she called a 'devastating' sense of humour. She hadn't mentioned his sexual prowess, since it wasn't her habit to talk in that way. 'Will you be taking those cats?' Boland had enquired. 'I don't want them here.' Her lover would willingly supply a home for her Siamese cats, she had replied, both of which she called 'Ciao'. Boland wondered if his successor even knew of their existence.

'I wonder what became,' Boland said, 'of Roche and Dead Smith?'

He didn't know why he said it, why he couldn't have accepted that the business between them was over. He should have shaken hands with Lairdman and left it at that, perhaps saying there were no hard feelings. He would never have to see the man again; once in a while he would feel sorry for the memory of him.

'Dead Smith?' Lairdman said.

'Big eejit with a funny eye. There's a barrister called Roche now; I often wonder if that's the same fellow.'

'I don't think I remember either of them.'

'Roche used to go around in a pin-striped blue suit. He looked like one of the masters.'

Lairdman shook his head. 'I'll say cheerio, Fergus. Again, my gratitude.'

'They were the bright sparks who washed your hair in a lavatory bowl.'

Boland had said to himself over and over again that Lairdman was welcome to her. He looked ahead to an easy widower's life, the house she had filled with her perversities and falsehoods for the last 12 years as silent as a peaceful sleep. He would clear out the memories of her because

155

naturally she wouldn't do that herself – the hoarded magazines, the empty medicine bottles, the clothes she had no
further use for, the cosmetics she'd pitched into the corners
of cupboards, the curtains and chair-covers clawed by her
cats. He would get Hanrahan to paint out the rooms. He
would cook his own meals, and Mrs Couglan would still
come every morning. Mrs Couglan wouldn't be exactly sorry
to see the back of her, either.

'I don't know why,' Lairdman said, 'you keep going on
about your schooldays.'

'Let me get you a decent drink before you go. Bring us
two big ones,' he called out to the barman, who was listening
to an anecdote the man in the gabardine coat was retailing
at the far end of the bar.

'No, really,' Lairdman protested. 'Really now.'

'Oh, go on, man. We're both in need of it.'

Lairdman had buttoned his black overcoat and drawn on
a pair of black leather gloves. Finger by finger he drew one
of the gloves off again. Boland could feel him thinking that,
for the sake of the woman who loved him, he must humour
the cuckold.

'It takes it out of you,' Boland said. 'An emotional thing
like this. Good luck to you.'

They drank, Lairdman awkward now because of what had
been said. He looked a bit like a priest, Boland thought, the
black attire and the way he wore it. He tried to imagine
the pair of them abroad, sitting down together in a French
restaurant, Lairdman being pernickety about a plate of food
he didn't like the look of. It didn't make sense, all this stuff
about a devastating sense of humour.

'I only mentioned the school,' Boland said, 'because it
was the other thing we had in common.'

'As a matter of fact, I'm a governor up there now.'

'Ah, go on!'

'That's why I said we'd maybe send the children there.'

'Well, doesn't that beat the band.'

'I'm pleased myself. I'm pleased they asked me.'

'Sure, anyone would be.'

Stupid he might be, Boland thought, but he was cute as
well the way he'd managed not to make a comment on the

156

Roche and Dead Smith business. Cuteness was the one thing you could never get away from in Dublin. Cute as weasels they were.

'You don't remember it?' he prompted.

'What's that?'

'The lavatory thing.'

'Look here, Boland – '

'I've offended you. I didn't mean that at all.'

'Of course you haven't offended me. It's just that I see no point in harping on things like that.'

'We'll talk of something else.'

'Actually, I'm a bit on the late side.'

The second glove was again drawn on, the buttons of the overcoat checked to see that all was well for the street. The glove was taken off again when Lairdman remembered there'd have to be a handshake.

'Thanks for everything,' he said.

For the second time, Boland surprised himself by being unable to leave well alone. He wondered if it was the whiskey; the long drive and then the whiskey on top of an empty stomach because of course there hadn't been anything in the house for his breakfast, not even a slice of bread. 'I'll come down and do you scrambled eggs and a few rashers,' she'd said the night before. 'You'll need something inside you before you set off.'

'I'm interested in what you say about sending your children there,' was what he heard himself saying. 'Would these be yours and Annabella's children you have in mind?'

Lairdman looked at him as if he'd gone out of his senses. His narrow mouth gaped in bewilderment. Boland didn't know if he was trying to smile or if some kind of rictus had set in.

'What other children are there?' Lairdman shook his head, still perplexed. He held his hand out, but Boland did not take it.

'I thought those might be the children you had in mind,' he said.

'I don't follow what you're saying.'

'She can't have children, Lairdman.'

'Oh now, look here – '

'That's a medical fact. The unfortunate woman is incapable of mothering children.'

'I think you're drunk. One after another you've had. I thought it a moment ago when you got maudlin about your schooldays. Annabella's told me a thing or two, you know.'

'She hasn't told you about the cats she's going to spring on you. She hasn't told you she can't give birth. She hasn't told you she gets so bored her face turns white with fury. It's best not to be around then, Lairdman. Take my tip on that.'

'She's told me you can't stay sober. She's told me you've been warned off every racecourse in Ireland.'

'I don't go racing, Lairdman, and apart from occasions like this I hardly drink at all. A lot less than our mutual friend, I can promise you.'

'You have been unable to give Annabella children. She's sorry for you, she doesn't blame you.'

'Annabella was never sorry for anyone in her life.'

'Now look here, Boland – '

'Look nowhere man. I've had 12 years of the woman. I'm obliging you by stepping aside. But there's no need for this talk of divorce, Lairdman, in England or anywhere else. I'm just telling you that. She'll come and live with you in your seven-room flat; she'll live in any house you care to buy, but if you wait till kingdom come you'll not find children trotting along. All you'll have is two Siamese cats that would bite the legs off you.'

'You're being despicable, Boland.'

'I'm telling you the truth.'

'You seem to have forgotten that Annabella and myself have talked about all this. She knew you'd take it hard. She knew there'd be bitterness. Well, I understand that. I've said I'm sorry.'

'You're a mean little blockboard man, Lairdman. You belong with your head held down in a lavatory bowl. Were you wringing wet when they let go of you? I'd love to have seen it, Lairdman.'

'Will you keep your damn voice down? And will you stop trying to pick a quarrel? I came out this morning in good faith. I'm aware of the delicacy of the thing, and I'm not saying I've been a saint. But I'll not stand here and be insulted. And I'll not hear Annabella insulted.'

'I think Dead Smith became a vet.'

'I don't care what he became.'

Abruptly, Lairdman was gone. Boland didn't turn his head, or otherwise acknowledge his departure. He examined the row of bottles behind the bar, and in a moment he lit a fresh cigarette.

For half an hour he remained on his own, where his usurper had left him. All he could think of was Lairdman as he remembered him, a boy who was pointed out because of what two bullies had done to him. The old cokeman, McArdle, used to laugh over the incident. Sometimes when the classroom radiator wasn't hot enough the boarders would go down to McArdle's coke-hole and sit around his furnace. He'd tell them obscene stories, all of them to do with the matron and cook, or else he told them about Lairdman. The more Boland thought about it all the more clearly he remembered Lairdman: not much different in appearance, the same trap of a mouth, a propelling pencil and a fountain pen clipped into the pocket of his jacket. He had a bicycle Boland could remember, a new one that had perhaps replaced an older one, a Golden Eagle. 'Oh, we met at a party Phyllis gave,' she had said, but there was no way of knowing how much truth there was in that, presumably none.

Boland ate his lunch in the dining room of the hotel, among people he did not know, who gave the impression of lunching there regularly. He didn't have to say he'd take nothing to drink because the waitress didn't ask him. There was water in a glass jug on the table, he'd be all right for the journey home, he decided.

'The cod,' he ordered. 'And the cream of celery.'

He remembered a time when the 13 boarders had smashed a window in an outhouse that no longer had a purpose. Most of the windowpanes were broken already, the roof had long ago tumbled in and one of the walls was so badly split that it had begun to disintegrate. It was forbidden for any boy to enter this small, crumbling building, and the boarders had not done so. They had stood 20 or so yards away throwing stones at the remaining windowpanes, as they might have thrown stones at a cockshoot. They had meant no harm, and did not realise that an outhouse which was so badly damaged already might be worthy of preservation. Ceremoniously the following morning the Belted Earl had taken his cane to them in the presence of the assembled day boys. Lairdman would have been watching, Boland reflected as he ate his soup: Lairdman might have brought it up just as he'd brought up the other matter, but of course that wasn't Lairdman's way. Lairdman considered himself a sophisticate; even in the days of his Golden Eagle he would have considered himself that.

Boland crumbled the bread on his side plate, picking up bits of it between mouthfuls of soup. He saw himself, one day in the future, entering the silence of his house. He saw himself on a summer evening pushing open the French windows of the drawing room and going out into the garden, strolling among its fuchsia bushes and apple trees. He'd known the house all his life; he'd actually been born in it. Opposite O'Connor Motors, it was the last one in the town, yellow-washed and ordinary, but a house he loved.

'Did you say the fish, sir?' the waitress enquired.

'Yes, I did.'

He'd been married in Dublin, she being the daughter of a Dublin wine merchant. The old man was still alive and so was her mother. 'You've taken on a handful,' the old man once had said, but he'd said it playfully because in those days Annabella had been a handful to delight in. What they thought of her now Boland had no idea.

'The plate's hot, sir,' the waitress warned.

'Thanks very much.'

People had been delighted when he brought her to live among them. They'd stopped him on the street and said he was lucky. He'd come back from Dublin with a crown of jewels, which was how they saw it. And yet those same people would be delighted when she left. The terrible frustration that possessed her – the denial of children through some mischance within her – turned beauty into wanton eccentricity. It was that that had happened, nothing else.

160

Slowly he ate his cod, with parsley sauce and cabbage and potatoes. Nobody would mention it much; they'd know what had happened and they'd say to one another that one day, probably, he'd marry again. He wondered if he would. He'd spoken airily of divorce to Lairdman, but in truth he knew nothing of divorce in Ireland these days. A marriage should wither away, he somehow felt, it should rot and die; it didn't seem quite like a cancer, to be swiftly cut out.

He ordered apple tart and cream, and later coffee came. He was glad it was all over: the purpose of his visit to Dublin had been to set a seal on everything that had happened, and in the encounter that had taken place the seal had at some point been set. The air had been cleared, he had accepted the truth that had been necessary to hear from someone else besides his wife. When first she'd told him he'd wondered if she could possibly be making it all up, and he'd wondered it since. Even while he'd waited in Buswell's bar he'd said to himself he wouldn't be surprised if no one turned up.

On the way to the car park two tinker children begged from him. He knew it wasn't coppers they were after, but his wallet or whatever else they could get their fingers on. One held out a box, the other pressed close to him, with a rug folded over her hands. Dublin was like that now. 'Go on, along with you,' he ordered them as harshly as he could.

It was because there hadn't been enough for her to do: he thought that as he eased the car through the heavy city traffic. And from the very start she hadn't taken to provincial life. A childless woman in a provincial town had all the time in the world to study its limitations. She had changed the furniture around, and had chosen the wallpapers that her Siamese cats had later damaged. But she'd resisted bridge and tennis, and had deplored the absence of even a cinema café. He'd thought he'd understood; so well used to the limitations himself, he was nevertheless aware that the society he had plunged her into was hardly scintillating. He'd driven her as often as he could to Dublin, before she'd taken to going on her own to visit Phyllis. For years he'd known she wasn't happy, but until she told him he'd never suspected she'd become involved with a man.

He stopped in Mullingar and had a cup of tea. The

Dublin evening papers had arrived before him: he read in the *Herald* that the Italian government had been successfully re-formed after the *Achille Lauro* incident; the dollar was slipping again; a meat-processing plant was to close in Cork. He dawdled over the paper, not wanting to go home. Lairdman would have telephoned her by now. 'Why don't you drive up this afternoon?' he might have said. Maybe all day she had been packing, knowing the encounter was only a formality. 'He won't stand in the way,' Lairdman would have said. 'He'll even supply grounds.' There'd be nothing to keep her, now that all three of them knew where they stood, and it was the kind of thing she'd do, pack up and go when she'd got him out of the way.

A coal fire was burning in the café. A rare welcome these days, he remarked to the woman who'd served him, and pulled a chair up close to it. 'I'd take another cup of tea,' he said.

The little white Volkswagen he'd bought her might be on the road to Dublin already. She wouldn't leave a note because she wouldn't consider it necessary. If the Volkswagen passed by now she would be puzzled at not meeting him on the road; she'd never notice his own car parked outside the café.

'Ah well, you'd need a fire,' the woman said, returning with his tea. 'A shocking foggy old month we're having.'

He drove on after he'd had a third cup of tea, keeping an eye out for the Volkswagen. Would she greet him with a touch on the horn? Or would he greet her? He didn't know if he would. Better to wait.

But over the next 50 or so miles there was no sign of his wife's car. And of course, he told himself, there was no reason why there should be: it was pure conjecture that she'd depart that afternoon, and the amount she had to pack made it unlikely that she could manage to do so in a day. For the next few miles he speculated on how, otherwise, her departure would be. Would Lairdman drive down to assist her? That had not been agreed, nor even touched upon as a possibility: he would instantly put his foot down if it was suggested. Would Phyllis arrive to help her? He would naturally have no objection to that. Certainly, the more he thought about it, the less likely was it that she would be

162

capable of completing the move on her own. She had a way of calling in other people when something difficult had to be undertaken. He imagined her sitting on the second step of the stairs, chattering on the telephone. 'Would you ever . . ?' she had a way of beginning her demands and her requests.

His headlights caught the familiar sign, in English and Irish, indicating that the town which was his home was the next one. He turned the radio on. 'Dancing in the dark,' a sensual female voice lilted, reminding him of the world he supposed his wife and Lairdman belonged to, the thrill of illicit love, tête-à-tête dancing, as the song implied. 'Poor Annabella,' he said aloud, while the music still played. Poor girl, ever to have got herself married to the inheritor of a country-town bakery. Lucky, in all fairness, the cocky little Lairdman had turned up. The music continued, and he imagined them running towards one another along an empty street, as lovers in a film. He imagined their embrace, and then their shared smile before they embraced again. As the dull third party, not even a villain, he had no further part to play.

But as Boland reached the first few houses on this side of the town he knew that none of that was right. Not only had the white Volkswagen not conveyed her to Lairdman in his absence, it would not do so tomorrow or the next day, or next week. It would not do so next month, or after Christmas, or in February, or in spring: it would not ever do so. It hadn't mattered reminding Lairdman of the ignominy he had suffered as a boy; it hadn't mattered reminding him that she was a liar, or insulting him by calling him mean. All that abuse was conventional in the circumstances, an expected element in the man-to-man confrontation, the courage for it engendered by an intake of John Jameson. Yet something had impelled him to go further: little men like Lairdman always wanted children. 'That's a total lie,' she'd have said already on the telephone, and Lairdman would have soothed her. But soothing wasn't going to be enough for either of them.

Boland turned the radio off. He drew the car up outside Donovan's public house and sat for a moment, swinging the

163

keys between his thumb and forefinger before going in and ordering a bottle of Smithwick's with lime. At the bar he greeted men he knew and stood with them drinking, listening to talk of racehorses and politics. They drifted away when a few more drinks had been taken but Boland remained there for a long time, wondering why he hadn't been able to let Lairdman take her from him.

ELIZABETH TALLENT

Listen to Reason

Have you got a nickel?
Have you got a dime?
If your name is Nicholas,
You're – all – mine.

Driving, Charlie was still singing, nonsensically and softly, though by now he must have been singing for himself, because five-year-old Nicholas's face was moody in sleep and his jacket had fallen away from his shoulder. A gesture Charlie resisted making repeated itself in his mind: his hand reaching to tug the jacket back up. An American, Charlie had a cautious sense of the dark English road before him. In London he took the Tube; he'd never had to adapt to driving on the left and ruby-red eyes shining in the verge, reflecting the Renault's headlamps. Headlights if you wanted to think Englishly, but Charlie didn't. In the dips of the road, mist had settled so densely the headlamps hardly pierced it.

His nothing songs for Nicholas meant exactly that – nothing – yet when Charlie brooded over this one, he found in it an accidental echo of his own father's declaration, when Charlie was small, that Charlie was going to nickel and dime him to death. This was said with that familiar confiding tilt of his father's head that had left Charlie believing he'd just been taken deeply, probably permanently, into his father's confidence, but Charlie had always believed wrong; he'd leaped too soon, when his father was only teasing, until finally Charlie had tired of leaping. When Charlie was nine and his father 40, cancer had come and swept away all of their normal, mutual chances for reconciliation. His father's death existed, a little live cinder of unhealing hurt, far back in Charlie's heart. This was what Charlie did not want his own son to live with, if (when) Charlie died: anger at having been left so incompletely understood.

165

If, when, he died. His mood had been bleak lately, though bleak moods were infrequent for Charlie.

He'd sworn he wouldn't leave England without visiting Hadrian's Wall, and Kyra had taken advantage of that, and of the fact that throughout their London year Charlie had spent cruelly little time with Nicholas, to pack father and son off in this rented Renault. Though he and Nicholas had been to Stonehenge only two weeks before, 'cruelly little time' was Kyra's phrase, coined in a tearful, accusing rage. This trip also left her with what she said she needed, a long weekend alone to pack the last of their stuff for the Heathrow scramble. Their New York odds and ends had never fitted in well with the dour English antiques that inhabited their chilly leased flat, and Charlie thought with relief of locking that narrow London door behind them for the last time. That they'd come to England at all was his fault. He'd been offered a year with a London publisher by his New York house, an offer too good to believe, then too good to refuse: Charlie's version, presented to his silent wife. Silent, but, he sensed, only half listening, so that Charlie's spirits rose. Kyra listened carefully indeed when she was going to fight.

Later, he wished she'd fought. Pennies were 'pee' to Nicholas now, and somehow, possibly from his sitter's son, he'd adopted that high pitch of nervous inquiry with which English schoolboys ended sentences. Worse, the righteous Scottish sitter had reported that on occasion Nicholas stole. Small things: a comb, a handkerchief with Victorian embroidery. Those, the sitter conveyed with lilting dis-approval, she hadn't minded losing. She hadn't wanted to trouble Kyra with the news. Then Nicholas stole a farthing because he liked its wren. That, the sitter minded very much. The farthing had been saved for her own boy. Its loss was traced to Nicholas, and, furiously shamed, he had gone to pry it from its hiding place under a seat cushion: a rumpus that Charlie, returning late, had found himself blamed for by his suddenly inconsolable wife. Stealing equalled stealing affection, Nicholas believed he must steal affection because his *father* was so unavailable, and Hadrian's Wall was Charlie's last chance to right the year-long wrong he'd inflicted – Kyra's reasoning, if you could call it reasoning.

Most of that year was behind them now. There was hardly anything left to get through: they would make it home to New York. Charlie breathed deep and tried to let virtue loosen what seemed to be a knot, a handspan-wide, constricting knot, of anguish in his chest.

Oh Charlie he's my darling,
Charlie he's a saint,
But if your name is Nicholas,
You like blue paint.

A nothing song of Charlie's, singing itself in Kyra's head as Brian's MG bowled down the hedgerowed lane. 'Charlie he's a saint' was funny. There was no warning hidden in it. There couldn't be, because Charlie didn't know that there was anything wrong. Her conviction that he did know, that was her guilt talking, not reason. Needing comfort, she would have lain her head on Brian's shoulder, but the seat belt he insisted on restrained her. It was funny realising so late, just before parting from him, that her English lover loved driving, especially driving fast, and that he resisted distraction while he was doing it.

Until lately, she'd been sure of her ability to distract him from anything. Brian was a slight, clear-headed person, orderly by nature – in spite of her, orderly. She'd known from the beginning that she was going to wage war on that quality in him, on his reasonableness and resourcefulness as well, though those were the very things that had drawn her to him. In the gloomy Indian restaurant where she'd first consented to sleep with him – consented to herself; he hadn't even as yet asked – she'd shaken her head extravagantly at a remark of his about Maggie Thatcher's strident voice, and felt her favourite earring unclasp and break on the parquet floor. She'd cupped the pieces in her palm, hating herself for the gesture she couldn't have helped – the line of argument she'd meant to follow was that 'strident' was a sexist term directed at unruly women, women who exposed themselves. The silver design and the wafer of its silver backing would join that stash of fragments she'd have mended on that faraway day when she got home to New York. Among the responses she was aware of, staring down at the pieces, was this self-reproach: in London she never got around to getting anything fixed. London had nullified her, countered initiative, washed away her New York self and left her with nothing else. She looked up as, without asking, he tipped the two fragments from her hand into his. Nesting the design neatly in its backing, he bit the earring lightly two or three times to seal the fit. Fastening it back on her earlobe, she'd felt his saliva there.

They were well into a small village when, from the corner of her eye, Kyra saw it: in the spring darkness it was another narrow English house, fronting the rain-pooled lane composedly, giving nothing away. When Brian drove by it, she thought in disappointment, oh, wrong one. It was only when the village petered out into dark fields again and he halted the MG, shaking his head, saying, 'You'll think I'm an idiot,' that she knew she'd been right, that had been the house where they were expected. She laughed, and teased the corner of his mouth with a gloved finger until he forgot himself enough to smile. He still hated making mistakes in front of her, and she still craved them from him, as proof that he was no longer so self-reliantly clear-headed after all.

In the car, idling in the cold field with its sullen smell of rained-on manure, he put his palms against her cheekbones so that his fingers were in her hair, and rocked her head back and forth so that she seemed to be saying *no no no*. This was a habit of his lately. Was it a parody of her way of denying him things, limiting their relationship, keeping its end always before his eyes? The top was down, the damp wind was blowing her hair into her face, and he cleared the strands away, saying, 'You can shake your head all you like, but I'm coming to New York next summer. I've decided.'

This had come up before. Her usual response was to draw a red herring across that path, to sidetrack him in such a way that the sidetracking felt final, but recently she'd been finding this harder to do. As her flight to New York and safety drew nearer, it was her emotions that were unruly, that had begun catching her off guard. This trip, when she'd never granted him so much time before, made her feel more

168

than usually precarious: what had she got herself into, and why?

Before she could think of an answer for him, he had the MG in reverse and moving fast enough so that the flat black fields whipped away and were replaced by dense hedgerows. He backed over a bridge resonant with the buckling sound of sodden old wood, then accelerated hard, startling her, where the lane gleamed under the first sombre housefronts. These ancient houses were steep and dark with disapproval, a strict unforgiving village parting crookedly down the middle to let the MG careen through insanely backwards. She stared over her shoulder, tears rinsing horizontally across her cheeks, and because her fist had lodged itself against her teeth, she sucked her knuckles, willing him to make no mistakes, willing her reflexes magically to second his. For fear of distracting him she made no sound. In the taillights' blaze, close under the rear tyres, a mouse dashed across the black-glass asphalt, *safe*. When the car lurched she didn't feel it as a skid. It was more as if the MG's body jarred sideways and there was one floating, eternal instant before the tyres caught and were snug underneath it again, the tailpipe grinding down along a rise in the road with a long, rusty rasp. The MG hugged backwards around another tight curve, past a small church, then threaded the needle of lane between high walls, the taillights dazzling the close-set flints into an array of quick, moving lights. The glaze of wet road steadied, the houses slowed, their sills and lamps and shutters stood out distinct. It was quiet, though she could have sworn a moment ago that someone had shouted out at them in a rage. Brian eased the car into the curb, really only an inadvertent shelving the road made below the flint housefront Kyra had noticed before because its window was lit.

One gentle, gauze-white window, shining into the street so peaceably it might have been the centre of the world. Kyra waited for Brian to move. When he did, it was to lean toward her and put his arms around her. When she didn't react, he gently dug his shoulder under her chin so that her chin was raised and he could breathe appalled apology – 'I'm sorry, so sorry' – down into her hair. The shout she had heard before started up again, in her head. A voice was shouting to her that he could have *killed* Charlie's wife, Nicholas's mother.

Inside the flint house, there was the echo-y, premonitory silence of adults keeping quiet for the sake of baby sleep. With painful alertness to the impression they were making, Kyra and Brian seated themselves on the leather sofa, only they sat down too near each other and had to rise, awkwardly together, and reseat themselves. If big, curly-headed Simon, judiciously feeding the flames in the tiled fireplace, observed the strain in this lovers' comedy routine, he gave no sign. He was Brian's oldest friend, and had seen him through the dissolution of his relationship with an actress, Pippa. Though when Brian told her this, Kyra wondered how much seeing through Brian, being Brian, had ever needed.

'It smells beautiful,' Kyra said, of the smoke wafting from the too small fireplace; the entire house was on such a tiny scale that she felt as if the dramatic, soot-darkened beams in the white plaster ceiling were close above her head.

Simon, kneeling, turned toward her. 'Do you know what we burn now?' His tone was accusing. He answered himself: 'Our elms. All our ruined, our dead and dying elms,' and Kyra felt, spreading out behind her, a luxuriant forest of unscathed American trees. Upstairs, a baby began to squall furiously loud.

Simon said sourly, 'It's not the air-raid siren at all, it's Joseph.'

In a detached way, as if to deflect Simon's mysterious anger, Kyra traced a seam in the leather and, between the cushions, found a dummy still bearing the crimp of Joseph's gums. 'Ah,' Simon said, 'thank you, I'll take that,' and extracted it from her fingers. Only then did she realise she'd been looking at it wistfully, and was embarrassed.

'Sounds in an excellent mood,' Brian said, of the wailing from above; he was as self-contained as ever, and Kyra had no idea how he felt. In the car, in the cold street, she'd refused to forgive him. She'd almost refused to come into this house at all, until he convinced her that there was no

170

alternative, that it would be absurd to drive back to London tonight.

'He's just tuning up,' Simon said. 'More to come, I'm afraid, unless Fiona manages a miracle. She sometimes does.'

Kyra wished bitterly that someone would sometime observe of her, so matter-of-factly, 'She sometimes does,' and understood with a start that she was jealous of this household, and of Fiona, as yet unseen.

Simon handed Kyra a drink and found his hostility of a moment ago ridiculous. What was it in Brian's women that sometimes brought it out in him, this rush of aggrieved aggression? Kyra rested the glass along her lower lip, then drank. She had dark hair, and the way it fell along her fine forehead and under her jaw proved there was no harm in her, none. Either she had a cold or she'd been crying, for her eyes were raw. Crying, Simon decided. Protectiveness gusted through him.

Simon was still observing Kyra when her mouth shaped a soft, shy O and Fiona entered, the baby braced against her shoulder. Simon and Brian exchanged a long look that neither could have interpreted easily, and Fiona did something backed by that stunning simplicity only she was capable of: bending forward, with a dislodging, easing twist of her shoulder, she handed the baby to Kyra, who rose to receive it. At almost the same instant, the women breathed to each other over the baby's head, 'Hello,' and 'Hello,' and then Fiona said, 'He's bored to tears with me.' Joseph was in Kyra's arms, and she said mindlessly, 'Oh, hey, you're heavier than you look.'

'Baby-worship time,' Simon said, not sourly, but on a note of graceful irony.

Joseph's breath, panting from tiny apple-seed nostrils against Kyra's face when she held him propped upright by his bottom, had a sweetness that stirred her stomach queasily; well, she'd felt nauseated in the car from Brian's stupidity. For an instant she hated the old cloth draped over her shoulder by Fiona, with sleight-of-hand deftness, in case he burped up; she disliked the way his baggy baby cheek was squashed in by her cheekbone when he bumbled his face to rest against hers. He caught a handful of her hair

171

and yanked, which made her want to snarl into his pink cowrie ear. Turning heftily, she looked anxiously at Brian, who drew her down onto the sofa and began to extricate her hair from Joseph's sticky fist. Fiona had disappeared into the kitchen.

'He's not willing to let you go, darling,' Brian said. 'Darling' roused her fury at him afresh. Kyra stood, and because the two men were sitting, standing conferred on her sudden princess status, and Joseph in an instant grew manageable, a blond baby boy-toy to flirt in her arms in front of the two men. It was as if they were both in love with her. Kyra put her dark forehead against Joseph's very fair one, guessing the picture this would make, and Joseph, more deceived than anyone by this act, opened his eyes absolutely round, and she sensed, within her uneasiness at being here at all, the faint pleasurable dawning of possessiveness, light at first and then mounting almost to a pressure, so that she forgot he was being studied and simply held Joseph, moving her lips in the down of his head, seeing the fair strands wave with her breath. Kyra began that standing-rocking, rolling into her left hip, cocking it, then rolling into the right, a self- and baby-seductive motion she could have carried on for an hour, and right in her arms Joseph gave up his war and fell asleep.

Wine in glasses that had been Fiona's great-grandmother's, and salad, and glossy black mussels in a bowl. 'Careful', said Simon, 'there's a duff one on top,' because you weren't supposed to eat those whose shells were slightly agape. To finish, cheese, crackers and port. When Kyra turned down the Brie, three English voices insisted: She must at least try it. At last Simon cleared the table while Fiona finished her wine and, with apologies for their being a weary old married couple, they went upstairs, leaving their guests the empty table, the wine bottle, and the small fire flickering across the quarry-tile floor. Brian stroked Kyra's hair and said, mock-accusingly, 'You liked them.' In London, when he'd told her how he wanted to spend this last, lied-for weekend, she'd been sure she would be nervous around this couple. 'More inexplicable still,' he said, 'they liked you.'

172

'You can tell, with Simon?'

Brian laughed. 'He is a riddle, when first you meet him.'

'He was so angry about the elms. I got a kind of "our tiny island, your huge imperialist continent" feeling from that.'

'I shouldn't hold it against him. I doubt he meant that.'

'I can't be manipulated out of knowing what I felt,' she said, and she waited for him to ask, 'Felt about?'

Instead he carefully traced her lower lip with one of his knuckles, studying her to see how much she disliked him at this particular moment, and something in her small, set face decided him, because he put his palms up to her cheekbones, asking, 'Make love?' and shook her head for her, *no no no.*

'Back to London would have been a good idea,' she said.

'It wasn't possible,' he said.

Kyra woke startled in Brian's arms, her cheek to his pale English chest to find that Fiona was bringing them tea. Right into the tiny guest bedroom.

Fiona put the tray down, kneeling among their fallen clothes, and aligned the teacup handles before pouring the tea. Her hair, the shade of her son's, swung over her face. Kyra closed her eyes and pretended to be asleep because that was slightly less embarrassing than being awake for this, and Brian said softly, 'Thank you; it looks marvellous,' to Fiona, who left, shutting the door nicely behind her. Brian's bathrobe fell from the door as it closed, and he jumped from the bed, padding across their tumbled things, and put it on before handing Kyra her tea.

She sat up in bed, balancing the cup and saucer on her knees. 'I don't forgive you for the car, you know.' She meant: Even though we made love, it wasn't me forgiving you.

'I think you do,' he said. He meant, she thought: You couldn't have held real resentment through our making love like that.

'That was dangerous of you.'

'Kyra, I've driven that lane for years, in all kinds of weather, I know it.'

'You can't.' Her logic felt like a death ray she was about to aim at him, and since it had usually gone the other way

173

– he annihilating some argument of hers with his formidable reasonableness – she felt pity for him, and an understanding coldness. 'You drove right by the house.'

'That was preoccupation, not a lack of – of familiarity with the place.' He finished most of his tea, and all of his biscuits. She gave him hers. In spite of her, they were almost on the brink of reconciliation. She fished for the last of the anger she still truly felt, and said, 'I don't want to stay.'

'We were supposed to have the weekend. You're not only disappointing me,' he said, 'you'll be disappointing them.'

His playing on a guilt he thought she could be made to feel made things easier. She was glad he'd done it. Whether she was angry at him or not, she should be; she wanted to be, and she wanted to go home.

The little car was purring away to keep up the level of its tepid interior heat, and its windscreen wipers, in quick, clocking strokes, showed the rainy, empty street before Kyra's flat. Brian had already shuttled her things from the boot of the car into the sheltered entryway, and sitting in the car with him was making her nervous, but she held her tongue out of some idea that she owed him a last-minute explanation.

The problem was, he wasn't allowing her to make anything sound final. His patience with her extended itself deftly, counteringly, before any move she thought to make. Often before, this tactic had kept her from making a definitive break with him, but she did not really see how either one of them could fail to accept that now, today, was definitive.

'New York is out,' she said. She meant his visit to New York.

'All right,' he said. 'Why?'

'Because I want my life to be all in one piece,' she said. 'Not part in New York, part here. Can you understand that?'

'I understand that Nicholas is the biggest piece.'

She let him have it that way: Nicholas was a reason he could accept.

'It's just sudden,' he said. 'I thought we'd have the whole weekend. To talk. To wander round. I thought we'd come to some other conclusion.'

'I know you wanted that to happen, but it wouldn't have.'

'You believe that,' he said. 'I think it would have done. And isn't it you who accuses *me* of deliberately ignoring what she feels to be true?'

She looked out at her street. 'All right,' she said. 'You think two more days would have changed things.'

'Yes.'

Midway through the flight, on an aeroplane crowded with sleepers, she rested her chin against Nicholas's head and whispered, 'From now on you have to be good.' She caught in Charlie's reading profile the absent-minded smile with which, though he wasn't truly listening, he monitored the tone of her voice; she counted this as a gift because it was a smile of contented, if uncomprehending, possessiveness. She chose her moment. He turned a page. She said, 'Charlie, I want a second child.'

Without quite taking his eyes from the page, he said, 'I always wondered how that decision got reached.' With his gaze downcast, his upper lip somehow longer than usual, the way it was when he was reading as an editor, he added, 'I mean, to have a second child.'

She said, 'Maybe it's like all other decisions: you only know it's a decision when you find yourself acting on it.'

He answered, 'Maybe,' with a touch of consternation she must have caused, turning to her. He went on, 'What made you decide now?'

She said softly, 'You,' and touching Nicholas's dreaming head, 'and him,' and remembering what other reasons there had been, she was glad that Charlie, his private shaft of reading light, could not see her clearly, seen even briefly, her face would have given her away.

Yet it would come to haunt her how often, in the weeks and months that followed, she dreamed she was back inside the speeding car.

ROSE TREMAIN

The Bellows of the Fire

The two things I cared about most in the world until this morning were my dog, Whisper, and the bungalow under the viaduct.

Whisper is black and white with black blobs round her eyes and my aunt Nellie Miller says she reminds her of a panda.

Whisper is a one-person panda. The one person she loves is me. She waits for me to get home from school with her nose in the letter-box flap.

The viaduct is about a mile from our house. In winter, I can't get to it before dark, but in summer I take Whisper there every day. Trains used to go over it, but the railway line was torn up before I was born, so I've always known it like it is now, which is like a roof garden of weeds.

On rainy days, I hardly stop on the viaduct to look at the bungalow, because down there in the mist and drizzle it looks a bit sorry for itself. But in the sunshine, you see that it isn't sorry for itself at all and that the people who live there give it so much love and attention, you can't imagine they've got time for normal life.

Despite what's happened and what may happen in the future, I still feel that if that bungalow was mine, I'd be one of the happiest people in Devon. The only thing I'd add to the garden would be a wall all round it to keep Whisper in, so that she couldn't roam off to the sea when I wasn't there and drown.

The sea's second on my list of places I like, except that the sea does something to me: it makes me long for things.

I sit down on the beach and stare out at invisible France, and this feeling of longing makes me dreamy as a fish. One of the things I long for is for time to pass.

It was my 14th birthday last week. We don't seem to cele-brate my birthday in our family any more and I think this is because my mother says it only reminds her how fast her life is slipping away.

The only birthday I remember well is when I was six. My mother still considered herself young then and we had a new car and we drove to Dartmoor. The plan was, we were going to make a fire and cook sausages in it. I thought this was the best idea my parents had ever had.

But in the car, on the way to Dartmoor, my brothers bagged all the good jobs in advance. 'Bags collect the wood.' 'Bags light the fire.' 'Bags be in charge of cooking.' Only after a long time did my mother remember me and say, 'What about you, Susan? What job are you going to do, dear?' I didn't know what other jobs there were. 'She can't do anything, she's too little,' said my brothers.

We drove for ages in silence, but then my father had an idea. 'You can be the bellows of the fire, Susie. That means you have to blow on it and your breath keeps it going.'

This didn't seem like a nice job to me. Blowing out cake candles was horrible enough. So I thought, I'm not going to breathe on their fire. I'm going to be absolutely quiet and hardly breathe at all. I'm going to be as silent as a stone.

Since then – or perhaps always, I don't know – I've been very quiet in my family. I notice things about them, like how they all love noise and seem to believe that happiness is *in* noise somewhere and that misery is in silence. They think that I'm a miserable person. What I think is that there are millions of things they'll never understand.

Our house is a modern house in a terrace of identical ones. Noise and mess from these houses spills out all over the puny little gardens and all over the street. If you were a visitor, from France or somewhere and you thought all of Britain was like our terrace, you'd say it was the most hideous country in the world. Getting away from our house is something I think about every day of my life. My brothers are trying to get work in this town. They're trying to get jobs, so they can stay on and live in houses like these ones, or worse. And girls I know at school, that's what they want too. They want to be beauticians or hairdressers in the crappy shopping arcade. If I thought that was going to happen to me, I'd drown myself.

I took Whisper to the sea this evening. I throw things into the waves and she gets them out. She's terrific at this, much better than other dogs we see. Then we lay in the sun while her coat dried and I told her the news that came this morning.

I like secrets. I'm going to keep this one as long as I can. It'll come out eventually, though, and then my mother will say, '*Film*, Susan? What film?' And I will tell her the story.

It's a story about a community. It's set in a town like ours, not far from the coast. It's based on something which actually happened, on a person who actually lived, a girl called Julie who was 14 and a fire raiser. She was a Girl Guide and her Dad worked for the town council. These things were important in the story, because the places where she started the fires were the places where new things were getting done, like a new Leisure Centre and a new Bingo Palace.

Being a Girl Guide, she knew how to start fires without matches or paraffin or anything, so there was never any evidence left lying about, and this is why it took the police ages and ages to track Julie down. And also, they decided all the wrong things to start with. They decided the fires were started by a person from an ethnic minority, who resented the clubs and places where he wasn't welcome, so all they were really looking for were young Indians or West Indian youths. It took them a year before they suspected the daughter of a town councillor, and by that time, seven fires had been raised and the Bingo Palace had burned to the ground. She was caught in the end only because she set fire to the Girl Guide hut.

So, anyway, the thing is, they're making a film about her. The TV company came down here months ago. They arranged auditions in all the schools. All they said was, you had to be about 14 and interested in acting. I haven't been in many school plays. When we did *The Insect Play*, I was only a moth with nothing to say. But I am very interested in acting, because in the last year I've realised that what I do all the time at home is *act*. I act the sort of person my family think I am, with nothing to say for herself and no opinions on anything, when inside me I'm not like that at all, I just don't let my opinions out. I'd rather save my breath. I plan, though. At school with one or two of the teachers and then on my walks to the viaduct and the sea, I plan a proper life.

Not that many people from our school went to the auditions. They thought it was going to be too hard, and anything that seems hard to them, they let it go. But it wasn't difficult. You had five minutes to look at the script and then you had to read out a speech from near the end of the film, where they ask Julie why she started the fires, and she tells them what she feels about communities like this one. She despises them. She thinks they've been hypnotised and corrupted. She thinks greed is all they understand.

It was quite a long, angry speech. When it came to my turn to read I pretended I was saying it all to my brothers and that they didn't understand a word of it and the more confused they looked, the more angrily the words came out. When I ended it, I knew I'd made an impression on the person who had asked me to read it. He was staring at me in amazement and then he said would I be able to come down to London in July for a second audition, which would be in front of a camera.

In the letter that came this morning, they told me that over 200 girls had been seen for the part of Julie and that now there are just six of us. And us six will go to London – not all together, but each of us on a different day – and we will all pretend to be Julie, the arsonist, and other real actors will pretend to be her Mum and Dad and everyone and they'll decide at the end of all that who they're going to cast.

When I think about this now, I realise that although I've longed to get away from this town and longed to be the owner of the bungalow under the viaduct, I've never before longed for anything I could actually have, *now*. Getting away and living in that little house were all way-into-the-future kinds of things, but this, this part in the film is waiting for someone now, this year, now, and I've got a one-in-six chance of getting it and I want it so badly that it's been impossible, since this morning, to concentrate on lessons or eat a school dinner because what I could feel all the time was my heart beating.

The only time I could feel calmer about it was on my walk with Whisper. What I told myself then was that I have had years of 'acting experience' at home and probably those other five girls have had none and what you see and hear of them is all there is. But me, I've been saving my breath. Saving it up for now.

When we walked back, by the time we got to the viaduct, I'd made myself believe – and I'm going to stick to this – that I am definitely the right person for this part and that the TV people are intelligent enough to recognise this and to offer it to me. And when I get it, that's going to be something.

But I still, to be on the safe side, looked for a long time at the bungalow under the viaduct and told myself that if you know how and where to look for them, there are loads of different ways you can be happy. Being an actress is one. Having a nice home in a place where there's silence is another. You just have to work at it all, slowly and carefully, like Dad made that fire catch on Dartmoor in the rain, one stick at a time.

ANGELA HUTH

Irish Coffee

It was Magda McCorn's custom to holiday alone. There was
not much choice in this matter, but even if there had been
she would probably have preferred it that way. She was
well acquainted with the many conveniences of the solitary
holiday and in the bad moments (which she would scarcely
admit to herself, let alone anyone else) remembered to
appreciate them.

Last year Mrs McCorn had gone to Sweden. The year
before, Norway. Now, she was sick of fish and twilight afternoons. A yearning for her late husband's country of birth
had assailed her one April afternoon, admiring the bilious
sweep of King Alfreds in her Cheltenham garden, and within
the week she was booked into a first-class hotel in Parknasilla, Co Kerry.

Mrs McCorn did little at random, and it was only after
thorough research that she chose Parknasilla. As her efficient
eye swept through the brochures, the name came back to
her with a sparkle of nostalgia. It was not her husband,
Patrick (born in the shadow of Croagh Patrick, a charming
Co Mayo man), but Commander Chariot, eligible bachelor
on a spring cruise to the Canaries some years back, who had
commended the place most warmly. They had been drinking
sherry at the ship's bar: the scene was an indelible picture in
Mrs McCorn's mind. Commander Chariot wore his panama,
despite the overcast skies, while Mrs McCorn had undone
the top button of her floral bolero which would indicate, she
felt, a nice distinction between normal reserve and long-
term possibility. But if the subtleties of his companion's
dress made any impression on the Commander, he did not
show it. His bleak grey eyes hovered on the horizon which
tilted a little perilously, for Mrs McCorn's sherry flushed
stomach, through the window behind the bar. He chatted
on in his charming, impervious way, about Parknasilla (often

181

visited in July) and other places he had enjoyed over the years. All the while calling her Mrs McCorn.

But then the Commander was not an easy man to get to know. The very first evening aboard, Mrs McCorn, well-trained antennae highly tuned for potential companions, sensed his reserve. Reserve, however, was a challenge rather than a deterrent to the good widow. On many occasions she had found herself quite exhausted from exercising her sympathy on shy fellow holiday-makers and often, as she wore them down she had recognised the breakthrough, the light, the reward: sometimes it was the offer of a drink or a game of bridge. On other occasions there were confidences, and it was these Mrs McCorn liked best. For in persuading a stranger to 'unwind his soul', as she called it, she felt of some real use, and the satisfaction kindled within her in the bleaker months of the year between holidays.

She had worked very hard upon Commander Chariot, trying to put him at his ease, to draw him from his shell, with the delicate lift of a sympathetic eyebrow, or an almost indistinguishable pat on the arm by her softly padded hand. And indeed, by the last night, amid the coloured rain of paper streamers, she had persuaded him to call her Magda. But she knew he had only complied with her wishes out of politeness. The name had not burst from his lips in a rush of warmth and natural friendliness, and Mrs McCorn had felt some disappointment. It was consolation, of course, to know the other passengers were firmly convinced a ship-board romance had flared between herself and the handsome Commander, and she would not give them any indication that the truth was quite different. She returned to Chel-tenham with the Commander's Suffolk address and the promise to 'drop in for a cup of tea if ever she was that way' (which, one day, she would most certainly arrange to be). The Commander made no such promises in return. In a brief farewell, he mentioned – in a voice that was almost callous, Mrs McCorn thought later, considering all the trouble she had taken – that Gloucestershire was not a part of the country he ever had occasion to visit. They did exchange Christmas cards, and Mrs McCorn rather boldly sent postcards from Norway and Sweden – by great strength

182

of will managing to refrain from saying 'wish you were here'. But her greetings from abroad remained unacknowledged and in terms of *development*, Mrs McCorn was bound to admit, the Commander was a failure.

But hope is often confused with inspiration, and on the journey to Ireland Mrs McCorn could not but help thinking that Fate may have planted the idea of Parknasilla in her head. On the aeroplane she bought herself a small bottle of brandy to quell the feeling of pleasant unease in her stomach: a glittery, excited feeling she had not experienced for many years. But the brandy's medicinal powers had no effect on a state which no medicine could cure, and by the time she set foot on Irish soil Mrs McCorn was as dithery as a girl, her heart a-flutter, her cheeks pink.

She walked into the lobby of the Grand Southern Hotel mid-afternoon of a fine July day, accompanied by her family of matching suitcases. She moved with head held high, bosom thrust forward, knowing that should her entrance cause a rustle of interest, then those who looked her way would take her for *someone*. She had persuaded her cautious hairdresser to be a little more generous with the Honey Glow rinse than usual and by great effort she had lost two pounds through cutting out her elevenses for the last month. She felt she exuded health at this, the beginning of her stay, which is more than can be said of most people, and it was with a symbolic flourish of wellbeing that she signed her name at the reception desk.

Then Magda McCorn, glowing in oatmeal dress with tailored jacket to match and a butterfly brooch (made from a deceased red admiral) sparkling on the lapel, tripped up the wide hotel stairs behind the friendly Irish porter. She admired the high Victorian passages, with their thick and shining white paint, and the ruby carpets. Commander Chariot was a man of taste, of course: he would only recommend the best in hotels. Should he not appear, then at least she would still have benefited from his recommendation and would thank him in a single sentence on the left-hand side of this year's Christmas card.

In her fine room overlooking the bay the porter relieved

himself of all her suitcases and asked if there was anything Mrs McCorn would be requiring? Mrs McCorn paused, smiled, fumbled in her bag for a tip, to give herself time. The only thing in the world she wanted was to know whether Commander Chariot, regular visitor to the Grand Southern, was expected. The porter would surely know. But Mrs McCorn was not a woman to indulge in questions that might bring forth a disappointing answer, and after a short, silent struggle, she decided to shake her head and give the man a pound. He could be useful in the future, should she change her mind.

When the porter had gone Mrs McCorn surveyed what was to be her room for the next two weeks with great satisfaction. Then she went to the window and looked out at the grey waters of the bay. There were palm trees in the hotel garden, reminding her this was a temperate climate, and, more distantly, wooded slopes that went down to the sea. I am going to be happy here, she thought, and sighed at the idea of such a luxury.

Some hours later – having furnished the room with small touches that made it more her own (crochet mat by the bedside table, magazines, travelling clock) – Magda McCorn returned downstairs. It was time to perform her first important task of a holiday: establish her presence. This she did by arming herself with a small glass of sherry, then drifting round the lounges (three of them, with open fires), nodding and smiling with fleeting friendliness in the direction of anyone who caught her glance. The idea was to stamp a firm image in the minds of the other guests: they should instantly understand that here among them was a middle-aged widow of considerable attractions, alone, but in good spirits and certainly not a case for sympathy. While her smile was calculated to indicate enthusiasm, should anyone wish to offer her to join in their conversation or their games, her firm choice of a chair near the window, and apparent engrossment in a book, conveyed also that she was a woman quite happy with her own resources. Her establishing over, her search for the Commander thwarted, Mrs McCorn set about hiding her disappointment in the pages of a light romance.

*

In the magnificent dining room of the Great Southern, Mrs McCorn had a single table by the window. There, she enjoyed a four-course dinner cooked by a French chef, and drank half a bottle of expensive claret. Nearby, at other tables, families with children, and several young married couples, chattered their way through the meal. Mrs McCorn did not envy them: it was her joy silently to watch the sun – which put her in mind of a crab apple rather than a tangerine, but then, as Patrick used to say, she was an original thinker – sink into the silver clouds which, if she half shut her eyes, looked like further promontories stretching from the bay. Her measure of wine finished, Mrs McCorn's thoughts took a philosophical turn: the frequent lack of clarity between boundaries (sea and sky, happiness and melancholy) struck her with some hard-to-articulate significance that sent a shiver up her spine. In fact it had been to Commander Chariot that she had tried to confide some of these private thoughts – as the sun then had been setting over Lanzarote – but he had shown a lack of response that Mrs McCorn had quite understood. It wasn't everybody who was blessed with such insights and after all they were of no practical use, and the Commander was a wholly practical man.

After dinner, to continue the establishing process, Mrs McCorn made her way to the lounge where the life of the hotel seemed to have gathered. There, an elderly lady wrapped in a mohair shawl, the occasional sequin twinkling in its furry wastes, played the piano. The prime of her piano-playing years was evidently over and, accompanied by a dolorous young man on the double bass, their rendering of Fifties tunes lacked spirit. It was as if the music was emerging from under a huge invisible cushion, oppressed. But it was good enough for Mrs McCorn. In her time she had had quite a reputation on the dance floor, although partnering her husband Patrick there had been little opportunity to show off her prowess at the quickstep. It would have been disloyal to complain, and she never did: although for all the happyish years of their marriage Magda McCorn secretly deplored the fact that her husband was such a lout on the dance floor. But her feeling for the dance, as she called it, never left her and here, suddenly, as of old she felt her toes privately wiggling in her patent pumps in time to the steady thump of *Hey There! You With The Stars In Your Eyes*, which, she recalled with a stab of nostalgia, had been played every night on the cruise to the Canaries.

Mrs McCorn chose herself a tactful armchair. That is, it was within reach of a middle-aged Norwegian couple, should they choose to talk to her, yet far enough away to make ignoring her within the bounds of politeness if that was how they felt. She gave them a small signalling smile and was delighted, though not surprised, when immediately they drew their own chairs closer to hers and began to converse in beautiful English.

Due to her holiday in Norway, Mrs McCorn was able to tell them many interesting things about their country, and to captivate their interest for some time. Occasionally she allowed her eyes to glance at the dance floor, where she observed the deplorable sight of unmusical men shunting their wives with not the slightest regard to the beat of the tune. The long-suffering expressions of the wives did not escape her, either. She felt for them, poor dears, and envied them, too. Varicose veins a-twinkle, at least they were on their feet.

Something of her feelings must have registered in Mrs McCorn's face for the Norwegian gentleman was standing, offering her his arm, asking her to dance. Taken so unawares, Mrs McCorn hardly knew whether to accept or refuse. But she saw the friendly smile of the Norwegian wife urging her, urging her, and knowing everything would be above board with the clinical Norwegian eyes of the wife following their every move, Mrs McCorn said yes.

On the small floor they lumbered round in imitation of a foxtrot. Mrs McCorn, confident that the delicate tracery on the back of her own calves was well hidden by her Dusky Sunbeam tights, gave a small shake of her hips to encourage her partner.

'You dance very well,' this spurred him to say, and Mrs McCorn began to enjoy herself. Should Commander Chariot come in now he could not fail to observe the way in which people were drawn to her wherever she went, and surely he would be moved to admiration.

Mrs McCorn's two-week holiday passed happily enough. She befriended many of the guests in the hotel, and every evening found herself in the desirable position of joining in games, drinks and conversations.

Her new acquaintances included many foreigners, and Mrs McCorn was able to let it be known that she was a much travelled woman herself – for all her quiet life in Cheltenham – with a flair for Continental cooking and some talent for making herself understood in French.

The pounds of flesh that Mrs McCorn had so industriously lost before coming to Ireland were soon regained, and indeed, increased, by her indulgence in the delicious food. But Mrs McCorn did not care. Realising that Fate had slipped up and been unkind in its choice of dates, and there was little hope that Commander Chariot would appear, she sought consolation in cooked breakfasts in bed (beautifully arranged trays, flat grey water unblinking in the bay outside her window), hearty lunches and enormous dinners. But as her plumpness did nothing to diminish her evident popularity, so she saw no reason for cutting back until she returned home.

On the last day of her visit Mrs McCorn – who for the most part had spent sedentary days – decided to join a trip to the Skellig Islands. She was all for a little adventure, and felt the breath of sea air would be of benefit to her complexion.

It dawned a disappointingly grey and misty day, a light drizzle swirling so weightless through the air you could not see it fall. Mrs McCorn contemplated abandoning the trip, but then felt that would be faint-hearted, and cheered herself with the thought that Irish weather was wonderfully changeable and at any moment the sun might drive away the cloud.

And indeed, by the time she was seated snugly in her poplin mackintosh and silk scarf on the fishing boat, along with some dozen foreign students, the gloom had begun to lift and the sun threw a first pale rope of light along the horizon. Mrs McCorn did not much like the bucking motion of the boat as it lumbered over the waves, but she sucked on boiled sweets and concentrated on the feeling of enjoying the proximity to so many young foreigners. She felt she was widening her horizons. Perhaps before the day was over she would find the chance to make herself known to them, although for the moment she could detect no openings. They were a dour lot: unwashed, unshaven, dirty clothes and unhealthy skin. But then Mrs McCorn, who was sensitive to the hardships of those less fortunate than herself, supposed they could not afford to live on anything but fish and chips on their camping holiday and was not surprised. She could have wished they had appeared friendlier, more willing to talk: a little conversation would have been agreeable, but perhaps they kept their interest for monuments rather than people.

After an hour of bumping over the grey area, Mrs McCorn and the other sightseers were rewarded by the sight of the first island. It loomed out of the misty sea like a single tooth. The fanciful thought came to Mrs McCorn that the whole Atlantic Ocean was a vast grey tongue, hissying and snapping and drooling with white-spittle foam, armed with its one hideous giant tooth. And the sky was a grim upper lip. The vast and dreadful mouth, made from the elements, only waited for the right time to swallow the boatload with a single flick of its lapping tongue . . . Mrs McCorn sucked harder on her raspberry drop and listened to the wails of 40,000 gannets, who fluttered round their island thickly as snowstorm. Occasionally one of them would swoop quite close to the boat, dismissing the passengers with its beady red eye, then diving into the waves to snap at an invisible fish.

The second island, their destination, came into sight. It was another monster rock, sheer and black and menacing, waves thundering round its base, thousands more gulls screaming their indignation at having to live in such a God forsaken spot. It was here 700 years ago that a small band of monks chose to build a monastery on its summit. To climb hundreds of steps to see the remains of this monastery was the aim of the expedition.

The boat moored at a small concrete pier. Mrs McCorn

looked about her in dismay. She had imagined it would be quite primitive, of course: a simple tea shop, perhaps, and a small cluster of cottages, but there was nothing. The petulant gulls were the only inhabitants, balancing on the edges of precarious rock nests, screaming all the while. Close to, the rock was no less intimidating. While the waves pounded upwards, other water streamed down the jagged sides. Mrs McCorn was afraid.

Gritting her teeth, remembering she was British, she followed the students up the dangerous little flight of steps. There, they abandoned her with peculiar speed, scampering up the steep path with an eagerness Mrs McCorn found herself unable to share. She followed them slowly, tucking the lunchbox the hotel had given her under one arm and telling herself she must persevere, however undesirable the climb to the top may seem.

Although Mrs McCorn's progress was very slow – students from another boat passed her with uncaring speed – she soon became out of breath and listened to her own panting against the dimmer noise of waves thudding far below. She was forced to conclude that she should have to rest before the top, or she might risk a heart attack. And who, then . . . She chose a small, flat rock at the edge of the steps, sat down, and unbuttoned her mackintosh. The hotel had provided her with an unimaginative lunch, but she found comfort in the sliced-bread sandwiches, tomatoes, biscuits and cheese. Her breathing returned to its normal pace, and after a while she began to feel cool again.

When she had finished eating Mrs McCorn looked about for somewhere to bury her empty lunchbox. There were no litter bins, of course, and the sea was much too far away to throw the wretched thing over the edge. Mrs McCorn scrabbled about the springy greenstuff that grew among the rocks, and eventually managed, by squishing it quite small, to hide the box. Plunging her hands into the greenery gave her a nasty turn; its cold sliminess was surprising. But she completed the job to her satisfaction and turned for another look at the bewildering expanse of grey Atlantic before continuing on her way.

The sky was whitish-grey, mists swirled blotchily about the sheer sides of rock. In the distance the sea kept up its perpetual snarl, and the gulls their angry screeching. Mrs McCorn had never felt so alone. To lift her spirits, she thought of the ordinary things of her life: her small, neat garden, her well-vacuumed carpets, her Silver Jubilee tin of biscuits, always full, in the kitchen, her cat Tibby, the absolute regularity of the parish newsletter – things which sometimes she found lacking in excitement, but which now she appreciated with all her heart. Then, for the first time that day, she thought of Commander Chariot.

As she did so, Mrs McCorn stood up. No point in dwelling on the unlikely, she thought, and at that moment a small chink of sun appeared in the sky, making the wet rocks glint. An omen, thought Mrs McCorn, and at once forced herself to abandon the idea as silly. But, trudging slowly up the rough steps once more, she could not cast aside the Commander. He filled her being in an unaccountable way: she longed for his presence. With him, this day on the island would be an agreeable adventure, instead of the frightening experience it was in reality. Alive in her mind, the Commander then spoke to Mrs McCorn in a voice so real he might have been at her side.

'Ruddy masochists, those monks must have been,' he said. ('Ruddy' was his favourite adjective.) And Mrs McCorn smiled.

Somehow, she got to the top. It was no great reward. A cluster of stone-built cells, gently rounded structures, putting Mrs McCorn in mind of a house martin's nest. Very uncomfortable, they must have been, with their slit windows and damp floors, the mists and rain flurrying about outside, and nothing to comfort in the sight of the grim Atlantic sea. Mrs McCorn ventured into one of the cells: it smelt wet and spooky. When her eyes had grown accustomed to the dark she noticed three of the students sitting on the floor in a corner. They passed an evil-smelling cigarette between them, and gave her an unfriendly look. Mrs McCorn hurried out.

She was quite cold by now, and thought with longing of the hotel bath and her warm candlewick dressing gown.

Only a few more hours . . . And it would, of course, be a good story to tell friends at home, not that she'd ever be up to describing the strange sense of horror that the island of rock had given her.

Before returning to the path to descend, Mrs McCorn leant over one of the ruined stone walls and looked down, down at the spumy sea battering for ever the base of the rock, and she listened to the endless evil screeching of the gulls. It was then it came to her why the silly old monks had chosen such a place to live: they had wanted to confront the devil head-on, and this was the perfect spot. There was no grain of comfort, of soft or easy living, on the rock land or the monster sea. The gannets were devils incarnate, the brief flashes of sun a simple mockery. On this island was the rough face of God, quite unlike the God Mrs McCorn was acquainted with in the church at Cheltenham, with its carpeted aisle and central heating. On this island, you'd have to be tougher than she, Mrs McCorn, to go on believing.

Physically weakened by such thoughts, and by the day's exposure to relentless elements, Mrs McCorn put the last of the boiled sweets in her mouth and began her slow descent. She found her knees were shaking and she was sweating quite hard into her poplin mackintosh. But for all the loneliness, she was glad there was no one here to witness the way in which the island had unnerved her – that is, except for Commander Chariot. He would have scoffed at any talk of devils and talked knowledgeably of the breeding habits of gannets, which would have been very cheering. As it was he was far from Ireland, or this place, with no thought of her. Mrs McCorn shuffled down the steps, one foot always forward like a small child, praying for the bottom.

Three hours later, in the safety of her hotel room, Mrs McCorn, although much happier, still found herself somewhat shaken. She packed her suitcase, so as to be ready for her departure in the morning, and it took her twice as long as usual. In her confusion she found she had put soft things at the bottom, and had to start all over again.

As it was her last night, Mrs McCorn felt it unnecessary to make quite the same effort she had made on previous evenings. She wore her plainest dress – very tight, now, across the stomach, and brushed half-heartedly at the mess the Skellig Islands had made of her hair. Somehow, she couldn't face drinks in the lounge – no energy, as yet, to recount the adventures of her day. She waited in her room until 8 o'clock, then went straight into the dining room.

She saw him at once. Commander Chariot was sitting at the window at a single table next to her own. Mrs McCorn's instant thought was to flee – to unpack her turquoise Lurex and change into that, and to have another go at her hair. But she was too late. He had seen her. He smiled, slightly.

Mrs McCorn followed the waiter to her table. She sat down and quickly ordered her dinner and half a bottle of wine. Then she allowed herself to look at the Commander, who was halfway through a plate of elaborate chops.

'Why, hello there, Mrs McCorn,' he said.

'Magda,' she said, with warmth and humour.

'Well I never, running into you here of all places.'

'It was your recommendation, you may remember.'

'Was it? Was it, now? Can't say I do remember. Anyway, here for long, are you?'

Mrs McCorn gave herself time to think before answering. Perhaps it would be possible to make new arrangements after dinner, to extend her stay for a few days. But there was the question of money (she had spent every penny of her holiday budget) and getting another flight back – too many complications.

'I'm leaving tomorrow morning, actually,' she said.

'Well, well, what a ruddy shame.' The Commander hustled a forkful of cauliflower into his mouth, shifting his eyes. His expression just might have been one of relief.

But this paranoid thought was quickly dispelled from Mrs McCorn's mind by the next turn in events: the Commander suggested he might join her at her table as they would only have one evening together.

Scarcely able to believe her good fortune, Mrs McCorn signalled to the waiter. He moved the Commander's place to Mrs McCorn's table, picked up the bottle of wine, and lifted an eyebrow at Mrs McCorn. Her heart thumping, Mrs

McCorn nodded. The waiter poured the Commander a glass of the wine: the Commander did not protest.

Outside, there was an orange sky over the bay, and a small hard gold sun. Mrs McCorn wondered if she should put to the Commander her funny idea about a *crab apple* sun. But she thought better of it, and said instead:

'It's been quite a few years, hasn't it? And you haven't changed at all.'

'No. Well. I manage to keep myself up to scratch.'

Indeed it was true he had not changed: no more grey hairs, no new wrinkles, the same handsome combination of angular bone and fine-drawn skin. Mrs McCorn found herself gazing at him in wonder and in disbelief. The only pity was the cruel timing. But she would not let herself think of the sadness of the morning. There was the whole night-time in which to play her cards with skill.

To keep a clear head, Mrs McCorn let the Commander drink all her wine, and ordered him another bottle. She delighted in his pleasure in the stuff: the way he sipped and swirled and sniffed with such expertise. They talked of their various trips, and the Commander acknowledged her cards from Norway and Sweden.

'I'm so glad they reached you. I thought that maybe – you know the foreign posts.'

'Oh, I *got* them all right. Should have written back, but I'm not much of a dab hand when it comes to letters myself.'

'I know just how you feel.' (This was a permissible lie. Mrs McCorn had no idea, as a great letter and postcard writer herself, how it must feel not to have the constant desire to keep in touch.)

By the end of the dinner, the Commander had a bright pink spot on both cheeks (crab apples again, thought Mrs McCorn). He was friendly and seemingly happy, but not exactly lively. There were long pauses between each comment he made, and the comments themselves were not of the stuff that remains for ever in the romantic memory. Mrs McCorn, remembering his long monologues about fishing and the Navy, wondered if there was anything troubling him. Given the right moment, she felt she should make a gentle enquiry.

'It's really quite lively, here, evenings,' she said. 'Shall we take our coffee in the lounge?'

The Commander followed. She led the way as far as the quiet room where the less lively guests read their papers round the fire, and the Commander indicated they should occupy the free sofa. But Mrs McCorn shook her head determinedly, and kept going till she reached two vacant chairs at the side of the dance floor. With a look of barely concealed pain on his face, as if the pianist's rendering of *Stardust* hurt his ears, the Commander lowered himself into one of the chairs. Mrs McCorn, meantime, was smiling and waving to nearby friends in some triumph: they had all heard about her friendship with the Commander and to be with him on this, her last night, was a proud occasion. So engrossed was she in acknowledging the waves and smiles – yet at the same time not wanting to encourage anyone to draw so near as to deflect the Commander's interest from herself – she was quite unaware that her own choice of seat was disagreeable to her companion. With the elation of a girl she summoned the waiter.

'Let's be devils, shall we, Commander, and treat ourselves to Irish coffees? She knew even as she made the suggestion the treat would be put on her bill, and she did not care. What did strike her, with a brief iciness of heart, was her own word *devil*. She remembered the lugubrious island of evil gulls she had so recently visited. But the dreadful experience seemed wonderfully far away now. She was back where she belonged, in a place of warmth and sentimental tunes and safety.

The Irish coffees came. Mrs McCorn sat back, revelling in the warm froth on her top lip as she sipped the sickly drink, one foot tapping the floor in time to the music. In truth, it would have been hard to have a conversation against the noise of the band, and the Commander, Mrs McCorn observed, was sunk in that pleasurable silence that is permitted between those of understanding. The broad-hipped dancers swayed about, sometimes giving their bodies a small flick to show some vestige of youth still lived under the middle-aged clothes. Mrs McCorn prayed the Commander would ask her to take the floor, to join them, to *show* them, but he did no such thing. And despite her vague sympathies for women's liberation, she felt it would not be quite the thing to make the proposal herself. She waved airily at one of the dancers, disguising her disappointment.

'I've made a lot of friends here,' she said. Commander Chariot nodded.

They had a second Irish coffee. The Commander, making much of his gallantry, paid with a lot of small change out of his pocket. The pianist struck up, by wonderful chance, *Hey There! You With The Stars In Your Eyes*. Mrs McCorn could restrain herself no longer.

'Do you remember, Commander?' she asked. 'Our tune? On the cruise?'

The Commander looked at her blankly.

'Can't say I do. Music's all the same to me. Wouldn't mind if I never heard another note in my life.'

Her ploy having failed, Mrs McCorn ordered two further glasses of Irish coffee – the Commander made no attempt, this time, to pay – so that he should not be aware of the deflation she felt.

They spent the next hour drinking Irish coffee, unspeaking, except to agree to another order. By 11 o'clock, Mrs McCorn felt both reckless and sick. The Commander, she noticed, had a cluster of sweat on both temples, and was flushed. Time, she thought.

'Well, I must be turning in, Commander. Early start tomorrow, for the plane.' Her words sounded thick as whipped cream. The Commander heaved himself up out of the deep chair and helped her to her feet.

'Jolly good idea,' he said.

Very slowly, Mrs McCorn made her way to the stairs. The pillars through which she threaded her way spun like acrobats' plates. When she tried to smile at various friends, her mouth slithered about in an uncontrollable way, and the feeling of nausea increased. But at last she achieved the foot of the stairs, and felt the mahogany banister solid beneath her liquid hand. She paused, turned carefully to the Commander, whose eyes were at half-mast, and whose mouth sagged.

'So it's *au revoir*, but not goodbye, I hope,' she slurred.

'*Au revoir* but not goodbye.' The Commander, too, held on to the banister, his hand only an inch away from Mrs McCorn's. The repetition of her own words gave her courage: in the floundering feather globe of her mind she realised it was her last chance.

'Nightcap, Commander? Just a small one?'

A long pause.

'Why not?' answered the Commander, eventually.

They negotiated the stairs, climbing each one as if it was a separate challenge, drifted like slurry along the moving ruby carpet to Mrs McCorn's room. There, the Commander dropped at once into the velvet armchair. Mrs McCorn hastily hid her peach Dacron nightie – nicely laid out by the maid – under her pillow and telephoned for two more Irish coffees.

In her own room, she felt better. The sickness seemed to have passed, her head rocked rather than span. The coffees came. Once more she and the Commander plunged their mouths into the comforting warm froth of cream, and sipped, without speaking. Mrs McCorn lost all sense of time. Her legs felt as if they were cast in swan's-down, her heart beat wildly as it had in all her imaginings of this climactic scene, and she realised it was no longer possible to continue her life without the Commander.

The next thing she knew she was on the floor by his chair (one shoe had fallen off), her hands running up his trouser legs. A strange moaning came from her lips.

'Commander, Commander! You are my life, I am your slave, your obedient servant, your SLAVE for ever!' She was dimly aware of her crescendoing voice; and the Commander's bony fingers trying to unlatch her hands from his grey flannel thighs.

'Get off, Mrs McCorn. Get *up*, Mrs McCorn. Don't be so ruddy stupid.' Through the humming in Mrs McCorn's ears, he sounded as if he meant to be stern, but the words lacked vigour.

'How can you say such cruel things to one who is your life, to one who has waited for you like Patience on a – ?'

'Get up, I say, Mrs McCorn. You're ruining the creases in my trousers.'

Mrs McCorn rose awkwardly as a zeppelin, poised above him for the merest second, then dropped on to his outspread knees, curling into a foetal position. Before he had time to protest, she had grabbed his jaw in one of her hands, squeezed his mouth into an open hole, and thrust her creamy lips on to his. For a blissful moment she managed to taste *his* Irish coffee and feel the small points of his teeth. She heard him moan, and lashed her tongue more wildly. But then she felt vicious fingers in her ribs, and drew back, crying out with pain.

'Get off, you silly old baggage! What the ruddy hell do you think you're doing?'

'Magda! Call me Magda . . .'

'I'll call the manager. Rape!'

The word struck Mrs McCorn like a blade. She unfurled herself, holding the sore ribs, stood.

'You don't understand, Commander.'

'I understand only too well, Mrs McCorn.'

'You've taken this all wrong.'

'You're blind drunk and disgusting with it.'

Somehow the words had little impact. They fell on Mrs McCorn's ears without wounding, but she felt it was incumbent upon her to protest.

'Commander! That's no way to speak when all I wanted – '

'I'm getting out of here.'

The Commander rose. His mouth was smeared with Mrs McCorn's Amber Fire lipstick, his sparse hair stood up in spikes. She felt sorry for him. He looked wounded, misunderstood. Mrs McCorn would have liked to put a gentle hand on his head, smooth the hair and say, there, it's all right now, it's all over. But she resisted.

The Commander moved to the door. He seemed both cowed and fed up.

'I'm sorry if I caused you any offence, Mrs McCorn,' he

said quietly in his normal voice, 'but a man has to protect himself from attack.'

'Quite.' Mrs McCorn nodded. She would have agreed to anything at that moment.

'And I realise you were overcome. Not yourself.'

'I'm sorry. Quite overcome. Not myself at all.'

'Well, I've survived worse things at sea.'

Gentleman to the last, thought Mrs McCorn.

'And now I must go to bed. You're not the only one with an early start. Tomorrow I'm off to the Skellig Islands.' He reached for the doorknob.

Mrs McCorn had been aware of her spirits rising as the Commander made his apology. All was not lost. But with this fresh, final piece of news they fell to a place so deep within her she had not previously been aware of its existence.

'The Skellig Islands?'

'Always wanted to go there. Well, goodnight.'

He left very quickly. When he had gone Mrs McCorn fell back on to the bed. Too weak to analyse the failure of the evening, too disheartened even to chide herself, she cried for a while, and then fell asleep.

The maid who brought her breakfast found her next morning, still dressed, on top of the bed, one shoe still on, make-up awry. Somehow Mrs McCorn roused herself and overcame this little embarrassment with considerable dignity, and even made a joke about the potent effects of Irish coffee. Then she hastened to repair herself and finish the packing.

Downstairs, she looked about for the Commander, but then she remembered the time of her own departure to the Skelligs yesterday, and realised he would already have gone. When she was given the bill she smiled at the huge sum the Irish coffees had amounted to, and with soft gentle fingers touched the headache that braided her forehead. Various friends from the hotel were there to see her off, and said how much she would be missed. Their declarations touched Mrs McCorn: at least she had made an impression in some quarters.

On the aeroplane over the Irish Sea, she found herself

imagining the Commander retracing her own steps of yesterday, or a million years ago, or whenever the thoroughly nasty day had been. But she imagined *he* was enjoying it, and she admired him for that. He was a man of vision in some ways but, unused to much contact with women, could be sympathised with for not recognising true worth when he saw it. Her conclusions about the Commander thus neatly parcelled in her mind, Mrs McCorn searched in her bag for a boiled sweet. And as the coast of England, dear England, came into sight, she decided that on this year's Christmas card, she would simply add *Did you enjoy the Skelligs?* Thereafter would follow months in which she could look forward to an answer, and life in Cheltenham would continue to be lived in hope.

EVA IBBOTSON

Lady in the Bath

When I was young I didn't think much about Madame Bonnard in the bath. I knew about her because I'd taken art history as part of my degree, but she didn't affect me much. I was too busy falling in love with unsuitable men or trying to convince myself that my job as an assistant in a research library in Battersea was a gateway to Higher Things, if only I could see what they were.

Then came the day when I fetched a 3kg tome on Sedimentary Rock for a young oil geologist called Bill Tranter. Bill had spent the last five years in those hot, sad places where oil unfortunately tends to happen and seemed entirely content with the old-fashioned formula of marriage and a family.

He proposed and I accepted. What's more, I knew exactly what it was I wanted, and meant to share with Bill. For if I hadn't thought much about Madame Bonnard in her bath, I was besotted with the way those turn-of-the-century French painters saw things. I wanted my life to shimmer with light like an Impressionist painting. I wanted there to be terraces and loosely tumbled fruit and hats that dipped and brimmed with flowers. I wanted to have rosy-skinned friends and boating parties and picnics among the poppies. Poplars and sun-drenched gardens and grapes with the bloom on them – all these and more I wanted, and meant to share with Bill.

Which was difficult because the firm that Bill worked for sent him to Newcastle upon Tyne.

I did my best. No one's ratatouille had more garlic in it than mine; I chased cats from my sooty window boxes and coaxed geraniums from the acid soil. I became known for the liquidity of my cheeses. If my friends weren't particularly rosy-skinned, they were voluble and warm, and when my children were born – two sons and then a daughter – I had no need to look to the Côte d'Azur for fulfilment and joy.

Except perhaps in that last hour before one could decently put them to bed, my children brought their own shimmer and sunshine.

Madame Bonnard in her bath floated on unregarded through those years though I had a postcard of her in my desk. I'd had rather too much freedom in my childhood: divorced parents, a rackety progressive school, so the restraints of family life suited me well enough. And Bill was a fantastic provider: he worked like a demon, travelled uncomplainingly to awful places, was regularly promoted. We moved to a house outside the town with a garden; we were happy.

Oh, we had rows, of course: all the monumental, classic rows of marriage. The Sex Row which started with Bill complaining that I was always too tired (which I was from staggering about half the night with armfuls of small children) and modulated, as time passed, into me complaining that *he* was always too tired (which he was from having just flown in from Kuwait or Bahrain). We had the Money Row which was about me wanting something frivolous *now* (a holiday, a hi-fi) and him wanting something sensible *then* (life insurance, a nest egg). And we had the row about his mother.

But we grew out of them gradually, as people do when they discover that being right isn't particularly interesting or useful. Bill wasn't artistic or romantic but he was steadily and unfashionably *good*. As for our children – well, there were never children like ours.

Then came the day when our daughter, the youngest of the three, went off to training college. That night, in a childless house, I looked into the mirror. And Madame Bonnard shot into the forefront of my mind and stayed there.

Madame Bonnard's name was Marthe. Pierre Bonnard – an absolutely marvellous Post-Impressionist painter – met her when she was 16 years old, making funeral wreaths in Paris. He used her as a model for a series of paintings that are staggering in their tender portrayal of physical passion, and took her to live with him. Thirty years later, he married her, was faithful to her – and never got over her death.

All right – but what about her *in the bath*?

Marthe was very keen on personal hygiene. Perhaps it was all those funeral wreaths when she was young. She spent hours in a tub carried to her bedroom, dribbling water from a sponge on to her breasts or scrubbing her back. And while she washed, he painted her.

Then came the day when they could afford a proper bathroom. I couldn't find much about that in the books, but I wouldn't be surprised if it wasn't one of the most important days in her life – a sort of piscine bar mitzvah, a wedding day . . . Now she could float stretched out, could rest the soap on her stomach, add hot water with her toe. And still her husband painted her. *Nude in Blue, Nude in Yellow* and always and again, *Nude in the Bath*.

Well, what's so odd about that, you may ask? A great many women (and I'm one of them) use the bathroom as womb and study, as sanctuary and solace. So what more natural than that a great painter of the nude should make a series of portraits of his wife in her bath? But Bonnard's paintings are quite something. They span the whole of Marthe's life and (we come now to the point, ladies and gentlemen) in them *she never gets any older*. At 20, she stands by the window, the tub beside her, a pensive, self-absorbed figure covered in light. And 40 years later, she floats in the water, an ever-young water sprite in an effulgence of rose and madder and sun-stippled green.

In the last of these paintings she is *65 years old* (the age, who knows, of Rembrandt's mother, of Whistler's mother – of anybody's mother) but to Bonnard she is as young as on the day they met.

And this, I thought, was love.

Was it surprising, then, that as I stood staring into the mirror I should think of Madame Bonnard with an intense and burning envy? For what I saw was a woman who had become middle-aged and would soon be old. My hair was not amusingly streaked with silver; it was going grey. The bags under my eyes, which I'd thought would vanish with a good night's sleep, were here to stay – and as I rubbed moisturiser into my forehead, it was my mother's hands I saw.

Well, you will say, so what? What of your husband? Surely he too was marked by time? Not so. Bill was two years older than me but he was very fit and very tanned and very, very busy. Bill jogged – at least he did till he snapped his Achilles tendon; he ate platefuls of bran and followed attentively the cancer-of-the-week articles in the Sunday papers. I did not think that he saw me as forever youthful. In those weeks after the children left, I did not think that he saw me at all – and I was scared.

I began to bring up the subject of Madame Bonnard in her bath among my friends as they drank coffee in my kitchen and they agreed with me. To be seen as eternally youthful was most truly to be seen with the eye of love.

'Not that Karl would know what I was talking about,' sighed Deborah.

Her husband was so obsessed by the coming nuclear holocaust that he regarded all personal relationships as futile, but it was odd how often the women with whom he posted CND leaflets through letter boxes were both pretty and young.

'It's all those hormones draining away,' I said bitterly. 'All those lovely oestrogens one needs so much.'

Janey, the most beautiful and elegant of my friends, was so sent by my descriptions of Madame Bonnard's Good Life in her blue-shuttered villa at Le Cannet that she went off to the library to research the French Impressionists.

'Mind you, being a water lily would be the best bet,' she said. 'Better than Madame Bonnard, even. No one ever gets tired of *them*.' And she opened a book of Monet reproductions so that we could pore over the lotus-like flowers floating in the drowned universe of the painter's garden pool. Pages and pages of them: Monet's obsession till the day of his death. 'No beastly diets or boring exercises if you're a water lily,' said Janey.

But we weren't water lilies; we were ageing women dreading the loss of love.

Unwisely – I see it now – I brought up the subject of

Madame Bonnard with my husband Bill. What I planned was a gentle, after-dinner conversation in which I'd tell him a bit about the Bonnard's estimable domestic life, hint at my fears, allow him to console me. 'I may not be a great painter, Laurie,' he would say, 'but to me you look just the same as you did when I first saw you standing on the library steps with the sunlight in your hair.'

After which we'd go upstairs and make some radiant, Post-Impressionist love.

It didn't, however, work out like that. Baked beans were making a come-back that spring as the Healthy Thing to Eat. (Later they slipped because of suspected food colouring in one of the brands.) Oily fish was in, too. Perhaps if we hadn't discussed Madame Bonnard among the debris of grilled mackerel and beans we'd have got on better. I produced my postcard of the floating Marthe at which Bill, after a longing look at his briefcase, peered with a furrowed brow.

'Look,' I said. 'She was 65 when that was painted and he sees her as a beautiful young girl.'

'More fool he,' said my husband, and as I retired, hurt, to bed he pulled out the documents he always brought home these days and started to work.

Three days later, he left for Lagos and no love – Post-Impressionist or otherwise – had been made.

My friends consoled me. They didn't say so, but I knew they suspected that Bill was turning his attentions elsewhere. He stayed at the factory later and later, set off earlier and earlier, played more and more squash – and he would never tell me, now, when to expect him from his trips abroad.

'We oughtn't to mind so much about love,' said Deb. 'All those feminists working so hard for us and we're just as drippy as our mothers.'

This reminded me of my mother who had recommended me, telephonically, to take a lover.

'Where do you take them *from*?' asked Janey gloomily – and indeed this is always the problem.

In the end we took not lovers but evening classes. I signed

on for Industrial Archeology which had vacancies, and Janey decided on Music Appreciation.

There are good reasons for taking classes in Industrial Archeology – the best being, probably, an interest in the subject. As a cure for a possibly lost love and the failure to be admired in the bath until the end of time the subject does not rate very high. Nor did Janey do any better with Music Appreciation.

'Do you realise, Laurie, you could fly from London to Amsterdam between the beginning of a Bruckner Symphony and the end?' she said, '*Easily*, you could.'

At the end of the summer, Deb's Karl finally took himself off with an 18-year-old redhead who understood about Nuclear Winter. Janey, who brought me the news, stood shaking with rage in my kitchen.

'When I think of what Deb's done for him all those years. Buying that miserable recycled loo paper and saving the skunks or the minks or whatever . . . Not to mention those shrivelled free-range tangerines grown by unoppressed Tunisians.'

And when Deb crept into my kitchen, swollen with weeping and blaming herself for being unattractive and overweight, I too could have murdered Karl.

Then, two months later, it was my turn.

I came in late one evening. The study door was open and Bill was on the phone. He had his back to me but the intensity, the despair in his voice almost winded me.

'I *can't*,' he was saying, 'Oh, God, I really can't do without you, Ingrid. There has to be something we can do.'

I walked on into the kitchen, managed to greet Bill normally, made a cup of tea. But I knew now why I'd been so frightened. I'd sensed Bill's desperation, the strain he was under. I didn't even feel bitter. Easy enough to imagine Ingrid: fair, curly-haired, a touch of Swedish blood, perhaps. And young, young, young . . .

I decided to say nothing. Years ago I'd fallen in love rather badly with my sons' music teacher. He was married too and it was heady and guilty and it passed. I think Bill knew at the time and I respected and admired him for keeping silence and letting me work it through.

But oh, God the wretchedness of the next few weeks! I wouldn't have believed anything could hurt so much. When I said Bill was good, I didn't mean stodgy and dull. I meant selfless and patient and concerned . . . and funny, too. Bill's left eyebrow had a kink in the middle; he knew everything there was to know about Marco Polo and I didn't love him as much as I had when we were first married, I loved him a great deal more.

I've always been struck by that bit in the Bible where it says: 'For he that hath, to him shall be given and he that hath not from him shall be taken even that which he hath.' Unpleasantly struck. Now, when I so desperately needed comfort, the beauties of nature were not available to me. I pounded sightlessly along Northumberland's glorious, empty beaches; leant against ancient oak trees which might have been pit props for all I gleaned from them.

And, hating myself, I began to behave like a jealous wife in a play, searching Bill's pockets, looking in drawers . . .

What I found was an entry in Bill's diary for Friday the 28th – a day on which he was absent in London.

'Flowers for Ingrid' it said – and then a pencilled address in a suburb on the other side of town.

And on Friday afternoon I was there, sitting in my car opposite No 15, North Terrace.

Not a typical love nest. A neat house in a modest row; there was a bird table in the garden; a blue-painted door.

It wasn't chance that I was there when the flowers came. I'd rung Interflora to ask when they delivered in Brenton. I saw the van draw up, the man get out and carry to the door of No 15 not a bunch of flowers but a basket . . . A great basket filled with dark red roses. A film star basket, an offering that belonged to the world of the Ritz, of those Hollywood movies of the Forties.

He rang the bell, the door was opened by a girl – and that was that.

She was the sweetest, prettiest thing you could imagine. Not in my most fevered Impressionist dreams could I have conjured up a more delectable creature. Her rich, blonde hair, shining with cleanliness, was loose down her back; her rosy cheeks caught the light in the way Renoir loved; she had a wide and generous mouth.

I got out of the car, pretending to look for something in the boot, and saw the way she smiled at the delivery man, pleased but a little puzzled. Then she picked up the card and read it and her face was transformed. 'Oh, how *lovely*!' she said with just a trace of a Geordie lilt in her voice – and she took the basket and buried her face in the roses, sniffing like a visionary, like an ecstatic puppy . . .

I went home.

Anguish is an odd thing. Bill had to go abroad again the following week. Alone in the house, I found myself sitting very still with my hands folded across my chest as if I could stop my internal organs – not my heart; less romantic-sounding and larger organs – from spilling out on to the ground. Then sometimes I would rush through the streets walking faster and faster as though I could leave it behind, the grinning gargoyle of my despair. Mostly, I marvelled that when I had had the incredible and undeserved benison of Bill's love, I'd spent so much time grumbling and fussing and arguing. How was it that I hadn't lived in a permanent state of bliss?

I became obsessed by the idea of behaving well.

'I must behave *well*,' I said to my friends who made everything so much worse by their unstinting sympathy.

I wrote away for refresher courses in librarianship so that I could support myself. I planned how to tell the children without once seeming to criticise Bill . . .

Curiously, I was in the bath when Bill came back from Aden.

'Good Lord,' he said, coming in to sit on the side of the tub and looking surprised because it was 10 o'clock on a Sunday morning and I was usually an early riser. 'You're worse than that Madame Bonnard of yours! How about getting out and grilling me a bit of bacon while I get out of these clothes?'

A mistake. Definitely a mistake on Bill's part to have mentioned that particular lady. Reaching for a towel, I began to yell.

'All right, you can sneer at the Bonnards, but they were

207

happy. He loved her. He didn't crucify her because she was growing old. He didn't turn away because she had a few wrinkles and her hair was going grey. He saw her as always young and . . .'

'Laurie, if you mention that creep to me again, you'll be sorry. If he wanted to live in cloud cuckoo land that's his business. Art is about lies.'

'It is *not*! How dare you say that!'

Bill sighed. He looked grey and exhausted. 'All right, then; it's about dreams. It's about visions. It's about how life might be, not how it is.'

'No, it's not about how life is – but perhaps that's a pity. Perhaps women shouldn't have to be afraid all the time about how they look.'

'I'm dead sure they shouldn't,' said Bill. 'And those with any sense aren't. They've got better things to worry about. Real things.'

'Oh yes? And what about you? If it's silly to worry about getting old, what's with all the jogging and squash and trying to look like an advertisement for Y-fronts? At least I'm not afraid to eat an egg!'

Bill had slumped down on the stool and when he spoke it was with resigned weariness like someone speaking to a recalcitrant child.

'If I go on about being fit it's because my job doesn't just depend on being fit but on being seen to be fit. Every day there's some new nonsense I can't be doing with. They've installed a computer in "Reference" instead of old Biggers who knew what you wanted as soon as you opened your mouth. Last week they sacked Johnston, at 52. Early retirement, they called it. He's got three children still at school. Clarke had a heart attack, sitting in the car park outside the factory with his redundancy slip in his hand and it was me they sent to tell the widow. Yesterday we turned back three times after take-off because they said there was a bomb on board. I don't tell you because there's no point in both of us being worried – but what do you suppose would happen to you if they turfed me out? The dole wouldn't keep you in *garlic*! And you moan on about that godforsaken woman in her bath! To be allowed to be the age one is without fear or

208

favour seems to me the biggest blessing one could hope for. I *don't* see you as 20. I never will and I don't want to. I see you as *you*.'

Hope licked its way along my veins; sustained me as I put on some clothes and went down to the kitchen to get some food. And died as I once more faced the truth.

'It's nice of you to pretend it's that,' I said. 'But I know the real reason. I know . . . about Ingrid.'

'What?'

'I heard you say that you . . . couldn't do without her.' Tears now, unstoppable ones, but no pity from my husband.

'Yes,' he said, looking at me with contempt. 'I did say it. And I meant it.'

He pushed his plate away, got up, and reached for an exotically wrapped parcel he'd left on the dresser. 'Get your coat,' said Bill.

'Where are we going?'

'To see Ingrid. No point in putting things off.'

By the time we stopped outside No 15 I was shivering so much I could hardly get out of the car, but Bill had no mercy. He strode up the path and rang the bell – and I followed.

She came to the door and she was prettier than ever in her Sunday morning *déshabille*: a sprigged dressing gown, bare feet. Sleepy too and just a little surprised.

'Good morning, Katy. I don't think you've met my wife? Is your mother in?'

'Yes, she is, Mr Tranter. I'll get her.' She led us into the sitting room, made us sit down. 'I'll get some coffee,' she said – and we heard her outside, calling 'Mum?'.

The woman who came into the room was grey-haired and plump and managed to conceal rather better than her daughter her surprise at this unexpected and awkwardly timed visit.

Bill got to his feet. 'My wife wanted to say how sorry she was about your leaving, Ingrid, and to bring you a small gift.' He motioned to the chair and I managed to pick up the parcel and hand it to Ingrid Vance.

Whom I knew, actually . . . Whom I had met several times

at office parties and spoken to often enough though Bill had not then used her Christian name. And who, I now gathered, had been sacked along with Dolly and Janet and been replaced by a large computerised printer in the basement to which Bill's letters were dispatched by chute and returned three days later . . . sometimes. If the kids who typed them in could read his handwriting and if the machine didn't take a sudden shine to one of Bill's brighter paragraphs and store it implacably somewhere in its bowels. It was a good printer and the vending machine which dispensed various unrecognisable fluids (when it was working, when Bill had 20 pence about his person) was a good vending machine and everyone understood that Ferguson & Plissfold had to move forward into the next century. Only the printer did not make a cup of Bovril when Bill had to miss his lunch or bring in the first daffodils or remember 20 years of office life.

And Mrs Vance's daughter was still at college.

'That's the only thing that worries me,' said Mrs Vance now, 'the way that Katy's carrying on.'

Katy came in then with the coffee and Bill faced her sternly, every inch her mother's boss. 'What's all this about you wanting to give up your last year at college?' he asked, frowning.

She flushed. 'It's only just to help out now that Mum's lost her job. Dad can't work, you know; not since his accident. A friend of mine's starting a dress shop and she said she'd take me on.'

'If you really want to make things hard for your mother,' said Bill, 'that's what you'll do. Throw up everything she's wanted for you.'

And Ingrid Vance threw him a glance of the deepest gratitude.

Which left the opening of the parcel, and Ingrid and I giving identical gasps as we saw the exquisitely embroidered Persian shawl.

'Oh, you shouldn't, Mrs Tranter. Not when the department's already sent such lovely roses!'

'That was your birthday present,' said Bill as we drove away, 'and it serves you right!'

When we got home I didn't apologise. I was too ashamed of my shoddiness, my self-absorption, to find the right words. Instead I went upstairs and fetched the postcard, and together we burnt her, poor Marthe Bonnard with her shimmering and ever-youthful limbs. And the love we made that night was not even remotely Post-Impressionist, but it was ours.

Life was good to me and my friends. Janey's husband was as steadfast as mine and Deb shacked up with a master baker who was a hundred times nicer than the sanctimonious Karl. I never again mentioned Madame Bonnard in her bath to Bill, but I confess that for Janey and Deb and me she went on floating over the roofs of our city: an ethereal, aquatic and much-envied wraith, for we did mind – yes, we did still mind – no longer being young.

Then one day she stopped floating and it happened like this.

Two years after I made such a fool of myself over Ingrid Vance, Bill took me to the South of France. He had a conference in Nice and I used my spare time to go on excursions round the countryside. And inevitably one of these was to Le Cannet to seek out the Bonnards' house.

I found it too. Blue shutters; a secret garden; the view he'd so loved to paint. Then, content and full of uplift, I went to a café and bought myself a pastis.

A very old man in a black beret sat at the next table. He asked what had brought me to the village and in my incorrect but enthusiastic French, I told him.

'Ah, yes,' he said, 'the Bonnards. My mother knew them. Her sister worked there for a time as *bonne*. A difficult job. She didn't stay'

'Why not?' I was desperately excited. This man's aunt might actually have run the immortal bath!

The old man shrugged. 'He was all right. A nice gentleman. But Madame . . . what a shrew! What a vixen! Such a temper . . . always scolding!'

'Really? But how could that be? When he painted her so beautifully? Those lovely pictures of her in the bath.'

'Exactly so,' said the old man, sipping his drink. 'Always

211

the same, year in, year out. My aunt heard her once, screaming at him. "Grow up, you old fool," she said to her husband. "Grow up!" Well, you can imagine . . . to deprive a woman of her dignity like that. At 60 to paint her like a silly little girl! Not that it was necessary for her to shout.' He broke off. 'I amuse you, Madame?'

I stopped giggling, apologised . . . asked if he would join me in another drink.

When the waiter came with two more pastis, I lifted my glass.

'To Art,' I said grandly.

The old man shook his head and put up a gnarled, brown-flecked and exceedingly beautiful hand.

'No, Madame,' he said. 'To Life!'

And we drank.

ANNE TYLER

Uncle Ahmad

He hadn't been in the United States an hour when he telephoned. 'I have a collect call for anyone,' the operator said, 'from Mr Ahmad Ardavi. Will you accept – '

'Hello? Hello?' Uncle Ahmad shouted. 'This is Ahmad! Ahmad is here!'

Elizabeth was the one who answered, and she wanted to get her husband but Uncle Ahmad didn't give her a chance. 'I'm coming!' he shouted. 'I've landed from Iran! I'm taking the train to Baltimore! Hassan is going to meet me?'

'Well, yes, surely, but don't you want to – '

'The 10pm train. Tell Hassan, Ahmad is on his way. So long! Bye bye!'

He hung up. There was a silence.

'Will you accept the charges?' the operator asked.

He was a black sheep – the gayest, the loudest, the wickedest, a frequenter of wrestling gyms and gambling joints, a heavy drinker in a Muslim family, an opium smoker, twice divorced, the kind of man who makes his friends' wives tighten their lips and shake their heads. Elizabeth had never met him but she felt she knew him well; she'd heard him discussed so often among visiting aunts and nieces. All the women in the family disapproved of him.

The men in the family adored him.

Her husband stood in front of the bedroom mirror and buttoned his shaggy sweater. Usually he never looked in the mirror. Even shaving, his eyes were focused on the reflection of the razor. But for Uncle Ahmad's sake he stood in front of the mirror with a sober, considering gaze, as if summing himself up. Elizabeth watched at his right, her thumbs hooked through the belt loops of her jeans. She wouldn't be meeting the train because it was after the children's bedtime. And anyway, she supposed that Hassan and his uncle would like a little time on their own. She saw herself as a blurry

213

blond liquid in the glass, hovering by Hassan's darker, more solid substance. He combed his hair, and smoothed his moustache with one cupped hand. 'I hope you won't mind his manners,' he said.

'Manners?'

'In good moods he eats rice with his fingers, sitting cross-legged on the floor.'

'The children will love it,' she said.

He didn't smile. He gathered objects from the bureau – billfold, keys, coins – and distributed them among his pockets. 'Back home,' he said, frowning at a ticket stub, 'the women keep telling him to use a spoon, lower his voice, show some consideration. They say he upsets their households.'

'I won't mind,' she told him.

'Once he brought Aunt Eshi a take-home pizza during Ramadan.'

'I don't even celebrate Ramadan.'

'She said that she was fasting so he sat down and ate it himself.'

'Believe me,' Elizabeth said, 'everything will go all right.'

'A *sausage* pizza,' said Hassan. He laughed. His face grew diamond-shaped, lighter, happier. For a moment, she could see how he must have looked as a child.

Uncle Ahmad turned out to be 7ft tall, lean, massively built, yellow as an onion. He had a handsome, leathery face and iron-grey sideburns; on top, he was perfectly bald. In fact, he reminded Elizabeth of a suntanned Mr Clean. He even stood like Mr Clean, when she opened the door to him – arms folded across his chest, feet wide apart between stacks of luggage. At first he just smiled down at her, with his golden, curiously Tartar eyes veiled and slitted; then he bellowed 'Elizabeth!' and flung out his arms and hugged her. He smelled of some cologne that was spicy and sharp; it prickled her nose like a sneeze. His chest was hard as bricks. She felt encased, protected. But he was not, after all, 7ft tall. It was only his way of standing, maybe, or his crashing voice or his assurance – his *presence*. She could easily look over his shoulder and see, behind him, Hassan coming up the sidewalk with three more pieces of luggage.

Once inside the house, Uncle Ahmad walked through the living room, rubbing his hands together and looking all around him. It was early spring, and cool; Elizabeth had lit a fire in the fireplace. 'Nice, very nice,' said Uncle Ahmad. 'How much this house costs? I'll take three.' He laughed, and then frowned at Elizabeth. 'Where are the children?' he asked.

'They've gone to bed.'

'What! Now?' He shot back a cuff (all his gestures were a mile wide) and looked at a huge gold watch. '10.30!' he said. 'Why you didn't let them wait for Uncle Ahmad?'

Elizabeth felt she'd already failed his test; she'd proved as fussy as any other woman. 'Well,' she said, 'maybe I could see if they're . . .'

But he said, 'In the morning, then,' and patted her shoulder. 'Wait! I'm forgetting.' He sprang to his biggest suitcase, opened it, and pulled out tissue-wrapped boxes. 'See what I brought you,' he told her. 'Pistachios, baklava . . .' He piled them in her arms. The spicy smell of his cologne advanced and retreated, advanced and retreated. He gave Hassan a blue silk tie. Then he took Hassan's head in his hands and kissed him on both cheeks. 'Ah, Hassan,' he said. 'I'm a lonely man. It's good to see you.' And he turned to Elizabeth and said, 'At home, I've lost all my friends. No one likes me.'

'Oh, surely that can't be true,' said Elizabeth.

He looked interested. 'Why not?' he asked her.

'Well, I mean . . .'

'I'm too much for them, I'm too much trouble. My friends say they want a rest. They say, "Go on, Ahmad, I'm tired, I don't want to be bothered any more. I want to sit here with my wife," they say. Now I have no one left. Could you bring me a Scotch, please.'

'Of course,' Elizabeth said.

She went out to the kitchen and poured a large tumbler, remembering that he supposedly drank Scotch by the quart. When she returned, he and Hassan were settled on the rug in front of the fire. Uncle Ahmad had his shoes and socks off, his shirt half unbuttoned, and his trousers rolled up to the knees. His feet were very long and highly arched; his

215

calves were ropy, muscular. He appeared to take up half the living room. 'Ah!' he cried when he saw her, and he reached for her hand and guided her down beside him. Then he drank the Scotch to the bottom, meanwhile encircling her with one arm. 'Excellent,' he said when he'd finished. He smiled at her, showing two rows of tobacco-stained, crumpled-looking teeth. 'I'll have more in a minute, not just yet,' he said. 'It's bad to drink too much if you plan to smoke.'

Elizabeth finally thought of the phrase to describe him: he was 'larger than life'. She rested, pleased, within the angle of his arm. She felt the house had grown fuller, somehow; her husband had a tousled, expansive look, and the living room was a tumult of tissue paper and open suitcases. Uncle Ahmad spoke at length, sometimes in Persian so she had to concentrate on his words. He was sick to death of Iran, he said. He'd had enough of those meagre little people at home. He was only here now for a month, it was all the time he could spare from the oil fields, but next spring when he turned 50 he was taking an early retirement, gathering all his money and getting out. Maybe he would live in America. 'Why not?' he said in English. 'I'm a millionaire several times over. And the language is no problem; at work I deal with Americans every day. I'll come and live in Baltimore near you, Hassan, near you, Elizabeth — my two favourite nephews.'

'We'd love it,' they said.

Then he took out his billfold, and found the black wafer of opium that he'd boiled down at home for his journey. He and Hassan drew close together to smoke a chunk of it in a tobacco pipe lined with Reynolds wrap. Their faces turned calm and beautiful; their skin took on a lemony glow. And even Elizabeth, who never smoked anything, began to feel gently bemused by the charred-roses smell of the haze that drifted over the living room.

The children loved him. He took Jenny for rides on his shoulders; for Hilary, he opened Coke bottles with his teeth. He made peculiar cork-popping sounds and then looked all around the room: 'Where it comes from? Eh? Where it comes from?' He shuffled cards to form bridges and twists and flying arcs, and then collapsed them into a deck again and threw back his head and laughed. His laugh could jar the house to its bones. The chains and medals on his grey-frizzed chest would jingle; his eyes would tilt and narrow. Jenny and Hilary were spellbound. They never thought he was funny, although he meant to be. They seemed to believe that he was some sort of genie. In the mornings their first question was, 'Is Uncle Ahmad still here?' – as if he might have vanished in the night. They asked the same thing when they came home from school; they raced through the house to find him, 'Where'd he go? Is he here?'

'*Boo!*' he would say, popping out, and immediately they took on the expectant, trustful look of children at a magic show, waiting to be dazzled.

But when he tired of playing he grew abrupt; he almost scared them. 'Enough,' he would say. He would drop to a chair, languidly raising one huge hand. 'Enough, go away.' And he would rest there, mournful and sulky-looking, with the corners of his mouth pulled down by two deep lines. 'Ah, ah,' he would tell the rug. He would pull out a Camel, light it with his slim gold lighter, hold it absently in those nicotine-stained fingers so burdened with massive gold-and-turquoise rings. Or he would take his amber prayer beads from his pocket and click them up and down – not idly, as other men did, but with a kind of knowing, scornful competence, two beads by two beads, and a careless flick when he reached the silk tassel at the end and started over, never once actually looking at the beads or appearing to realise that he held them. 'Ah, Lizzie,' he would say, stretching out his feet, 'I'm an old man, old man . . .'

He called her Lizzie. She had never been called Lizzie in her life, never would have allowed it, but from Uncle Ahmad it seemed an honour. Everything he did was touched with some kind of exotic yellow light. Yellow, in fact was his colour – the colour of his skin, his eyes, his teeth, his buffed nails, his prayer beads, and his jewellery. Even his shirts were yellowish, most of them: ivory silk, no doubt expensive, blousing at the cuffs and waist and open nearly to his navel. He could have been a pirate or a riverboat gambler – any-thing at all. Elizabeth's friend Ada, coming to return a casserole, gaped at him once from the doorway and later asked, in a whisper, 'Why is Yul Brynner sitting in your living room?'

And Elizabeth, newly rich, spread her hands and smiled and said, 'Don't ask *me*; I guess he just likes it here.'

He told Hassan that he felt life had cheated him. 'What does it amount to?' he asked. (He said this in Persian, over the pipe, long after Elizabeth was in bed. Later Hassan would repeat it all to her, frowning, as if studying each word a second time before he passed it on.)

'What have I got out of it?' Uncle Ahmad asked. 'I've had a hard lot, my childhood was wretched. You never knew your grandfather but he was a selfish, stingy man. All his wealth went for his own pleasures. He kept wives, women, he travelled through Europe picking up the latest ideas . . . but we were never even given proper schooling. He wore an enormous coat made of some kind of rare white fur from Russia but we children were in rags. I tell you, Hassan, our family has always lived a life without supports. We don't sustain each other, we look only inward, we're all depressives . . . oh, if we could be the way I dream of! Upholding each other, giving courage, love, strength. But these Ardavis, it takes all the courage they have just to get through the day.

'Your father had it better; he was the oldest, your grand-father's favourite. Not that he was any happier, poor creature. But me, I was always in disgrace. I don't know why. I'm a likable person, am I not? But he couldn't stand the sight of me. So I said, "Ah well, wait and see, when I grow up I'll be rich, somehow. I won't want for anything, I won't have to ask a thing from anyone." And that's what happened. I've done well, Hassan. And I did it on my own. I have drawers full of shirts I've never even worn yet. My shoes are made in Rome; my suits in London. Sometimes I buy an armload of jewellery and travel through Tehran making peace with the aunts. You think they don't give in then? They're glad of me, underneath. They have some need of me.

'But money, what is money? My first wife, Maryam . . . well, she was a youthful mistake, never mind. But then Pari!

I bought her everything, gave her all she asked, new dresses every day of the year. When her clothes were ready to be laundered, she threw them out and bought new. But still, she wasn't satisfied. I couldn't so much as clean my teeth at the table; she found it offensive. "*I* paid for this table," I told her. "I paid for the meat that is stuck in my teeth, paid for the toothpick too. Do I have a right to clean my teeth, or not?" A woman like that takes the fun out of life, Hassan-jun.

'She turned mean and niggling, small-minded as all women do, in the end. Forever complaining, finding fault. She said I was too noisy, too uncouth, too self-centred. Then she started plucking her eyebrows and they got that puffy look. I said, "Enough! I've had enough of women!" Oh, the odd one here and there, but still . . . and she's already ruined my son. Remember Jamal? He's a weakling, a girl, his mother wouldn't even let me teach him to wrestle. "Oh no, you'll hurt him, you're so rough, you think nothing of pushing people around . . ." Now he works in the Bank Melli, some sissy job, I never even see him. Is this what it amounts to? Is this all I'm getting?

'Ah, baba,' he said, tugging his ear, 'sometimes it seems to me that I've worn out my life before I've come to the end of it.'

And he laughed, but then shook his head, and pulled down the corners of his mouth as he held a match to his pipe.

His cologne took over the house. The children carried it to school on their clothes, and their friends asked what that smell was. His clutter of cast-off shoes, crumpled cigarette packs, and paisley silk handkerchiefs mounted in every room. His laundry (ribbed underwear of navy and brown and other surprising colours) tinted everyone else's. He enveloped them all.

In the mornings he rose late, after Hassan and the children were gone, and he would lope down barefoot to the kitchen and make tea on the gas range. A gigantic splash of flame nearly obscured the little kettle. (Everything he did was so extravagant.) When Elizabeth came in he said, 'Lizzie,' and absently draped an arm across her shoulders.

He wasn't himself till he'd had his tea – two or three glasses, which he drank while sucking a sugar cube behind his upper front teeth. Then gradually his energy collected and rose, at least enough for him to say, 'Well! What we are planning to do today?'

Like a child, he had to be kept amused. And his favourite amusement was shopping. His life really began at 10am when the stores opened.

At Hutzler's, or Stewart's, or Towson Plaza, he raced down the aisles collecting shirts and ties. He bought $57 worth of men's toiletries. He barely stood still, rumbling with impatience, while a nervous salesman measured him for a suit. Then he was off again, tearing through the sweater department, choosing cardigans and turtlenecks, and after that a new set of suitcases to put them in. He reminded Elizabeth of those contest winners who are given 60 seconds to gather as many free groceries as possible.

Over lunch, at some McDonald's or drugstore counter, he checked off items on a long list of Persian squiggles. His hands were so large that his fountain pen seemed about to snap, and his rings got in the way. With one contemptuous stripping motion he wrung them all off; they clattered like hailstones across the paper. 'Now,' he said. 'Shirts, cravats . . .' Elizabeth tried on one of the rings. It was big as a napkin ring and warm, almost hot.

'Where can I find a raincoat like Hassan's?' he asked. 'I want one.'

'Oh . . . Hutzler's, maybe.' She felt suddenly tired. It seemed too much trouble to eat. 'Tell me,' she said, 'don't they have clothes in Iran? Are they too expensive, or what?'

'Eh?' he said absently. 'No, no, we have plenty, but I want American clothes. I want a coat like Hassan's. I want all Hassan owns, I want it all.'

He laughed. The other customers turned and stared, with the same sort of hopeful expression that the children wore in his presence.

After lunch, they often went to the dimestore. He had a weakness for ingenious utensils – like Elizabeth's perforated spoon for making tea. He bought three of those. And three Buttoneers for attaching buttons without thread, three Trac

II razors, three adhesive-backed telephone pencils. He paid with fistfuls of $10 bills whose supply seemed inexhaustible. Or sometimes he signed a traveller's cheque – his signature in English, 'Ahmad Ardavi', surprisingly small and crooked.

Then at 2 or 2.30, he would suddenly lose interest; he would seem to deflate. 'We'll go,' he would tell her. They made their way to the car, whose back windows were a mass of packages. Uncle Ahmad limped heavily, like a returning soldier. Settling in the car, he would sigh, 'Lizzie, Lizzie, Lizzie,' and allow himself to be chauffeured home in silence.

Once when they reached the house there was a department store brochure lying on the doorstep, with a man's bulky-knit sweater pictured on the cover. 'Aha!' said Uncle Ahmad, peering down at it. '*That's* what I want! See that? I want it in beige.'

'Uncle Ahmad,' said Elizabeth. 'You have it.'

'I do?'

'You bought it last week, for $40. You've got everything. What more do you need?' She was annoyed, and her voice clearly showed it, but Uncle Ahmad didn't take offence. In fact, he seemed delighted. 'You're right,' he said. 'I'm a greedy man. I want it all. Isn't that so?' And he flung back his head and laughed. 'I want! I want! I want!' he said.

To Elizabeth, his mouth looked like a cavern, and she couldn't believe the number of packages in his great, long, sinewy arms.

Uncle Ahmad grew restless and called up all the relatives in America. He got them from Hassan's address book. Elizabeth thought he was having his afternoon opium but instead he was sitting on her bed dialling Chicago, Boston, and Minneapolis on the upstairs extension. When she came in with a stack of fresh sheets she found him there, talking Persian. 'No, baba, come, there's lots of room, what's life without you to share it?' Elizabeth listened, leaning in the doorframe. She noticed the leather address book open on his knee. No telling how many people he had called before this one. There were so many Ardavis getting their education in the States these days that they could have formed a school

221

of their own. When he'd hung up she said, 'Uncle Ahmad, who was that?'

'Your dear cousin Kurosh,' he said. 'It's been much too long Hassan hasn't seen him.'

But he looked uncomfortable, and when Elizabeth went on standing there he scratched his head, thought a moment, and finally closed the address book and rose. 'I'll just go have a little smoke,' he told her.

In the evening, when Hassan came home, Uncle Ahmad told him he'd invited a few guests for the weekend.

'You did what?' Hassan said.

'Just close family, Hassan-jun.'

'But that could be 200 people!'

'Dear one,' said Uncle Ahmad, 'what's wrong with a little party now and then? You're too quiet here. I'm a man, Hassan, I need fun, excitement, I need *life*!' And he flung his arms wide. 'I am not the kind of person who can drag about on his own all the time,' he said.

'Phone them,' said Hassan.

'Eh?'

'Telephone them. Uninvite them.'

'Hassan! I can't do that.'

'You think we're back home?' Hassan asked. 'You think we're in Tehran with 20 servants to make the beds and cook the rice? If you want to see them, go there. Or talk to us first, invite one at a time. Elizabeth can't be expected to manage without notice.'

Uncle Ahmad lowered his arms and looked at Elizabeth. He waited. Now was the moment, she knew, for her to step forward and say that of course she could manage, let him have his party; she wasn't one of his niggling female relatives. But she didn't, though she suspected that even Hassan was hoping she would. She just sat quiet and watched the children's card game as if none of this had anything to do with her.

Then Uncle Ahmad said, 'Very well, Hassan,' and went away to the phone. They heard him dial a number and speak; and then another number, and another . . . 'How many people *were* there?' asked Hassan.

'I don't know,' Elizabeth said.

'The phone bill alone . . . you have to watch him more closely.'

'How can I? As it is, I'm buying his clothes, brewing his tea, following after his opium pipe with a can of Glade . . . I'd have to put him on a leash.'

'Yes, well,' said Hassan, and he sank into a chair and frowned into space. 'The thing is, I always liked him so much.'

'Well, of course,' said Elizabeth.

'He was my favourite relative.'

'Of course, Hassan, he's wonderful.'

'But now I don't know,' said Hassan. 'It's difficult.'

And he went on frowning into space, gently shaking his head.

Uncle Ahmad did uninvite everyone he could think of, but he forgot about two people – Kurosh and a second cousin by marriage named Hamid. Or else he overlooked them on purpose. At any rate, Kurosh arrived on Saturday afternoon with a pregnant Iranian wife and two crying babies, and Hamid wasn't far behind. They had to be supplied with makeshift beds, since Uncle Ahmad had the only guest room. They had to be given a steady stream of tea and Scotch, and mounds of rice. The men smoked their pipe and grew serene and philosophical, but the babies went on crying and Kurosh's wife seemed very unhappy. She said she'd been married by proxy, Kurosh had been in New Jersey and she in Tehran for the wedding, which was a very large affair with the bride all in white and the groom only a tinted photograph on the table next to the gifts. She wished he were *still* a tinted photograph, she said. She sighed and rubbed her abdomen, which was straining her embroidered velvet tunic.

Squinting against the smoke, adrift in a sea of pistachio shells, Elizabeth reminded herself that not everyone could lay claim to such a colourful family. Most of her friends had married Americans. Their in-laws were unremarkable. Their husbands had perhaps a couple of dull sisters, a few pallid nieces and nephews, a dowdy mother in a flowered hat. She imagined the mother arriving for Sunday dinner after church, bringing *Peanuts* books for the grandchildren. She'd be wearing short white gloves and an Orlon double-knit dress; her face would be plain, sweet, pocketed with comely wrinkles. A sad little ache started up in Elizabeth's chest.

'Ah, Lizzie-jun,' said Uncle Ahmad, with his Tartar eyes alight, 'isn't this true meaning of life? Food and drink and a pipe to smoke, and your dear ones gathered all around?'

There was only a little ice cream in the bottom of the carton, and she stretched it to fill two bowls for the girls. It was Friday night and she still hadn't found the time to do this week's grocery shopping. She set the bowls on the table and went to get spoons, and returned to see Uncle Ahmad lifting Hilary's scoop of ice cream in his fingers. 'Uncle *Ahmad*!' Jenny shrieked. Uncle Ahmad laughed, holding his mouth open wide, his lower jaw jutting forward, his fist dripping ice cream across the tablecloth. Elizabeth rapped a spoon on a glass, sharply, like an after-dinner speaker. 'Put it back,' she said.

He turned and stared, his mouth still open, his fist still dripping, the laughter fading. Hassan lowered the evening paper.

'Put it back in the bowl,' she said.

He looked at Hassan. Hassan nodded. 'Back,' he said.

Slowly, Uncle Ahmad opened his fist and let the ice cream fall into the bowl.

'Well,' he said, tucking his ticket in his coat pocket, 'I think I have everything.'

'We hate to see you go,' said Elizabeth.

She was dying to see him go. She'd been waiting for this the whole month, it seemed now. She couldn't believe she'd ever welcomed his coming, or willingly padded across the floor to him with his tumblers of Scotch. But there was only another half minute to endure, so she could smile and say, 'I hope you have an easy trip.'

'Thank you, Elizabeth,' said Uncle Ahmad, and he bent to kiss her. His face felt fine-grained and hard. But this was early morning, not his best time, and when she drew away she thought he had a shrivelled, skull-like look. The yellow of his skin was brassy, almost curry-coloured. When he lifted the children, a grunt escaped him.

'You'll come and visit, yes?' he asked them. 'My two little gypsies. I'll buy you gypsy earrings.'

He held a child in the crook of each arm. Standing like that, with his feet planted wide, he suddenly became the man she'd first met – gigantic, powerful, generous. She felt a pang at the thought of losing him. And she guessed from his averted gaze that he wouldn't be coming back. He lowered the children gently to the floor. He slapped his pockets and told Hassan, 'So. I'm ready, I think.'

Then at the door he turned and called, 'Okay! Ahmad is going! So long! Bye bye!'

And he walked on out, leaving his smell of spice and burnt flowers, leaving the house somehow bigger than before, and emptier, as if he had taken more than just himself. He might, Elizabeth thought, have carried off something of theirs as well. She had never known till now that people who are larger than life become that way by consuming chunks of other people's lives, so they are missed forever afterwards like an arm, or a leg, or a piece of a heart.

PENELOPE LIVELY

Clara's Day

When Clara Tilling was $15\frac{1}{2}$ she took off all her clothes one morning in school assembly. She walked naked through the lines of girls, past the headmistress at her lectern and the other staff ranged behind her, and out into the entrance lobby. She had left off her bra and pants already, so that all she had to do was unbutton her blouse, remove it and drop it to the floor, and then undo the zipper of her skirt and let that fall. She slipped her feet out of her shoes at the same time and so walked barefoot as well as naked. It all happened very quickly. One or two people giggled and a sort of rustling noise ran through the assembly hall, like a sudden wind among trees. The Head hesitated for a moment – she was reading out the tennis team list – and then went on again, firmly. Clara opened the big glass doors and let herself out.

The entrance lobby was empty. The floor was highly polished and she could see her own reflection, a foreshortened pink blur. There was a big bright modern painting on one wall and several comfortable chairs for waiting parents arranged round an enormous rubber plant and ashtrays on chrome stalks. Clara had sat there herself once, with her mother, waiting for an interview with the Head.

She walked along the corridor to her form room, which was also quite empty, with thick gold bars of sunlight falling on the desks and a peaceful feeling, as though no one had been here for a long time nor ever would come. Clara opened the cupboard in the corner, took out one of the science overalls and put it on, and then sat down at her desk. After about a minute Mrs Mayhew came in carrying her clothes and her shoes. She said, 'I should put these on now, Clara,' and stood beside her while she did so. 'Would you like to go home?' she asked, and when Clara said that she wouldn't, thank you, Mrs Mayhew went on briskly, 'Right you are then, Clara. You'd better get on with some prep, then, till the first period.'

226

All morning people kept coming up to her to say 'Well done!' or just to pat her on the back. She was a celebrity right up till dinner time but after that it tailed off a bit. Half way through the morning one of the prefects came in and told her the Head wanted to see her straight after school.

The Head's study was more like a sitting room, except for the big paper-strewn desk that she sat behind. There were squashy chairs and nice pictures on the walls and photos of the Head's husband and her children on the mantelpiece and a Marks & Spencer carrier bag dumped down in one corner. The window was open onto the playing fields from which came the cheerful incomprehensible noise like birds singing, of people calling to each other. Except for the distant rumble of traffic you wouldn't think you were in London.

The Head was busy writing when Clara came in; she just looked up to say, 'Hello, Clara. Sit down. Do you mind if I just finish these reports off? I won't be a minute.' She went on writing and Clara sat and looked at the photo of her husband, who had square sensible-looking glasses and her three boys who were all the same but different sizes. Then the Head slapped the pile of reports together and pushed her chair back. 'There . . . Well now . . . So what was all that about, this morning?'

'I don't know,' said Clara.

The Head looked at her, thoughtfully, and Clara looked back. Just before the silence became really embarrassing the Head pushed a hand through her short untidy fair hair, making it even untidier, and said, 'I daresay you don't. Were you trying to attract attention?'

Clara considered. 'Well, I would, wouldn't I? Doing a thing like that. I mean – you'd be bound to.'

The Head nodded. 'Quite. Silly question.'

'Oh, no,' said Clara hastily, 'I meant you'd be bound to attract attention. Not be bound to be trying to.'

The Head, a linguist, also considered. 'Well . . . That's a fine point, I think. How do you feel about it now?'

Clara tried to examine her feelings, which slithered away like fish. In the end she said, 'I don't really feel anything,' which was, in a way, truthful.

The Head nodded again. She looked at her husband on the mantelpiece, almost as though asking for advice. 'Everything all right at home?'

'Oh fine,' Clara assured her. 'Absolutely fine.'

'Good,' said the Head. 'Of course . . . I was just thinking, there are quite a lot of people in Four B with separated parents, aren't there? Bryony and Susie Tallance and Rachel.'

'And Midge,' said Clara. 'And Lucy Potter.'

'Yes. Five. Six, with you.'

'Twenty-five per cent,' said Clara. 'Just about.'

'Quite. As a matter of fact that's the national average, did you know? One marriage in four.'

'No, I didn't actually,' said Clara.

'Well, it is, I'm afraid. Anyway . . .' She looked over at her husband again. 'You're not fussing about O-levels, are you?'

'Not really,' said Clara. 'I mean, I don't *like* exams, but I don't mind as much as some people.'

'Your Mocks were fine,' said the Head. 'Physics and Chemistry could have been a bit better. But there shouldn't be any great problems there. So . . . Are you still going around with Liz Raymond?'

'Mostly,' said Clara. 'And Stephanie.'

'I want people to come and talk to me if there's anything they're worried about,' said the Head. 'Even things that may seem silly. You know. It doesn't have to be large obvious things. Exams and stuff. Anything.'

'Yes,' said Clara.

The phone rang. The Head picked it up and said no, she hadn't, and yes, she'd be along as soon as she could and tell them to wait. She put the receiver down and said, 'It wasn't like you, Clara, was it? I mean – there are a few people one wouldn't be *all* that surprised, if they suddenly did something idiotic or unexpected. But you aren't really like that, are you?'

Clara agreed that she wasn't, really.

'I'll be writing a note to your mother. And if you have an urge to do something like that again come and have a talk to me first, right?' The Head smiled and Clara smiled back. That was all, evidently. Clara got up and left. As she was closing the door she saw the Head looking after her, not smiling now, her expression rather bleak.

Most of the school had gone home but all those in Clara's form who had boyfriends at St Benet's, which was practically everyone, were hanging around the bus station deliberately not catching buses because St Benet's came out half an hour later. Clara hung around for a bit too, just to be sociable, and then got on her bus. She sat on the top deck by herself and looked down onto the pavements. It was very hot; everyone young had bare legs, road menders were stripped to the waist, everywhere there was flesh – brown backs and white knees and glimpses of the hair under people's arms and the clefts between breasts and buttocks. In the park, the grass was strewn with sunbathers; there were girls in bikinis sprawled like starfish, face down with a rag of material between their legs and the strings of the top half undone. Clara, with no bra or pants on, could feel warm air washing around between her skin and her clothes. Coming down the stairs as the bus approached her stop she had to hold down her skirt in case it blew up.

Her mother was already home. She worked part-time as a dentist's receptionist and had what were called flexible hours, which meant more or less that she worked when it suited her. Afternoons, nowadays, often didn't suit because Stan, her friend, who was an actor, was only free in the afternoons.

Stan wasn't there today, though. Clara came into the kitchen where her mother was drinking tea and looking at a magazine. 'Hi!' she said. 'Any news?' which was what she said most days. Clara said that there was no news and her mother went on reading an article in the magazine called, Clara could see upside down across the table 'Orgasm – Fact or Fantasy?' Presently she yawned, pushed the magazine over to Clara and went upstairs to have a bath. Clara had another cup of tea and leafed through the magazine, which was mostly advertisements for tampons and deodorants, and then began to do her prep.

The Head's letter came a couple of days later. Clara heard the post flop onto the doormat and when she looked over the bannister she knew at once what the typed envelope must be. At the same moment Stan, who had stayed the night, came out of her mother's room on his way to the bathroom. He wore underpants and had a towel slung round his neck like a football scarf, and was humming to himself. When he saw her he said, 'Wotcha! How's tricks, then?' and Clara pulled her dressing gown more closely round her and said, 'Fine, thanks.'

'That's the stuff,' said Stan vaguely, 'Hey – I got you a couple of tickets for the show. Bring a friend, OK?' He was a stocky muscular man with a lot of black hair on his chest. The smell of him, across the landing, was powerful – a huge inescapable wave of man smell: sweat and aftershave and something you could not put your finger on. Clara always knew when he was in the house before she opened the sitting room door because whiffs of him gusted about the place. She said, 'Thanks very much. That would be super,' and edged into her room.

When she came down they were both having breakfast. Her mother was just opening the post. She said, 'Coffee on the stove, lovey. Oh goody – my tax rebate's come.' She opened the Head's letter and began to read. First she stared at it with a puzzled look and then she began to laugh. She clapped her hand over her mouth, spluttering. 'I don't *believe* it!' she cried. 'Clara, I simply do not believe it! Stan, just listen to this . . . Isn't she the most incredible girl! Guess what she did! She took off all her clothes in school assembly and walked out starkers!' She handed the letter to Stan and went on laughing.

Stan read the letter. Grinning hugely, he looked up at Clara. 'She'll have done it for a dare, I bet. Good on yer, Clara. Terrific! God, I wish I'd been there!' He patted Clara's arm and Clara froze. She went completely rigid, as though she had turned to cement, and when eventually she moved a leg it seemed as though it should make a cracking noise.

Her mother had stopped laughing and was talking again. ' . . . the last thing anyone would have expected of you, lovey. You've always been such a prude. Ever since you were a

230

toddler. Talk about modest! Honestly, Stan, she was hilarious, as a little kid – I can see her now, sitting on the beach at Camber clutching a towel round her in case anyone got a glimpse of her bum when she was changing. Aged 10. And when her bust grew she used to sit hunched over like a spoon so no one would notice it. And if she had to strip off for the doctor you'd have thought he'd been about to rape her, from her expression. Even now I can't get her out of that Victorian one-piece school regulation bathing costume – and it's not as though she's not got a good shape.'

'Smashing!' said Stan, slurping his coffee.

' . . . spot of puppy fat still but that's going, good hips, my legs if I may say so. Which is what makes this such an absolute scream. Honestly, sweetie, I wouldn't have thought you had it in you. I mean, I've not been allowed to see her in the buff myself since she was 12. Honestly, I've wondered once or twice if there was something *wrong* with the girl.' Her mother beamed across the breakfast table. 'Anyway, old Mrs Whatsit doesn't seem to be making a fuss. She just thinks I ought to know. More coffee, anyone? God, look at the time! And I said I'd be in early today . . . I'm off. Leave the breakfast things, lovey – we'll do them later. Coming, Stan?'

Clara went on sitting at the table. She ate a piece of toast and drank her coffee. Her mother and Stan bustled about collecting her purse and his jacket and banged out of the house, shouting goodbye. The front gate clicked, the car door slammed, and then Clara began to cry, the tears dripping from her chin onto her folded arms and her face screwed up like a small child's.

RUTH RENDELL

Fen Hall

When children paint a picture of a tree they always do the trunk brown. But trees seldom have brown trunks. Birches are silver, beeches pewter colour, planes grey and yellow, walnuts black and the bark of oaks, chestnuts and sycamores green with lichen. Pringle had never noticed any of this until he came to Fen Hall. After that, once his eyes had been opened and he had seen what things were really like, he would have painted trees with bark in different colours but next term he stopped doing art. It was just as well, he had never been very good at it, and perhaps by then he wouldn't have felt like painting trees anyway. Or even looking at them much.

Mr Liddon met them at the station in an old Volvo estate car. They were loaded down with camping gear, the tent and sleeping bags and cooking pots and a Calor gas burner in case it was too windy to keep a fire going. It had been very windy lately, the summer cool and sunless. Mr Liddon was Pringle's father's friend and Pringle had met him once before, years ago when he was a little kid, but still it was up to him to introduce the others. He spoke with wary politeness.

'This is John and this is Roger. They're brothers.'

Pringle didn't say anything about Roger always being called Hodge. He sensed that Mr Liddon wouldn't call him Hodge any more than he would call *him* Pringle. He was right.

'Parents well, are they, Peregrine?'

Pringle said yes. He could see a gleam in John's eye that augured teasing to come.

Hodge, who was always thinking of his stomach, said: 'Could we stop on the way, Mr Liddon, and buy some food?'

Mr Liddon cast up his eyes. Pringle could tell he was going to be 'one of those' grown-ups. They all got into the car with their stuff and a mile or so out of town Mr Liddon

232

stopped at a self-service shop. He didn't go inside with them which was just as well. He would only have called what they bought junk food.

Fen Hall turned out to be about seven miles away. They went through a village called Fedgford and a little way beyond it turned down a lane that passed through a wood.

'That's where you'll have your camp,' Mr Liddon said.

Of necessity, because the lane was no more than a rough track, he was driving slowly. He pointed in among the trees. The wood had a mysterious look as if full of secrets. In the aisles between the trees the light was greenish-gold and misty. There was a muted twittering of birds and a cooing of doves. Pringle began to feel excited. It was nicer than he had expected. A little further on the wood petered out into a plantation of tall straight trees with green trunks growing in rows, the ground between them all overgrown with a spiky plant that had a curious prehistoric look to it.

'Those trees are poplars,' Mr Liddon said. You could tell he was a schoolteacher. 'They're grown as a crop.'

This was a novel idea to Pringle. 'What sort of a crop?'

'Twenty-five years after they're planted they're cut down and used for making matchsticks. If they don't fall down first. We had a couple go over in the gales last winter.'

Pringle wasn't listening. He had seen the house. It was like a house in a dream, he thought, though he didn't quite know what he meant by that. Houses he saw in actual dreams were much like his own or John and Hodge's, suburban Surrey semi-detached. This house, when all the trees were left behind and no twig or leaf or festoon of wild clematis obscured it, stood basking in the sunshine with the confidence of something alive, as if secure in its own perfection. Dark mulberry colour, of small Tudor bricks, it had a roof of many irregular planes and gables and a cluster of chimneys like candles. The windows with the sun on them were plates of gold between the mullions. Under the eaves swallows had built their lumpy sagging nests.

'Leave your stuff in the car. I'll be taking you back up to the wood in 10 minutes. Just thought you'd like to get your bearings, see where everything is first. There's the outside

233

tap over there which you'll use of course. And you'll find a shovel and an axe in there which I rely on you to replace.'

It was going to be the biggest house Pringle had ever set foot in – not counting places like Hampton Court and Woburn. Fen Hall. It looked and the name sounded like a house in a book, not real at all. The front door was of oak, studded with iron and set back under a porch that was dark and carved with roses. Mr Liddon took them in the back way. He took them into a kitchen that was exactly Pringle's idea of the lowest sort of slum.

He was shocked. At first he couldn't see much because it had been bright outside but he could smell something dank and frowsty. When his vision adjusted he found they were in a huge room or cavern with two small windows and about 400 square feet of squalor between them. Islanded were a small white electric oven and a small white fridge. The floor was of brick, very uneven, the walls of irregular green-painted peeling plaster with a bubbly kind of growth coming through it. Stacks of dirty dishes filled a stone sink of the kind his mother had bought at a sale and made a cactus garden in. The whole place was grossly untidy with piles of washing lying about. John and Hodge, having taken it all in, were standing there with blank faces and shifting eyes.

Mr Liddon's manner had changed slightly. He no longer kept up the hectoring tone. While explaining to them that this was where they must come if they needed anything, to the back door, he began a kind of ineffectual tidying up, cramming things into the old wooden cupboards, sweeping crumbs off the table and dropping them into the sink.

John said: 'Is it all right for us to have a fire?'

'So long as you're careful. Not if the wind gets up again. I don't have to tell you where the wood is, you'll find it lying about.' Mr Liddon opened a door and called, 'Flora!'

A stone-flagged passage could be seen beyond. No one came. Pringle knew Mr Liddon had a wife, though no children. His parents had told him only that Mr and Mrs Liddon had bought a marvellous house in the country a year before and he and a couple of his friends could go and camp in the grounds if they wanted to. Further information he had picked up when they didn't know he was listening. Tony

Liddon hadn't had two halfpennies to rub together until his aunt died and left him a bit of money. It couldn't have been much surely. Anyway he had spent it all on Fen Hall, he had always wanted an old place like that. The upkeep was going to be a drain on him and goodness knows how he would manage.

Pringle hadn't been much interested in all this. Now it came back to him. Mr Liddon and his father had been at university together but Mr Liddon hadn't had a wife then. Pringle had never met the wife and nor had his parents. Anyway it was clear they were not to wait for her. They got back into the car and went to find a suitable camping site.

It was a relief when Mr Liddon went away and left them to it. The obvious place to camp was on the high ground in a clearing and to make their fire in a hollow Mr Liddon said was probably a disused gravel pit. The sun was low, making long shafts of light that pierced the groves of birch and crabapple. Mistletoe hung in the oak trees like green birds' nests. It was warm and murmurous with flies. John was adept at putting up the tent and gave them orders.

'Peregrine,' he said. 'Like a sort of mad bird.'

Hodge capered about, his thumbs in his ears and his hands flapping. 'Tweet, tweet, mad bird. His master chains him up like a dog. Tweet, tweet, birdie!'

'I'd rather be a hunting falcon than Roger the lodger the sod,' said Pringle and he shoved Hodge and they both fell over and rolled about grappling on the ground until John kicked them and told them to give him a hand, he couldn't do the lot on his own.

It was good in the camp that night, not windy but still and mild after the bad summer they'd had. They made a fire and cooked tomato soup and fish fingers and ate a whole packet of the biscuits called iced bears. They were in their bags in the tent, John reading the *Observer's Book of Common Insects*, Pringle a thriller set in a Japanese prison camp his parents would have taken away if they'd known about it, and Hodge listening to his radio, when Mr Liddon came up with a torch to check on them.

'Just to see if you're OK. Everything shipshape and Bristol fashion?'

Pringle thought that an odd thing to say considering the mess in his own house. Mr Liddon made a fuss about the candles they had lit and they promised to put them out, though of course they didn't. It was very silent in the night up there in the wood, the deepest silence that Pringle had ever known, a quiet that was somehow heavy as if some great dark beast had lain down on the wood and quelled every sound beneath under its dense soft fur.

He didn't think of this for very long because he was asleep two minutes after they blew the candles out.

Next morning the weather wasn't so nice. It was dull and cool for August. John saw a Brimstone butterfly which pleased him because the species was getting rarer. They all walked into Fedgford and bought sausages and then found they hadn't a frying pan. Pringle went down to the house on his own to see if he could borrow one.

Unlike most men Mr Liddon would be at home because of the school holidays. Pringle expected to see him working in the garden which even he could see was a mess. But he wasn't anywhere about. Pringle banged on the back door with his fist – there was neither bell nor knocker – but no one came. The door wasn't locked. He wondered if it would be all right to go in and then he went in.

The mess in the kitchen was rather worse. A large white and tabby cat was on the table eating something it probably shouldn't have been eating out of a paper bag. Pringle had a curious feeling that it would somehow be quite permissible for him to go on into the house. Something told him – though it was not a something based on observation or even guesswork – that Mr Liddon wasn't in. He went into the passage he had seen the day before through the open door. This led into a large stone-flagged hall. The place was dark with heavy dark beams going up the walls and across the ceilings and it was cold. It smelled of damp. The smell was like mushrooms that have been left in a paper bag at the back of the fridge and forgotten. Pringle pushed open a likely looking door, some instinct making him give a warning cough.

The room was enormous, its ceiling all carved beams and

236

cobwebs. Even Pringle could see that the few small bits of furniture in it would have been more suitable for the living room of a bungalow. A woman was standing by the tall, diamond-paned, mullioned window, holding something blue and sparkling up to the light. She was strangely dressed in a long skirt, her hair falling loosely down her back, and she stood so still, gazing at the blue object with both arms raised, that for a moment Pringle had an uneasy feeling she wasn't a woman at all but the ghost of a woman. Then she turned round and smiled.

'Hallo,' she said. 'Are you one of our campers?'

She was at least as old as Mr Liddon but her hair hung down like one of the girls' at school. Her face was pale and not pretty yet when she smiled it was a wonderful face. Pringle registered that, staring at her. It was a face of radiant kind sensitivity, though it was to be some years before he could express what he had felt in those terms.

'I'm Pringle,' he said, and because he sensed that she would understand, 'I'm called Peregrine really but I get people to call me Pringle.'

'I don't blame you. I'd do the same in your place.' She had a quiet unaffected voice. 'I'm Flora Liddon. You can call me Flora.'

He didn't think he could do that and knew he would end up calling her nothing. 'I came to see if I could borrow a frying pan.'

'Of course you can.' She added, 'If I can find one.' She held the thing in her hand out to him and he saw it was a small glass bottle. 'Do you think it's pretty?'

He looked at it doubtfully. It was just a bottle. On the window sill behind her were more bottles, mostly of clear colourless glass but among them dark green ones with fluted sides.

'There are wonderful things to be found here. You can dig and find rubbish heaps that go back to Elizabethan times. And there was a Roman settlement down by the river. Would you like to see a Roman coin?'

It was black, misshapen, lumpy, with an ugly man's head on it. She showed him a jar of thick bubbly green glass and said it was the best piece of glass she'd found to date. They

237

went out to the kitchen. Finding a frying pan wasn't easy but talking to her was. By the time she had washed up a pan which she had found full of congealed fat he had told her all about the camp and their walk to Fedgford and what the butcher had said: 'I hope you're going to wash yourselves before you cook my nice clean sausages.'

And she told him what a lot needed doing to the house and grounds and how they'd have to do it all themselves because they hadn't much money. She wasn't any good at painting or sewing or gardening or even housework, come to that. Pottering about and looking at things was what she liked.

' "What is this life, if full of care, we have no time to stand and stare?" '

He knew where that came from. W H Davies, the Supertramp. They had done it at school.

'I'd have been a good tramp,' she said. 'It would have suited me.'

The smile radiated her plain face.

They cooked the sausages for lunch and went on an insect-hunting expedition with John. The dragonflies he had promised them down by the river were not to be seen but he found what he said was a caddis, though it looked like a bit of twig to Pringle. Hodge ate five Mars bars during the course of the afternoon. They came upon the white and tabby cat with a mouse in its jaws. Undeterred by an audience, it bit the mouse in two and the tiny heart rolled out. Hodge said faintly, 'I think I'm going to be sick,' and was. They still resolved to have a cat-watch on the morrow and see how many mice it caught in a day.

By that time the weather was better. The sun didn't shine but it had got warmer again. They found the cat in the poplar plantation, stalking something among the prehistoric weeds John said were called horse tails. The poplars had trunks almost as green as grass and their leafy tops, very high up there in the pale blue sky, made rustling whispering sounds in the breeze. That was when Pringle noticed about tree trunks not being brown. The trunks of the Scotch pines were a clear pinkish-red, as bright as flowers when for a moment the sun shone. He pointed this out to the others but they didn't seem interested.

'You sound like our auntie,' said Hodge. 'She does flower arrangements for the church.'

'And throws up when she sees a bit of blood, I expect,' said Pringle. 'It runs in your family.'

Hodge lunged at him and he tripped Hodge up and they rolled about wrestling among the horse tails. By four in the afternoon the cat had caught six mice. Flora came out and told them the cat's name was Tabby which obscurely pleased Pringle. If she had said Snowflake or Persephone or some other daft name people called animals he would have felt differently about her, though he couldn't possibly have said why. He wouldn't have liked her so much.

A man turned up in a Land Rover as they were making their way back to camp. He said he had been to the house and knocked but no one seemed to be at home. Would they give Mr or Mrs Liddon a message from him? His name was Porter, Michael Porter, and he was an archaeologist in an amateur sort of way, Mr Liddon knew all about it, and they were digging in the lower meadow and they'd come on a dump of 19th-century stuff. He was going to dig deeper, uncover the next layer, so if Mrs Liddon was interested in the top now was her chance to have a look.

'Can we as well?' said Pringle.

Porter said they were welcome. No one would be working there next day. He had just heard the weather forecast on his car radio and gale force winds were promised. Was that their camp up there? Make sure the tent was well anchored down, he said, and he drove off up the lane.

Pringle checked the tent. It seemed firm enough. They got into it and fastened the flap but they were afraid to light the candles and had John's storm lantern on instead. The wood was silent no longer. The wind made loud siren-like howls and a rushing rending sound like canvas being torn. When that happened the tent flapped and bellied like a sail on a ship at sea. Sometimes the wind stopped altogether and there were a few seconds of silence and calm. Then it came back with a rush and a roar. John was reading Frohawk's *Complete Book of British Butterflies*, Pringle the Japanese prison camp thriller and Hodge was trying to listen to his radio. But it wasn't much use and after a while they put the lantern out and lay in the dark.

About five minutes afterwards there came the strongest gust of wind so far, one of the canvas-tearing gusts but 10 times fiercer than the last; and then, from the south of them, down towards the house, a tremendous rending crash.

John said, 'I think we'll have to do something.' His voice was brisk but it wasn't quite steady and Pringle knew he was as scared as they were. 'We'll have to get out of here.'

Pringle put the lantern on again. It was just 10.

'The tent's going to lift off,' said Hodge.

Crawling out of his sleeping bag, Pringle was wondering what they ought to do, if it would be all right, or awful, to go down to the house, when the tent flap was pulled open and Mr Liddon put his head in. He looked cross.

'Come on, the lot of you. You can't stay here. Bring your sleeping bags and we'll find you somewhere in the house for the night.'

A note in his voice made it sound as if the storm were their fault. Pringle found his shoes, stuck his feet into them and rolled up his sleeping bag. John carried the lantern. Mr Liddon shone his own torch to light their way. In the wood there was shelter but none in the lane and the wind buffeted them as they walked. It was all noise, you couldn't see much, but as they passed the plantation Mr Liddon swung the light up and Pringle saw what had made the crash. One of the poplars had gone over and was lying on its side with its roots in the air.

For some reason – perhaps because it was just about on this spot that they had met Michael Porter – John remembered the message. Mr Liddon said OK and thanks. They went into the house through the back door. A tile blew off the roof and crashed on to the path just as the door closed behind them.

There were beds up in the bedrooms but without blankets or sheets on them and the mattresses were damp. Pringle thought them spooky bedrooms, dirty and draped with spiders' webs, and he wasn't sorry they weren't going to sleep there. There was the same smell of old mushrooms and a smell of paint as well where Mr Liddon had started work on a ceiling.

At the end of the passage, looking out of a window, Flora stood in a nightgown with a shawl over it. Pringle, who sometimes read ghost stories, saw her as the Grey Lady of Fen Hall. She was in the dark, the better to see the forked lightning that had begun to leap on the horizon beyond the river.

'I love to watch a storm,' she said, turning and smiling at them.

Mr Liddon had snapped a light on. 'Where are these boys to sleep?'

It was as if it didn't concern her. She wasn't unkind but she wasn't involved either. 'Oh, in the drawing room, I should think.'

'We have seven bedrooms.'

Flora said no more. A long roll of thunder shook the house. Mr Liddon took them downstairs and through the drawing room into a sort of study where they helped him make up beds of cushions on the floor. The wind howled round the house and Pringle heard another tile go. He lay in the dark, listening to the storm. The others were asleep, he could tell by their steady breathing. Inside the bags it was quite warm and he felt snug and safe. After a while he heard Mr Liddon and Flora quarrelling on the other side of the door.

Pringle's parents quarrelled a lot and he hated it, it was the worst thing in the world, though less bad now than when he was younger. He could only just hear Mr Liddon and Flora and only disjointed words, abusive and angry on the man's part, indifferent, amused on the woman's, until one sentence rang out clearly. Her voice was penetrating though it was so quiet:

'We want such different things!'

He wished they would stop. And suddenly they did, with the coming of the rain. The rain came, exploded rather, crashing at the windows and on the old sagging depleted roof. It was strange that a sound like that, a loud constant roar, could send you to sleep . . .

241

She was in the kitchen when he went out there in the morning. John and Hodge slept on, in spite of the bright watery sunshine that streamed through the dirty diamond window panes. A clean world outside, new-washed. Indoors the same chaos, the kitchen with the same smell of fungus and dirty dishcloths, though the windows were open. Flora sat at the table on which sprawled a welter of plates, indefinable garments, bits of bread and fruit rinds, an open can of cat food. She was drinking coffee and Tabby lay on her lap.

'There's plenty in the pot if you want some.'

She was the first grown-up in whose house he had stayed who didn't ask him how he had slept. Nor was she going to cook breakfast for him. She told him where the eggs were and bread and butter. Pringle remembered he still hadn't returned her frying pan which might be the only one she had.

He made himself a pile of toast and found a jar of marmalade. The grass and the paths, he could see through an open window, were littered with broken bits of twig and leaf. A cock pheasant strutted across the shaggy lawn.

'Did the storm damage a lot of things?' he asked.

'I don't know. Tony got up early to look. There may be more poplars down.'

Pringle ate his toast. The cat had begun to purr in an irregular throbbing way. Her hand kneaded its ears and neck. She spoke, but not perhaps to Pringle or the cat, or for them if they cared to hear.

'So many people are like that. The whole of life is a preparation for life, not living.'

Pringle didn't know what to say. He said nothing. She got up and walked away, still carrying the cat, and then after a while he heard music coming faintly from a distant part of the house.

There were two poplars down in the plantation and each had left a crater four or five feet deep. As they went up the lane to check on their camp, Pringle and John and Hodge had a good look at them, their green trunks laid low, their tangled roots in the air. Apart from everything having got a bit blown about up at the camp and the stuff they had left

242

out soaked through, there was no real damage done. The wood itself had afforded protection to their tent.

It seemed a good time to return the frying pan. After that they would have to walk to Fedgford for more food – unless one of the Liddons offered a lift. It was with an eye to this, Pringle had to admit, that he was taking the pan back.

But Mr Liddon, never one to waste time, was already at work in the plantation. He had lugged a chain saw up there and was preparing to cut up the poplars where they lay. When he saw them in the lane he came over.

'How did you sleep?'

Pringle said, 'OK, thanks,' but Hodge, who had been very resentful about not being given a hot drink or something to eat, muttered that he had been too hungry to sleep. Mr Liddon took no notice. He seemed jumpy and nervous. He said to Pringle that if they were going to the house would they tell Mrs Liddon – he never called her Flora to them – that there was what looked like a dump of Victorian glass in the crater where the bigger poplar had stood.

'They must have planted the trees over the top without knowing.'

Pringle looked into the crater and sure enough he could see bits of coloured glass and a bottleneck and a jug or tankard handle protruding from the tumbled soil. He left the others there, fascinated by the chain saw, and went to take the frying pan back. Flora was in the drawing room, playing records of tinkly piano music. She jumped up, quite excited, when he told her about the bottle dump.

They walked back to the plantation together, Tabby following, walking a little way behind them like a dog. Pringle knew he hadn't a hope of getting that lift now. Mr Liddon had already got the crown of the big poplar sawn off. In the short time since the storm its pale silvery-green leaves had begun to wither. John asked if they could have a go with the chain saw but Mr Liddon said not so likely, did they think he was crazy? And if they wanted to get to the butcher before the shop closed for lunch they had better get going now.

Flora, her long skirt hitched up, had clambered down

243

into the crater. If she had stood up in it her head and shoulders, perhaps all of her from the waist up, would have come above its rim, for poplars have shallow roots. But she didn't stand up. She squatted down, using her trowel, extracting small glass objects from the leafmould. The chain saw whined, slicing through the top of the poplar trunk. Pringle, watching with the others, had a feeling something was wrong about the way Mr Liddon was doing it. He didn't know what though. He could only think of a funny film he had once seen in which a man, sitting on a branch, sawed away at the bit between him and the tree trunk, necessarily falling off himself when the branch fell. But Mr Liddon wasn't sitting on anything. He was just sawing up a fallen tree from the crown to the bole. The saw sliced through again, making four short logs now as well as the bole.

'Cut along now, you boys,' he said. 'You don't want to waste the day mooning about here.'

Flora looked up and winked at Pringle. It wasn't unkind, just conspiratorial, and she smiled too, holding up a small glowing red glass bottle for him to see. He and John and Hodge moved slowly off, reluctantly, dawdling because the walk ahead would be boring and long. Through the horse tails, up the bank, looking back when the saw whined again.

But Pringle wasn't actually looking when it happened. None of them was. They had had their final look and had begun to trudge up the lane. The sound made them turn, a kind of swishing lurch and then a heavy plopping, sickening, dull crash. They cried out, all three of them, but no one else did, not Flora or Mr Liddon. Neither of them made a sound.

Mr Liddon was standing with his arms held out, his mouth open and his eyes staring. The pile of logs lay beside him but the tree trunk was gone, sprung back roots and all when the last saw cut went through, tipped the balance and made its base heavier than its top. Pringle put his hand over his mouth and held it there. Hodge, who was nothing more than a fat baby really, had begun to cry. Fearfully, slowly, they converged, all four of them, on the now upright tree under whose roots she lay.

The police came and a farmer and his son and some men

from round about. Between them they got the tree over on its side again but by then Flora was dead. Perhaps she died as soon as the bole and the mass of roots hit her. Pringle wasn't there to see. Mr Liddon had put the plantation out of bounds and said they were to stay in camp until someone came to drive them to the station. It was Michael Porter who turned up in the late afternoon and checked they'd got everything packed up and the camp site tidied. He told them Flora was dead. They got to the station in his Land Rover in time to catch the 5.15 for London.

On the way to the station he didn't mention the bottle dump he had told them about. Pringle wondered if Mr Liddon had ever said anything to Flora about it. All the way home in the train he kept thinking of something odd. The first time he went up the lane to the camp that morning he was sure there hadn't been any glass in the tree crater. He would have seen the gleam of it and he hadn't. He didn't say anything to John and Hodge, though. What would have been the point?

Three years afterwards Pringle's parents got an invitation to Mr Liddon's wedding. He was marrying the daughter of a wealthy local builder and the reception was to be at Fen Hall, the house in the wood. Pringle didn't go, being too old now to tag about after his parents. He had gone off trees anyway.

ANNE TYLER

Your Place is Empty

Early in October, Hassan Ardavi invited his mother to come from Iran for a visit. His mother accepted immediately. It wasn't clear how long the visit was to last. Hassan's wife thought three months would be a good length of time. Hassan himself had planned on six months, and said so in his letter of invitation. But his mother felt that after such a long trip six months would be too short, and she was counting on staying a year. Hassan's little girl, who wasn't yet two, had no idea of time at all. She was told that her grandmother was coming but she soon forgot about it.

Hassan's wife was named Elizabeth, not an easy word for Iranians to pronounce. She would have been recognised as American the world over – a blonde, pretty girl with long bones and an ungraceful way of walking. One of her strong points was an ability to pick up foreign languages, and before her mother-in-law's arrival she bought a textbook and taught herself Persian.

'*Salaam aleikum*,' she told the mirror every morning. Her daughter watched, startled, from her place on the potty-chair. Elizabeth ran through possible situations in her mind and looked up the words for them. 'Would you like more tea? Do you take sugar?'

At suppertime she spoke Persian to her husband, who looked amused at the new tone she gave his language with her flat, factual American voice. He wrote to his mother and told her Elizabeth had a surprise for her.

Their house was a three-storey brick Colonial, but only the first two storeys were in use. Now they cleared the third of its trunks and china barrels and *National Geographics*, and they moved in a few pieces of furniture. Elizabeth sewed flowered curtains for the window. She was unusually careful with them; to a foreign mother-in-law, fine seams might matter. Also, Hassan bought a pocket compass, which he

246

placed in the top dresser drawer. 'For her prayers,' he said. 'She'll want to face Mecca. She prays three times a day.'

'But which direction is Mecca from here?' Elizabeth asked.

Hassan only shrugged. He had never said the prayers himself, not even as a child. His earliest memory was of tickling the soles of his mother's feet while she prayed steadfastly on; everyone knew it was forbidden to pause once you'd started.

Mrs Ardavi felt nervous about the descent from the plane. She inched down the staircase sideways, one hand tight on the railing, the other clutching her shawl. It was night, and cold. The air seemed curiously opaque. She arrived on solid ground and stood collecting herself – a small, stocky woman in black, with a kerchief over her smooth grey hair. She held her back very straight, as if she had just had her feelings hurt. In picturing this moment she had always thought Hassan would be waiting beside the plane, but there was no sign of him. Blue lights dotted the darkness behind her, an angular terminal loomed ahead, and an official was herding the passengers towards a plate-glass door. She followed, entangled in a web of meaningless sounds such as those you might hear in a fever dream.

Immigration. Baggage Claims. Customs. To all she spread her hands and beamed and shrugged, showing she spoke no English. Meanwhile her fellow-passengers waved to a blur of faces beyond a glass wall. It seemed they all knew people here; she was the only one who didn't. She had issued from the plane like a newborn baby, speechless and friendless. And the customs official didn't seem pleased with her. She had brought too many gifts. She had stuffed her bags with them, discarding all but the most necessary pieces of her clothing so that she would have more room. There were silver tea sets and gold jewellery for her daughter-in-law, and for her grand-daughter a doll dressed in the complicated costume of a nomad tribe, an embroidered sheepskin vest, and two religious medals on chains – one a disc inscribed with the name of Allah, the other a tiny gold Koran with a very effective prayer for long life folded up within it. The customs official sifted gold through his fingers like sand and frowned at the Koran. 'Have I done something wrong?' she asked. But of course he didn't understand her. Though you'd think, really, that if he would just *listen* hard enough, just meet her eyes once . . . it was a very simple language, there was no reason why it shouldn't come through to him.

For Hassan, she'd brought food. She had gathered all his favourite foods and put them in a drawstring bag embroidered with peacocks. When the official opened the bag he said something under his breath and called another man over. Together they unwrapped tiny newspaper packets and sniffed at various herbs. 'Sumac,' she told them. 'Powder of lemons. Shambalileh.' They gazed at her blankly. They untied a small cloth sack and rummaged through the kashk she had brought for soup. It rolled beneath their fingers and across the counter – hard white balls of yoghurt curd, stuck with bits of sheep hair and manure. Some peasant had laboured for hours to make that kashk. Mrs Ardavi picked up one piece and replaced it firmly in the sack. Maybe the official understood her meaning: she was running out of patience. He threw up his hands. He slid her belongings down the counter. She was free to go.

Free to go where?

Dazed and stumbling, a pyramid of knobby parcels and bags, scraps of velvet and brocade and tapestry, she made her way to the glass wall. A door opened out of nowhere and a stranger blocked her path. 'Khanom Jun,' he said. It was a name that only her children would use, but she passed him blindly and he had to touch her arm before she would look up.

He had put on weight. She didn't know him. The last time she'd seen him he was a thin, stoop-shouldered medical student disappearing into an Air France jet without a backward glance. 'Khanom Jun, it's me,' this stranger said, but she went on searching his face with cloudy eyes. No doubt he was a bearer of bad news. Was that it? A recurrent dream had warned her that she would never see her son again – that he would die on his way to the airport, or had already been dead for months but no one wanted to break the news; some second or third cousin in America had continued

248

signing Hassan's name to his cheerful, anonymous letters. Now here was this man with greying hair and a thick moustache, his clothes American but his face Iranian, his eyes sadly familiar, as if they belonged to someone else. 'Don't you believe me?' he said. He kissed her on both cheeks. It was his smell she recognised first – a pleasantly bitter, herb-like smell that brought her the image of Hassan as a child, reaching thin arms around her neck. 'It's you, Hassan,' she said, and then she started crying against his grey tweed shoulder.

They were quiet during the long drive home. Once she reached over to touch his face, having wanted to do so for miles. None of the out-of-focus snapshots he'd sent had prepared her for the way he had aged. 'How long has it been?' she asked. 'Twelve years?' But both of them knew to the day how long it had been. All those letters of hers: 'My dear Hassan, ten years now and still your place is empty.' 'Eleven years and still . . .'

Hassan squinted through the windshield at the oncoming headlights. His mother started fretting over her kerchief, which she knew she ought not to have worn. She'd been told so by her youngest sister, who had been to America twice. 'It marks you,' her sister had said. But that square of silk was the last, shrunken reminder of the veil she used to hide beneath, before the previous Shah had banished such things. At her age, how could she expose herself? And then her teeth; her teeth were a problem, too. Her youngest sister had said, 'You ought to get dentures made, I'm sure there aren't three whole teeth in your head.' But Mrs Ardavi was scared of dentists. Now she covered her mouth with one hand and looked sideways at Hassan, though so far he hadn't seemed to notice. He was busy manoeuvring his car into the right-hand lane.

This silence was the last thing she had expected. For weeks she'd been saving up stray bits of gossip, weaving together the family stories she would tell him. There were three hundred people in her family – most of them related to each other in three or four different ways, all leading intricate and scandalous lives she had planned to discuss in detail, but instead she stared sadly out of the window. You'd think Hassan would ask. You'd think they could have a better conversation than this, after such a long time. Disappointment made her cross, and now she stubbornly refused to speak even when she saw something she wanted to comment on, some imposing building or unfamiliar brand of car sliding past her into the darkness.

By the time they arrived it was nearly midnight. None of the houses were lit but Hassan's – worn brick, older than she would have expected. 'Here we are,' said Hassan. The competence with which he parked the car, fitting it neatly into a small space by the kerb, put him firmly on the other side of the fence, the American side. She would have to face her daughter-in-law alone. As they climbed the front steps she whispered, 'How do you say it again?'

'Say what?' Hassan asked.

'Her name. Lizabet?'

'Elizabeth. Like Elizabeth Taylor. *You* know.'

'Yes, yes, of course,' said his mother. Then she lifted her chin, holding tight to the straps of her handbag.

Elizabeth was wearing blue jeans and a pair of fluffy slippers. Her hair was blonde as corn silk, cut short and straight, and her face had the grave, sleepy look of a child's. As soon as she had opened the door she said, '*Salaam aleikum.*' Mrs Ardavi, overcome with relief at the Persian greeting, threw her arms around her and kissed both cheeks. Then they led her into the living room, which looked comfortable but a little too plain. The furniture was straight-edged, the rugs uninteresting, though the curtains had a nice figured pattern that caught her eye. In one corner sat a shiny red kiddie car complete with licence plates. 'Is that the child's?' she asked. 'Hilary's?' She hesitated over the name. 'Could I see her?'

'*Now?*' said Hassan.

But Elizabeth told him, 'That's all right.' (Women understood these things.) She beckoned to her mother-in-law. They climbed the stairs together, up to the second floor, into a little room that smelled of milk and rubber and talcum powder, smells she would know anywhere. Even in the half-light from the hallway, she could tell that Hilary was beautiful. She had black, tumbling hair, long black lashes, and skin of a tone they called wheat-coloured, lighter than Hassan's. 'There,' said Elizabeth. 'Thank you,' said Mrs Ardavi. Her voice was formal, but this was her first grand-child and it took her a moment to recover herself. Then they stepped back into the hallway. 'I brought her some medals,' she whispered. 'I hope you don't mind.'

'Medals?' said Elizabeth. She repeated the word anxiously, mispronouncing it.

'Only an Allah and a Koran, both very tiny. You'll hardly know they're there. I'm not used to seeing a child without a medal. It worries me.'

Automatically her fingers traced a chain around her neck, ending in the hollow of her collarbone. Elizabeth nodded, looking relieved. '*Oh* yes. Medals,' she said.

'Is that all right?'

'Yes, of course.'

Mrs Ardavi took heart. 'Hassan laughs,' she said. 'He doesn't believe in these things. But when he left I put a prayer in his suitcase pocket, and you see he's been pro-tected. Now if Hilary wore a medal, I could sleep nights.'

'Of course,' Elizabeth said again.

When they re-entered the living room, Mrs Ardavi was smiling, and she kissed Hassan on the top of his head before she sat down.

American days were tightly scheduled, divided not into morning and afternoon but into 9.00, 9.30, and so forth, each half-hour possessing its own set activity. It was marvel-lous. Mrs Ardavi wrote to her sisters: 'They're more organised here. My daughter-in-law never wastes a minute.' How terrible, her sisters wrote back. They were all in Teheran, drinking cup after cup of tea and idly guessing who might come and visit. 'No, you misunderstand,' Mrs Ardavi protested. 'I like it this way. I'm fitting in wonder-fully.' And to her youngest sister she wrote, 'You'd think I was American. No one guesses otherwise.' This wasn't true, of course, but she hoped it would be true in the future.

Hassan was a doctor. He worked long hours, from six in the morning until six at night. While she was still washing for her morning prayers she could hear him tiptoe down the stairs and out of the front door. His car would start up, a distant rumble far below her, and from her bathroom window she could watch it swing out from beneath a tatter of red leaves and round the corner and disappear. Then she would sigh and return to her sink. Before prayers she had to wash her face, her hands, and the soles of her feet. She had to draw her wet fingers down the parting in her hair. After that she returned to her room, where she swathed herself tightly in her long black veil and knelt on a beaded velvet prayer mat. East was where the window was, curtained by chintz and misted over. On the east wall she hung a lithograph of the Caliph Ali and a colour snapshot of her third son, Babak, whose marriage she had arranged just a few months before this visit. If Babak hadn't married, she never could have come. He was the youngest, spoiled by being the only son at home. It had taken her three years to find a wife for him. (One was too modern, one too lazy, one so perfect she had been suspicious.) But finally the proper girl had turned up, modest and well-mannered and sufficiently wide of hip, and Mrs Ardavi and the bridal couple had settled in a fine new house on the outskirts of Teheran. Now every time she prayed, she added a word of thanks that at last she had a home for her old age. After that, she unwound her veil and laid it carefully in a drawer. From another drawer she took thick cotton stockings and elastic garters; she stuffed her swollen feet into open-toed vinyl sandals. Unless she was going out, she wore a housecoat. It amazed her how wasteful Americans were with their clothing.

Downstairs, Elizabeth would have started her tea and buttered a piece of toast for her. Elizabeth and Hilary ate bacon and eggs, but bacon of course was unclean and Mrs Ardavi never accepted any. Nor had it even been offered to her, except once, jokingly, by Hassan. The distinctive, smoky smell rose to meet her as she descended the stairs. 'What does it taste like?' she always asked. She was dying to know. But Elizabeth's vocabulary didn't cover the taste of bacon; she only said it was salty and then laughed and gave up. They had learned very early to travel a well-worn conversational path, avoiding the dead ends caused by unfamiliar words. 'Did you sleep well?' Elizabeth always asked in her funny, childish accent, and Mrs Ardavi answered, 'So-so.' Then they would turn and watch Hilary, who sat on a booster seat eating scrambled eggs, a thin chain of Persian gold crossing the back of her neck. Conversation was easier, or even unnecessary, as long as Hilary was there.

In the mornings Elizabeth cleaned the house. Mrs Ardavi used that time for letter writing. She had dozens of letters to write, to all her aunts and uncles and her thirteen sisters. (Her father had had three wives, and a surprising number of children even for that day and age.) Then there was Babak. His wife was in her second month of pregnancy, so Mrs Ardavi wrote long accounts of the American child-rearing methods. 'There are some things I don't agree with,' she wrote. 'They let Hilary play outdoors by herself, with not even a servant to keep an eye on her.' Then she would trail off and gaze thoughtfully at Hilary, who sat on the floor watching a television programme called *Captain Kangaroo*.

Mrs Ardavi's own childhood had been murky and grim. From the age of nine she was wrapped in a veil, one corner of it clenched in her teeth to hide her face whenever she appeared on the streets. Her father, a respected man high up in public life, used to chase servant girls through the halls and trap them, giggling, in vacant bedrooms. At the age of ten she was forced to watch her mother bleed to death in childbirth, and when she screamed the midwife had struck her across the face and held her down till she had properly kissed her mother goodbye. There seemed no connection at all between her and this little overalled American. At times, when Hilary had one of her temper tantrums, Mrs Ardavi waited in horror for Elizabeth to slap her and then, when no slap came, felt a mixture of relief and anger. 'In Iran – ' she would begin, and if Hassan was there he always said, 'But this is not Iran, remember?'

After lunch Hilary took a nap, and Mrs Ardavi went upstairs to say her noontime prayers and take a nap as well. Then she might do a little laundry in her bathtub. Laundry was a problem here. Although she liked Elizabeth, the fact was that the girl was a Christian, and therefore unclean; it would never do to have a Christian wash a Muslim's clothes.

The automatic drier was also unclean, having contained, at some point, a Christian's underwear. So she had to ask Hassan to buy her a drying rack. It came unassembled. Elizabeth put it together for her, stick by stick, and then Mrs Ardavi held it under her shower and rinsed it off, hoping that would be enough to remove any taint. The Koran didn't cover this sort of situation.

When Hilary was up from her nap they walked her to the park – Elizabeth in her eternal blue jeans and Mrs Ardavi in her kerchief and shawl, taking short painful steps in small shoes that bulged over her bunions. They still hadn't seen to her teeth, although by now Hassan had noticed them. She was hoping he might forget about the dentist, but then she saw him remembering every time she laughed and revealed her five brown teeth set wide apart.

At the park she laughed a great deal. It was her only way of communicating with the other women. They sat on the benches ringing the playground, and while Elizabeth translated their questions Mrs Ardavi laughed and nodded at them over and over. 'They want to know if you like it here,' Elizabeth said. Mrs Ardavi answered at length, but Elizabeth's translation was very short. Then gradually the other women forgot her, and conversation rattled on while she sat silent and watched each speaker's lips. The few recognisable words – 'telephone', 'television', 'radio' – gave her the impression that American conversations were largely technical, even among women. Their gestures were wide and slow, disproving her youngest sister's statement that in America everyone was in a hurry. On the contrary, these women were dreamlike, moving singly or in twos across wide flat spaces beneath white November skies when they departed.

Later, at home, Mrs Ardavi would say, 'The red-haired girl, is she pregnant? Is the fat girl happy in her marriage?' She asked with some urgency, plucking Elizabeth's sleeve when she was slow to answer. People's private lives fascinated her. On Saturday trips to the supermarket she liked to single out some interesting stranger. 'What's the matter with that *jerky*-moving man? That girl, is she one of your dark-skinned people?' Elizabeth answered too softly, and never seemed to follow Mrs Ardavi's pointing finger.

Supper was difficult; Mrs Ardavi didn't like American food. Even when Elizabeth made something Iranian, it had an American taste to it – the vegetables still faintly crisp, the onions transparent rather than nicely blackened. 'Vegetables not thoroughly cooked retain a certain acidity,' Mrs Ardavi said, laying down her fork. 'This is a cause of constipation and stomach aches. At night I often have heartburn. It's been three full days since I moved my bowels.' Elizabeth merely bent over her plate, offering no symptoms of her own in return. Hassan said, 'At the table, Khanom? At the table?'

Eventually she decided to cook supper herself. Over Elizabeth's protests she began at three every afternoon, filling the house with the smell of dillweed and arranging pots on counters and cabinets and finally, when there was no more space, on the floor. She squatted on the floor with her skirt tucked between her knees and stirred great bowls of minced greens while behind her, on the gas range, four different pots of food bubbled and steamed. The kitchen was becoming more homelike, she thought. A bowl of yoghurt brewed beside the stove, a kettle of rice soaked in the sink, and the top of the dishwasher was curlicued with the yellow dye from saffron. In one corner sat the pudding pan, black on the bottom from the times she had cooked down sugar to make a sweet for her intestines. 'Now, this is your rest period,' she always told Elizabeth. 'Come to the table in three hours and be surprised.' But Elizabeth only hovered around the kitchen, disturbing the serene, steam-filled air with clatters and slams as she put away pots or pacing between stove and sink, her arms folded across her chest. At supper she ate little: Mrs Ardavi wondered how Americans got so tall on such small suppers. Hassan, on the other hand, had second and third helpings. 'I must be gaining five pounds a week,' he said. 'None of my clothes fit.'

'That's good to hear,' said his mother. And Elizabeth added something but in English, which Hassan answered in English also. Often now they broke into English for paragraphs at a time – Elizabeth speaking softly, looking at her plate, and Hassan answering at length and sometimes reaching across the table to cover her hand.

At night, after her evening prayers, Mrs Ardavi watched television on the living-room couch. She brought her veil downstairs and wrapped it around her to keep the draughts away. Her shoes lay on the rug beneath her, and scattered down the length of the couch were her knitting bag, her sack of burnt sugar, her magnifying glass, and *My First Golden Dictionary*. Elizabeth read novels in an easy chair, and Hassan watched TV so that he could translate the difficult parts of the plot. Not that Mrs Ardavi had much trouble. American plots were easy to guess at, particularly the Westerns. And when the programme was boring – a documentary or a special news feature – she could pass the time by talking to Hassan. 'Your cousin Farah wrote,' she said. 'Do you remember her? A homely girl, too dark. She's getting a divorce and in my opinion it's fortunate; he's from a lower class. Do you remember Farah?'

Hassan only grunted, his eyes on the screen. He was interested in American politics. So was she, for that matter. She had wept for President Kennedy, and carried Jackie's picture in her purse. But these news programmes were long and dry, and if Hassan wouldn't talk she was forced to turn at last to her *Golden Dictionary*.

In her childhood, she had been taught by expensive foreign tutors. Her mind was her great gift, the compensation for a large, plain face and a stocky figure. But now what she had learned seemed lost, forgotten utterly or fogged by years, so that Hassan gave a snort whenever she told him some fact that she had dredged up from her memory. It seemed that everything she studied now had to penetrate through a great thick layer before it reached her mind. 'Tonk you,' she practised. 'Tonk you. Tonk you.' 'Thank you,' Hassan corrected her. He pointed out useful words in her dictionary – grocery-store words, household words – but she grew impatient with their woodenness. What she wanted was the language to display her personality, her famous courtesy and her magical intuition about the inside lives of other people. Nightly she learned 'salt', 'bread', 'spoon', but

256

with an inner sense of dullness, and every morning when she woke her English was once again confined to 'thank you' and 'NBC'.

Elizabeth, meanwhile, read on, finishing one book and reaching for the next without even glancing up. Hassan chewed a thumbnail and watched a senator. He shouldn't be disturbed, of course, but time after time his mother felt the silence and the whispery turning of pages stretching her nerves until she had to speak. 'Hassan?'

'Hmm.'

'My chest seems tight. I'm sure a cold is coming on. Don't you have a tonic?'

'No,' said Hassan.

He dispensed medicines all day; he listened to complaints. Common sense told her to stop, but she persisted, encouraged by some demon that wouldn't let her tongue lie still. 'Don't you have some syrup? What about that liquid you gave me for constipation? Would that help?'

'No, it wouldn't,' said Hassan.

He drove her on, somehow. The less he gave, the more she had to ask. 'Well, aspirin? Vitamins?' Until Hassan said, 'Will you just let met *watch*?' Then she could lapse into silence again, or even gather up the clutter of her belongings and bid the two of them good night.

She slept badly. Often she lay awake for hours fingering the edge of the sheet and staring at the ceiling. Memories crowded in on her, old grievances and fears, injustices that had never been righted. For the first time in years she thought of her husband, a gentle, weak man given to surprising outbursts of temper. She hadn't loved him when she married him, and at his death from a liver ailment six years later her main feeling had been resentment. Was it fair to be widowed so young, while other women were supported and protected? She had moved from her husband's home back to the old family estate, where five of her sisters still lived. There she had stayed till Babak's wedding, drinking tea all day with her sisters and pulling the strings by which the rest of the family was attached. Marriages were arranged, funerals attended, childbirth discussed in fine detail; servants' disputes were settled, and feuds patched up and then restarted. Her husband's face had quickly faded, leaving only a vacant spot in her mind. But now she could see him so clearly – a wasted figure on his deathbed, beard untrimmed, turban coming loose, eyes imploring her for something more than an absentminded pat on the cheek as she passed through his room on her way to check the children.

She saw the thin faces of her three small boys as they sat on the rug eating rice. Hassan was the stubborn, mischievous one, with perpetual scabs on his knees. Babak was the cuddly one. Ali was the oldest, who had caused so much worry – weak, like his father, demanding, but capable of turning suddenly charming. Four years ago he had died of a brain haemorrhage, slumping over a dinner table in faraway Shīrāz, where he'd gone to be free of his wife, who was also his double first cousin. Ever since he was born he had disturbed his mother's sleep, first because she worried over what he would amount to and now, after his death, because she lay awake listing all she had done wrong with him. She had been too lenient. No, too harsh. There was no telling. Mistakes she had made floated on the ceiling like ghosts – allowances she'd made when she knew she shouldn't have, protections he had not deserved, blows which perhaps he had not deserved either.

She would have liked to talk to Hassan about it, but any time she tried he changed the subject. Maybe he was angry about the way he had heard of Ali's death. It was customary to break such news gradually. She had started a series of tactful letters, beginning by saying that Ali was seriously ill when in truth he was already buried. Something in the letter had given her away – perhaps her plans for a rest cure by the seaside, which she never would have considered if she'd had an ailing son at home. Hassan had telephoned overseas, taking three nights to reach her. 'Tell me what's wrong,' he said. 'I know there's something.' When her tears kept her from answering, he asked, 'Is he dead?' His voice sounded angry, but that might have been due to a poor connection. And when he hung up, cutting her off before she could say all she wanted, she thought, I should have told him straight out. I had forgotten that about him. Now when she spoke of Ali he listened politely, with his face frozen. She would have told him anything, all about the death and burial and that witch of a wife throwing herself, too late, into the grave; but Hassan never asked.

Death was moving in on her. Oh, not on her personally (the women in her family lived a century or longer, burying the men one by one) but on everybody around her, all the cousins and uncles and brothers-in-law. No sooner had she laid away her mourning clothes than it was time to bring them out again. Recently she had begun to feel she would outlive her two other sons as well, and she fought off sleep because of the dreams it brought – Babak lying stiff and cold in his grave, Hassan crumpled over in some dark American alley. Terrifying images would zoom at her out of the night. In the end she had to wrap herself in her veil and sleep instead on the Persian rug, which had the dusty smell of home and was, anyway, more comfortable than her unsteady foreign mattress.

At Christmas time, Hassan and Elizabeth gave Mrs Ardavi a brightly coloured American dress with short sleeves. She wore it to an Iranian party, even leaving off her kerchief in a sudden fit of daring. Everyone commented on how nice she looked. 'Really you fit right in,' a girl told her. 'May I write to my mother about you? She was over here for a year and a half and never once stepped out of the house without her kerchief.' Mrs Ardavi beamed. It was true she would never have associated with these people at home – children of civil servants and bank clerks, newly rich now they'd finished medical school. The wives called their husbands 'Doctor' even in direct address. But still it felt good to be speaking so much Persian; her tongue nearly ran away with her. 'I see you're expecting a baby,' she said to one of the wives. 'Is it your first? I could tell by your eyes. Now don't be nervous. I had three myself; my mother had seven and never felt a pain in her life. She would squat down to serve my father's breakfast and "Eh?" she would say. "Aga Jun, it's the baby!" and there it would be on the floor between her feet, waiting for her to cut the cord and finish pouring the tea.' She neglected to mention how her mother had died. All her natural tact came back to her, her gift with words and her knowledge of how to hold an audience. She bubbled and sparkled like a girl, and her face fell when it was time to go home.

After the party, she spent two or three days noticing more keenly than ever the loss of her language, and talking more feverishly when Hassan came home in the evening. This business of being a foreigner was something changeable. Boundaries kept shifting, and sometimes it was she who was the foreigner but other times Elizabeth, or even Hassan. (Wasn't it true, she often wondered, that there was a greater distance between men and women than between Americans and Iranians, or even *Eskimos* and Iranians?) Hassan was the foreigner when she and Elizabeth conspired to hide a miniature Koran in his glove compartment; he would have laughed at them. 'You see,' she told Elizabeth, 'I know there's nothing to it, but it makes me feel better. When my sons were born I took them all to the bath attendant to have their blood let. People say it brings long life. I know that's superstition, but whenever afterwards I saw those ridges down their backs I felt safe. Don't you understand?' And Elizabeth said, 'Of course.' She smuggled the Koran into the car herself, and hid it beneath the Texaco maps. Hassan saw nothing.

Hilary was a foreigner forever. She dodged her grand-mother's yearning hands, and when the grown-ups spoke Persian she fretted and misbehaved and pulled on Elizabeth's sleeve. Mrs Ardavi had to remind herself constantly not to kiss the child too much, not to reach out for a hug, not to offer her lap. In this country people kept more separate. They kept so separate that at times she felt hurt. They tried to be so subtle, so undemonstrative. She would never understand this place.

In January they took her to a dentist, who made clucking noises when he looked in her mouth. 'What does he say?' she asked. 'Tell me the worst.' But Hassan was talking in a low voice to Elizabeth, and he waved her aside. They seemed to be having a misunderstanding of some sort. 'What does he say, Hassan?'

'Just a minute.'

260

She craned around in the high-backed chair, fighting off the dentist's little mirror. 'I have to know,' she told Hassan. 'He says your teeth are terrible. They have to be extracted and the gums surgically smoothed. He wants to know if you'll be here for another few months, he can't schedule you till later.'

A cold lump of fear settled in her stomach. Unfortunately she *would* be here; it had only been three months so far and she was planning to stay a year. So she had to watch numbly while her life was signed away, whole strings of appointments made and little white cards filled out. And Hassan didn't even look sympathetic. He was still involved in whatever this argument was with Elizabeth. The two of them failed to notice how her hands were shaking.

It snowed all January, the worst snow they had had in years. When she came downstairs in the mornings she found the kitchen icy cold, criss-crossed by draughts. 'This sort of cold enters your bones,' she told Elizabeth. 'I'm sure to fall sick.' Elizabeth only nodded. Some morning now her face was pale and puffy, as if she had a secret worry, but Mrs Ardavi had learned that it was better not to ask about it.

Early in February there was a sudden warm spell. Snow melted and all the trees dripped in the sunshine. 'We're going for a walk.' Elizabeth said, and Mrs Ardavi said, 'I'll come too.' In spite of the warmth she toiled upstairs for her woollen shawl. She didn't like to take chances. And she worried over Hilary's bare ears. 'Won't she catch cold?' she asked. 'I think we should cover her head.'

'She'll be all right,' said Elizabeth, and then shut her face in a certain stubborn way she had.

In the park, Elizabeth and Hilary made snowballs from the last of the snow and threw them at each other, narrowly missing Mrs Ardavi, who stood watching with her arms folded and her hands tucked in her sleeves.

The next morning, something was wrong with Hilary. She sat at the breakfast table and cried steadily, refusing all food. 'Now, now,' her grandmother said, 'won't you tell old Ka Jun what's wrong?' But when she came close Hilary screamed louder. By noon she was worse. Elizabeth called

261

Hassan, and he came home immediately and laid a hand on Hilary's forehead and said she should go to the paediatrician. He drove them there himself. 'It's her ears, I'm sure of it,' Mrs Ardavi said in the waiting room. For some reason Hassan grew angry. 'Do you always know better than the experts?' he asked her. 'What are we coming to the doctor for? We could have talked to you and saved the trip.' His mother lowered her eyes and examined her handbag straps. She understood that he was anxious, but all the same her feelings were hurt and when they rose to go into the office she stayed behind.

Later Hassan came back and sat down again. 'There's an infection in her middle ear,' he told her. 'The doctor's going to give her a shot of penicillin.' His mother nodded, careful not to annoy him by reminding him she had thought as much. Then Hilary started crying. She must be getting her shot now. Mrs Ardavi herself was terrified of needles, and she sat gripping her handbag until her fingers turned white, staring around the waiting room, which seemed pathetically cheerful with its worn wooden toys and nursery-school paintings. Her own ear ached in sympathy. She thought of a time when she had boxed Ali's ears too hard and he had wept all that day and gone to sleep sucking his thumb.

While Hassan was there she was careful not to say anything, but the following morning at breakfast she said, 'Elizabeth dear, do you remember that walk we took the day before yesterday?'

'Yes,' said Elizabeth. She was squeezing oranges for Hilary, who'd grown cheerful again and was eating a huge breakfast.

'Remember I said Hilary should wear a hat? Now you see you should have been more careful. Because of you she fell sick; she could have died. Do you see that now?'

'No,' said Elizabeth.

Was her Persian that scanty? Lately it seemed to have shrunk and hardened, like a stale piece of bread. Mrs Ardavi sighed and tried again. 'Without a hat, you see – ' she began. But Elizabeth set down her orange, picked up Hilary, and walked out of the room. Mrs Ardavi stared after her, wondering if she'd said something wrong.

For the rest of the day, Elizabeth was busy in her room. She was cleaning out bureaux and cupboards. A couple of times Mrs Ardavi advanced as far as the doorway, where she stood awkwardly watching. Hilary sat on the floor playing with a discarded perfume bottle. Everything, it seemed, was about to be thrown away – buttonless blouses and stretched-out sweaters, stockings and combs and empty lipstick tubes. 'Could I be of any help?' Mrs Ardavi asked, but Elizabeth said, 'Oh, no. Thank you very much.' Her voice was cheerful. Yet when Hassan came home he went upstairs and stayed a long time, and the door remained shut behind him.

Supper that night was an especially fine stew, Hassan's favourite ever since childhood, but he didn't say a word about it. He hardly spoke at all, in fact. Then later, when Elizabeth was upstairs putting Hilary to bed, he said,' Khanom Jun, I want to talk to you.'

'Yes, Hassan,' she said, laying aside her knitting. She was frightened by his seriousness, the black weight of his moustache, and her own father's deep black eyes. But what had she done? She knotted her hands and looked up at him, swallowing.

'I understand you've been interfering,' he said.

'I, Hassan?'

'Elizabeth isn't the kind you can do that with. And she's raising the child just fine on her own.'

'Well, of course she is,' said his mother. 'Did I ever say otherwise?'

'Show it, then. Don't offer criticisms.'

'Very well,' she said. She picked up her knitting and began counting stitches, as if she'd forgotten the conversation entirely. But that evening she was unusually quiet, and at nine o'clock she excused herself to go to bed. 'So early?' Hassan asked.

'I'm tired,' she told him, and left with her back very straight.

Her room surrounded her like a nest. She had built up layers of herself on every surface – tapestries and bits of lace and lengths of Paisley. The bureau was covered with gilt-framed pictures of the saints, and snapshots of her sisters at family gatherings. On the windowsill were little plants in

263

orange and aqua plastic pots – her favourite American colours. Her bedside table held bottles of medicine, ivory prayer beads, and a tiny brick of holy earth. The rest of the house was bare and shiny, impersonal; this room was as comforting as her shawl.

Still, she didn't sleep well. Ghosts rose up again, tugging at her thoughts. Why did things turn out so badly for her? Her father had preferred her brothers, a fact that crushed her even after all these years. Her husband had had three children by her and then complained that she was cold. And what comfort were children? If she had stayed in Iran any longer Babak would have asked her to move; she'd seen it coming. There'd been some disrespect creeping into his bride's behaviour, some unwillingness to take advice, which Babak had overlooked even when his mother pointed it out to him. And Hassan was worse – always so stubborn, much too independent. She had offered him anything if he would just stay in Iran but he had said no; he was set on leaving her. And he had flatly refused to take along his cousin Shora as his wife, though everyone pointed out how lonely he would be. He was so anxious to break away, to get *going*, to come to this hardhearted country and take up with a Christian girl. Oh, she should have laughed when he left, and saved her tears for someone more deserving. She never should have come here, she never should have asked anything of him again. When finally she went to sleep it seemed that her eyes remained open, burning large and dry beneath her lids.

In the morning she had a toothache. She could hardly walk for the pain. It was only Friday (the first of her dental appointments was for Monday), but the dentist made time for her during the afternoon and pulled the tooth. Elizabeth said it wouldn't hurt, but it did. Elizabeth treated it as something insignificant, merely a small break in her schedule which required the hiring of a babysitter. She wouldn't even call Hassan home from work. 'What could he do?' she asked.

So when Hassan returned that evening it was all a surprise to him – the sight of his mother with a bloody cotton cylinder hanging out over her lower lip like a long tooth.

'What *happened* to you?' he asked. To make it worse, Hilary was screaming and had been all afternoon. Mrs Ardavi put her hands over her ears, wincing. 'Will you make that child hush?' Hassan told Elizabeth. 'I think we should get my mother to bed.' He guided her towards the stairs, and she allowed herself to lean on him. 'It's mainly my heart,' she said. 'You know how scared I am of dentists.' When he had folded back her bedspread and helped her to lie down she closed her eyes gratefully, resting one arm across her forehead. Even the comfort of hot tea was denied her; she had to stay on cold foods for twelve hours. Hassan fixed her a glass of ice water. He was very considerate, she thought. He seemed as shaken at the sight of her as Hilary had been. All during the evening he kept coming to check on her, and twice in the night she heard him climbing the stairs to listen at her door. When she moaned he called, 'Are you awake?'

'Of course,' she said.

'Can I get you anything?'

'No, no.'

In the morning she descended the stairs with slow, groping feet, keeping a tight hold on the railing. 'It was a very hard night,' she said. 'At four my gum started throbbing. Is that normal? I think these American pain pills are constipating. Maybe a little prune juice would restore my regularity.'

'I'll get it,' Hassan said. 'You sit down. Did you take the milk of magnesia?'

'Oh, yes, but I'm afraid it wasn't enough,' she said.

Elizabeth handed Hassan a platter of bacon, not looking at him.

After breakfast, while Hassan and his mother were still sitting over their tea, Elizabeth started cleaning the kitchen. She made quite a bit of noise. She sorted the silverware and then went through a tangle of utensils, discarding bent spatulas and rusty tongs. 'May I help?' asked Mrs Ardavi. Elizabeth shook her head. She seemed to have these fits of throwing things away. Now she was standing on the counter to take everything from the upper cabinets – crackers, cereals, half-empty bottles of spices. On the very top shelf was a flowered tin confectioner's box with Persian lettering on it, forgotten since the day Mrs Ardavi had brought it. 'My!' said Mrs Ardavi. 'Won't Hilary be surprised!' Elizabeth pried the lid off. Out flew a cloud of insects, greyish-brown with V-shaped wings. They brushed past Elizabeth's face and fluttered through her hair and swarmed towards the ceiling, where they dimmed the light fixture. Elizabeth flung the box as far from her as possible and climbed down from the counter. 'Goodness!' said Mrs Ardavi. 'Why, we have those at home!' Hassan lowered his teacup. Mixed nuts and dried currants rolled every which way on the floor; more insects swung towards the ceiling. Elizabeth sat on the nearest chair and buried her head in her hands. 'Elizabeth?' said Hassan.

But she wouldn't look at him. In the end she simply rose and went upstairs, shutting the bedroom door with a gentle, definite click which they heard all the way down in the kitchen because they were listening so hard.

'Excuse me,' Hassan said to his mother.

She nodded and stared into her tea.

After he was gone she went to find Hilary, and she set her on her knee, babbling various folk rhymes to her while straining her ears towards the silence overhead. But Hilary squirmed off her lap and went to play with a truck. Then Hassan came downstairs again. He didn't say a word about Elizabeth.

On the following day, when Mrs Ardavi's tooth was better, she and Hassan had a little talk upstairs in her room. They were very polite with each other. Hassan asked his mother how long they could hope for her to stay. His mother said she hadn't really thought about it. Hassan said that in America it was the custom to have houseguests for three months only. After that they moved to a separate apartment nearby, which he'd be glad to provide for her as soon as he could find one, maybe next week. 'Ah, an apartment,' said his mother, looking impressed. But she had never lived alone a day in her life, and so after a suitable pause she said that she would hate to put him to so much expense. 'Especially,' she said, 'when I'm going in such a short time anyway, since I'm homesick for my sisters.'

'Well, then,' said Hassan.

At supper that night, Hassan announced that his mother was missing her sisters and would like to leave. Elizabeth lowered her glass. 'Leave?' she said.

Mrs Ardavi said, 'And Babak's wife, of course, will be asking for me when the baby arrives.'

'Well . . . but what about the dentist? You were supposed to start your appointments on Monday.'

'It's not important,' Mrs Ardavi said.

'But we set up all those – '

'There are plenty of dentists she can see at home,' Hassan told Elizabeth. 'We have dentists in Iran, for God's sake. Do you imagine we're barbarians?'

'No,' Elizabeth said.

On the evening of the third of March, Hassan drove his mother to the airport. He was worrying about the road, which was slippery after a snowfall. He couldn't find much to say to his mother. And once they had arrived he deliberately kept the conversation to trivia – the verifying of tickets, checking of departure times, weighing of baggage. Her baggage was fourteen pounds overweight. It didn't make sense; all she had were her clothes and a few small gifts for her sisters. 'Why is it so heavy?' Hassan asked. 'What have you got in there?' But his mother only said, 'I don't know,' and straightened her shawl, looking elsewhere. Hassan bent to open a tooled-leather suitcase. Inside he found three empty urn-shaped wine bottles, the permanent-press sheets from her bed, and a sample box of detergent that had come in yesterday's mail. 'Listen,' Hassan, 'do you know how much I'd have to pay to fly these things over? What's the matter with you?'

'I wanted to show my sisters,' his mother said.

'Well, forget it. Now, what else have you got?'

But something about her – the vague, childlike eyes set upon some faraway object – made him give in. He opened no more bags. He even regretted his sharpness, and when her flight was announced he hugged her closely and kissed the top of her head. 'Go with God,' he said.

'Goodbye, Hassan.'

She set off down the corridor by herself, straggling behind a line of businessmen. They all wore hats. His mother wore her scarf, and of all the travellers she alone, securely kerchiefed and shawled, setting her small shoes resolutely on the gleaming tiles, seemed undeniably a foreigner.

WILLIAM TREVOR

The Property of Colette Nervi

Drumgawnie the crossroads was known as, and for miles around the land was called Drumgawnie also. There was a single shop at the crossroads, next to a pink house with its roof gone. There was an abandoned mill, with tall grain stores no longer used for any purpose. Drumgawnie Rath, a ring of standing stones that pre-dated history, was half a mile across the fields where Odd Garvey grazed his cattle.

It was in 1959, an arbitrary date as far as the people who lived in and around Drumgawnie were concerned, that visitors began to take interest in the stones, drawing their cars up by the mill and the grain stores. English or French people they usually were, spring or summertime tourists who always called in at the shop to enquire the way. Mrs Mullalley, who owned the shop, had thought of erecting a small sign but in the end had abandoned the notion on the grounds that one day perhaps a visitor might glance about her premises and purchase something. None ever had.

'You have to cross the little stream,' she informed a French couple in the early summer of 1968. 'Continue on past where you've drawn your car in and then there's rocks you can step on to see you over the bit of water. Go neither right nor left after that until you'll strike the stones standing up in the grass.'

In her bedroom Dolores Mullalley, then aged twenty-two, watched from her window, the lacy half-curtain pulled back at the edge. She had heard the car coming to a halt by the mill, and minutes later foreign voices had become louder as the visitors approached the shop. She had pushed herself up from her bed and jumped across to the window. The woman was wearing a black leather coat, a thin woman with a smiling, slanted face, strange looking and beautiful. The man had a moustache and a pipe.

Dolores imagined these foreign people asking her mother about the standing stones, and her mother telling them, using the same expressions she always did. When her mother wasn't there and Dolores gave the directions herself she never used expressions like 'to see you over the bit of water' or 'you'll strike the stones standing up in the grass'. All that was her mother's old-fashioned way of putting things. Dolores simply said that the visitors must cross the stream at a place they'd see and then keep straight on. Her father, no longer alive, had once carried her to see the standing stones and she hadn't found them much to look at. But a visitor who had spent a whole afternoon examining them and had afterwards returned to the shop to verify the way to the Rossaphin road, had stated that they were the most extraordinary stones of their kind in the whole of Europe. 'I think he was maybe drunk,' Dolores's mother had commented, and her father had agreed.

As soon as they left the shop the Frenchman took the woman's arm affectionately, both of them laughing at something or other. Dolores watched them walking on the left-hand side of the road, towards the mill and the towering grain stores. There had been prosperity in the place once, both her father and her mother had said, at the time when the mill operated. Its owner had lived in the pink distempered house with the fallen-in roof, a man called Mr Hackett, who had grown some special kind of plums in his garden.

The French couple stood for a moment by their car, a small, bright red vehicle, hired in Dublin, Dolores guessed. A group of English people and an American woman, returning from the stones some years ago had been unable to start theirs and had telephoned the Dan Ryan car-hire organisation from the shop. It was then, for the first time, that Dolores had realised it was possible for visitors from other countries to hire motor cars and to drive all over Ireland in them.

The Frenchman removed the pipe from his mouth and knocked it out on the edge of his shoe. He unlocked one of the car doors and took from it two pairs of short green gumboots, which he and the woman put on. They stowed their shoes in the car and then the man put his arms about his companion. He bent her head backwards, leaning his body against her and pushing his lips on to hers, Dolores

270

guessed, although she could not quite see that detail of the embrace. He released the woman and she at once placed her hands, fingers splayed out, on his black hair, drawing his face down to hers again. After a moment they separated and set off jauntily, hand in hand, their arms stretched across the path they walked along. On either side of them nettles and dock grew in great profusion; daisy heads and butter-cups decorated the grass of the path, ragwort was everywhere. The afternoon was sunny, puffy little clouds were stationary in the sky. On the red roof of the car there was what appeared to be a shadow, small and rectangular and vividly black: it was an object, Dolores realised when she screwed her eyes up, not a shadow at all. Carelessly the two had left it there.

She dropped the edge of the half-curtain and limped back to her bed, where she had been reading *Holster in the Dust* by Tom K Kane. She picked a cigarette from a packet of Afton Major, open on the candlewick counterpane. She lit it and inhaled. Because of her bad leg she lay down for an hour or so almost every afternoon, unless it was the time of year when the seed potatoes had to be put in on the slope at the back or the later time the grown potatoes had to be gathered. Years ago, when Dolores was twelve, old Dr Riordan had suggested that a rest in the afternoon might be a relief. The leg, shrivelled to the bone as a result of infantile paralysis, necessitated the use of a crutch, although in making her way across her bedroom or the kitchen, or sometimes moving about in the shop, Dolores could manage without this aid, limping from one steadying surface to the next. *The evening sun-rays reddened the canyon*, she read. *Dust was acrid in One-Draw's nostrils and grimy on his cheeks.* Her father had bought these yellow-backed books of the Wild West Library, which were closely printed on absorbent paper, a perpendicular line down the centre of each page, separating the prose as in a newspaper. Their soft covers were tattered now, creases running through horses and riders and gunsmoke, limp spines bent and split. Her father had bought one in Mackie's the newsagent's every Friday, making the journey to Rossaphin in the horse and cart, taking Dolores with him. He had brought to the town the carrots and cabbages he grew on the slope, turnips and potatoes when he had them, plums from the forgotten garden next door. A waste of time, Dolores's mother had always maintained, because of the small profit there'd been, and when Mr Mullalley died the practice had ceased and the horse had been sold. The cart was still in the yard at the back, its faded orange-painted wood just beginning to rot. Even though her father had died fourteen years ago Dolores still missed those weekly journeys and the feeling of excitement they engendered.

The shop, patronised by everyone in the neighbourhood, kept Mrs Mullalley and her daughter going. The bus dropped off newspapers there, groceries and confectionery were stocked, and a rudimentary post office maintained. At the time of Drumgawnie's greater prosperity, Mrs Mullalley's father had run it profitably, with a public house as well. Dolores's own father, once employed in Mr Hackett's milling business, had married into the shop after the closing of the mill. In his lifetime it was still thought that Dolores's affliction might miraculously right itself as she grew up, but this had not happened. He died in the kitchen armchair, having complained for several months of pains in the chest which Dr Riordan had not taken seriously. 'Well, Mother of God, isn't it the most surprising thing in three decades of practising medicine?' Dolores remembered him saying in the kitchen, the body already covered with a bed-sheet. 'Riordan was drunk as a fish,' her mother was afterwards to remark. 'His breath would've knocked you down.' Not used to that particular smell, Dolores had imagined it to be a variation of the disinfectant she associated with Dr Riordan's house in Rossaphin.

One-Draw slid from the saddle. His eyes were slits, measuring the distance. 'Cassidy!' he shouted. 'Reach, Cassidy!' There was no reply, no movement. Not a sound in the canyon.

Dolores folded down the corner of the page to keep her place. She lit another Afton Major. There was never any pain in her leg; it was just the ugliness of it, the difficult, unattractive movement, the crutch she hated so. She'd become used over the years to all the cumbersome arrangements that had to be made for her, the school bus coming specially to the crossroads to take her to the convent in Rossaphin, the Crowleys calling in on a Sunday to take her and her mother to mass in their Ford. Once a year, three weeks before Christmas, she and her mother went for the day to shop in Rossaphin, driven on that occasion also by the Crowleys. They had a meal in Love's Café and didn't return to the crossroads until six o'clock. Her mother had to get special permission to close the post-office counter, which was something Father Keane was able to arrange, just as it was he who persuaded the Crowleys to be kind in the way they were.

Now and again, between one December and the next, Dolores managed to get in to Rossaphin on the bus, but the journey home again had to be arranged carefully and in advance, with the co-operation of one of the drivers who called regularly at the shop. Phelan who brought the bread was no good because he came out in the morning, but the Mitchelstown Cheese man always passed through Rossaphin in the late afternoon and then came on to the crossroads, and Jimmy Reilly, who brought the bacon, came in the afternoon also. Having chosen a particular day and made the arrangement to meet one or other of the delivery men at a time and a place, Dolores usually had three hours or a bit more on her own. Her mother didn't like it though; her mother worried in case the van men might forget. Neither of them ever had, but something once did go wrong with Jimmy Reilly's engine and Dolores was left waiting outside the Provincial Bank until five o'clock when she should have been collected at two. A boy had come up to her with a message, and then Father Keane had appeared on his bicycle. He rang the bell of the bank and the manager's wife had allowed Dolores to sit on a chair in the hall until the Crowleys arrived in their Ford. The tears were running down her mother's cheeks when eventually she arrived back at the crossroads, and after that Dolores never again went into Rossaphin on her own.

She squashed her cigarette butt on the ashtray that lay beside *Holster in the Dust* on the candlewick counterpane. The ashtray was made of glass, with green letters advertising 7-Up on it, a free gift from one of the delivery men. She'd easily finish *Holster in the Dust* tonight, Dolores considered, she'd even start *Guns of the Apache Country*. She'd read both of them before, but not recently.

She tidied the counterpane, brushing the wrinkles from it. She paused for a moment by the looking-glass on her dressing-table to smear fresh lipstick on to her lips and to run a comb through her long black hair. Her face was round, her chin a pleasant curve. Her father had told her that her eyes were like a dog's he'd once owned, meaning it as a compliment. They were brown and serious, as if all the time Dolores was intent on thoughts she chose not to share with other people. But mostly what she thought about were the adventures of the Wild West Library.

'Are you rested, pet?' her mother enquired in the shop. 'You didn't smoke too much?'

'Only two,' Dolores lied.

'You're better off without, pet.'

Dolores nodded. 'That's a well-dressed pair went up to the stones.'

'Did you see them? You should stay lying down, pet.'

'I'll look after the shop now.'

Her mother said that Mrs Connell hadn't come in for her bread yet, nor Whelan for his *Independent*. 'French those people said they were.'

She sliced a couple of rashers as she spoke and took them away on the palm of her hand, through the small store-room at the back of the shop, into the kitchen. In a moment the smell of frying would drift through the store-room, as it did every evening at this time, and soon after that Dolores would put up the wire shutter on the post-office counter and lock the drawer where the postal orders and the stamps and the registration book were kept. She'd take the key into the kitchen with her when eventually she went to sit down to her tea. She would hang it on a hook on the dresser, but the shop itself would remain open and anyone who came into it would rap on the counter for attention, knowing that that was expected.

'Mademoiselle,' the Frenchman said, and went on talking.

Dolores couldn't understand him. He wasn't smiling any more, and his thin companion in her leather coat wasn't smiling either. They were agitated: the man kept gesturing, moving his hands about; the woman frowned, muttering in French to herself. Dolores shook her head. '*Je ne sais pas,*' the Frenchman said. '*Peut-être-ici.*'

He looked around the shop. The woman looked also, on the counter, on the post-office counter, on the cartons that had arrived yesterday and had not yet been opened, on the floor.

'I didn't catch what you said,' Dolores explained, but the woman continued to speak French.

'*Le sac. Le sac noir.*'

'The handbag of my friend,' the man said. 'We lose the handbag.'

'Lose?'

'I place it,' the woman said. 'It is that I place it.'

Dolores reached for her crutch. She lifted the flap of the counter and helped in the search. She called loudly to her mother and when her mother arrived, wiping her hands on her apron, she explained that a handbag had been lost, that it might have been left in the shop.

'I would have noticed,' Mrs Mullalley said, quickly.

'*Ah, oui, oui,*' the man agreed.

'She was carrying a handbag,' Mrs Mullalley said, a defensive note entering her voice. 'She definitely walked out of the shop with it. A square handbag, under her arm.'

Dolores tried to remember: had the woman had a handbag when they walked together to the car? Had she had it when they'd embraced? And then she did remember: the square dark shadow on the red roof, too vivid to be just a shadow.

'She put it on top of the car,' she said, and as she spoke she seemed to see what at the time had passed unnoticed: the woman's arm raised in the moment just before the embrace, the handbag in her hand and then on the red metal that glittered in the sunlight. Dolores had been too intent on the embrace to have observed this properly, but she was certain it had happened.

'Oh yes,' she said, nodding to lend emphasis to her claim. 'You put it on the roof of your car.'

'You observe?' the Frenchman asked.

'I saw from a window upstairs.'

'Ah, merci, mademoiselle. Merci beaucoup.' It was the woman who spoke. The man thanked Dolores in English.

She watched, leaning against the doorway of the shop. Her mother accompanied the French couple across the road and then disappeared from sight because of the incline down to the mill. Dolores had sensed her mother's anxiety, the feeling there'd been in her mother's mind that an accusation was being made. She thought of going upstairs to her bedroom to watch again from the window and was about to do so when the smell of burning bacon wafted from the kitchen. Hurriedly, she shuffled through the shop and the store-room.

'They never found it,' her mother said, returning ten minutes later. 'They moved the car to see if it had fallen off. They'd been up and down to the stones four times, they said, looking on the path in case she dropped it.'

'She put it on the car, she couldn't have dropped it.'

'Ah, sure, you can't watch them.'

'So it's gone, is it?'

'They wrote down an address for me in case it would surface some day. She was down in the mouth, that woman.'

Dolores saw the beautiful, slanted face pulled further to one side, the mouth dragged into a corner of itself, tears threatening. The man would put his arm around the smartly-clad shoulders, so very slight beneath the leather. He would comfort his lover and promise her another handbag because people like that, who could hire a motor car, who could come all the way from France to see some stones in a field, wouldn't have to bother about the expense.

'Did you tell them to go to the gardai at Rossaphin?'

'I didn't mention the gardai to them,' Mrs Mullalley spoke firmly again, and Dolores knew that she hadn't suggested the police because she didn't want it to become known that a handbag had disappeared in this manner at the crossroads. 'Sure, won't they find the thing in their motor car somewhere?'

Dolores nodded, silently agreeing that somehow or other that would be the outcome of the matter. When they had returned from the stones the woman must have taken the handbag from the roof without noticing what she was doing and she must have bundled it into the car without noticing either. She cut a piece of fried bread and dipped it into the little mound of salt on the side of her plate. She began to think about One-Draw Hagan and his enemy, Red Cassidy.

'Only Henry Garvey was about,' her mother continued, 'driving in the old man's heifers. He'd have been too far away to catch what was going on.'

Dolores nodded again. Perhaps when the lovers returned to the car there had been another embrace, which had driven everything from their minds – like in *Travellin' Saddles* when Big Daunty found his Indian love and both of them went into a swoon, lost to the world. *Colette Nervi*, it said on the piece of paper the French lovers had given her mother. 19 *rue St Just, Toulouse, France*. They had insisted on giving her money also, so that she could send them a letter in case the handbag ever turned up.

Henry Garvey was a large, slow man of forty, known in the neighbourhood for his laziness and his easy-going nature. His uncle, Odd Garvey, had outlived both of Henry's parents, and the two lived together in the farmhouse which the whole Garvey family had once occupied. Odd Garvey, small and wizened in his old age, had never married – due to meanness, so it was locally said. He was reputed to be affected in the head, though this impression which he gave was perhaps no more than another reflection of a miserly nature. The farmhouse which he occupied with his nephew was in need of considerable repair, its roof leaky, its walls wet with rising damp. Henry spent as little time as he could there, preferring to ride his mother's ancient bicycle into Rossaphin every morning and to remain there until it was time to fetch the heifers in. He laid bets and drank in a number of selected public houses while waiting for the afternoon's racing to begin. He bet on greyhounds as well as horses, and had been known in one bar or another to offer odds on a variety of propositions, including the year of his uncle's decease. A permanent smile split his sun-burned face, the easy, lazy smile of a man who was never in

277

a hurry. Sometimes in the evenings he rode back into Rossaphin again, to drink more stout and to talk about racehorses. His uncle owned the farmhouse and the heifers, Henry the fields and the brood of turkeys he fattened every year for Christmas. He received payment from his uncle for the grazing of the heifers and from two other farmers for the grass he let them have on an annual basis: with his turkey profits, this made him a living of a kind. His four sisters had long ago left the neighbourhood, only one of them remaining in Ireland.

'There was foreign people over at the stones,' he reported to his uncle on the evening the French couple had come. 'Jabbering away.'

'Did you approach them? Did you charge them the price for going over our fields?'

Henry vaguely wagged his head and knowing that such a charge had not been made the old man continued to grumble, his empty gums squashing up baked beans before he swallowed them. Because he had difficulty with crusts, he tore pieces of bread from the centre of a slice and dipped the soft white lumps into the sauce that went with the beans. Mumbling through this food, he said that the number of people who nowadays crossed their land was a disgrace. It was a favourite mealtime topic: every day, whether there had been visitors to the standing stones or not, the old man urged Henry to protest to the gardai or the Board of Works or somebody at the courthouse in Rossaphin. He was convinced that a substantial sum of money was owing to the Garvey family because no toll had ever been charged on the right of way to Drumgawnie Rath. Now, at eighty-six, he was too old to do anything about it. He hadn't been to mass for ten years, or spoken to anyone except his nephew for six.

In Henry's view the old man could have kept himself normal by picking up the groceries and the newspaper every day in Mrs Mullalley's shop. In a normal manner he could have whiled away his time with Mrs Mullalley or the daughter instead of skulking behind the trees, looking out for visitors. But he wouldn't enter the shop because he couldn't bear to hand over money to anyone, so Henry had to see to everything like that. Not that he particularly minded. He had a basket which he hung from the handlebars of his bicycle and he actually enjoyed loitering in shops, Mrs Mullalley's or anyone else's. He would light a cigarette and sometimes in Mullalley's he might have a bottle of lemonade. He would lean his back against the counter and listen to the Mullalley girl going on about the Wild West stories she read. She was a decent enough looking creature in her way, the only pity was the leg she was afflicted with.

'Dressed up to the nines they were,' Henry continued in the kitchen. 'A useless type of person, I'd say.'

His uncle emitted a sucking noise. The footsteps made by the visitors wore the grass down. Another thing was, the Board of Works should be informed that cars were being left without charge on the piece of verge by the mill.

'I don't think it's a matter for the Board of Works.'

'Why wouldn't it be? Didn't the Board man come to see me in 1949? Wasn't it the Board drew attention to the stones before any stranger knew they were there?'

'If it's anyone's concern I'd say it was the County Council's.'

'Go into the courthouse in that case. Go into the head clerk and say we're deprived of grass for the cattle due to footsteps wearing it down.'

Henry promised that he would do as he was asked. He always promised when the subject came up. He ate his beans and bread and drank several cups of tea. He didn't say that there were other ways of charging for the use of the path through the fields. He didn't explain that you could get what was owing to you if you were sharp with your eyes and used the intelligence you were born with.

Four years after the French woman's mishap with her handbag Dolores became aware – in the late summer of 1972 – of Henry Garvey's interest in her. During that July and August his manner changed. He no longer stood with his back to her, for instance, smiling through the open door at the roadway outside while she told him the plot of another Wild West novel. Instead he faced her, leaning an elbow on the counter. He even lifted his eyes to her face and scrutinised it. Now and again his glance moved over her long dark hair and over her shoulders. Once she'd noticed him looking at her hands.

It had never occurred to Dolores, twenty-six now, that romance would come her way. One cold January day, ages ago, the Crowleys had driven her and her mother to the cinema in Ballyreddy, sixteen miles beyond Rossaphin, for the Sunday Matinée. Father Keane had had a hand in the arrangement – had no doubt said that it would be an act of charity – and the Crowleys, seeking through his good offices a chance of heavenly life, had acceded easily to his wish. *From Here to Eternity* the film had been, and Dolores had never forgotten any of it, far richer in romance than anything in her father's Wild West library. But that was as close as she had so far come to the world of love and passion, and what neither the intercession of Father Keane nor the kindness of the Crowleys could achieve for her was a place among the Friday-night dancers in Rossaphin. Dolores had never been inside the Electric Dance Hall and she guessed she never would. There would be no point: she knew that and accepted it. Yet sometimes she dreamed that miraculously she danced beneath fairyland lights to the music she'd heard on the radio, and was sad for a moment after she woke up. She knew such a miracle could never, ever happen.

'I had him backed both ways,' Henry Garvey said towards the end of that August. 'I was fortunate all right.'

He had been talking about the horse, Wonder Boy, a day or two before. It was running on some English racecourse, destined to make him a fortune. He had told her about a greyhound called Trumpeter, which had won at Limerick, and another greyhound called Smashero. His uncle had died, nearly two years ago now, and she and her mother had gone to the funeral in Rossaphin, driven by the Crowleys. Afterwards they'd all had a cup of tea in Love's Café and Mrs Mullalley had taken the opportunity to purchase some oilcloth in Bolger's.

Even though old Garvey had been poor company, it was apparent enough that Henry had become lonely in the farmhouse. He came more often to the shop and lingered there longer than he used to. And then, one morning when

Dolores was in the middle of telling him the plot of *Kid Kelly*, she found him scrutinising her even more closely than before. Her mother was present on that occasion and Dolores knew she had observed and had understood, Henry Garvey's interest. After he'd gone her mother was beside herself with delight, although she didn't say a word. Dolores heard her humming in the kitchen, and her manner was so sprightly when Jimmy Reilly delivered the bacon in the afternoon that he asked her if she'd won the sweep.

'D'you know what it is,' Henry Garvey said at the beginning of September, 'I'm uncertain what to do with myself.'

As he spoke, he pushed his cigarette packet across the counter at her. She was sitting on the stool which Father Keane had given her as a present, its legs cut down to just the right height. She could sit on it and lean on the counter, just like Henry Garvey was leaning now, on a level with him.

'The old farmhouse above is shook,' he said.

Her mother was not there. Her mother had taken to slipping out to the potato slope whenever Henry Garvey appeared, even if it was raining. Dolores knew that the news of the courtship had been passed on to the Crowleys and to the van men who called at the shop, to Father Keane and to all the people who came to the crossroads for their groceries. When she rested in the afternoons she could hear the excited tone of her mother's voice in the shop below. She was never able to make out the words but she knew that the latest of Henry Garvey's attentions was being retailed.

'I'm wondering,' he said at the beginning of September, 'would I sell the old fellow's heifers?'

She made a slight gesture with the hand that held the cigarette, a shrug of the fingers that was intended to imply that Henry Garvey was his own master, and must make his own decisions.

'I have the acres all right, but sure what use is the old house to me? Isn't it falling down on account of the old fellow wouldn't permit a bit of cement to be applied to it?'

Dolores, who had never seen the farmhouse, made the same gesture again.

'And sure you could hardly call them heifers any more. Wouldn't I be better without the trouble of those lassies?'

He turned his ample smile towards her, the red-brick flesh of his face screwed up into small bulges. She had only once seen him wearing a tie and that was at the funeral of his uncle. On Sundays he went to a later mass than her mother and herself: she supposed he'd put the tie on for that also.

'Another factor is,' he continued, 'I need a new bicycle.'

In the shop, and in the rooms above it and behind it, on the slope out at the back, he could take her father's place. He could occupy the chair in which her father had so abruptly died. He could marry into the shop and the house just as her father had, and he would bring with him the rent for the grazing of his fields. Her father had brought nothing.

'What I'm wondering is,' he said, 'could I learn to drive a car?'

She did not reply. She did not even make the same gesture again. She saw herself stepping out of the car he spoke of, the point of the crutch secure on the pavement. She saw herself limping beside him towards the cinema at Ballyreddy, up the steps and down the long passage with framed photographs of film stars on the walls. She saw herself in Rossaphin, not having to wait outside the Provincial Bank for Jimmy Reilly and his van, but going at her leisure in and out of the shops. On a Sunday, mass would be attended when it was convenient, no need to fit in with the Crowleys. And would there be any harm in going, just once, into the Electric Dance Hall, and standing there for a while, looking at the dancers and listening to the music?

'I'm sure you could drive a car,' she said. 'If Phelan can drive that bread van I'd say you could drive a car.'

'The old bike was a good machine in its day, but the mudguards is overtaken by the rust.'

'A car would be handy for you, Henry.'

'There's nothing I like better than talking about matters like that to you.'

He paid the compliment without looking at her, gazing as he used to, out into the roadway. He was nearly twenty years older than she was, but no other man would ever come into this shop and say he liked talking to her about bicycles and cars. No other man would examine her hair and her hands – or if he did he'd stop it in a hurry, like the new young conductor on the long-distance bus had when he'd realised she was crippled and misshapen.

Henry Garvey left the shop after he'd paid the compliment, and when her mother came in from the back Dolores told her he was considering buying a car. Her mother would have already said prayers, begging the Virgin to make it all right, begging that a crippled woman should not one day find herself alone at the crossroads. The paralysis had been a shock out of nowhere: the attentions of Henry Garvey were just as unexpected, a surprise that came surely from God.

'A car?' her mother said. 'Ah, wouldn't that be grand, pet?'

The crossroads was nearer to the town than the farmhouse was, the journey would be shorter, and easier without the stony track that led down to the farm. Often, lounging in the shop, he'd smelt a bit of cooking going on in the kitchen; he remembered Mullalley in his day, selling stamps and weighing out potatoes. He liked it when she told him about Kid Kelly and Two-Draw Hagan, and she appeared to be interested when he outlined his chances in a race.

'That's fixed so,' he said to her on the day they arranged the marriage. 'Sure, it'll be suitable for the pair of us.'

He gave her a present, a necklace he'd found in the handbag he'd taken years ago as payment for all the strangers who had walked across the fields. There were little blue jewels in it: twenty-two of them, she told him, because she'd counted them. A week or so later he pushed the handbag itself across the counter at her. He'd found it with the necklace, he said, among his mother's possessions. Tim Durcan was teaching him to drive a car, he said.

Dolores had known when Henry Garvey gave her the necklace that Mrs Garvey had never possessed such a piece of jewellery. Her mother had known also, but had not said anything. It wasn't until the handbag had appeared that both of them guessed Henry Garvey had stolen the French woman's property. They still did not say anything. In the drawer where the postal orders and the registration book were kept there remained the scrap of paper on which Colette Nervi had written down her address. It had been there for all the intervening time, together with the small sum of money for postage in case the handbag ever came to light. Mrs Mullalley destroyed the scrap of paper after Dolores had received her presents and looking in the drawer one day Dolores discovered that she had done so.

The wedding was to take place in June. Two girls Dolores had been at the convent with were to be bridesmaids, and one of Henry Garvey's bar-room companions had agreed to act as best man. Everyone for miles around Drumgawnie was invited, all the shop's customers, the same people who'd attended Mr Mullalley's funeral nineteen years ago, and Odd Garvey's funeral. The Crowleys were invited, and some Rossaphin people, Jimmy Reilly and Phelan the bread man. Some of the other van drivers lived too far beyond the district but all of them brought gifts for Dolores a week or so before the wedding day.

Father Keane had a crutch painted white and had asked Mrs Crowley to cover the arm support in lace to match the wedding dress. Dolores thought she'd never seen a crutch look so pretty, and wondered if it was a marriage tradition for crippled brides, but did not ask. Henry Garvey's farm-house was up for sale, the cattle had already been sold. Mrs Mullalley had arranged to move out of her room, into the one that had always been Dolores's. 'The simplest thing,' she said, not dwelling upon the subject.

'I don't know will he ever communicate the knack of it,' Henry Garvey said, referring to Tim Durcan's efforts to teach him to drive a motor car. The car had a way of jumping about with him, juddering and stalling before he even got it started. He had heavy feet, Tim Durcan explained: a man driving a car needed to be sensitive with the clutch and the accelerator. 'You'd think it would be easy,' Henry said to Dolores, and she softly encouraged him, urging him to persevere. There would be nothing nicer, she continued in the same soft voice, than having a car. The white crutch was in her bedroom, in a corner by the dressing-table, waiting for the day in June. She had covered the lace on the arm-support with a piece of brown paper in case it got dirty.

On the night before the wedding Dolores wondered what else there had been in the handbag. Money would have been bet on a horse or a greyhound, keys perhaps thrown away; somewhere in the unsold farmhouse there'd be a make-up compact. In a month's time there was to be an auction of the furniture and the few remaining bits of farm machinery: before that happened she would find the compact and hide it carefully away. She would not keep her money in the black handbag, nor her cigarettes and matches; she would not be seen in the shops with it. She would be careful with the gifts of Henry Garvey in case, after all, the lovers from France had reported the loss to the gardai. Henry Garvey would never notice that the necklace was never seen at her neck because he was not the kind to notice things; nor was he the kind to realise that you had to be careful. She felt drowsily comforted by knowing what she must do but when she turned the light out and attempted to sleep a chilliness possessed her: what if Henry Garvey rode over in the morning on his mother's bicycle to say he'd made a mistake? What if he stood with his back to the counter the way he used to, gazing with his smile out into the roadway? He would not say that the folly of the marriage had at last been borne in upon him. He would not say that he had seen in his mind's eye the ugliness of his bride's body, the shrivelled limb distorting everything. He would not say it had suddenly occurred to him that the awkward, dragging movement when she walked without her crutch was more than he could look at for the remainder of his life. 'I gave you stolen presents,' he'd say instead, 'I'm too ashamed to marry you.' And then he'd mount the bicycle and ride away like one of the cowboys of the Wild West.

In the darkness she lit another cigarette, calming herself. If he'd rather, he could have this room on his own and she could share her mother's. Being a bachelor for so long, that might be a preference he'd have. She'd hate it, in with her mother, but there was an empty back room, never used, which one day might be fixed up for her. There would be a bed and a wardrobe up at the farm.

She turned the light on and read. She finished *Silent Prairie* and began one she hadn't read for ages, *King Cann Strikes Gold!* by Chas D Wasser. At half-past six she heard her mother moving.

He made a cup of tea in the kitchen. No one would buy the place, the way the roof and the kitchen wall were. The wall would hardly last the winter, the crack had widened suddenly, nearly nine inches it must be now. The old furniture would fetch maybe a hundred pounds.

At the kitchen table he stirred sugar into his tea. He wondered if he'd ever manage the driving. And if he did, he wondered if Mrs Mullalley would stand the price of a car. It was a matter he hadn't mentioned yet, but with all the trouble he was going to over the learning wouldn't she tumble to it that he had done his share? The three of them were in it together, with the farmhouse the way it was and the girl the way she was. It was only a pity there hadn't been a ring in that handbag he'd taken as payment for the use of the path across his fields. Still and all, he'd got seven to one on Derby Joan with the money there'd been in the purse, which easily covered the cost of the ring he'd had to buy.

He drank his tea and then moved over to the sink to shave himself. They stocked razor blades in the shop, which would be useful too.

In front of the altar she leant on the white crutch, wishing she could manage without it but knowing that the effort would be too much. Father Keane's voice whispered at them, and she could sense the delight in it, the joy that he truly felt. Beside her, Henry Garvey was wearing a tie, as she had known he would.

She had to kneel, which was always difficult, but in time the ceremony was over and she made her way down the aisle, careful on the tiles, one hand gripping the wooden cross-piece of the crutch, the other holding on to him. Hidden beneath her wedding-dress, the necklace that had been stolen from Colette Nervi was cool on the flesh of her

286

neck, and in those moments in the aisle Dolores recalled the embrace. She saw the lovers as they had been that day, the woman's leather coat, the man knocking out his pipe. Sunlight glimmered on the red, polished car, and enriched the green of the foliage. The woman's fingers were splayed out on her lover's dark head; the two faces were pressed into each other like the faces of the man and the woman in *From Here to Eternity*.

EVA IBBOTSON

Theatre Street

Her name was Madame Lavarre. Trained at La Scala, she had danced in all the capitals of Europe, taught with her famous countryman, Cecchetti, in Russia.

Now she was old, the ramrod back held firm against the rigours of arthritis, the dyed hair piled high above a raddled, made-up face. Old, but deeply formidable as she surveyed the new intake for the ballet school she now ran in London.

It was a late winter morning in 1931. Pavlova, killed by overworked, had died two months before; Diaghilev, too, was dead, but they had done their work. Even the English, who prided themselves on being Philistines, wanted their daughters – if not yet their sons – to dance. That morning, over thirty children had been brought to the tall, yellow stucco house in Regent's Park which housed the prestigious Lavarre Academy of Dance. Of these, fifteen had already been rejected. Now, Madame turned her attention to the survivors. They had been weighed and measured, their hearing tested, their ability to sing in tune ascertained. Even so, another five would have to go.

'You can dance now, *mes enfants*,' she said. 'Do anything you wish. Just follow the music.'

The meek little woman at the piano played a Delibes waltz and the children danced. Three revealed themselves immediately as unmusical. There was one boy who was clearly gifted, another who – desperately as she needed boys – would have to go.

But these decisions were taken beneath the level of her consciousness. She was watching only one child.

Someone had taught her, and taught her well. There was no precociousness, no dangerous attempt to go up on her toes, yet at nine she had already tasted the control that alone brings freedom. A narrow little face, fawn hair cut in a fringe, large brown eyes. She had been shy at the interview

288

but now she was wholly absorbed. 'Even with her eyelashes, she dances,' thought Madame.

She motioned to the pianist to stop and gave instructions to the two assistant teachers who gently led the casualties away. 'Come here,' said Madame to the child with fawn hair, and she came, biting her lip, holding back the tears, for this summons could only mean that she had failed.

'Dancers don't grimace,' said Madame Lavarre. She led her to the window embrasure and stabbed her cane at the pianist who broke into a march.

She was alone, now, with the child. Outside, snow had begun to fall. She could have been back in Russia, at the school in Theatre Street . . .

'What is your name?'

'Alexandra, Madame.'

'And who taught you to dance, Alexandra?'

'My mother.'

The voice was low, sweet, but absolutely English. Why then this absurd sense of familiarity?

'Mothers are usually a disaster. Is yours a dancer?'

'Yes, Madame. At least she was.'

The pride in the child's voice was unmistakeable.

'What is her name?'

The little girl was silent. Silky lashes curtained the downcast eyes. 'I must not say. She told me not to tell.'

'Nevertheless, you *will* tell.' The old woman's face was hooded as an eagle's. She tapped with her dreaded cane on the floor.

The child stood trapped. 'Do exactly what they tell you sweetheart,' her mother had said. 'Just do what they ask.'

'Starislova,' she said. 'Giovanna Starislova. That was her name.'

A long pause. It was impossible that this fierce and terrifying old lady could be crying, yet something glittered in the coal-black eyes.

'Is she here?'

'She is downstairs, Madame. In the hall. She wouldn't come upstairs with the other – '

289

But Madame, flinging an imperious '*Continuez!*' at her underlings, was already at the door.

It had begun many years earlier in a now vanished world. On the fifteenth of April, 1912, to be exact, with the visit of a young English officer, Captain Alex Hamilton, to the Imperial Ballet School in St Petersburg.

He was in Russia as *aide de camp* to his Brigadier who was heading a military delegation sent to discuss the establishment of a joint garrison in Badakhshan, that notorious trouble spot north of the Hindu Kush, and had already tasted Russian hospitality at its most lavish: at a banquet at Prince Yussoupov's palace from which the guests were still being carried two days later, at a dinner in the mess of the Chevalier Guards which had ended in a dawn visit to the islands, and – more decorously – at a luncheon at the beautiful palace of Tsarskoe Selo with the Tsar, his wife and four pretty daughters.

Now, politely concealing his boredom, he entered with the Brigadier, a fellow officer seconded from the Indian Army, and Count Zinov, his Russian host, the portals of the Tsar's own ballet school in Theatre Street.

He was aware that an honour was being conferred on him. In Vienna, he would have been shown the Spanish Riding School with its 'white pearls', the horses of Lippiza; the Italians would have taken him to the opera. The Russians showed him the cradle of the art they had brought to a perfection unequalled anywhere in the world – the ballet.

Not every visitor was taken to Theatre Street, Rossi's lovely, silent row of ochre-coloured and garlanded buildings whose high, bare rooms – half palace, half convent – housed the school. At ten years old they came here, small girls with anxious eyes clutching their shoe bags, to be paraded, measured, prodded and examined and – if admitted – put through eight years of the hardest training in the world. Small vestal virgins, these girls in their blue wool dresses, their white aprons, their relentlessly braided and pulled back hair. They slept in dormitories, all fifty of them, moved everywhere under the gaze of a posse of governesses, were forbidden to speak even to the boys on the floor above with whom they practised their polkas and mazurkas.

Then, at eighteen, they joined the Maryinsky Ballet, to become for the twenty or so years of their working life, snowflakes or swans or sugar plum fairies ... Or once, every so often, that other thing. From the door Alex was now entering had emerged Pavlova, anguished about her thinness and frailty ... Karsavina, destined to be Diaghilev's darling ... and that eighth wonder of the world, Nijinsky.

These hallowed ghosts were entirely invisible to Alex Hamilton as he crossed the hallway, to be greeted by the formidable Principal, Varvara Ivanovna. He was in every way a product of his class, trained to conceal anything which might single him out for attention. If nothing could be done about his good looks, his wide grey eyes, it was at least possible to barber and brush his hair so as to minimise its russet glint, its spring. His high intelligence he dealt with by speaking as seldom as possible. His knowledge of foreign languages – so deeply un-British – could be glossed over by a man who had, after all, won the Sword of Honour in his last year at Sandhurst. At twenty-six it was inevitable that he should have known and pleased women, but the only emotion he had hitherto found uncontrollable was the homesickness which had attacked him when he woke, at the age of seven, in the barred dormitory of his prep school and realised that as a result of some crime he was not aware of having committed, he was banished – perhaps for ever – from the adored gardens and streams and sunlit water meadows of his Wiltshire home.

It is perhaps worth adding that he was not musical. An unfortunate experience at *Tosca* when the heroine, after leaping off the battlements, had apparently bounced and reappeared, had left him with a distaste for opera. The only ballet he had ever seen – a *divertissement* from *Coppelia* inserted into a revue at the Alhambra, had bored him stiff.

But the Principal was welcoming them in French and the Brigadier's bulbous nose twitched at Alex, instructing him to take over the conversation. Following her through an archway, they encountered a crocodile of tiny girls in fur-trimmed pelisses, each with a neatly rolled towel under her arm, bound for the weekly ritual of the steam bath in a distant courtyard; passed through a vestibule where a huddle of infant Ice Maidens, pursued by maids with hairbrushes, waited to be conveyed to a matinée at the Maryinsky – and were led upstairs.

Explaining the routine of the school as she went, Varvara Ivanovna took them through a dining room with oil-cloth covered tables, threw open the door of a classroom to reveal a pigtailed row of girls having a lesson in notation, another in which pinafored pupils were dutifully drawing a vase filled with acanthus leaves . . . And down a long corridor hung with portraits: of Taglioni, the first Sylphide of them all, whose ballet shoes, when she retired, had been cooked and eaten by her besotted admirers . . . of Legnani, whose thirty-two *fouettés*, when she first came to Russia, had had every child in Theatre Street pirouetting and turning in an agony of emulation.

They had come to the heart of the building and every-where, escaping even the heavy double doors with their crests of Romanov eagles, came snatches of music. Fragments of Brahms waltzes, of *études* by Chopin or by some unknown hack, repeated again and again, relentlessly rhythmical, their only function, however exalted their source, to serve the *battements* and *glissées* and *arabesques* that were these children's alphabet.

'You will wish to see our advanced class, I imagine,' said the Principal. 'The girls who next year will leave us to join the *corps de ballet*. Some of them are already very talented.' She consulted the watch pinned to her belt. 'They will be in Room Five.'

Alex translated, the Brigadier nodded and Count Zinov pulled his moustache happily at the thought of the seven-teen-year-olds. Suppressing a sigh, for he had hoped still to visit a Cossack officer who had promised to show him his horses, Alex stood aside for his superiors as Varvara Ivanovna opened yet another door.

The room they entered now was high and bare with three long windows, a *barre* running round the walls and, everywhere, mirrors. There was a white and golden stove, a portrait of the Tsar . . . a wooden floor raked like the stage of the Maryinsky. In the corner, beside them as they entered, was a middle-aged woman, ugly as a toad, coaxing with stumpy, mottled fingers, a soaring phrase from a Schubert Impromptu out of the upright piano.

And all round the walls, girls in white practice dresses, one hand on the *barre* . . .

'*Continuez, s'il vous plaît*,' ordered the Principal. 'These gentlemen wish to see the class at work.'

The pianist resumed her phrase. The girls, who had paused with demure and downcast eyes, lifted their heads.

'Let me have your *pliés* again,' ordered the *maîtress de ballet*, 'One, two . . . good . . . *ronds de jambe* . . . Lydia, your *porte de bras* . . . *demi-plié* . . . *tendu devant* . . . up . . . *demi-plié* in fourth . . . close . . .'

Alex looked on idly. Five girls on the far wall beneath the portrait of the Tsar; six on the wall next to the corridor . . . another six along the window. It was this row he watched absently. Two very dark girls . . . a fair one . . . one with red hair . . .

And then a voice in his head pronouncing with ice-cold clarity, the words: '*This is the one.*'

He did not at first understand what had happened, it was so patently impossible and absurd. Indeed, he shook his head as at some trifling accident, and let his eye travel again to the beginning of the row.

The first girl, dark, with a narrow Byzantine head; the second, dark also though a little taller; the third with that grey-eyed blonde beauty that Puskin gave his heroines; then the redhead . . . And now, as he reached the girl who was fifth in line, he ducked mentally, leaving a space, and came to the last one, another dark-haired Circassian beauty.

Then carefully, painstakingly, he let his eye travel back to the girl who was fifth in line – and again, clear as a bell, the voice in his head said: 'Yes.'

The fragment of Schubert gave way to a phrase from Bellini and the girls went into their *battements*.

His face taut, Alex studied her.

She had a neat and elegant head, but so did all the other girls. Her arms were delicate and perfectly proportioned, her neck high and almost unnaturally slender – but it was so with all of them: how could it be otherwise, hand-picked and measured as they were? She moved with flawless grace and musicality – and if she had not done so would long ago have been sent away so what was noteworthy in that? Her brown hair was scraped back off a high forehead, just one curl escaping its bondage, cupped her small ear. Her eyes, too, were brown, but only brown – not liquid with Oriental promise as with the girl who stood beside her.

Why, then? For God's sake, *why*?

The music had stopped. The girls stood quietly, their feet in the fifth position, their eyes cast down. Except for this one girl; a good girl, hitherto known for her modesty and quietness, who now lifted her head, looked directly and with an expression of the most extraordinary happiness at the handsome English officer – and smiled.

Her name was Vanni. Giovanna, really, for the route that classical ballet had taken – Milan to Paris, Paris to St Petersburg – was reflected in her ancestry. Both her parents had been dancers and came to settle at the Maryinsky. At ten, dressed in white muslin, Vanni had carried her shoe bag through the portals of the Ballet School for her audition as inevitably as Alex, dressed in grey shorts and a blazer with towers on the pocket, had climbed into his prep school train.

She was an excellent pupil, industrious, obedient. Her teachers liked her; she got on well with the other girls.

Then, at a quarter past three on the fifteenth of April, a week after her seventeenth birthday, in the middle of a *cou de pied en devant* she felt . . . something.

When the music stopped, she turned and saw in the group of people standing by the piano, only one man. A man who, in the now silent room, crossed calmly and deliberately the expanse of empty floor, and came to stand, as she had known he would, in front of her.

It was a piece of extraordinary effrontery. The Principal hissed; the Brigadier stared, unable to believe his eyes; the other girls giggled nervously. The Tsar himself would have hesitated thus to single out one girl.

'What is your name?' said Alex. He spoke in French, the language of the dance, and urgently, for it could only be minutes before they were separated.

'Vanni. Giovanna Starislova. My school number is 157. I shall be here till May 1913, then at the Maryinsky.'

She had understood at once; given him what he needed.

'I'm Alex Hamilton of the 14th Fusiliers. My home is Winterbourne Hall in Wiltshire.'

She nodded, a frown mark between her eyes as she memorised these English names. Quickly, he took possession of his territory. A small bridge of freckles over the nose, gold glints in the brown eyes, lashes which shone like sunflower seeds . . . There was a tiny mole on her left cheek: a fleeting scent of camomile came from her hair.

'She is good,' he thought blissfully. 'A good girl.' It was a bonus, unexpected.

'I will come back,' he said. His voice was very low but each word as distinct as when he briefed his soldiers. 'I don't know when, but I shall return.'

She had folded her slender hands as women do in prayer. Now she tilted them towards him so that her fingertips rested for a brief moment on his tunic.

'I will wait,' she said.

Alex returned to England. Vanni was sent for by the Principal and questioned.

The questions yielded nothing. No, said Vanni standing with downcast eyes in her blue serge dress, she had never seen the Englishman before, he had written no notes to her, made no assignations.

Then why had she smiled in that brazen manner, asked Varvara Ivanovna, who could still recall the unmistakeable radiance, the *intention* behind that smile.

Vanni shook her head. She did not know. But though usually so well-behaved and obedient, she did not apologise, and the Principal decided not to prolong the interview for even at the mention of the Englishman, the girl became illumined, as if she had swallowed a small and private sun.

So Vanni was punished – deprived of permission to visit her parents for three successive Sundays – and watched. But there were no further misdemeanours.

When a boy on the floor above sent her a red tissue rose from his Easter Cake she returned it. No letters came from England and at rehearsals, when the older pupils went to augment the cupids and nymphs of the *corps de ballet*, she was conspicuous for *not* making sheep's eyes at the handsome *premier danseur*, Vassilov.

If she was still watched when she returned for her last year at the school it was for a different reason.

'There is something a little interesting, now, in her work,' said Cecchetti, the most famous dancing master in the world, to Sonia Lavarre who taught the senior class. 'And she seems stronger.'

But what he meant was 'happier'.

In May 1913, a year after Alex's visit, she left the school in Theatre Street and became a member of the *corps de ballet* at the Maryinsky Theatre. Her salary was six hundred roubles a month, her future assured. For her parents – for Vanni herself, as they believed – it was the fulfilment of a dream.

Back with his regiment on Salisbury Plain, Alex threw himself into his work. In the summer he took his battalion to Scotland for manoeuvres. Getting his men fit, turning them into first-class soldiers, occupied him physically. At night, in his tent, he read the technical manuals which poured from the world's presses now that his profession was growing ever more complex and scientific. And when his army duties permitted, he went down to Winterbourne, the estate which, since the death of his father two years earlier, had been wholly his.

It was a place of unsurpassed and Arcadian loveliness. A Queen Anne house of rosy brick faced south across sloping lawns which merged with water meadows fragrant, in summer, with yellow iris and cuckoo-pint and clover. Sheltered by verdant hills, Alex's farmlands were rich and lush; the cows that grazed in his fields were the fattest, the most reposeful cows in the Southern Counties; his sheep moved in dreamy clusters as if waiting to be addressed by The Good Shepherd Himself. With Alex's position at Winter-bourne went the Mastership of the Hunt, a seat on the Bench, an elaborate system of duties to tenants and fellow landowners alike.

It could not be – surely to God it *could not* be – that to share these duties he proposed to install a dancing girl, probably of low birth, whom he had glimpsed for five minutes in a strange, barbaric land?

For as the months passed, the memory of that extra-ordinary encounter became more and more blurred and dream-like. He could remember Vanni's posture at the *barre*, but her face, increasingly, eluded him. So when his stately, widowed mother told him that the Stanton-Darcys were coming for the weekend and bringing Diana, Alex was pleased. He had attended Diana's coming out ball, sat next to her at hunt dinners. She was twenty-one, sweet, with curls as yellow as butter, large blue eyes and a soft voice.

Diana came. The weekend was a great success. She went with Alex round the farms, the tenants took to her, his factor presented her with an adorable bulldog puppy. She was already a little in love with him – being in love with the handsome, foxy-haired Captain Hamilton had been the fashion among the debutantes of her year. Yet somehow it happened that three months later she became engaged to the Earl of Farlington's youngest son, for girls with blonde curls and big blue eyes do not lie about unclaimed for long.

Alex's mother swallowed her disappointment and tried again. Selena Fordington was an heiress – unnecessary in view of Alex's considerable wealth, but agreeable nonetheless; a quiet, intelligent girl whose plainness vanished as soon as she became animated. Alex liked her enormously, took her to Ascot and Henley – and introduced her to his best friend, who promptly married her.

A year had passed since his visit to Russia, and his longing to be ordinary, not to be singled out in this bizarre way, grew steadily. Yet the following winter he stood aside and let Pippa Latham go. Pippa, his childhood love, a tomboy with the lightest hands in the hunting field and a wild sense of humour, who returned from India a raven-haired beauty with a figure to send men mad . . .

It was time then, to return to Russia and lay his ghosts. His and hers, for Vanni – if she remembered him at all – was probably living under the protection of a wealthy balletomane, or even married to a dancer with hamstrings like hawsers and long hair. He would take her out for a meal, perhaps, buy her a keepsake . . . They would laugh together about what had seemed to happen in that high, bare room in Theatre Street, wish each other luck . . . And he would return to his country a free and normal man.

Thus at the end of May, 1914, having collected the long leave owing to him, Alex set off again for Russia.

His host, the hospitable Count Zinov, was overjoyed to see him, but apologetic.

'It is the last night of the Maryinsky season – a gala performance of *Swan Lake*. It would be hard for my wife and me to miss it but if you did not feel like joining us we could arrange for you to dine with a friend. I know you do not care for the ballet.'

'I would be honoured to accompany you,' Alex replied.

The Maryinsky is a blue and silver theatre, sumptuous beyond belief. The chandeliers, all fire and dew, drew sparks from the tiaras of the women, the medals of the men. The Tsar was in his box with his wife and two eldest daughters. The Grand Duchess Olga had put up her hair.

In the Zinovs' *loge*, Alex joined in the applause for the conductor. Tchaikovsky's luscious, soaring music began . . . The curtain rose.

Act One: A courtyard in Prince Siegfried's Palace . . . The courtiers parade in cloth of gold. The peasantry arrive with gifts for the Prince. They dance. They dance, it seems to Alex, for a remarkably long time. The King and Queen approach their son. It is his birthday they inform him in elaborate mime. It is time he chose a bride.

But the Prince – the great Vassilov in suitably straining tights – does not wish to marry. He grows pensive . . .

The music changes; becomes dark and tragic. Swans, seemingly, are flying overhead. The prince is excited. He will go and hunt them. His courtiers follow.

The curtain falls.

An interval . . . champagne . . . a French Countess in the next box flirting outrageously with Alex.

And now, Act Two. This, of course, is the act that *is* the ballet. A moonlit glade . . . A lake . . . A romantic ruin, some equally romantic trees. To the world's best loved ballet music, the doomed Swan Queen enters on her points. She is in a white tutu with a tiny crown on her lovely head, and on the night in question is greeted with sighs of adoration for she is danced by the fabled Kschessinskaya, once the mistress of the Tsar.

The crown on her head is useful, for were she to be danced by anyone less exquisite, it might not be easy, at once, to distinguish her from her encircling and protective swans.

Just how many swans there are in *Swan Lake* depends, of course, on the finances and traditions of the company, but there are a remarkable number, and the discipline and precision with which they conduct themselves can make or mar this masterpiece. Perfect unity, the ability to act as one is what the Russians demand, and get, from their *corps*. Identical in calf-length tutus, their hair hidden by circlets of feathers, their arms and faces blanched by powder, these relentlessly drilled girls would have made peas in a pod look idiosyncratic.

So now, despairing at her fate (for she is, of course, an enchanted princess) Odette glides forward. A row of fifteen swans *jeté* from stage left towards her, so far away on the vast stage that their faces are nothing but a blur. Fifteen more come from stage right. Ten swans enter diagonally from both the upstage corners. And from the centre, as if from the lake itself, the last row of girls, their fluttering arms crossed at the wrists, doing their impeccable *battements* . . .

The first swan, the second, the third . . .

At which point the voice in Alex's head which had been silent for two years, said: '*That one.*'

Two hours later, he waited at the stage door among a crowd of students and admirers.

The orchestra came out first: tired men in shabby over-coats carrying their instruments. Then the first group of girls, chattering like starlings, excited at the prospect of the long summer break ahead . . . and another . . .

And now three girls: a curly red-head, a dark Circassian beauty, and in the middle –

'Come on, Vannoushka,' begged the curly-haired Olga.

'No . . . you go on.' Vanni had stopped, hesitant and bewildered, like a fawn at the edge of an unfamiliar clearing. 'I feel . . . so strange.'

Alex had been hidden at the back of the crowd. Now he came forward, walked up to her, bared his head.

'We met two years ago, in Theatre Street. I said I would return. Do you remember?'

And she said: 'Yes.'

They went to Paris, the Mecca of all Russians. When they arrived, he booked two rooms at the luxurious Hotel Achilles in the Rue St Honoré. They dined in its magnificent res-taurant, strolled in the Tuileries Gardens. Then he took her upstairs, let her into her room, and went on into his own room next door.

An hour later, leaning out of the window, he heard what is perhaps the most heart-rending sound in the world; the sound of someone trying *not* to cry.

He ran from his room.

'What is it, Vanni?' he said, throwing open her door. 'For God's sake, my darling, what's the matter?'

She was sitting in her white nightdress on the edge of the four-poster bed. Her long brown hair was loose about her shoulders and the tears were rolling silently, steadily down her face.

'Why did you bring me, then?' she managed to say. 'If I . . . don't please you. You knew I was not pretty . . . You *knew* . . .'

Appalled, he began to babble . . . about marriage . . . about respect. He was going to the Embassy tomorrow to arrange . . . 'But it is not tomorrow,' she said, bewildered. 'It is now. It is today.'

The years of his idiot upbringing, the taboos and conventions he had drunk in with his mother's milk, dropped from him. He took her in his arms.

And from that moment, all that night and the next night and the next, always and always, it was today.

They moved to a little hotel in a narrow street on the Left Bank. Their room was on the top floor under the steep, grey roof. If she leant out – but it was necessary for him to hold her legs – she could just see the silver ribbon of the Seine. It was hot as summer advanced, the pigeons made an appalling din under the eaves and they spoke of moving on – to the Dordogne with its golden castles and wild delphiniums and walnut trees . . . or to Tuscany with its blue, hazed hills.

But they didn't move. They stayed in Paris, dazed by their happiness, watching the city empty for summer.

It is, of course, religion that is meant to do it, meant to make people take true delight in momentariness, meant to make them aspire to goodness, to let go of the clamorous self. Alas, it is so very much more often a complete, requited and all too human love.

A dancer's body is a kind of miracle. She seemed to talk with her feet, the back of her neck, her small, soft ears. As she moved about their little room, learning it by heart, touching with questing fingertips the brass knobs of the bed, the chest of drawers, the buttons of his jacket as it lay across a chair, he could not take his eyes from her fluent grace. Yet she had the gift of all true dancers: she could be absolutely, heart-stoppingly still.

They lived like children. He had had servants or batmen all his life; she had been brought up in an institution. To go to the baker, buy a long *baguette*, sit on a park bench crumbling it for each other and the birds, was an enchantment. They fed each other grapes in the Bois, spent dreamy afternoons gliding down the river in a *bâteau mouche* . . . In the sun, she grew golden: the brown hair lightened; hair, eyes, skin merged in a honey-coloured glow.

Alex disapproved. 'When we came you had eight freckles

across the bridge of your nose,' he said, pulling her towards him in the Luxembourg Gardens and getting a Gallic nod of approval from the park keeper. 'Now you've got twelve. I don't remember giving you permission to change.'

'It's happiness,' she said. 'Happiness gives you freckles, everyone knows that.'

'Rubbish. I shall buy you a parasol.'

So he bought her a most expensive, sky-blue parasol, much-fringed and embroidered with forget-me-nots – and the same afternoon threw it off the *Pont Neuf* because it prevented him from kissing her.

A wealthy and a generous man, it had been his intention to buy her beautiful clothes, present her with jewels, but here his luck was out. To the information, conveyed by Alex as they breakfasted off hot chocolate and *croissants* on the pavement of their personal café, that they were bound for the *couture* houses of the Rue de la Paix, she reacted with wide-eyed despair. 'Ah, no, Alex; they will take me from you and put me in booths and there will be ladies with pins!' Nor could he lure her into Cartier with its magnificent display of rings and brooches.

Then one Sunday, at the *marché aux puces*, as they wandered between the barrows, she suddenly picked up a small gold heart on a chain. On one side was engraved the word: *Mizpah*. She turned it over. 'Look, Alex, the words are in English! Read them.'

'*The Lord watch between me and thee when we are absent one from another,*' he read. He looked at her face. She was learning English quickly; she had understood. 'You want it?'

'Please.'

'It's only a trumpery thing,' he complained – but he paid without bargaining, the absurd price the stallholder asked, and as he bent to fasten it round her neck, he kissed her suddenly, unashamed, on the throat and said huskily: 'He *will* watch, my beloved. He will watch between us.'

Alex continued to besiege the Embassy, the immigration office, more determined than ever to take her back to England and arrange their marriage, but they were beset by delays. She had not brought the right papers from Russia; till her parents sent them, they were helpless.

'Incompetent, bureaucratic idiots!' raged Alex when the official he was dealing with dared to go on holiday.

But there was one absolute solution, one unfailing panacea, nowadays, for anything which vexed Alex. On the first night, in their room under the eaves, Vanni had begun herself to unpin her hair, and he had forced down her hand and said: 'No. That's my job. That is for me to do.' Now, always before love, he would say, 'Come here,' standing with his back to the window and she would come to him and bend her head and then carefully, methodically, he would remove one by one the hairpins with which she secured her heavy, high-piled tresses. 'Things must be done *properly*,' he would say, laying the pins neatly in a row on the sill. 'No cheating.' And it was only when he had laid the last pin beside the others that he allowed himself to pick her up, the cool silk of her loosened tresses running down his arms, and carry her to bed.

'Yes, but what about my *soul*,' she protested. 'I am, after all, mostly Russian. Souls are important to us.'

'I'm mad about your soul, *je t'assure*,' he murmured. 'I see it quite clearly – a sort of soft, blue-grey colour. The colour of peace. Afterwards I will tell you . . .'

And afterwards he did tell her. He spoke to her, indeed, as he had not believed it was possible to speak to another human being.

'It must be reincarnation,' she said. 'That's the only way one can explain the way we knew each other just like that.'

'Nonsense,' he murmured. 'You may have been one of Tutenkhamen's temple dancers but I'm damned certain I wasn't his High Priest.'

'No, you were certainly not a High Priest,' she said demurely, 'but perhaps you were a great Crusader on a horse . . . and you saw me in the slave market at Antioch. There were hundreds of slaves, all very beautiful, tied up in chains, but you saw me and said – '

'*This is the one*,' quoted Alex.

'Yes.' She looked at him sideways. 'You're sure it was me you wanted, not Olga? She has such marvellous red hair. Or

Lydia? Someone has written an ode to Lydia's kneecaps, did you know? Are you *sure* it was me?'

'Well, I *think* it was you,' said Alex, lazily teasing. 'But I'm not absolutely certain. Perhaps if you would just come a little closer . . .'

'But I'm already very close,' she protested, not unreasonably, for her head lay against his chest.

'Not close enough.' His voice, suddenly, was rough, anguished, as he was gripped by one of those damnable intimations of mortality that are the concomitant of passion.

But it was not mortality that they thought of much during that sweet and carefree summer of 1914. It was rather of the future that Alex spoke, lying in the dark after love – and of his home. And she would listen as to a marvellous fairy tale, learning her way in imagination out of the French windows of the drawing room, down the smooth lawns to the lake with its tangled yellow water lilies and the stream over which the kingfishers skimmed. She learnt the name of his farms: Midstead . . . South Mill . . . and of his fields: Ellesmere . . . High Pasture . . . Paradise . . .

'*Paradise!*' she exclaimed. 'You have a field called Paradise?'

She heard about his dogs: the gentle wolfhound, Flynn, and the bull terrier bitch, Mangle: and about the Winterbourne oak, as old and venerable as the house itself.

'And there you will live, my darling, and be my wife and my love,' Alex would finish.

'Ah, yes,' she would agree, rubbing her cheek against his face. 'I shall be a great lady and pour milk into my tea and eat ham and eggs and ride on big horses in the fog,' said Vanni, whose image of England had been implanted at a very early age.

They were strolling hand in hand along the Quai aux Fleurs when a newsboy came by calling his 'Extra!'

'What is it?' asked Vanni as Alex bought a paper.

'Just some Austrian Archduke's been bumped off,' he said lightly.

'Oh,' she said, relieved. Russia had an unending supply of Archdukes which were constantly being blown up by devout revolutionaries. It was sad, of course, especially when they had been patrons of the ballet.

Alex, in the days that followed, was gayer and more light-hearted than ever, but he redoubled his onslaught on the Embassy – and at night he had to steel himself not to hurry over his hairpins, not to tumble them on the floor, so desperate was his need to be beside her.

They had most of July, still, to hope as the world hoped. Then Germany declared general mobilisation. France followed. And a telegram came recalling Alex.

For the rest of her life, Vanni needed no map of Hades. Not Dante's limbo with its damned and swirling souls, not the black River Styx. Just Platform One of the Gare du Nord on a bright day in summer.

A well-kept station, geraniums in hanging baskets, sunlight slanting through the glass. All around them, women sobbing and men hugging their girls. And Alex, in uniform again, standing quite still beside the train that was to take her back to Russia, folding and unfolding her small hands like a fan.

'It'll be over by Christmas,' they heard a young soldier say – and Alex turned his head, a look of naked envy on his face as he glanced at someone so foolish and so young.

Then the doors began to slam and she turned to climb into the carriage.

'Wait!', he said, and lifted her hat a little – a brave hat trimmed with marguerites – and pulled one silver hairpin from her hair. And then he stood back and let her go.

Vanni had three weeks before the opening of the new season to get her body back into shape. It was not enough but she did it. Her parents had gone to live in the country; she moved into an apartment on the Fontanka with Olga and Lydia – and she danced.

In October, they gave her one of the slave dances in *Prince Igor* and the *pas de trois* in *La Bayadère*. She was made a *coryphée* . . .

Her modest success passed in a haze. She lived for letters from the front.

'There's a letter from France,' Grisha, the old doorman, would say as she came in for her morning class, his eyes shining with happiness on her behalf.

'There's a letter, *Vannoushka*,' Olga would whisper, hurrying into the *foyer de danse* for a rehearsal. 'Hurry, you just have time.'

Even Vassilov, the Apollo of the Maryinsky, stopped her once on the way to his dressing room to tell her that the post had come.

Alex wrote little of the danger, the horrors he saw daily. It was only indirectly that she gathered he had been promoted, had won the MC after only four months of fighting. It was the future – always and only the future that Alex wrote about: their marriage and their life together at Winterbourne.

In the spring, she had a letter from England. He had been hit in the shoulder; he was in hospital; it was nothing.

Vanni rejoiced. He was in hospital; he was safe! Her exultation showed in her work. They give her the Columbine in *Harlequinade*.

She had rejoiced too soon. The wound healed well; Alex refused convalescence and insisted on returning to his men. In July he was back on the Somme.

Then, on a bright October morning, Vanni came into the theatre and found Grisha slumped over his table. It was ten o'clock in the morning but he was already drunk.

'It may not be . . .' he murmured, and picked up a black-rimmed envelope from Britain.

But it was.

His mother, swallowing her disapproval of the foreign girl who had ensnared her son, had kept her promise to him. She wrote of his incredible bravery, the devotion of his men, the last confused and horrific battle in which, until the shell that destroyed his dugout, he had conducted himself with the heroism that was already becoming a legend. He had been awarded the DSO . . .

'Oh, God, why doesn't she cry!' raged Olga in the days that followed. 'I cannot bear it!'

But Vanni could manage nothing: not to eat or talk – or cry . . . Only to dance.

One afternoon, Cecchetti found her on the deserted stage after a matinée.

'So,' he said, tapping her with his stick. 'Why are you still here, may one ask?'

She curtseyed. 'I'm sorry, Maestro.'

He examined her. What had happened to her was betrayed in a strange darkening of her hair, her eyes. 'It does not occur to you, perhaps, that you are fortunate?'

Somehow she managed to smile. 'No,' she murmured. 'It does . . . not occur to me.'

He sat down on a stage rock and motioned her to do likewise.

'Grief,' he said. 'Sorrow . . . Everyone experiences them. Each day now, there are women who get letters like yours. Sons, husbands, lovers are killed. Their world ends. And what can they do with this grief? Nothing. It is locked inside them; useless. But you . . .'

She was looking at him, trying very hard as she did these days, to turn the sounds that came from people's mouths into recognisable words.

'You are an artist. For you, sorrow is a force that can be harnessed. It has a use.'

Vanni shook her head. 'I'm not like that,' she said. 'I'm not a great dancer.'

'No. Not yet.' He paused. 'Vassilov wants you,' said the old man. 'That's why I came. We're giving you *La Sylphide*.'

'*Vassilov!*' She jumped up, incredulous. 'Vassilov wants to dance with *me*!'

So began one of the most illustrious partnerships in the history of ballet. Anton Vassilov, at the time they began to dance together, was at the height of his fame: a tall, marvellously built dancer of the old school. Vanni brought him her youth, the hunger for work caused by her all-consuming grief. He brought her authority, prestige, the glamour of his name.

The war was going badly for the Russians. Food was scarce; fuel had to be begged for. They danced now for men, many of them wounded, who had seen what no man should see and live. Yet these were marvellous nights at the Mar-

307

yinsky – these last nights of the Romanov Empire when Vassilov and the little Starislova gave new meaning to the great *ballets blancs* of the classical repertoire. Men died, that awful year of 1917, with a piece of ribbon from Vanni's ballet shoes in the pocket of their tunics. She was carried shoulder high through the streets after her first *Giselle*.

The revolution did not greatly affect the company. The new regime treated them well. No one could have been less politically minded than Vanni and her good-natured, easy-going partner. Yet in the spring of 1918 they found themselves fleeing the country with forged passports, their dancers' bodies swathed in old coats, walking bent and stiff. On the way to a rehearsal they had rescued a little countess, trying to make her way into a food queue, from the sport and jeering of the crowd. Someone denounced them as 'Enemies of the People'. An anonymous phone call at three in the morning warned them that they were to be taken for questioning and urged them to leave at once.

At the Finnish border they were stopped by the ragged peasant soldiers who guarded the new republic. One of them, searching their meagre possessions, saw the glint of the golden heart Vanni wore round her throat. (*The Lord watch between me and thee . . .*)

'Give it me,' he said in his thick dialect.

She stepped back. 'If you want it, you must kill me first,' she said quietly.

He cursed, scowled – and let her go.

They were in Finland and free. Free to walk through two hundred miles of forest to the coast . . . and to arrive, at last, on a day as foggy as any Vanni had imagined, in a grimy, northern English port.

Their fame had long since spread to Europe. De Witte, that gifted impresario, built his London season round them. They had never danced better. There was a new *rapprochement* between them born of the hardships they had shared, and it showed in their work. If her Odette and Giselle now reached a new perfection it was partly because of Vassilov's unselfish partnering. For now he loved Vanni; he wanted them to marry.

'Why not?' he demanded. 'Yes, I know all about the Englishman but it is *three years*!'

She did not know why not. He was a good man, had shown unexpected courage on their nightmare journey; he could make her laugh.

It was to please Vanni that Vassilov gave up his precious free time to go on the dismal, inconvenient tours of hospitals and army camps on which she insisted, travelling with only an accompanist, a reduced group of girls, to perform on rickety stages to puzzled soldiers who would greatly have preferred the chorus from *Chu Chin Chow*.

But the day before she was due to dance at an army camp near Devizes, she travelled alone, for Vassilov had a sore throat. She booked in at the Red Lion and next morning took the bus to Winterbourne.

The gate stood open. The elms lining the avenue were just touched with the first gold of autumn.

She knew it all. The lake on her left with the tangled water lilies . . . the stream . . . and yes, there – a skimming streak of blue – was the kingfisher.

The house, now. Serene, lovely – but shuttered, dead.

No, not quite. An old man, a caretaker, presumably, came out of a side door towards her.

'Can I help you, miss?'

'I am wondering . . .' Her English was still uncertain and fragmented. 'Is the lady . . . Mrs Hamilton . . . The mother of my . . .' But it seemed she still couldn't say Alex's name.

The old man stared at her. 'Mrs Hamilton died more than two years ago. In the winter of 1916. Had a stroke and was gone in a couple of hours.'

'I see . . . There is no one here, then?'

'No one, miss.'

She thanked him and turned away. The last link with Alex, then, was gone. And then she saw his tree: the great oak that he had loved so much. ('It was a whole world to me, Vanni, that tree. There were squirrels in it and little mice and hollows that filled with water when it rained. I used to spend hours in that tree.')

She walked up to it, rested her back against the trunk.

And felt, suddenly an incredible sense of release. It was

as if the grief and anguish that had weighed her down was physically lifted from her. She felt a lightness and something else she could not at first believe.

'I'm happy,' thought Vanni wonderingly. '*Happy*!'

The debt of sorrow she owed her love was paid, then. She was free. And in that instant she saw as clearly as if she really stood before her, the image of a child: her child, a girl, fair-haired and lightly made, waiting to be born – and dance.

So precise was the moment of her rebirth that Vanni looked at her watch. A quarter past twelve. Then she walked lightly to the gate.

Back at the hotel, she wondered whether to ring Vassilov and tell him that she was ready, now, to marry him. But there was time. Everything would unfold in its own way.

Three hours later, at the army camp, she danced a *pas seul* from *La Fille Mal Gardée* and a tommy called Ron Smith, who could barely spell his own name, became a lifelong balletomane. Then, as always, she accompanied the camp commandant and the doctor on a tour of the hospital.

It was in a magnificent Palladian mansion, a little way from the camp. Long windows, high bare rooms in which men sat playing cards or writing letters, their crutches against their beds . . .

A very silent room, now, with the really sick: the shell-shock cases, those with head wounds.

The room had been the private gymnasium of the nobleman who had given his house. There were wooden bars round the walls, a bare parquet floor. And rows of beds . . . eight down one side of the wall by the windows, eight by the left-hand wall, another eight facing her. Identical white beds with grey blankets, many of them screened by identical screens.

Vanni stopped. Her thoughts came to her in Russian, sometimes in Italian or French. But it was in English, now, that the voice in her head stated matter-of-factly: '*That one.*'

What happened next should have been easy enough to ascertain, yet to the last there were different versions. On one thing, however, everyone was agreed. The famous ballerina moved up to the third bed from the left and in a voice from which the charming, foreign hesitancy was entirely absent, said: 'Take away the screen.'

This done, there were revealed, to the extreme annoyance of the Matron, two of the prettiest nurses, who should have been elsewhere, leaning in concern over patient Number 59613. Really, was there no limit to the fuss that had to be made over this admittedly heroic major with his medals and his amnesia? After all, other men had been decorated three times for bravery, had been grievously wounded and left for dead. Yet even in his present state, the man seemed to possess an unquenchable glamour.

'What are you doing here?' she now said angrily to the nurses. 'Why aren't you in the sluices?'

But the girls were ready with their defence.

'We heard him speak, Matron. A name, it sounded like. We thought he might be coming round.'

'At a quarter past twelve, it was,' said the second nurse, pleased to show her efficiency.

'Rubbish,' said the Matron. 'The patient's been in a deep coma ever since he was repatriated.'

To this interchange the visiting ballerina paid no attention. Instead, she removed, for some reason, her small, pill-box hat and handed it to the commandant to hold as if he was a footman. Then she moved over to the bed and knelt down.

She knelt, and she waited. Then, after a while, quietly and without emotion, she pronounced the patient's Christian name.

And now again, there was disagreement. That the man stirred on the pillow and turned his head was indisputable. Indisputable, too, that he smiled, a slow, incredibly peaceful smile quite without awe or incredulity.

At this point, on account of the smile, the nurses were already crying so that their testimony is not really worth much. The ballerina, on the other hand, did not cry. Rather, as the man's emaciated, still shapely hand, lifted itself from the pillow, she bent her head so that he found, first, her high piled shining hair.

'He was just *stroking* her hair,' said the first nurse afterwards: a nice girl, decently brought up, who hunted with the Quorn.

'Oh, yes?' said the second, who was deplorably Cockney and working class.

And it had to be admitted that the Major's long, chiselled fingers seemed to move through the brown tresses with a sense of undoubted purpose – to come to rest, with what was surely a kind of familiarity, on the first hair pin . . . the second, and the third. It was probably just an accident – for he was still pitifully weak – that the pins should fall one by one on to the blankets so that presently the dancer's quiet, transfigured face was entirely framed in her loosened hair . . .

But if a certain disquiet nevertheless remained, if the action did not seem to be *quite* that of an English officer and gentleman, the first words with which the gallant major signalled his return to health and sanity were as reassuring and high-minded as anyone could wish.

'Sanctuary,' said Alex Hamilton, and smiled once more, and slept.

'Vanni! *Doushenka! Milenkaya!*' For all her seventy years, Madame Lavarre ran down the last flight of stairs and the elegant woman standing in the hall turned and, absurdly, in her Chanel coat and sable muff, she curtseyed. To be pulled to her feet, embraced and addressed in a spate of Russian.

'Oh, you bad, bad girl!' scolded Madame, 'To give it all up just like that! After such a *Giselle*.' She shook her head. 'How you must have suffered. What a struggle!'

Vanni smiled. 'No. There was no struggle. I never had to think not for a moment. As soon as I found him again, all I wanted was to be with him.'

'Yes, I can see it in your face, your happiness. He must be a good man, I think, not only a brave soldier. So you have no regrets?'

'None.' But Vanni's eyes rested, now, with an infinity of love on the child who had followed Madame and stood quietly waiting on the upstairs landing. 'Is she – ' she began, but found she could not trust her voice.

'She is accepted, of course,' said Madame Lavarre. She

paused. Then, throwing common sense, caution, even wisdom to the winds, she put an arm round Vanni and answered the question in her former pupil's gentle eyes. 'Do not fear: *doushenka*,' she said, too softly for the child to hear. 'She is one of us. She will dance!'